Secret Lives

Two women. Two generations.
One War

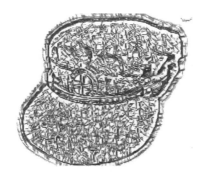

Anna

JENSEN

Just a short note about language before we continue our sojourn into the world of garden spaces. I am a most English author, despite having lived in South Africa for many years; I therefore use British English phraseology and spelling rather than American, so please forgive me if anything isn't clear or isn't spelt as you might expect.

Contents

To all those who live their lives in secret. May you know yourselves seen, known and loved by the Author of all.

Alice

February 1942

•⁻ •⁻•• •• ⁻•⁻• •

A lice clutched her suitcase until its handle bit into her icy flesh. The mid-morning sun didn't reach the station platform where she waited. She wished she'd remembered to wear gloves. She wished a lot of things.

She patted her hat with her free hand, sure the soft bottle-green fabric must be crumpled and smudged with soot from the train ride. The gentleman sitting opposite her had insisted on keeping the window open for the whole journey. Smoke had billowed in on a bitter wind as they traversed the Fens from Cambridge, causing Alice to alternately cough and shiver.

She was glad to finally arrive at Bletchley Station. The gentleman, whose name she never asked, helped her get her suitcase down from the rack above their heads. She staggered under its weight towards the door and down the steps to the platform. *What on earth did I pack in here?* Alice tried to appear at ease with her burden as her audience of one waved goodbye.

Now she was alone on the platform, all her fellow travellers having been greeted and whisked away by friends or family. What should she do? Alice had been told she would also be met at the station and taken to the boarding house that was arranged for her. But there was no one left on the platform, except for an elderly-looking stationmaster preparing for the next train to arrive.

Stuffing her hand into the pocket of her overcoat — a coat several sizes too big on account of it having been borrowed from her brother — she wondered what to do. She could ask the stationmaster for directions, but she didn't know where she was staying. She could find the waiting room in the hope that there was a fire lit for her to warm herself. But she was worried whoever came to meet her wouldn't know that's where she was and so might leave again, thinking she had decided not to come after all. Or she could remain standing here and contemplate the many ways a person could die from exposure, and calculate how long it might take given certain atmospheric conditions.

Alice chuckled at that. Father was always saying she was a walking abacus, performing sums of varying complexities on everything she encountered. She knew mathematics was her refuge, the safe place she always ran to when confronted with the realities of a sometimes hostile world, but it was kind of Father to encourage her. Even if he didn't understand her.

Once more looking up and down the deserted platform, Alice wondered what she had let herself in for this time. It had all been such a lark when she finished that prize crossword from *The Daily Telegraph*. Egged on by Mavis and Vera as they timed her with an old stopwatch, she felt certain she must have solved it far quicker than anyone else her age. Dropping the completed entry into the post box outside college, Alice felt a flush of pride. The whole episode was quickly dismissed from her mind as studying for impending exams took priority over everything else.

That was until Professor Wilkins called her into his study a few weeks later. Alice was both mystified and terrified. Had she made some terrible mistake on one of her papers? Was she to be 'sent down' for not making the grade?

She dressed carefully for the appointment, borrowing from Mavis a neat tweed skirt and jacket. Alice hated such outfits but felt the occasion warranted it. Smoothing the newly-set waves of indignant blonde curls, she knocked on the Prof's door.

'Come!' came the immediate response.

As she opened the door and entered, Alice inhaled the smell of pipe smoke and old papers. The rush of familiarity calmed her. Although she had been in the Prof's study just once or twice, the atmosphere was so reminiscent of her father's study at the vicarage she felt immediately at home.

Professor Wilkins stood from behind his desk and motioned to a chair in front of her. As Alice sat, she became aware of someone standing in the shadows of the room, far from where the sunlight streamed in through the open sash window. Willing herself not to look at whoever it was, she focused her attention on the now-seated Professor. He was fiddling with his pipe, puffing and blowing while he held a match to its contents. Pungent smoke billowed upwards. Satisfied, he looked up. For some moments there was silence while the brightness of his eyes searched the darkest recesses of Alice's soul. Or so it seemed.

'Well, Miss Stallard,' Wilkins began. 'I understand you have been indulging in a little competitive frivolity in your spare time?' As he spoke he shuffled through the papers strewn across his desk, plucking from amongst them what looked like a piece of old newspaper. A piece of old newspaper with a completed crossword visible.

Alice groaned. *Was that what this was about? How had he heard about that? And more to the point, how has my entry ended up on his desk?* She would quiz the wretched Mavis and Vera once she was back at their rooms.

'Um,' she mumbled.

The professor waved her explanation away before it even got started.

'No matter. What is done is done.' He looked at the paper in his hand once more, then turned to the figure still standing in the shadows. 'A good score, you say? One of the quickest you've seen? Yes, yes, I suppose Miss Stallard does have a certain aptitude for these things.'

As he spoke, the figure took a step or two into the room and Alice could see him for the first time. He extended his hand in greeting.

'Good morning, Miss Stallard. I must congratulate you on your excellent crossword skills!' His voice was rich and educated. Alice could easily imagine him ordering around soldiers on the battlefield...

Recalling herself to the present with a start, Alice realised someone was talking to her. She hadn't heard anyone approach but now turned to see a nervous-looking young man, this one in uniform, staring at her. Gosh, was she talking out loud? She did that quite often, her thoughts on display for all to hear.

'Oh, I'm so sorry, miles away. I didn't hear you walk over, what did you say?' Her words tumbled out in a rush of embarrassment and nerves.

He took a step backward, removing his cap as he did so. 'Beg pardon, ma'am, but would you be Miss...' he glanced at the piece of paper he held, 'Miss Alice Stallard?'

Miss Alice Stallard nodded.

'Ah, I'm glad you're still here,' the soldier smiled, looking surer of himself now her identity was established. 'I'm Corporal Fitch, sent to pick you up from the train and take you to your digs. Got delayed — sorry — a supply train came through at just the wrong time and I got caught at the crossing. Had to wait for ages. Here, let me take that.' He reached for Alice's suitcase, which she relinquished with a sigh of relief. She massaged her frozen fingers with her other hand.

'Is it always this cold here?' she asked, while hurrying to keep up with her chauffeur. Thank goodness she wasn't wearing the ridiculous shoes Vera wanted her to wear. She would have been flat on her face if she had.

Corporal Fitch didn't reply. He was hurrying towards a muddy green car — *a Ford something-or-other?* — parked underneath the stationmaster's office window. He slung Alice's suitcase on the back seat and glanced at his watch.

'Miss Stallard, I'm afraid I'll have to take you to where you will be staying and then ask you to make your own way to the Park. I have another engagement which I will be late for if I wait while you get settled in.'

The Park? What park? 'That's no problem. Do I have time for a cup of tea? Don't worry, I'm joking. I'll run upstairs and leave my suitcase on the bed then run straight back out again. How will I know where to go?'

'You can ask your landlady for directions. It's not far; the other side of the railway line.' Fitch negotiated his way out of the parking area and into the narrow lane. Almost as an afterthought he added, 'Don't tell her why you want to go to the Park though...'

'Don't worry about that. I don't know why I'm going there myself. No one's told me anything, just to catch that train and meet you and then find a Mr Saunders.'

Fitch didn't look surprised. He gave a curt nod. 'Mm, sounds about right. Oh, before I forget — you'll need this to gain access to the Park later.'

He dug around in his breast pocket with one hand while he kept the other on the steering wheel. He pulled out a green sheet of paper, folded in two.

'Your gate pass.'

Alice took it from him and stowed it in her shoulder bag. *Where am I going, that I need a gate pass to get in? What is this place? And what am I going to be doing there?*

Knowing that only time would provide answers to her many questions, Alice looked out of the window. After crossing the railway line, Corporal Fitch drove past the Park Hotel. She could make out a couple of people sitting in the hotel lounge — a man reading a newspaper, a lady knitting. They continued on for a few more streets then turned left into Albert Street.

'Right, here you are then.' He climbed out of the car and came around the front to open the door for Alice.

'Thank you. And thank you for carrying my suitcase at the station. I can manage from here. You'd best be off!'

Fitch ignored her and grabbed her case. He strode up to one of the houses and knocked on the shiny red door. Net curtains covered the downstairs windows on either side of the entrance. The one on the right twitched, a face appeared, then the curtain fell back into place. Within seconds the door was opened by a plump, middle-aged woman in a flowery apron and fluffy pink carpet slippers.

'Well, it's about time, young man. Really, why you young people can't tell the time, I'm sure I don't know.'

'Sorry Mrs Anderson, train was late...' Fitch blushed, looked down at his polished shoes. Alice chuckled. *Has the confident Corporal Fitch met his match in this Mrs Anderson? Perhaps he doesn't have somewhere else to be; he just wants to escape.* 'This is Miss Stallard. Miss Stallard, meet Mrs Anderson. You will be billeted with her for the duration of your stay.'

Alice stepped forward, held out her hand.

'Good afternoon, Mrs Anderson. My sincere apologies for the delay. I think there was a problem on the line.'

'Well, you're here now. Come in and I'll show you to your room. And as for you, young man, be off with you. You look like a cat on a hot tin roof, jiggling around so.'

Corporal Fitch didn't need to be told twice. He directed a half-salute at the two women, murmured a hasty farewell and climbed back into his car. He coaxed the engine into life, performed a perfect three-point turn and roared off down the road.

Mrs Anderson ushered Alice into a tiny hallway which smelt of old boots and wet carpet. The wallpaper was a diamond pattern of an indeterminate colour on account of the dim light bulb dangling from the ceiling. A narrow table, cluttered with keys and pens and a ration card, took up most of the floor space. Above it hung a gilt-framed mirror, splotchy with age. Turning to close the door behind her, Alice was confronted with a row of pegs on which hung several coats, a bright purple scarf and the familiar brown box containing a gas mask.

To the right of the hallway, Alice glimpsed the sitting room. Chintz-covered armchairs were grouped around a fireplace beside which stood a Bakelite wireless radio set. The mantelpiece sported several framed photographs. A carriage clock sat in pride of place, ticking rhythmically in the quiet house. A painting of a girl sitting on a stool hung from the picture rail of the chimney breast. *Little Miss Muffet sat on her tuffet...*

The door to the left was closed. The parlour? Kitchen? Alice wasn't sure. And she wasn't about to be given a chance to find out.

'Don't dawdle, child. I don't have all day.' Mrs Anderson lumbered ahead up the stairs, steadying herself on the bannister rail as she went. Her lungs wheezed in protest.

'Sorry, yes of course. Corporal Fitch told me I have to hurry as I have an appointment at the Park. I was hoping you might tell me the quickest way to get there?' Alice grabbed her case and followed Mrs Anderson to an upstairs landing.

'Here's your room.' Ignoring the question, Mrs Anderson pushed open a door the moment Alice reached the top of the stairs. She squeezed past, inhaling her landlady's generous spray of perfume as she did so. 'Breakfast at half past seven every morning, unless you're on nights and don't get back in time. A plate will be left in the oven for you. Lunch at the Park. Dinner at 5 o'clock sharp. Again, a plate will be put aside if you're late. No smoking. No drinking. No visitors.'

Alice nodded. Rules were alright. Bit of a nuisance, but alright.

'I'll leave you to arrange your things.'

Alice plonked her case down on the orange candlewick bedspread. The room faced the street, windowpanes taped up in case of bombing raids. Blackout curtains hung from the rail. A dark wardrobe brooded in the corner. Next to the bed was a nightstand; a chipped jug and bowl for her daily ablutions and an ancient-looking table lamp with fringed shade crowded its surface. The faded blue wallpaper was peeling in the corners. On the floor, a threadbare carpet of mustard yellow completed the appalling colour scheme.

Knowing she would have to leave unpacking until later, Alice was relieved to find the jug was full of water. She splashed a little into the bowl, rolled up the sleeves of her coat and blouse and pushed her hat further back on her head. Scooping up the water in her cupped hands, she splashed it over her face, the shock of cold making her gasp. She grabbed the stiff face towel from a hook on the wall and patted herself dry. She was going to need some of that face cream Mavis always used if she didn't want to look like an old lady by the time this was over.

Poking around in her shoulder bag for the compact mirror she carried, Alice checked her appearance. Her lipstick needed a touch up. She played around with the hat until her curls looked less squashed. A last look around her new home and Alice was ready.

The wireless was on in the sitting room. Alice knocked on the closed door.

'Mrs Anderson? I'm off. I wonder — could you give me directions to the Park?'

A chair creaked and Alice heard the shuffle of slippers. The door opened so suddenly it made her jump backwards in surprise.

'Follow where that young corporal went racing off to earlier— up the street and then use the footbridge over the railway. The Park is on your left. Big iron gates. You can't miss it.'

'Thank you. Oh, er, Mrs Anderson? Sorry to disturb you again. I don't have a key...'

'Under the mat. Make sure you put it back when you've used it.'

Alice exited the claustrophobia of Mrs Anderson's hallway. The rush of fresh air revived her as she stepped out onto the pavement. Checking there was indeed a key hidden under the mat before slamming the door closed, Alice turned left and followed the directions given to her.

Alice

The Interview

• ─ • ─ •• •• ─ • ─ • •

Alice soon reached the footbridge over the railway line. There was no one around. She watched a robin, his red breast bobbing in and out of the bushes. She glanced over the side of the bridge, checked for any activity at the station below. There was none. A thin streak of smoke rising upward from the chimney was the only indication that the station master was still on duty.

Stumbling down the metal stairs on the other side, Alice felt the flutter of butterflies in her stomach. For the second time in a few days, she began to wonder what on earth she was doing. *Here I am, going to a job — is it a job? — I know nothing about, with no one I know. Or anyone who knows me. 'Courage, Child!' as Father would say.*

A few yards further and Alice was in front of the ornate iron gates to the Park. A guard hut stood off to one side. As she was wondering what to do next, a man in military uniform stepped out and approached her.

'We're not open to the public, Miss. Move along.'

'I — I was told to report here, for an interview?'

'Oh, I see. Do you have a gate pass?' Although mollified, the guard still regarded Alice with suspicion. He took the piece of paper and unfolded it with care. 'You are Miss Alice Stallard? Of The Vicarage, Wisbech? Your identity card, please.'

Alice rummaged in her bag for the green cardboard document and handed it over to the guard. It had seen better days — the corners were curled and there was a coffee stain on the back cover.

'Sorry,' she muttered, hanging her head in shame.

ANNA JENSEN

'I should think so too, young lady. These are vital documents during our troubled times. You should take better care of it.' He held the identity card in one hand, the gate pass in the other, scrutinising each paper in turn. He appeared satisfied. With a nod, he returned the identity card to Alice; the gate pass he carried into the hut and, as far as Alice could tell, added it to a pile of similar slips of paper.

'Right you are then, Miss Stallard. If you'd like to follow me...' He pulled a bunch of keys from his pocket. Leaving the hut open and turning his attention to the gate, he used one of the larger keys in the lock. He beckoned Alice through.

She stepped through the gap and waited for the guard to close and relock the gate. An ugly, red-brick house with arched entranceway loomed ahead, fronted by an expanse of frost-tinged lawns. Black smoke curled upwards from a couple of brooding chimney stacks. The blackout curtains were not yet drawn, although lights were switched on in several of the rooms. In the centre of the lawn the iced-over water of a pond glistened.

Alice turned back to the guard, impatient for him to finish fiddling with the gate and escort her somewhere warmer.

With a jingle of keys, the guard marched off down the path to the right without saying a word. Alice hurried to catch up with him. Within a few more strides, they reached a small hut, not much larger than the one at the gate.

In response to a sharp knock on the peeling green paint, a muffled command to 'Come!' bid them enter. Stepping in ahead of Alice, the guard announced her presence to the hut's occupant.

'Good, good, well move aside, let the poor girl in. She must be freezing out there.'

Alice was shivering from more than the frigid air. The sound of the man's voice terrified her. She imagined him to be tall and ramrod straight, his greying hair cut neat and sharp.

He was none of those things. He wore a brown, loose-fitting cardigan over a blue and white checked shirt. The top button was undone, a red tie loose at the neck. His hair, far from being either grey or neat, was a busy halo of dark curls framing his face. He wore a pair of round spectacles —

held together on one side with a piece of string — which magnified his brown eyes. *You look like an owl who needs his feathers trimmed...*

'Do sit, Miss Stallard. Corporal, shut the door behind you, be a good man.'

He settled back into his chair and reached for a pile of papers which he shuffled through for a few moments, jotting notes on some with a worn-down pencil. Alice sat in silence. How the man could sit there without a hat or coat on, she wasn't sure. It was no warmer inside the hut than it had been outside. The only difference was the lack of fresh air. A musty, closed-in smell permeated the room. She twisted her fingers together, hoping he would hurry up.

Eventually the man looked up.

'Allow me to introduce myself, Miss Stallard. I am Mr Saunders. My job here at the Park is to run through the basics with all our newest recruits, make sure you know what arrangements are made, that sort of thing. I understand you did rather well with that crossword puzzle?'

How does everyone know about that?

'I believe so, yes. Bit of luck, really. I'm reading mathematics at Cambridge — well, I was — but I do love to play around with words too. Sort of number patterns with the alphabet, if you know what I mean?' Words tumbled over one another in their nervous rush to escape. A blush rose on Alice's neck and across her cheeks.

'Oh, don't be shy, Miss Stallard. There are plenty more just like you here. And they all love to share their achievements, if you see what I mean...' He glanced back at the papers. 'Anyway, to business. You have already met Mrs Anderson, I believe? Yes, I see from your expression that you have. Anyway, your remuneration will be £150 per year until you turn 21 — you are currently 19, I understand — out of which you must pay Mrs Anderson the going rate for your board and lodging.

'You will be allotted a few days of leave, although depending on whatever crisis is on at the time, they may be withdrawn. At short notice, I might add.

'There are three shifts here at the Park; eight in the morning until four in the afternoon; four in the afternoon until midnight; and midnight until eight in the morning. As you are billeted in Bletchley itself and therefore quite close to the Park — you're lucky with that, I must tell you — you will provide your own transport back and forth. There are several dedicated buses which run, but these are reserved for those living in outlying areas. I suggest a bicycle might be a good option.'

Alice nodded.

'I must impress upon you the need for *absolute* discretion about your position here. Is that understood? No one must know that you work here, at the Park, nor must they know what you do here.' He held up a hand before Alice could interrupt him. 'You will inform your friends and family that you are working with a group of academics near Oxford. Nothing more. Your postal address will be issued to you in due course. Please do not use any other address than the one provided.

'On your first day of active duty, you will attend a series of lectures providing more details about security procedures and so forth. You will also sign the Official Secrets Act. Be under no illusions, this is not a mere 'rubber stamp' affair; there are serious consequences should you break any of its conditions, ranging from dismissal to prison and, ultimately, death.'

Alice raised her hand an inch or two, as though still at school and nervous to ask the teacher a question.

'Yes? Is there something I have not made clear?'

'Well, sir — Mr Saunders — I appreciate all the information you have given me. But, um, there seems to be something you have left out...'

He removed his spectacles and squeezed his temples.

'Miss Stallard, I thought I made myself abundantly clear about everything that concerns your time here at the Park.'

'Well, yes, sir. But you haven't mentioned what I will be doing here. You know, what job I'm here for.'

Mr Saunders replaced his spectacles with a sigh.

'No, I have not. Nor shall I be doing so. You will receive notification when you are to return here. At that time, once the aforementioned Act has been signed, you will be told your duties.' He took out his pocket watch and checked the time. 'May I suggest you make your way back to Mrs Anderson's billet? You will probably have missed dinner already, but I understand she keeps something to one side for her boarders. Do you have a torch with you? I'm sure it will be quite dark. Must close the blackouts, while I think of it.'

He rose and busied himself at the windows. He waved a hand of dismissal at Alice.

'Thank you, sir, yes I do have a small light with me. Thank you for your time, sir.'

Alice let herself out. The man was right — it was dark. The blackouts were up at all the windows of the mansion, tiny chinks of light showing where they didn't quite fit. She flicked on the small torch she'd brought with her, keeping its beam low and close to her body. Groping her way back to the gate, she mouthed a silent prayer of thanks for her dear father who had managed to get hold of the torch especially for her.

The click of her heels on the paving sounded loud in the quiet stillness of night and she wasn't surprised to find the guard waiting for her. He held the gate open as she passed through.

'Goodnight, Miss. Mind how you go.'

The steps up the railway bridge were even more slippery than earlier. Alice held on to the handrail despite the cold of the metal. Already encumbered with her shoulder bag and gas mask, the addition of the torch made her extra cautious. An owl hooted in the distance. The sky was moonless, the clouds of earlier in the day now leaking a steady drizzle.

Once over the bridge and back at street level on the other side, Alice felt more confident and extended her stride. She wriggled gloves from her pocket over numb fingers. She was eager to get back to her billet, if not because she expected a warm welcome from her landlady, at least so she could get out of the freezing night air. She clenched and unclenched her jaw in hopes of relieving some of the icy numbness, opening and closing her mouth as she hurried through the deserted Bletchley streets.

Noise spilled out onto the pavement as she hurried past the hotel. Someone was playing the piano, hammering away at the keys. Alice winced. Raucous voices pounded out the words to 'It's A Long Way to Tipperary.' *Wrong war, but it seems to be going down well.*

Once past the shaded lights of the hotel's entrance, the intense darkness was disorientating, and she missed the turn to Albert Street. Alice recognised her mistake when she reached the Post Office. Knowing she hadn't seen that on the short drive from the station earlier, she retraced her steps. Her feet ached inside her shoes. Her back and shoulders were sore from all the walking. The gurgle of her stomach reminded her she hadn't eaten anything since leaving Cambridge early that morning.

I wonder what delights Mrs Anderson has in store for me to eat this evening? Alice shone the torch onto her watch face. Long past dinnertime.

With relief, Alice found herself at last in more familiar territory. On her right was the entrance to Albert Street. A car, headlamps covered until they resembled the slits of a cat's eyes, rumbled past her. It splashed through a puddle on the corner, the water spraying Alice's lower body.

Cold, wet and hungry, she started to cry. *Why did I listen to those silly girls? I could be with them, warm and cosy beside some fireplace, eating crumpets dripping in butter. I'm being ridiculous. We would hardly be able to find the crumpets, much less the butter.*

Pulling herself together with a shake and a straightening of the shoulders, Alice peered at the numbers fixed to each door until she reached number 18. Alice bobbed down, trying not to get the hem of her skirt any wetter than it was already, and lifted the doormat. She groped around in search of the key but couldn't feel anything through her gloves. Removing her glove with her teeth, she tried again.

She shone her torch over the area, feeling around for any cracks where the key could have fallen. Success. She grasped the key between freezing fingers, not wanting it to fall to the ground where she would have to scrabble around to find it again. Pushing it into the lock, she opened the door into the tiny hallway. Alice dumped her bag, gas mask and torch on the bottom step of the stairs, then turned to return the key to its place under the mat outside.

'Good grief, girl. Were you born in a barn? Shut the door.' The disgruntled voice of Mrs Anderson greeted Alice. 'And you're late.

There's a plate on the table in the kitchen. Down the passageway at the back.'

Wondering how on earth any draught was able to reach Mrs Anderson behind her closed sitting room door, Alice hurried to replace the key and shut out the night air. She hung her sodden overcoat on the only spare peg available; her hat joined the rest of her belongings at the bottom of the stairs. It was time to find her meal.

A small paraffin lamp was burning on the kitchen table, it's vapours vying for attention with the acrid smell of Jeyes Fluid. Alice's eyes watered. Turned down low, the dirty yellow flame tortured and stretched the dark shadows of the room into shapes too grotesque for Alice's exhausted imagination. She tried the switch beside the door. Nothing. Hence the lamp on the table. She stepped further into the room and fiddled with the knob on the lantern, coaxing the flame higher and brighter. *That's better.*

An over-sized ceramic sink and draining board were mounted under the window. Net curtains, tied back with dainty lace ribbons, did their best to camouflage the fabric blackout curtains. Drying-up cloths hung over a tap protruding from the wall. On a rail underneath the sink Alice could make out a metal wash tub and a rippled washboard. A basket was stuffed full of clothes waiting for wash day. She didn't relish the prospect.

The stove filled the rest of that side of the kitchen; a dull copper kettle took up one of its two rings. Kitchen cabinets lined the opposite wall, doors hanging on crooked hinges, drawers stuck somewhere between open and closed.

To the left of the door where Alice stood, a refrigerator hummed. She guessed the door on the other side of the room, next to the sink, led out to the back yard and the privy. She would investigate that later. For now, she needed her tea.

A heavy wooden table occupied the centre of the room, six unmatched chairs pushed around its edges. Next to the lamp, a red and white checked drying cloth covered what was likely to be Alice's dinner.

Before examining its contents, Alice splashed water into the bottom of the kettle and lit the gas. As she waited for it to boil, she searched through the cupboards in search of tea things. She found a battered cannister of tea leaves and a set of china cups and saucers. She took one down for herself, hoping it wouldn't be too chipped.

With everything laid out on the kitchen table, she lifted the cloth from the plate in front of her. A pile of powdered scrambled egg, cold and congealed, was dolloped beside a pale pink slice of luncheon meat. A couple of slices of tomato completed the meal. Alice sighed.

She was fifteen, nearly sixteen, when war was declared, and rationing was introduced. To everyone's surprise the magnificent teas enjoyed in the vicarage continued; her mother still managed to put together a fantastic spread — cold meats and baby potatoes or a lettuce or two from the garden. And there was always cake, either rustled up by her mother while she was out at school or donated by a grateful parishioner, limited resources pooled and shared. The kettle was kept hot, pushed on or off the hot plate of the old cooking range depending on how urgent the need for tea may be.

The kettle in her current kitchen was hissing and spitting. Alice poured the water over the leaves in a teapot lurking under a brown hand-crocheted tea cosy. Making sure she didn't add too much water, she replaced the kettle on the stove and carried the half-full teapot to the table. She pulled out a chair, being careful to ensure it didn't scrape on the black and dirty-white floor tiles, or get caught on one of the cotton floor rugs. She sat with a weary sigh and pulled the plate of food towards her.

Alice lowered her head in prayer. 'For what I am about to receive may the Lord make me truly thankful. And I don't just mean the food, Lord. All of it. This place. Mrs Anderson. The job I don't even know I'm doing....Amen.' She swallowed a sob with a scoop of egg.

Alice finished her meal, washing it down with a second cup of tea. Overcome with exhaustion now that her hunger was satisfied, she stumbled over to the sink. Pouring the last of the water from the kettle over her plate and tea things, Alice rubbed them with the only cloth she could find. The dregs of tea went down the sink and she rinsed out the tea pot. Sure that drying up and putting away were all part of the rules and regulations associated with Mrs Anderson's Boarding Establishment, Alice forced her weary body to cooperate.

Realising she was going to have to visit the privy before she would be able to settle down to sleep, she opened the outer door. The rain had stopped, a gentle wind having blown the remaining clouds away. Stars studded the night sky, twinkling and winking at Alice as she took the few steps down the path to the privy. Their beauty arrested her progress. A favourite Scripture flitted into her mind. "Lift up your eyes on high and see: who created these? He who brings out their host by number, calling them all by name." *Am I numbered? Do you call me out by name, right here, right now?*

Not wanting to waste any more time — or freeze without her coat — by exploring her surroundings more than necessary, Alice finished in the privy and returned to the relative warmth of the kitchen. She decided to damp down the lamp rather than put it out, hoping Mrs Anderson would come through and blow it out when she was ready for bed.

Out in the gloomy passageway, it took a while for Alice's eyes to adjust. She stood still, waiting until she could make out the staircase. The wireless was still on in the sitting room, although the evening concert had finished; Alice could hear the measured tones of a BBC newsreader.

At last able to see where she was going, Alice crept along, gathered her belongings, and climbed up to her room. The third stair gave a loud squeak of disapproval as she stepped on it. The sound was loud in the quiet hallway. *Must remember that when I come home late.*

'Goodnight, Mrs Anderson....' Alice hoped her landlady wouldn't appear in the doorway, eager for either a bedtime chat or to complain about something more that she had done wrong.

She didn't. 'Goodnight, dear. Sleep tight and don't let the bed bugs bite!' *That's kind. Or is she being serious?*

Concerned at what she may find under the orange bedspread, Alice hurried the rest of the way upstairs. She pushed the bedroom door open with her hip. Dumping her stuff on the bed, she took a couple of steps over to the window; she needed to draw the thick blackout curtains before turning on the bedside lamp. She pulled and tugged at the stiff material, worried the whole rail would come crashing down on top of her at any moment. With one final sharp yank, the last remaining glimpse of the outside world was gone.

The darkness was complete. Alice knocked her shin against the end of the bed. She bit her lip to prevent crying out, her heart racing as she struggled to keep the instant claustrophobia from taking over. Patting her way along the bed, she made it back across the room without further incident. She switched the light on with a sigh of relief.

Too tired to do anything about unpacking, she perched on the side of the bed and reached down to take off her shoes, again thankful to have gone with her head rather than Vera's heart in her choice of footwear. *I would never have survived the day.* She flopped back on the bed still fully clothed and closed her eyes.

Rosie

February 1998

●━● ━━━ ●●● ●● ●

R osie sprinted up the lane from school, her thick plait thumping between her shoulder-blades as she ran. She knew Mum would disapprove, admonish her for being so-unladylike as she raced up the narrow lane. But she didn't care. It was Friday and she'd been cooped up at a desk all day. She'd slung her bag over her shoulder and stuffed her hat into her pocket. She stretched her legs in long, loping strides. The air, although cold on her face, revived her from the stupor she had fallen into during History — the last lesson of the day.

They were studying the Second World War this year. Expecting to enjoy it, Rosie was frustrated and disappointed at how boring Mrs Norris was managing to make it. The teacher sat behind her desk at the front of the classroom reading page after page from the textbook. Sitting at the back of the classroom, Rosie strained to hear the teacher's breathy whisper. Her attention kept wandering, lured by the window next to her. Clouds scudded past as the wind picked up. Laura flicked a pellet of rolled up tissue at her. Right on target it clipped Rosie's earlobe.

'Ow!' Her voice was louder than anticipated.

'Do you have something to add, Rosie? No? Then may I ask you the courtesy of concentrating on the matter in hand? Now, where was I?' Mrs Norris resumed her monotonous droning.

Rosie glared at Laura. Her shoulders were shaking with laughter as she tried to contain her delight at her friend's reprimand. Rosie looked away, knowing if they made eye contact, she would be in trouble again, this time for giggling.

The two girls were best friends since nursery school. Both families farmed land in the lush green hills of Somerset. They were drawn to one another from their first day of meeting, playing with tractors in the sand pit rather than the dress-up clothes in the Wendy house. Progressing to the same primary school together, their friendship solidified into a defensive alliance, protecting one another from the kids from town who mocked their accents or declared they smelt of cows.

They were nearing the end of their school career, with A-levels a few months away. Neither quite knew what they wanted to do or where they wanted to go next. There were half-started conversations about taking a Gap Year and backpacking around the world. The next minute they dreamed of illustrious careers in high finance or academia.

The bell rang for the end of the school day. Rosie and Laura shoved books into bags and shrugged into their puffer jackets. Rosie coiled a long, hand-knitted scarf around her neck.

'Stupid. Why did you do that? You know how she hates being interrupted. She loses her place and then has to start all over again.' She tried to sound cross but knew she wasn't doing a good job of it.

'Oh, and of course you were paying close attention, right? I saw you, looking out the window. Was Mike practising kicking for posts out on the field, or something?'

Rosie knew she was blushing. Rather than reply she pulled her gloves out of her jacket pocket and pretended to busy herself with putting them on.

'Ha, got you!' She knew Laura wouldn't let it go.

Thank goodness it's the weekend. She'll have forgotten by Monday. 'No, actually, I was looking at the weather. You know, how farm girls always do?' She stuck her tongue out at her friend and ran down the corridor before Laura could thump her arm. 'C'mon, else we'll miss the bus.'

The driver shook his head as they scrambled up the steps into the bus.

'Sorry, Pete, didn't mean to be late...'

'You say that every time, cheeky miss.' He closed the doors with a whoosh. 'Sit down so we can get going.'

They found a couple of spare seats halfway down the bus, and sat with their bags on their laps. The other Sixth Formers took up the whole of the back row. They sprawled over each other, laughing and swearing.

The younger kids kept their heads down low, making sure they weren't noticed or picked on.

Pete roared the idling engine into life and set off in a cloud of foul-smelling diesel fumes, turning out of the school gates to a mighty cheer from the back row. He drove through the streets of Winscombe, depositing passengers along the way. By the time they reached the edge of town, only a few of the farm children were left. They all spread out, glad to have the bus to themselves at last. Someone unplugged their headphones and the music from their phone filled the bus with 'My Heart Will Go On' — the current Number One, if Sunday evening's chart show was anything to go by.

'Wonder who it will be this week?' Laura loved music, knew all the bands and their latest songs.

'I dunno. Don't really care. I can't believe you still listen to that. It's what we did as kids.' Rosie, on the other hand, preferred to roam the hills behind the farmhouse or read the latest science fiction trilogy in her spare time. 'What you doing this weekend?'

'Not sure. Dad said something about getting the sheep pens sorted. Guess it'll be chores for me. What about you?'

'Gran's coming.' Rosie's eyes lit up at the prospect. 'And Gramps as well of course.'

'You are so lucky, having such cool grandparents. Mine just sit there and demand tea all the time.'

This was a familiar conversation. And it was true — Rosie's grandparents were very cool. Especially Gran.

It was the thought of Gran already at home that spurred Rosie to hasten the last few metres to the farmhouse. She banged open the door and threw her bag down. Bending to remove her shoes, she struggled with the damp laces. She sniffed, her nose running from the contrast between the outside chill and the warmth of the radiator next to her. Giving up the impossible task of loosening the knots in her laces, she yanked her shoes off instead, flinging them onto the shoe rack next to her mother's yellow and red polka dot wellington boots and her father's more sober green ones.

'Gran, I'm home!' She grabbed a hanger from the coats cupboard and draped her jacket and scarf over it. She stuffed her hat and gloves in the pocket, then hung the whole lot back on the rail. Making sure the outside door was properly closed — *don't let the heat out, child* — she skated off down the hallway, her thick socks sliding along the polished parquet floor. 'Gran, where're you?'

'In here dear. Beside the fire your father has kindly stoked up for us.' Gran never sounded as old as she was. There was no shake or tremor in the voice that called from the sitting room. 'Shall I be pouring tea?'

'Gran! It's so wonderful to see you.' Rosie flung herself across the room, throwing her arms around her grandmother's neck. Pulling away after an exchange of kisses, Rosie noticed the tea table set out. 'Yes, please, I'd love some tea. Where's everyone else?'

Her grandmother busied herself with the tea things, choosing a china mug with care. She poured in a splash of milk then lifted the teapot to pour its aromatic contents into Rosie's cup.

'Here you are, dear. You look quite flushed. Did you run from the bus?' Rosie took her tea and nodded. 'Ha, I thought you would. Oh, the others. Your mother is out taking Emma to ballet and your father has gone with Gramps to look at the pigs. Or something. So they left me in charge for when you came home. I brought cake — would you like some?'

Rosie smiled. She knew there would be cake. There always was when Gran came to visit. It was like a week-long Mad Hatter's Tea Party, with her own Granny Alice the centre of the wonderland.

'Yes, please Gran. Which one is it today?'

'Coffee and walnut — my favourite. And your Gramps doesn't like it much, so there's more for us.' She winked.

Rosie laughed. 'You are mean to poor old Gramps.'

'Oh, not really. There's a chocolate cake in that other tin. He's well taken care of, don't you worry. Is this big enough for you?'

'That's enough to feed a horse, but yes, as I'm hungry enough to eat a horse, that's perfect— thank you.' The slice of cake dwarfed the delicate tea plate Gran passed over to Rosie. The aroma of coffee and rich butter icing made her mouth water. Taking the seat opposite Gran, Rosie balanced the tea plate on the arm of the chair.

Gran cut herself a sliver of cake, miniscule in comparison to the doorstop-sized piece she had presented to Rosie.

'Are you on a diet, Granny? I've never seen you take such a small piece of cake before.'

'You cheeky thing. No, child, I'm still full from lunch — we stopped at The Swan on the drive over and I indulged in their largest portion of steak and kidney pie. They serve the best there is for miles around.' As she spoke, Gran topped up her own tea cup and returned to the deep armchair that she commandeered whenever she visited. She still managed to look elegant despite disappearing amongst the overstuffed cushions. 'So how was your day, dear? Are you feeling ready for those 'mock' exams you have to write?'

Rosie looked up in surprise, her mouth full of cake. She swallowed. 'How do you always know so much, Gran?'

'Oh, you know, I listen to the radio, read the paper. I keep my ear to the ground.' She chuckled and took a dainty forkful of her own cake.

Rosie did know. The radio was always on in her grandparents' home, with current affairs news shows or classical afternoon concerts playing. Gramps listened to Test Match special whenever he got the chance.

When not pottering about in their garden, they sat in wicker armchairs in the conservatory, admiring the view or reading the paper — *The Times* for Gramps and *The Guardian* for Gran. 'To get the perspective from the other side, dear...' — with the doors thrown open on all but the most inclement day. A freshly-brewed pot of coffee in the morning, or tea in the afternoon, sat on the table between them. A heater was tucked away in a corner in case the chill got too much for them; it was rarely used.

There was a television, used mainly for watching reruns of old films or travel and nature documentaries, but it was in the sitting room on the other side of the house; they preferred to be near the garden.

Gran was waiting for an answer, looking at Rosie over the top of her teacup.

'Oh, my day was alright I suppose. Glad it's Friday. And that you're here. Mock exams? Yes, I suppose I'm ready. I still have some extra studying to do — we haven't quite finished all the sections yet, especially in Bio — Biology. So frustrating. I just want to be done.'

'I never got on with Biology. Definitely not my subject.' Gran replaced her cup in its saucer with a rattle. 'And your favourite subject? Mine was Maths. And English as well I suppose.'

'Ugh, definitely not Maths. I thought History would be the one I liked most. It probably would be if it wasn't for the teacher.'

'Mm, teachers make all the difference, don't they?'

'We're doing the Second World War. I was looking forward to it but it's just a bunch of facts and figures, boring stuff that doesn't mean anything. I want to know what it was like, y'know, what it felt like for people living through it.' Rosie paused and picked up the last of her cake in her fingers, licking them clean when she was finished. She gulped down some tea, then stood up to return everything to the tea table. 'That was delicious, Gran — thank you. I might have to try some of Gramps' chocolate cake later, you know, check if it's as nice.'

She perched on the arm of Gran's chair.

'Gran, you were in the War weren't you?' Rosie longed to know more, to hear something from real life. 'I bet you could teach me more than Mrs Norris ever could. You must have done stuff, been places, seen people; and you're the best at telling stories.' That was true. Rosie remembered bedtimes with her sister, sitting up in the bed they shared while Gran entertained them with tale after tale — the first Man on the Moon, the Queen's Coronation and years later, her Silver Jubilee. *But never about the War.*

'Ha, you think flattery will get everywhere, don't you? I'm sure I can't add much to what you're learning at school.'

'No, come on Gran, there must be something...' Before Rosie could press Gran any further, the back door slammed. Voices, animated and loud from being outdoors, approached through the house. The door to the sitting room burst open and Samson and Delilah bounded in, wagging their tails in sheer joy as they rushed over to where Rosie sat. They showered her with slobbery kisses.

'Dogs! Samson, Delilah, come back here!' Rosie's father tried to sound cross but they all knew he was too fond of them to ever get properly angry. 'You're full of mud.'

'Ugh, you really are. Go, outside with you both.' Rosie shoved the furry bodies away from her.

They rushed out, leaving behind muddy pawprints and the smell of wet dog. Rosie knew from their wild barking that Dad was feeding them treats in the kitchen. *Mum will go mad when she gets back.*

'I'd better clear some of this up, before Mum gets home. Back in a sec, Gran.'

'You are a good girl, Rosie. Your mother is right to be proud of you.' She smiled and waved her granddaughter away.

'Oh, hi Gramps. I need to get a broom or something. Maybe I should take the pot and make some fresh tea.'

Rosie's grandfather strode into the room, a peaked cap in his hand.

'Rosie, there you are. We missed you earlier — pity you weren't back in time to come and look around the farm with your father and me.' Rosie reached up and kissed him on the cheek. It was cold and dry.

'Gramps. You're freezing. Go and sit next to the fire with Gran and I'll get that tea. Give me your cap — I'll hang it up for you.' Rosie plucked the cap from his hand, ushering him to the armchair she had just vacated. She gave the fire a quick poke and threw on a couple more logs which sparked, flames leaping up the chimney. Sure that her grandparents were settled, she grabbed the tea pot and headed for the kitchen. 'Dad, I'm home. Why did you let the dogs through...?'

Rosie returned with the tea, and a dustpan and brush. Her father followed along behind.

'You need a damp cloth, Rosie-Posie. The mud will still be wet, surely? The brush won't help. Well, it will help to spread it about a bit, I suppose.'

Rosie ignored him. 'More tea, Gran? And you, Gramps?'

She took Gran's cup, about to top it a second time.

'Oh no, thank you dear. I'm quite awash with tea. It's all I've done since getting here; drink tea. Bill, you'll have some though, won't you?'

'What? Oh, tea, yes thank you Rosie, dear.'

Rosie drew another of the cups towards her, added the milk and a couple of teaspoons of sugar then poured in the tea. It looked a bit pale and weak. *Hope he doesn't notice.*

'And some of Gran's delicious coffee cake, Gramps?' She laughed at his horrified expression. 'Only joking. She's brought chocolate cake for you. And Dad — tea?'

'I'll get some in a minute thanks. Let it stew for a bit first.' He winked at his daughter. She shook her head and glared at him.

'Here you go, Gramps.'

Gramps gave a grunt of gratitude as he took the plate from Rosie. Ignoring the fork, he used fingers to break off a chunk of cake. 'Don't need that. Got my own in-built forks right here.' He chuckled. A crumb went down the wrong way. Rosie grabbed the plate from him as he coughed until his eyes watered. 'What did you put in that there cake, Alice — feathers? I'm alright, lass, you can give me my cake back.'

Rosie noticed Gran didn't seem to join in the joke. A concerned expression showed on her face, creases appearing between her eyes and around her mouth as she watched Gramps pick at a swirl of icing, avoiding her gaze.

Embarrassed, Rosie turned away and grabbed the dustpan and brush. 'Better get this sorted out, before Mum and Emma are home.' She knelt down and rubbed at the mud carried in by the dogs. She managed to sweep up a few of the dryer clumps; the rest sort of blended in with the patterned rug. 'That'll do. Dad, your tea will be ready, I should think. I'm going up to my room — want to get out of my uniform and stuff.'

'Thanks, Rosie-P. We'll call you down when Mum's home. Alice, you sure I can't pour you some more?'

Rosie hurried out of the room, taking the dustpan and brush with her. Too many people were clustered around the blazing fire and the sitting room was stuffy and claustrophobic. She tipped the contents of the dustpan into the kitchen bin and put everything into the cupboard in the scullery.

She ran up the stairs to her bedroom. She flung herself onto the bed and stuffed her face into a pillow. *They can't be getting old, they can't.* Hot tears stung her eyes as she pictured the contorted face of Gramps coughing over a few crumbs. She knew it was something more than a bit of food gone down the wrong way; Gran's face said everything. As did the determined way Gramps ignored his wife. They were usually so caring of one another, nodding when the other spoke or reaching across to pat a hand in agreement. It was what Rosie loved about them so much, that deep connection between them. They were the kind of couple who didn't finish each other's sentences; they finished each other's thoughts.

Rosie rolled over, sitting up to wipe her eyes and nose. It was getting dark. The earlier wind carried with it cold, winter rain. Fat, heavy rain drops spattered against the windowpane and slithered downwards in narrow pathways lit by a dim moonshine.

A car drew up outside. She heard the slam of doors, then the draught of cold air wafting up the stairs as the front door was pushed open. Mum and Emma were home.

'Hi everyone. We're back. Mum, Dad, did you get some tea? Rosie, how was your day? Tim, did you let the dogs in?' Mum arrived everywhere a bit like a hurricane — full of energy and noise. Rosie pictured her pulling off her coat and discarding it on top of the boot shelf — to be hung up later — impatient to get into the house and find out what everyone else was doing. Emma, on the contrary, would be removing her coat and hanging it in the cupboard. On the hanger with her name on. Her neat bun of hair, essential accessory for every young ballerina, still immaculate despite the bobble hat she wore. Slipping out of her fur-lined boots, she would already be pirouetting towards the sitting room to greet her grandparents.

Rosie stayed silent, not yet ready to return downstairs. Leaving the bedside lamp switched off, she got up to pull her curtains closed. Pausing for a moment, she gazed out of the window to the hills in the distance. The silhouettes of bare winter trees formed a line of deep purple on the far horizon, indistinct through the gloom. The darker shapes of storm clouds brooded over the landscape, scudding across the sky as the wind hounded them onwards. A sudden gust splattered more rain against the window, making Rosie jump. She yanked the curtains closed.

Rosie plugged in the lava lamp on her desk. The unlit room burst into orange and yellow life. Globs of lazy colour collided, rose, dipped, separated as heat warmed the liquid in its glass tube. Plopping back down onto the bed and grabbing her favourite old teddy bear from her pillow,

Rosie hugged it to herself. Gran had given it to her when she was a baby. It was worn and missing one of its beady black eyes. Its tummy was bare from years of constant rubbing.

'Teddy, what will I do when they're gone?'

She knew she was overreacting — it was only one coughing fit, after all. But they were always so vital, so vigorous, she couldn't imagine them growing properly old. Like Laura's grandparents, who already lived in 'sheltered accommodation', spending their days in weary stillness or attending hospital appointments.

And there's so much I don't know about them. Especially Gran. Anytime Rosie tried to get her grandmother talking about the past, she changed the subject or busied herself with some activity or other. Rosie had tried quizzing Mum about it a few times.

'What do you know about Gran, Mum? You know, before she met Gramps and had you and stuff?'

'Um, not much really. I hardly knew my grandparents. He was a vicar, I think. Or maybe they just lived in a vicarage, I'm not sure. There are no photographs or anything.'

'But what about her friends? Don't they know?'

'Well, I only know Vera. And they're always as thick as thieves when they get together. No-one can get a word in edgeways once they're on a roll.'

That was true. Vera was Gran's glamorous friend — fashionable and expensive hairdos, manicured fingernails, a thick string of pearls hugging her throat. Her clothes were straight from the designers, her shoes soft Italian leather. And yet despite the intimidating outward appearance and posh accent, Rosie liked her, delighted whenever she came to visit. The gifts brought for herself and Emma helped, of course. As the girls grew older, Vera showed genuine interest in them, asking about their hobbies, their hopes and dreams.

'You know, Teddy, they're not gone yet are they? I'm going to find out all I can while I can. Why not? I'm sure there's nothing either of them need to hide.' *Yes, that's what I'll do. When the exams are all over, I'll go down and stay with them, do a bit of investigating. It'll be fun, after all the stress of exams. I'm sure Gran will talk to me. She has to, at some point.*

'Rosie? Are you up there? Tea's ready.'

'Coming Mum. Just getting changed.' Rosie pulled a tissue from the box at her elbow and blew her nose. She stripped off her school uniform and replaced it with the torn jeans and slouchy black jumper that were a home 'uniform', she wore them so often. She pulled a clean pair of thick hiking socks from the drawer and tucked them into her pocket. She would wear them downstairs on the cold kitchen floor instead of slippers.

Alice

Bletchley Park

I t was several days before Alice was summoned back to the Park. Unable to sit hour after hour in Mrs Anderson's spare bedroom, she decided to explore the town. After getting so disorientated and lost on her first night, the next morning she retraced her steps back to the Park, making sure she knew her way next time she walked at night. She ticked off landmarks as she went — the house with the ceramic dog decorating the doorstep; the broken window at Number 6. Once on the main road she turned to look back at the entrance to Albert Street, searching for anything which would help her recognise which street was hers. She noticed a jagged paving stone, perhaps broken by a car clipping the corner. It wasn't much, but at least it was something she could look out for.

Now she had her bearings and was confident she would find her way home, Alice was happy to dawdle. By mid-morning a few rays of sunshine filtered through the clouds and she started to feel warm. She pulled the green hat from her head and ruffled her fingers through her hair. A young man in uniform, watching her from the other side of the road, whistled.

'Hello gorgeous! When did you get to town?' He wore the pale blue uniform of the Royal Air Force. His short dark hair and his shiny shoes indicated he was also a recent arrival.

Alice knew better than to encourage him. It was flattering to be noticed though. She smiled then hurried away.

'No, don't go. There's a war on, remember? What's your name at least?'

It would be rude not to reply. Alice stopped walking and turned to look back over her shoulder.

'Alice. Miss Stallard to you though.' *Gosh, did I say that? Mavis would be proud of me.*

'Well, Miss Stallard-to-you-though, I'm pleased to make your acquaintance. And I'm Frank. Just plain Frank.' He took a few steps towards her, about to cross the road.

'It's nice to meet you too, Frank. But I must be off. Good-day.' Alice succeeded in stopping his approach. She ducked into the closest shop — the butcher's — and pretended to wait in the queue until she was sure Frank was no longer there. Alice wrinkled her nose at the smell of fresh raw meat — never her favourite.

'Miss, what can I get you? I've got a nice bit of tongue here?'

'Oh, thank you. Sorry, I won't be buying today. Another time though.' Certain the coast was clear, Alice darted back out into the street.

She heard the butcher muttering as she closed the door behind her. 'All these new people in town. That Park has a lot to answer for...Mrs Tidman, what can I get you? Nice bit of tongue?'

Alice resumed her stroll towards the footbridge and the Park beyond. The hotel, devoid of the song and laughter of the other evening, looked tired and forlorn. The curtains were pulled back, windows thrown open to the pale sunshine. A fire burned in the grate of the lounge. An older lady stood behind the bar, polishing glasses and returning them to hang above her head. She spotted Alice as she passed the window and waved a hello.

'Hope to see you in here one day soon, my dear. We serve good food. Cheap too. All the girls from the Park come in here when they get desperate for something nice.'

Alice returned the wave but didn't speak. She wasn't sure what to say. *Don't think I'm supposed to visit hotel lounges without a chaperone. Mother would have a fit if she suspected I was even thinking about it.*

Another lady, wearing a starched white apron and carrying a feather duster, pushed her way into the room.

'Morning, Mrs Richards. How are you today? Lots of clearing up from last night, as you can see. Oh, and how's Mr Richards? Is his leg feeling any better?'

Alice left the two women to their chores and gossip. In contrast to her previous visit, the road leading up to the Park gates beyond the railway bridge was busy with buses, a couple of covered trucks and several cars. Men and women, in military uniform and civilian clothes, milled about. Some were boarding the bus at the back of the line while others disembarked from the one at the front. An army sergeant — she assumed from the commanding tone of his voice — yelled instructions from the rear of one of the trucks. A dark blue car attempted to squeeze past the chaos and enter the Park. It was met with a vociferous hooting of horns and several 'Oi, watch out's' from the pedestrians.

Alice kept well out of the way. A gate sentry appeared, different to the one on duty the previous day, a clipboard in hand. He was accosted by the bossy sergeant, arms gesticulating as he made his wishes plain; he wanted access, and he wanted it now.

'It's not called the lunatic asylum for nothing. As you can see...' A girl of about her age, with neat dark hair and hazelnut-brown eyes, stuck out her hand in welcome. 'Charlotte. But my friends call me Lottie. You're new here, are you? I don't know everyone, but I never forget a face and I definitely haven't seen yours before.'

'Yes, I arrived late yesterday. Alice. Alice Stallard.' The girls shook hands. 'What is this place though? You know, besides a loony bin?'

'Oh, you've not started here yet then? It is all very confusing to begin with, isn't it? They just tell you not to ask questions and do the job you've been told to do.' She paused, the roar of the truck's engine drowning out her words. 'And of course, you can't tell anyone what your job is once you do know. Or where you work, come to think of it.'

Charlotte — Lottie — wore a khaki tunic over a knee-length skirt. She carried a cap under one arm. Sensible-looking brown lace-up shoes completed the image of a woman in wartime.

'I'm ATS — Auxiliary Territorial Service. Or Adventure Through Service as they'd like us to think.' She laughed. 'It's not that bad. Although we don't look nearly as glamorous as they do, do we?'

Alice turned to stare at the group of girls Lottie pointed out. She had to admit, they did look smarter in their navy-blue Women's Royal Naval Service uniforms. One girl's buttons were so well-polished, they glinted in the light filtering through the leafless trees above them.

'Well...' not wanting to offend a possible future friend, she hesitated in delivering a verdict.

'Ha, you don't need to be polite. We still look like a sack of spuds, even though they did a bit of a fiddle with some darts and a belt a while back.' Lottie glanced at her watch and pulled her cap down over her waves of hair. 'I'd best be off. Don't want to be late for my shift. I'll see you around, Alice. Where are you staying?'

'Albert Street. Mrs Anderson.'

Lottie grimaced in sympathy. 'At least you're close to the Park, you won't need to catch one of those infernal buses. Drive at snail's pace and they're always freezing. And you're close to the hotel. Join us for drinks one evening. It's fun. And we need to make fun to survive this place, let me tell you. Anyway, must dash.'

Lottie hurried over to the Wrens, greeting each of them with a squeal and kiss on each cheek. They linked arms and wandered in through the gates to their mysterious duties.

Friday morning and still Alice had heard nothing from the Park. Mrs Anderson was out at some church function, helping women serve tea to other women. She surprised Alice with an invitation to join her.

'You poor dear. All this way and then nothing to do but mope around at home. I don't know why they bother with bringing so many of you out here. Well, if you're sure you don't want to come along?' She wrapped herself in her thick winter coat and pulled her hat down low over her eyes. 'It's bitter out today. Full of fog since last night. Still hasn't cleared.'

As Mrs Anderson opened the door, Alice saw she was right. A thick mist swirled up and down the street, obscuring the other side of the road.

Alice and her landlady had come to an understanding; as long as she kept out of the way, was quiet and tidied up after herself, Alice was welcome in Mrs Anderson's home. She wasn't yet on the level of being invited into the sitting room to listen to evening programmes on the wireless, but at least there was no longer the animosity which had greeted her arrival earlier in the week.

'Thank you for inviting me, Mrs Anderson. I'm sure I will be fine here at home for a couple of hours. Enjoy your morning.'

As it turned out, Alice was glad she had stayed at home. Around 11 o'clock, there was a sharp knock at the door. Unsure whether she should answer it while the lady of the house was out, Alice peered down through her bedroom window to see who it was.

Parked at the kerb was the same dirty green car which had collected her from the station earlier in the week. On the doorstep, Corporal Fitch lifted his hand, preparing to knock again.

Alice tapped on the window to get his attention. He looked up and smiled. She waved and indicated she was coming down.

'Hello.' The corporal had removed his cap despite the damp. He gave a half-salute.

Not sure what kind of salute with which she should return the gesture, Alice resorted to the three Brownie fingers of her childhood.

'Ha, very clever. I'm so used to being with all the officers and so on, I forget that civilians are here as well. Sorry.'

'Good morning, Corporal Fitch. I'm afraid Mrs Anderson isn't here at the moment, but I'm sure she'd love to see you when she gets back. Why don't you come in and wait?' Alice laughed as a look of panic crossed the expressive Fitch face.

'No, no, I'm not stopping. It's you I came to see anyway.' He took a handkerchief from his pocket and blew his nose. 'Excuse me, caught a dratted cold...You are to report to the Park at twelve noon sharp. For a briefing.'

'A briefing? What am I to be briefed about? Will I be told what I'm doing here?'

'Ah, lass, you need to learn to ask fewer questions. Actually, not ask any at all and rather get on with doing what you're told.'

Why won't anyone tell me anything? I only want to know what I'm doing here. Out loud, Alice tried not to sound defensive. After all, the man was doing his job.

'Thank you, Corporal Fitch, I'll go and get myself ready.' She was about to bid Fitch farewell and close the door when she remembered something; a certain document the sentry on duty at the gate from the other day still had tucked away in his office. The blood rushed to her cheeks. *How stupid of me. I suppose I didn't think I was going back.* 'Um, there is one thing...'

'This, perhaps?' With a flourish, Corporal Fitch produced a folded square of paper from his pocket. It was his turn to laugh. 'Don't worry, that was a temporary pass, for the interview. This is your new — permanent — one. Whatever you do, don't lose it. Big trouble if you do.'

'Oh, thank you so much, that's kind of you to bring it around for me.' Alice grabbed the gate pass from the Corporal's outstretched hand.

'You're welcome. Right, I need to be on my way. 12 o'clock. Don't be late.'

'But who do I report to?'

But Fitch didn't hear over the car's starter motor. He replaced his cap on his head and raised a hand in farewell. He was soon out of sight, swallowed by the fog which was even thicker than earlier.

Oh, well, I was told not to ask questions. I suppose someone will tell me what to do when I need to do it.

Alice ran up the stairs back to her room. She scrubbed her face with a flannel cloth, gave her unruly curls as much of a comb as she dared and painted her lips with Elizabeth Arden's 'Victory Red'; another gift from the girls. *As though lipstick will win the war.*

Once out in the street, she hurried past the hotel where lunch was being served, the mouthwatering smell a considerable contrast to the sparse meal Alice was used to being served at Mrs Anderson's. She checked her watch and increased her pace; Fitch's warning about not being late spurred her on.

The entrance to the Park was again busy with traffic and people. Alice looked around for Lottie. Or even Corporal Fitch. But she saw no one she recognised. She was relieved to see she wasn't the only one in civilian clothes — *mufti*, so Vera told her, although how she knew, Alice had no idea.

'Don't just stand there, girl. You're in the way. Watch out! Did no one ever teach you how to cross a road?'

A despatch rider on a motorcycle, his goggles perched on top of his head, missed Alice by an inch or two as she darted towards the gates. 'Hey! Watch it!'

'Sorry.'

Yet another sentry was on duty. Alice pulled out her gate pass and waited while he ran his fingers over a clipboard, searching for her name.

'Ah, Miss Alice Stallard. Ballroom in the Mansion at twelve noon.'

Ballroom? Am I going to a dance?! This gets more ridiculous by the minute.

'Thank you. Um, where exactly might that be?'

'Follow the path over to the house, in at the main entrance, first door on your left.'

Alice followed the directions. By the time she reached the doors of the old mansion, she was shaking with nerves. Men and women appeared out of nowhere, their voices and footsteps muffled by the persistent fog. They seemed not to notice Alice. Or, if they did, they ignored her. Heads down and collars turned up against the damp, they rushed past her intent on whatever mission awaited them.

Wondering what mission lay ahead of her in the next few minutes, Alice unwound her scarf under the shelter of the mansion's impressive front porch. The size of the columns, the weight of the door in front of her, the glimpse of stately staircase did nothing to calm Alice's beating heart. Taking a deep breath, she pushed her way through the doors and went in search of the ballroom.

At least it doesn't look as though we're dancing then...

Chairs of all types were ranged in rows on the ballroom floor. Alice chose one near the back. Around twenty or so others were already seated, many of them girls similar in age to Alice. A few seemed to know each other, or at least to have met previously, as they sat in small groups chatting. Most sat alone. Alice was intimidated by the grandiose, oak-panelled surroundings, the girls in soft cardigans knitted in the latest shades, pearls hanging around their necks, the men handsome in suits and ties. There was a burst of laughter from a group seated near the front, inappropriate and loud; hands clamped over mouths and shoulders shaking as they tried to silence the joke.

Over by the windows a couple of men stopped their conversation, glancing at the source of the sudden outburst with slight smiles on their lips. They rolled their eyes at each other, then continued their discussion. They kept looking around the room as though checking for new arrivals. After a few late stragglers had taken their seats with embarrassed apologies, the older of the two men walked to the front.

He cleared his throat to get everyone's already undivided attention and began his speech.

Alice couldn't remember all the details of what was said that afternoon. Once the words 'Official Secrets Act' and 'Treason' were mentioned, she was unable to hear much more. The older man was replaced by the younger who issued a series of dire warnings about what the outcome would be should they ever breathe a word to anyone — 'Anyone, mind you — not your mother or father, not your best friend. And definitely not your latest sweetheart!' This latter comment he directed at the giggling group from earlier. Alice was pleased to notice they wore expressions of serious concern. She could see one of the girls twisting a pair of grey gloves into a corkscrew of anxiety.

The lecturer brought his speech to its climax. 'Should any of you be discovered breaking the Official Secrets Act, either intentionally or otherwise — and mark my words, you will be discovered — the full force of the law will be brought to bear, resulting in your internment. Or death.'

No one was talking now, almost not breathing.

The men moved over to a table at the side of the room. One picked up a clipboard and began calling out names. The other, a Wing Commander Alice later discovered, passed a wad of documents to the summoned individual sitting opposite him. She — or he, although there were a mere half a dozen or so men in today's intake — took the pen and signed their name. A few stood up with a show of bravado, smiling as though signing such a document was an everyday occurrence. Most sidled over to the other side of the room, heads down, eyes averted. Alice thought one girl, younger than herself, wiped tears with a handkerchief.

'Miss Stallard. Miss Stallard?'

With a jolt, Alice realised it was her turn to go up. *Why did I sit at the back? Everyone will be watching me.* She kept her eyes fixed on the table ahead, trying not to look flustered or break into a run.

'Good afternoon, Miss Stallard, do take a seat.' The younger man ticked her name off his list and indicated the chair.

'Thank you.'

'Miss Stallard,' the Wing Commander took over, 'do you understand all you have been told this afternoon? That you are here under strict rules of secrecy and that you will face due penalty should you break those rules?'

Alice nodded. She didn't trust her voice enough to use it.

The Wing Commander glared at her for a couple of seconds, his blue eyes searching her for any signs of rebellion. Satisfied, he held out a pen and pushed a set of papers across the table.

Taking the pen with a shaking hand, Alice stared at the papers in front of her. The letters blurred and bobbed around as though either the document or Alice were immersed in water. A finger stretched across and pointed to a large 'X' at the bottom of the first page.

'Here. Sign here, Miss Stallard.'

Alice did as she was told. Her scrawl was added to the yellowish pages, a dark commitment to keep quiet, come what may.

'Please wait over there, Miss Stallard. Someone will come through shortly and explain your duties and so on.' The Wing Commander indicated the right-hand side of the ballroom.

'Thank you, sir.' Alice pushed her chair back and moved across the room on wobbly legs, to wait underneath a gilt-framed portrait of a man in a fur-lined robe, little dogs scampering around his feet. Over the next fifteen minutes, she was joined by another girl and one of the men. They exchanged greetings without properly introducing themselves. They awaited their fate in silence. Alice glanced out of the window, surprised to be able to see the lawn and pond beyond, a mallard duck waddling over its frozen surface. The fog had lifted; everything was crisp and clear in the golden glow of a late afternoon sun.

Alice threw her things into her suitcase. Not expecting to be asked to move so soon after her arrival in Bletchley, she muttered to herself as she packed.

'Bedford. Why Bedford? Oh, where is my nightgown? Of all the places... This case is never going to close. How did I get everything in here before?'

Mrs Anderson clumped up the stairs.

'Have you got someone in there with you, Miss Stallard? You know my rule on visitors. Just because you're up and leaving doesn't mean you can carry on however you fancy.'

Alice turned to see Mrs Anderson leaning against the door frame, her chest heaving as she tried to catch her breath.

She laughed. 'Oh, you startled me, Mrs Anderson. No, sorry, I always do that when I have a lot on my mind — talk to myself, that is. I have to get all this packed and be at the station in time to take the next train to Bedford, and it doesn't seem to fit in as well as it did when I came.'

Blouses and skirts still spilled out from the suitcase and across the bed.

'Well, if you would fold your clothes for a start, I dare say they would fit in perfectly well.' Mrs Anderson sighed, pushed herself into the room and over to the bed, wafting a powerful, sweet perfume as she moved. She picked up a long skirt and shook her head. 'Here, let me help you.'

Alice passed each errant item of clothing to Mrs Anderson and watched as the efficient older woman folded and placed everything in careful piles inside the suitcase.

Finished, Mrs Anderson reached over and closed the lid, locking the brass catches with a firm click.

'There, you see. "A place for everything and everything in its place," as my old mother used to say. Even in a suitcase.' She straightened up.

'You know, I wasn't keen when the billeting officer ordered me to have someone stay in my spare room. I've been on my own so long, I'm used to it. My own ways, you know. Well, I have to admit, I am going to miss having you here. You know, another body about the place. Someone to know if I survived the night, that sort of thing.'

'You've been most kind, Mrs Anderson — thank you. I hope you get someone lovely soon. I'm sure you will — new people seem to arrive at the Park all the time, don't they?'

Mrs Anderson replied with a snort. 'Well, you'd best get off, Miss Stallard. I wish you a pleasant journey.'

Alice

Bedford

```
•⎯ •⎯•• •• ⎯•⎯• •
```

A lice was grateful for Mrs Anderson's farewell blessing but didn't find it a pleasant trip at all. This time, her train was packed with child evacuees on their way to bomb-free refuges. Sweaty, over-excited bodies added to the fug of cigarette smoke swirling through the carriage. Alice fished her handkerchief from a pocket, holding it to her nose. The children were wide-eyed and miserable. Some held hands, others cried in isolation. Alice wanted to cry with them. So many were dressed in what must be their Sunday best, shoes polished and hair brushed; the boys with sharp partings, the girls' long locks tied in pigtails. One little boy, probably no older than about five, sat next to Alice sucking his thumb. The rhythmic motion of the train, the clackety-clack of the wheels over winter tracks, the stuffy warmth of the carriage and the trauma of farewells soon got the better of him. His head drooped and he flopped over onto Alice's shoulder who put her arm around him, settling him in her lap instead. She stroked his hair.

Where are you going, little man? And where are you from? What have those eyes seen already, those ears heard? Where is your mummy? And what of your dad? And who will be there to tuck you into bed tonight?

The train arrived at Bedford station. Alice shook the boy awake and helped him with his suitcase and gas mask. He gave her a kiss on the cheek by way of thanks, then he was herded out of the carriage and down onto the platform with all the other boys and girls. Forming a ragged crocodile, they were led towards a group of people clustered at the far end of the platform. Alice tried to see who 'her' little boy was presented to. *Hopefully that man who looks like Father Christmas.*

As for Alice, there was no Corporal Fitch to greet her this time; there was no Corporal Anybody. Alice pulled a crumpled piece of paper from her pocket and read again the address of her latest billet. *Mr and Mrs Minton-Brown, 6 St Andrew's Road, Bedford.*

Approaching the stationmaster, she asked for directions.

'That's a fair trek, that is, young lady. Best you get a lift with one of those taxis at the front of the station.'

'Oh, I'm sure I can walk.'

'Don't you worry about the money, miss — there's a war on. You're obviously not here on your holidays. Tell the driver Joe sent you.'

Within twenty minutes, the taxi was pulling up at a large, red-brick house. A small patch of grass and dark green shrubs created a garden at the front of the property. Alice walked up the pathway of neat paving to a shiny black door. A polished brass knocker, letterbox and keyhole flashed a welcome.

A bit smarter than Mrs Anderson's.

The door was flung open before she had chance to raise her hand to the knocker. A woman about her mother's age stood in the doorway. She wore a pale blue cotton dress over which a checked yellow and green apron was tied. The woman wiped her hands on the apron, leaving white flour marks on the fabric.

'Mrs Minton-Brown? I'm...'

'Miss Alice Stallard? Yes, we've been expecting you. Well, I have — my husband is out at the bank. He's the manager, you know. Come in, come in, you're most welcome. Sorry about the flour, I'm in the kitchen baking up a storm for tea later.'

That explained the summer dress despite the overcast February day. Taken aback at the effusive welcome, so in contrast to that of Mrs Anderson just a week earlier, Alice took a moment to recollect her manners.

'Thank you, yes, I am Alice. Shall I leave my case here?' At a nod from her hostess, she put the case down beside the coat stand, where she hung up her overcoat. She followed Mrs Minton-Brown to the kitchen where she was already filling a kettle with water and offering tea.

The room was large and modern, full of the gadgets and appliances Alice saw in magazines; a twin-tub washing machine, a stove slotted in between two sets of cupboards with cream wooden doors. Around the walls, at eye level, glass fronted cabinets displayed a range of pretty crockery. A gleaming white fridge took pride of place opposite the stove. At the far end of the room, a walk-in pantry cupboard stood open. Neat stacks of tins and packets filled the shelves.

The central table was covered with all the paraphernalia of pie-making. A pie plate full of steaming carrots, turnips and potatoes awaited its lid, a circle of pastry already rolled and ready. On the stove, a pot simmered, the tart aroma of blackberries, apples and sugar making Alice's mouth water.

'I'm sure you'd love a cup of tea. I saved our coupons and got some Typhoo especially. Please sit down. I must get this pie in the oven otherwise there won't be any dinner tonight.' She stirred the contents of the pie dish. 'Only a few pieces of meat today, I'm afraid. The butcher didn't have much left by the time I got there this morning. I think it's time we kept chickens. We've got the space, after all.'

Alice turned in her seat to look out of the windows, open despite the weather, at the garden beyond. There was no lawn at this side of the house; furrows of rich, dark soil were planted with vegetables. At the far end of the garden, beside a hedge of holly, three or four fruit trees sheltered a wooden shed. A small patio with a wooden table and bench provided an area for the gardeners to rest and admire their handiwork.

'Thank you, Mrs Minter-Brown, tea would be lovely. And your pie smells delicious.'

'Goodness, what a mouthful — do call me Emily, dear.'

Emily finished assembling the pie and put it in the oven. She returned her attention to the tea-making.

'Now that you've had some refreshment, let me show you your room. I hope you'll be happy here. Although we never know how long our guests are with us, we do try to make it a home from home for you all.'

Alice's new bedroom was as different to the one in Albert Street as everything else about this billet. It was bright and airy and looked down over the small front garden. A pale-yellow quilted bedspread matched the curtains hanging at the window, and a simple wallpaper decorated the walls with cornflowers and daisies.

Emily left Alice to unpack and freshen up. The young woman relaxed for the first time since leaving Cambridge. *This is going to be a wonderful eight weeks, I just know it.*

Tomorrow she would start her training over the road. At the top-secret Cryptography School for Coders.

Alice's first evening with the Minton-Browns passed in something of a blur. Mr Minton-Brown — 'please, call me Harry'— arrived home at about half past five. The blackout curtains were already up at the windows. Emily was laying the table in the small dining room, a fire crackling in the grate and candles lit on the table. The evening concert was playing on the wireless.

Mr Minton-Brown parked his black Ford Anglia out on the street, walked up the garden path and in through the front door with such a cheery hello, Alice's nerves about meeting another new host evaporated.

'Emily, I'm home. Goodness, that smells delicious. Did you manage to get a decent cut of pie meat, then? You have been busy.' He removed his hat and coat and hung them over the hooks in the hallway and stored a brown leather briefcase under the hall table. Alice stood in the shadows of the kitchen doorway. 'Ah, good evening. Miss Stallard, isn't it? Yes, the billeting officer said you would be arriving today. Welcome to our home. I understand you will be staying for approximately eight weeks. For a typing course? Very good, I'm sure.'

Typing course? Remembering the document she had signed the day before, Alice realised this was how her life would be for the foreseeable future — a series of half-truths and white lies, told on her behalf by people she did not know and would never meet.

'Oh, yes, that's right — a typing course. I'm lucky to have been chosen for it. Only a handful got through the selection process.' Mr Minton-Brown looked puzzled. *Stupid. Anyone can get on a typing course.*

She continued, not allowing a gap for any questions. 'Anyway, it's awfully good of you both to put me up. Your home is lovely.'

'Thank you, we hope you will be happy here. Emily dear, are we to sit for dinner, or should we have a drink first?' He kissed his wife on the cheek.

'Well, we could have something small, to welcome Alice.' Emily wriggled free from her husband. 'Do you want to pour some sherry for each of us, while I go and finish the meal?'

'Oh, not for me thank you. I — I don't drink. But thank you for the offer. Mrs Minton-Brown — sorry, Emily — let me help you with that.' Alice retreated into the kitchen.

The pie was delicious, and more satisfying than anything Alice had eaten in weeks. She hid a yawn behind the starched cotton serviette laid at her place.

'Oh, you poor dear, you must be exhausted. You're excused from the clearing up — for tonight only, mind.' Emily winked.

'Thank you, you're very kind. I am tired, I must admit. Thank you for a delicious meal. It was lovely.' Alice rose from her place, laid the serviette to the side of her empty plate, and moved towards the door. 'Goodnight, both of you. And thank you again.'

She didn't sleep well, despite the good food and the comfortable bed. She tossed and turned, anxious for morning to come and yet dreading what morning might bring. She heard Emily and her husband climb the stairs to their own bedroom at the other side of the house. They had left a light on in the hallway downstairs. A faint glow shone under Alice's bedroom door long after she knew her hosts must be asleep.

Alice woke to the sound of the door slamming and the Ford Anglia's engine bursting into life. She rolled over and looked at the foldaway alarm clock she had put on her bedside table the night before.

'Oh no! I'm late.' Alice picked up the clock and shook it. The time was correct; she must have forgotten to set the alarm the night before. *What an awful way to start.* She threw back the covers on the bed and rushed to open the blackouts. The dark blue of night was giving way to the paler blue of early morning. A faint pink tinge could be seen over the roofs of the houses opposite. A thrush hopped along the branches of the shrubs below her window.

Deciding to skip breakfast in favour of arriving at school on time, Alice laced up her shoes, buttoned up her overcoat and pulled down her hat before pausing at the door to call a quick 'goodbye' to Emily. A muffled, 'Have a lovely day' responded from the upstairs bedroom.

Alice hurried along St Andrew's Road, careful not to slip on the patches of frost that had appeared overnight. Within a few minutes, she stood at the gate of another red-bricked property. A brass nameplate was attached to the gate post, its lettering 'International Services Bureau' partially hidden by the overhanging hedge. Assuming this was the right place, Alice pushed open the gate and walked in through doors propped open despite the morning chill.

Inside, the property showed signs of its conversion from family home to war-requisitioned office and classroom space. The flooring was patterned linoleum. Walls were painted pale green; damp showed through in dirty patches on the once-white ceiling. To her right, a frosted-glass door indicated a reception office.

Alice knocked. A woman's voice responded.

'Come in! And shut the door behind you, it's freezing out there.'

A woman in civilian clothes of white blouse and grey cardigan sat behind an old-fashioned oak desk which consumed most of the available floor space. There was room only for the woman's chair, a filing cabinet in one corner and a gas heater in the other. Forced to stand, Alice tried not to fidget.

'Miss Alice Stallard. Sent from Bletchley Park, ma'am.'

'Oh, you can cut the ma'am thing. Miss Winters will do. Yes, we're expecting you.'

Alice felt hot in the stuffy room. The window behind Miss Winters was shut, ensuring no fresh air could sneak in uninvited.

Miss Winters pulled a sheet of paper towards her, tapping a pen against her teeth as she read.

'Right we are then. Let's take you to the classroom. You've lots of work ahead of you.'

The classroom was upstairs at the back of the converted house. Alice took her place with two other women and six men who were to start the course with her. They all smiled and nodded at one another; proper introductions could wait until later.

A school blackboard was at the front of the 'classroom', a man in brown trousers and an olive-green shirt beside it.

'Good morning, one and all. I am Mr Clyde. Today we will begin your training in the art of codes and code breaking. Shall we begin?'

He turned away from his pupils and wrote a series of letters on the blackboard.

And so began one of the most fascinating lectures Alice thought she would ever attend.

They covered the history of ciphers and codes. 'From as far back as the Egyptian Pharaohs, ciphers and codes have been used to pass on secret messages. Messages only the initiated could interpret and understand...'

They discussed the various types of codes. 'Of course, there is the simple method of using a book common to both parties. The message will contain a set of numbers indicating the page, line, word and letter to be used from which the text is created.'

They practised coding a plain text message using a simple Caesar cipher, shifting the letters of the alphabet one, two, six places across. 'As you can see, the letter A will now be enciphered as B, or C, or G...'

This was all well-known to Alice, and from a quick glance around the room, also to everyone else. One of the men at the front was staring out of the window. Another stretched and yawned. The girl closest to Alice was doodling on her notepad, a complicated pattern of flowers and birds spreading across the page.

Alice allowed her mind to wander, tracing a knot of wood in the desktop with her finger. She remembered all the messages she and her brother Tom had sent to each other, when they were young. They'd used an old copy of *The Times* as their 'control', hiding it in an outhouse to make sure it wasn't thrown away. They took turns to scurry outside, create an encoded note, then run back into the house where they would push the note into a hole in the floorboards of their playroom. The recipient would retrieve the note, then take their place outside with *The Times* and translate the message.

Usually, it was nothing more exciting than 'You smell!' or 'Mum says don't be late for dinner'. Even so, it was tremendous fun and kept them occupied during the long summer holiday break from school.

Alice returned her attention to Mr Clyde who was drawing a grid on his blackboard, now wiped clean of previous notes. At the top was scrawled 'Playfair Cipher'. Underneath the title, Mr Clyde wrote the name 'CHARLES' and under that the message 'meet me at hammersmith bridge tonight'.

'And now for some fun. Have any of you heard of the Playfair cipher?' The window-gazer raised his hand a couple of inches, then lowered it, possibly uncertain if he was thinking of the right thing. No one else moved. 'The Playfair cipher is so-called because of its use by one Lyon Playfair, a scientist, politician, and one-time Postmaster-General who was made first Baron Playfair of St Andrews in September 1892. However, the invention of the code is credited to Sir Charles Wheatstone.' He underlined the word CHARLES with his piece of chalk.

'Using his name as the keyword, we can follow Wheatstone's own development of the code. First, we need to create an alphabet square, like so...

CHARL
ESBDF
GI/JKMN
OPQTU
VWXYZ

'Next, we divide our message to be sent into pairs — digraphs —like this...

ME – ET – ME – AT – HA – MX – ME – RS – MI – TH – BR – ID – GE – TO – NI – GH – TX

...adding an 'x' where there are two letters the same, and at the end to ensure there are two letters in each digraph. Understand?'

They all nodded whilst copying from the board into their notebooks.

'So we start to encipher our message, using the alphabet grid created from our keyword 'CHARLES'. Scanning the rows and columns in the grid for the corresponding message digraphs, and following a specific set of rules as given by Wheatstone, we can quickly create our encoded note, like so...'

Plain text: ME – ET – ME – AT – HA – MX – ME – RS – MI – TH – BR – ID – GE – TO – NI – GH – TX

Ciphertext: GD – DO – GD – RQ – AR – KY – GD – HD – NK – PR – DA – MS – OG – UP – GK – IC – QY

For the rest of the afternoon, the group marshalled letters across the blackboard and in their notepads with the precision of soldiers learning to square bash a patrol ground.

Alice

Homework

•⁻ •⁻•• •• ⁻•⁻• •

TRANSPOSITION KEYS

The cryptography school's students were greeted with a new heading on the blackboard on their second week of attendance. Mr Clyde was rubbing his hands together, a broad smile of delight spread across his face.

'And now, dear pupils, we get to do some real work. First, we need some grids drawing up.'

Alice pulled the ruler out of her pencil case and began drawing horizontal lines across the page of her notebook. Once finished, she swivelled the page and ran her pencil down the other way. The paper was filled with small squares.

She looked up to find Mr Clyde writing on the blackboard.

CARELESS TALK COSTS LIVES

As though we need the reminder. I hate not being able to tell Mr and Mrs M-B what I'm doing here every day. It feels so wrong, so dishonest.

There was no time to worry further; Mr Clyde was speaking again.

'Right, all finished? Good. I'm sure you're all familiar with the sentence on the board.' Several of them groaned. 'Yes, yes, I know. It is true though. Once you're finished here and out in the big bad world of war, you'll understand what all the fuss is about.'

He stopped speaking and reached for the glass of water he kept on the corner of his desk. Alice noticed his hand was shaking. She looked up at him. A fine line of sweat beaded his forehead. He wiped it with the back of his free hand, took another sip of water. *Poor man. What have you seen? The last war, or this one?*

Mr Clyde replaced the glass on his desk. Swallowing a cough, he managed to compose himself and return his attention to the blackboard and his waiting students.

'This is the key we will use to encrypt our message. Firstly, we need to make this a string of letters rather than an actual phrase — so remove the spaces between each of the individual words. The next step is to sequentially number each of the letters in our key. Starting at the first A as 1, the second A as 2 and so on, I would like you to write out the numbers.'

Alice bent her head and wrote the sentence in the squares of her grid. She scanned through the letters, numbering them as she went along.

All finished, she looked up. The other girls were also finished, as were a couple of the men. The others were still working their way through the puzzle. Mr Clyde nodded at her.

'Well done all those already finished. I know this is a painstaking process, but it is vital to get it right. As you will see in the next step.'

He tossed his piece of chalk up and down and whistled through his teeth while waiting for the others to finish.

At last, all pencils were down on the desks and heads raised.

'Okay. We need to send a message to our fellow agents. How about this?' He tapped away on the board for a couple of seconds.

THE OPERATION TO DEMOLISH THE BUNKER IS TOMORROW AT ELEVEN RENDEZVOUS AT SIX AT FARMER JACQUES

They all nodded.

'Will we be given explosives as well sir?' It was Bill Smythers. He always played the clown. A couple of others sniggered.

Mr Clyde glared. Usually happy to share a joke, this time there was no smile on his lips.

'Mr Smythers, may I remind you we are in the serious business of war? One day, you may well be out in the field with some dynamite you will be asked to detonate. I suggest you focus on this aspect of your task, so you know when and where you are to fulfil such a duty.'

'Sorry, sir. Yes, of course sir.' A chastened Bill picked up his pencil and began copying the sentence from the board.

'What are you doing, Mr Smythers? I haven't explained the next step yet.'

Bill blushed, his pale skin turning bright red from his neck to the tips of his ears. Alice looked away, embarrassed on his behalf.

Mr Clyde turned back to the rest of the class. 'Anyone else have anything to say, or shall I continue?' The silent response satisfied him. 'So, now we must fit this sentence into our transposition grid. How do you think we do that? Anyone? Yes, Alice?'

'Do we write the message as another string of letters under the two rows we already have? Or...?'

'That's exactly it. Go on then, all of you.'

'What do we with the blank squares?' This time it was Mary asking the question.

'For now, just put an X. Everyone finished? Right, next step. We take the letters from each column and group them together to create our encrypted text. Like this.' More chalk on board.

TTLF HHEA EEVR OBEM PUNE ENRR RKEJ AENA TRDC IIEQ OSZU NTVE TOOS OMUX DOSX ERAX MRTX OOSX LWIX IAXX STAX HETX

'This is the completed message which the agent can send, either in text like this or, as is the case if they are radioing through to HQ, in Morse code. Of course, the received message must be decrypted into plain text before it can be read. That's all for today; we will consider how the receiving station would unscramble the message tomorrow.'

Alice paid little attention to her walk home that night. It started snowing during the afternoon; her footsteps were muffled by the thick carpet that covered the uncleared pavement. A car drove past, its wipers flicking backwards and forwards, the driver peering forward. Alice kept her head bowed, her hands stuffed deep in her pockets. She chewed on her bottom lip, deep in concentration. She was so absorbed in her thoughts, she walked straight past Harry's car parked on the road, only realising when she was a few houses further along. *Ugh, silly goose.*

She retraced her steps and hurried up the path. Pushing open the door, she called out, 'Sorry I'm late.'

'Oh, that's alright, Alice. We're here, in the dining room already. I hope you don't mind, I've served ours. Harry is starving today for some reason.'

Alice threw her outdoor clothes over the hallway pegs and made for the dining room. Emily was serving a thick casserole of carrots, turnips and beef shin onto her plate. The smell was, as usual, incredible. Realising she was more hungry than she thought, Alice took her place. Harry said grace.

'You're even quieter that usual tonight, Alice. Is anything the matter?' Harry looked at her over the top of his spectacles.

'Oh, gosh, sorry, were you talking to me? No, no, there's nothing the matter. I had an interesting day today. I think I was still going through it in my mind. Sorry.' She smiled at both Harry and Emily. 'How was your day, Harry? I see you got home before the snow started to come down.'

'Yes, I decided to leave the bank early, didn't want to get trapped there overnight.' He laughed. 'Oh, Emily, do you know who came in today? Mrs Laver. I haven't seen her in weeks. I was asking about her Reg. Seems it's all very hush-hush, he isn't allowed to tell anyone where he is or what he's doing. Not even his wife.'

'Oh, that's not right, is it? Poor Daphne. She must be out of her mind with worry. More stew, Alice?' Emily held out another spoon of casserole.

'Goodness, no thank you, Emily, you served me an enormous portion the first time round. Could I take your plates, if you're both finished? I hope you don't mind, but I won't join you for the evening concert tonight. I — I need to do some reading before tomorrow.'

'You're welcome to read in the sitting room, you know. It's much warmer by the fire. We can keep the volume down low, can't we dear?'

Harry nodded. 'Yes, of course. What is it you have to read, Alice? Anything we would find interesting?'

'Please don't go to any trouble. I'm quite happy in my room — it's so cosy, I never feel cold there. And no, Harry, it isn't anything interesting at all! Far from it, actually.' Alice pulled a face. Emily laughed.

'Very well, you carry on. But come down for some tea before you settle in to bed, won't you?'

'Yes, I'd like that — thank you.'

Alice piled up all the plates and carried them through to the kitchen. Impatient to get upstairs to her room so she could work on her idea, she didn't wait for the water to get hot. She added extra washing liquid to the sink and dumped the plates into the cold soapy water. Leaving them to soak, she returned to the dining room to collect the other dishes. Emily and Harry were still there.

'We can bring these through, Alice, don't worry. You said you wanted to get on with your reading this evening.' Emily always noticed the needs of others, put herself out to ensure they were met. *I wonder who notices what you need?*

'I suppose you've also got some letters to write, do you?' Harry, with more questions. 'Are you learning shorthand on your course, as well as typing? Yes, of course you will be.'

'Yes, that's right, I do have some letters to see to this evening, as well as the reading I want to do.' For once, it wasn't a lie Alice was telling. She was going to attend to some letters; just not the sort Harry was meaning. 'But I'll do my chores first. Really, there's no hurry. Thank you though. You enjoy a night off, Emily.'

Alice gathered up the serving dishes, smiled at them both and pushed back out through the door. As she hurried to the kitchen, she heard their quiet conversation continue as Emily and Harry left the table.

The crockery needed a quick wipe with the cloth by the time she attended to it. Stacking the plates on the drying rack, Alice tackled the serving bowls and cooking pots next. These required a bit more of a scrub, and her hands were raw from the cold water by the time she was finished. Alice examined her red fingers; she didn't want to get chilblains. Satisfied they only needed a good dry and some Vaseline rubbing into her fingertips and around her nails before she went to bed later, she reached for the plates to put away. As she picked up the first, her elbow caught on the edge of the table, the china almost slipping from her fingers. *Ouch. More haste, less speed, Alice. You don't want to go breaking anything.*

She took more care with the remaining plates, glasses and pots. She put the knives and forks back into their drawer and grabbed the dishcloth to wipe down the counters.

Finally, she was finished, and she could escape to her room. And the evening she had planned.

She raced up the stairs, taking them two at a time. Once in her room, Alice pulled closed the blackouts. Fumbling in the dim light from the stairs, she felt for the switch on her bedside lamp. Once able to see what she was doing, Alice retrieved her suitcase from where it was stowed under the bed and wedged it against the closed door; she needed to be sure of privacy for the task she intended for the evening.

Something had occurred to her after this afternoon's lecture, an idea she wanted to try out before her next lesson. It was what had kept her so distracted on her walk home, caused her to pass Harry's parked car without seeing it. If she was right, she thought Mr Clyde would be impressed indeed. Alice sat at the desk-cum-dressing table with a fresh notebook spread out in front of her. The students were not allowed to bring home the books and papers they used at the school. Instead, everything was left in a neat pile on their desks, behind a locked classroom door. *Secrets, secrets, so many silly secrets.* It was like being a child, whispering to one another in the playground. Fun, but surely unnecessary?

Alice sucked on the end of her pencil for a few minutes. She was able to recall with considerable accuracy anything once she saw it written down, a gift which had helped her through many exams at school.

Frowning in concentration, Alice traced out the letters of the code from earlier that afternoon. She wanted to pretend she was seeing the coded message for the first time, with no prior knowledge of the instructions it contained. Using the key — which she assumed a friendly recipient of the message would have in their possession — she thought she could work backwards and unscramble the sets of letters and so reassemble the 'clear text'.

She wrote out the groups of four letters, numbering them in order as she went.

1TTLF 2HHEA 3EEVR 4OBEM 5PUNE 6ENRR 7RKEJ 8AENA 9TRDC 10 IIEQ 11OSZU 12NTVE 13TOOS 14OMUX 15DOSX 16ERAX 17MRTX 18OOSX 19LWIX 20IAXX 21STAX 22HETX

If I put those back into columns in the order the key says they should be...

Alice created a grid of squares like the one she drew up at the school. First, she filled in the key they were using — CARELESS TALK COSTS LIVES — taking out all the spaces between the words. Scanning across the new phrase, she entered in the numbers associated with each letter. Next, drawing arrows and lines across her page, Alice worked out where each of the four-letter code groups should fit into her grid.

Neat, tidy handwriting was an essential; twice she misread the letter 'O', thinking it was a 'D', and had to start again.

Nearly there...

'Alice, dear, I'm putting the kettle on for tea. Will you come down?' Alice jumped at the sound of Emily's voice from the bottom of the stairs. Her hand lurched across the page, a squiggly line through her precious grid.

Drat. Now look what you made me do. 'I'll be done in five minutes, thank you, Emily.'

'Good. I'll get everything ready. Mr Barlow had a few digestive biscuits in the shop today; we'll have a couple of those.'

Alice ignored her. She was so close, she knew it.

A few minutes more and half a pencil left, Alice sighed with satisfaction. She leant back in her chair, arms stretching behind her head.

The plain text message was clear in front of her.

THE OPERATION TO DEMOLISH THE BUNKER IS TOMORROW AT ELEVEN RENDEZVOUS AT SIX AT FARMER JACQUES

'I've done it, I've actually done it.' Alice laughed out loud. She remembered about the tea. And the biscuits. *Better hurry if I want to get one.*

Shoving her suitcase back under the bed, Alice opened the door and reached to turn off the light. As she leant forward, she caught sight of the notebook on the other table. *Agh!* The booklet was still open, the pages on full display to anyone who wanted to look. Alice trusted both Emily and Harry, of course, but she knew if she didn't form this secrecy habit now, when it didn't matter, she would never get it right when it did. Hastening back to her makeshift desk, she closed over the notebook, then pushed it under her mattress as the safest place to keep it. Satisfied with her security arrangements, Alice turned off the light and went downstairs to Emily and Harry.

'Ah, here she is! How was the reading? And the letter writing? Get everything done?' Harry looked at her over the top of his newspaper. 'I must say, you are a most diligent student, Alice. I would have you working in the bank with me anytime. I should put a word in with Phyllis. She heads up the typing pool, y'know?'

'Don't be silly, Harry, darling. I'm sure Alice has other things in mind rather than working in the bank. Don't you?' She winked at Alice. 'Besides, she's doing the course at the request of the War Office. They must have a, well, more exciting, post in mind for her.'

'Yes, you're right of course, dear. But maybe after this wretched war is over, eh?'

Emily poured Alice her tea into a delicate cup and saucer. They always used the best china in the evening. It was decorated with an intricate pattern of pink roses, yellow primroses, and a trail of green leaves.

'Please don't bring out anything special for me, Mrs Minton-Brown,' Alice had said on her first evening.

'We always use this set after dinner; we like the excuse to get it out and enjoy it. Why buy something only to leave it hidden away? And please, I really would prefer if you called me Emily.'

Emily held a plate of digestives towards Alice. On one of the best china plates, of course.

'Thank you, I would love one. And yes, thank you, Harry, I did get everything finished. Oh yes, alright then, I will have a second biscuit, they're such a treat.' Alice alternated her attention between Harry and Emily, a conversational tennis spectator. She took her tea and biscuits and retreated to her seat in the window.

They sat munching and sipping in companionable silence. The wireless was on low, waiting for the news bulletin to start. The fire glowed in the grate.

'You poor thing, you must be shattered. Having to work in the evening too.' Emily picked up her knitting again.

'I don't know about me. You seem to work all day and all night, Emily. What are you making now?'

'Socks! Apparently, the army need even more.' Alice watched as the needles plucked and pulled at the dark grey yarn at Emily's feet, surprised at how she didn't look at her creations while she worked. Within a few minutes, she was already casting off the stitches of one sock and getting ready to start the next. 'And yes, I suppose I do work whatever hours the Lord sends. You know, the wife of Proverbs 31?' She chuckled.

Alice wasn't used to anyone but her parents quoting the Bible. It reinforced her conviction that this was the best billet she could have wished for. A wave of homesickness washed over her, unexpected in its suddenness and intensity. She bent her head to wipe away a couple of tears; she didn't want Emily to notice. She would either be concerned that she wasn't being a good enough hostess — which couldn't be further from the truth — or she would be kind. And that would make Alice cry even more.

'Ssh, the news is about to start...' Harry turned up the volume of the wireless. The chimes of Big Ben filled the peaceful sitting room.

'I'll leave you to it, if you don't mind. I think, as you say, working in the evening as well as during the day isn't so good for me. I'm exhausted — I can hardly keep my eyes open.' Alice rose from where she sat and returned her cup and saucer to the tea tray. As she turned to leave, Emily put down her knitting, squeezing Alice's hand before she was able to move away.

'We do pray for you, Alice dear.' She spoke in such a low voice, Alice struggled to hear her words over the sound of the newsreader. Alice couldn't speak. Her throat was constricted and tight, her vision blurred as more tears threatened to spill over.

Emily patted her hand again, then let go. 'You get up to bed. It will be better in the morning. You'll see.'

Alice laboured up to her bedroom, the euphoria of her earlier accomplishment eclipsed by overwhelming tiredness. Her fingers fumbled with the buttons on her blouse, slowing her progress and delaying the moment when she could collapse into bed. She burst into tears. It was her first real cry since she had posted the crossword all those weeks ago; the swallowed sobs at Mrs Anderson's didn't count.

What have I done?

Rosie

June 1998

●▬● ▬▬▬ ●●● ●● ●

R osie threw her pen down and watched as it skidded across a desk piled high with papers and textbooks.

'I've had enough.' With a groan, she stretched and pushed out of her chair. 'Mum! Can I make lunch? Mum?'

'I'm down in the office, Rosie, finishing off these accounts for your dad. What did you say?'

Rosie wandered downstairs, following Mum's voice to the farm office at the front of the house. Filing cabinet drawers gaped open, coloured labels fastened to metal dividers sticking up like warning flags. Invoices and receipts overflowed the in and out boxes Mum kept on the corner of the desk. She swivelled around in her chair, pushing a pair of reading glasses up into her hair as she turned to Rosie.

'Sorry, what were you saying? Or yelling, I should say.'

Before Rosie could reply, the printer burst into life, the clack clack of paper feeding into the rollers distracting Mum's attention away from her. Rosie rolled her eyes.

'I'm getting lunch. See you in the kitchen when you're done.'

'Yes, right, won't be long.'

Rosie was cutting thick slices of warm homemade bread when Mum came through.

'Well, thank goodness that's done for another week or so. Not my favourite task around the place, I must say. Do you want cheese and tomato sandwiches or would you rather have soup?'

'A sandwich I think.' Mum passed over cheese, a few slices of ham and a couple of tomatoes for Rosie. 'Thanks. And I'm done too. Done studying. It's History tomorrow and I've gone through everything so many times I can't think straight.'

'And that's your last exam, isn't it? Well done, Rosie-P, you've worked hard for your A-levels. Your dad and I are proud of you. I'm sure you can take the rest of the day off.' She winked at her daughter. Picking up their lunch plates she walked towards the open back door. 'Let's have these outside. You can bring a couple of glasses of water. Or juice if you prefer.'

'Water's fine.' Rosie poured water into two tall glasses and plucked a sprig of fragrant mint from the pot on the windowsill. 'I'll add a bit of flavour to mine though.'

A paved patio stretched along the length of the house. There was a view across the garden to a small stream burbling its way through the farm. Dragonflies flitted in the shade of the hawthorn bushes clustered on its banks. Mum sat at the wooden picnic table, her face tipped towards the sun.

'This is the life, isn't it?' She bit into her sandwich, tomato seeds squirting out and running down her chin. She wiped them away with the back of her hand. 'Delicious. So, dad and I were wondering, once the exams are over, if you'd had any thoughts about what you fancy doing when you're finished? Emma will still be at school, and we don't have the pickers coming in for another few weeks, so you won't be needed to help with anything on the farm straight away. What about going away somewhere, maybe with Laura?'

Rosie swallowed a gulp of water. 'Well, I wondered about going to see Gran and Gramps for a bit. I don't suppose I'll see them as much once I'm away at uni and it would be fun to go and visit them on my own for a change. You know, find out what they do all day, that kind of thing.'

'That's kind of you, Rosie, but wouldn't you want to go somewhere more exciting, let your hair down a bit? There won't be much happening in the village, I shouldn't think. There's the pub and the community centre, but that's about it. Oh, and the church of course. But that won't be like church here, with all you youngsters involved and everything. I think it's a bit old-ladyish from what Mum's said.'

'I quite fancy some peace and quiet after the last few months. And Laura and me could always go away for a weekend later in the holidays, if we can be spared. Or a day in London, something like that. Besides, I can keep an eye on Gramps for you.'

The harsh winter had taken its toll on her grandfather's health, with more than one trip to the hospital causing some alarm to the family. There was talk about selling the cottage, moving closer to town into some kind of sheltered accommodation. But both he and Gran resisted the idea and his steady return to strength convinced everyone they could remain in their own home for a while longer.

'Yes, that's true. It might be a good idea. But only for a few days, maybe a week or so. I do think you'd find it more boring than you expect.' Mum stood up, brushing crumbs from her lap. 'Anyway, we can chat to your dad about it some more later. I need to go and clear up all my mess in the office before getting started with tea. Chops and mash tonight.'

Rosie drained her glass. 'And I'll force myself to work a little longer. Just in case I've forgotten something.'

Back in her room, Rosie ignored her textbooks and study notes. Instead, she grabbed a sheet of paper and plonked down on the bed. Chewing the end of her pen, she grinned. Her plan had worked. Her resolve from earlier in the year, to visit Gran and Gramps and see what discoveries she could make about their past, was still strong. But she couldn't see a way to make it happen; they always visited as a family, and never for more than a few days at a time. Mum had been up and down quite a bit with Gramps, helping with hospital appointments and that kind of thing but Rosie wasn't included in those trips. Besides, they were hardly the time for detective work.

But here was an ideal opportunity. Rosie could go there for a week or two on her own while the rest of the family were still busy. Slotting into her grandparents' lives would make it easier to chat, to ask a question or two when she got the chance. It would seem less like an interrogation, less threatening. And Mum would be happy, knowing someone would be able to report on whether they were coping at home or not.

Rosie pulled the pen from her mouth and began writing. There were certain questions she was determined to have answered.

Why don't you talk about the War?

She scratched that out. *Bit confrontational to start with, maybe.*

What was the War really like?

That's better.

What was rationing like?
What was the Blitz like?

They're innocent questions, surely? Now for something a little deeper maybe.

Where did you live during the War?
What work did you do?
Do you have any photographs?

I'm going to ask it...

Why don't you talk about the war?

Rosie read through the questions. How could any of them be a problem to answer? Except the last one. But that was silly; what reason could there be for not talking about something that everyone already knew about?

Satisfied with her 'studies', Rosie folded the paper in half and lay it on the bed next to her. Rolling over on to her side, she closed her eyes.

I'll have a quick nap before tea.

Alice

Next Steps

.— .—.. .. —.—.. .

Emily was right; a good night's sleep was all Alice needed. She woke up early, refreshed and once more excited about her discovery of the evening before. She hurried to get dressed and prepare herself for the day. Hefting the mattress up, she pulled out the notebook for a quick read-through of her work to refresh her memory; just as papers and notes were not allowed out of the top-secret coding school, neither were any allowed in.

Satisfied she knew it well enough to jot down once in the classroom, Alice pushed the book back under the mattress, smoothed down the bedspread and stepped over to remove the blackout curtains. It was still a few minutes before dawn; the stars, bright in a clear sky, illuminated the road and patch of garden below her. More snow had fallen during the night, soft mounds piled up against the gate posts. An icicle dangled from the outside window frame. A car lumbered past, the driver slow in the treacherous conditions of ice and the slits of headlight to see by.

Alice watched it drive past then peered at the glowing hands of her watch. Time for breakfast.

She found Emily already in the kitchen, a pot of tea warm under a blue and white knitted tea cosy. Emily stood at the stove, stirring a steaming pot of porridge oats.

'Good morning, Emily. I wasn't expecting you to be up already. I hope I didn't disturb you?'

'Morning, Alice. How are you this morning? Did you sleep well? I'm sure you feel better for it?' Emily wiped her hands on the apron wrapped around her waist. 'No, you didn't disturb me at all. Harry has a meeting in London today and needs an early start. So, I set the alarm for a few minutes earlier than usual, to make you both some porridge oats for a change before you head off for the day.'

'Gosh, thank you. That is kind of you. Here. let me set the table for us then.'

'Thank you, dear. And pour us our tea while you're at it. You can leave Harry's in the pot — he'll be down in a moment. No point in it going cold.'

Alice clattered around with bowls and spoons while Emily attended to the porridge. It was unusual for them to be together at this time of day. Harry was the first out, followed soon afterwards by Alice. Emily always got up to make tea and cook something for them both — powdered eggs, toast, bacon if she could get it — but then retreated upstairs while the others organised themselves.

Alice poured the strong dark tea into the two cups. She would have liked some sugar, but, since the start of war and rationing, she was trying to train herself to go without. *I'd rather my share was used to bake a cake.* Passing Emily her tea, Alice pulled a chair out for herself. She sat without speaking, chewing her lip and sipping at her tea. She didn't want to talk too much in case the memorised letters of her decrypted code rearranged themselves into something different. Or fell out of her mind altogether.

'There you are. Eat up. As I say, don't worry to wait for Harry, he'll be here in a moment.'

As Emily finished speaking, the sound of her husband clumping down the stairs and along the hallway indicated he was indeed on his way.

The kitchen was soon filled with his nervous presence. He kept fiddling with his tie and smoothing his hair. He slurped at the tea Emily put in front of him but barely touched the bowl of porridge.

'Harry! You need to eat before you go. You know they probably won't provide anything once you get there.'

Harry picked up his spoon for a couple of mouthfuls before a glancing at his watch. 'Goodness, is that the time?' He gulped the last dregs of his tea, gave Emily a kiss on the cheek. 'Thank you, darling, sorry, I don't have time to have any more. Can't miss the early train.'

He was already out in the hallway, pulling on his overcoat, grabbing his hat and scarf. He picked up his leather briefcase from beside the hall table and unlatched the door. An icy blast blew through to the kitchen. Alice shivered. *Maybe I should run up and fetch a cardigan before I leave. The classroom is full of draughts — it'll be freezing today.*

Harry slammed the front door behind him with a 'Bye, have a good day.' Alice could hear the car engine stutter and complain at being woken from its night-time slumber. Coaxed into life and off on its way to the station, silence returned to St Andrew's Road.

'I must also be off, Emily.' She gathered the plates and bowls and carried them to the sink. 'I want to get in a bit early, go through some of the...reading I was doing last night.'

'Yes, of course, you get off, Alice. And have a good day. Be careful of the ice on the pavement — it will be bad after the extra snowfall last night.'

'Thank you, Emily. Yes, I'll be careful. And thank you for breakfast. And everything.' Alice avoided eye contact as she spoke, not wanting the emotion of last night to return. She hurried to fetch her cardigan and get out of the house.

Alice made it to the school gates in one piece, although not without some slipping and sliding along the way. She hurried through the doors and up to the classroom. Still locked. Mr Clyde must be running late, on account of the weather.

Alice slid down and sat on the carpeted floor, her back against the wall. She closed her eyes, visualising the page of letters and numbers stored back in her bedroom.

'Miss Stallard? Is that you? Are you quite alright?' It was Mr Clyde.

Oh, how embarrassing. 'Yes, Mr Clyde, I am quite fine, thank you for asking.' Alice stood up; no easy task encumbered as she was with overcoat, hat, gloves, gas mask and handbag. 'Sir — Mr Clyde — I wonder if I could have a moment of your time before the others arrive?'

The man stopped fiddling with the key in the lock and looked up at Alice. 'Yes, I suppose so. Come in then. Just let me get this dratted door unlocked. I must speak to Fred about it. Always sticking.'

A bit more wiggling and there was a satisfying click. Mr Clyde held open the door for Alice to pass through, then closed it behind them both.

'So, what do you want to talk to me about, Miss Stallard? Are you finding the course somewhat taxing? Would you like me to go back over the example we used for transposition keys? I know it can take a few times of trying before one fully grasps all the concepts.' As he spoke, he flicked on the lights and bent to switch on the gas heater at the front of the room.

Alice, meanwhile, went straight to her desk. Turning to a blank page in her notebook, she filled in a new grid from memory. Having finished getting the classroom ready, Mr Clyde came and looked over her shoulder.

'What...what on earth are you doing? Don't you know you aren't allowed to take anything — and I mean ANYTHING — out of this room at the end of the day?' He began to pace backwards and forwards behind Alice, running his hands through his hair. 'And I thought we had impressed upon you all the need for total and utter secrecy around the work you are doing. I will have to report this to Major Masters. Immediately.'

He started to move towards the door.

'No, Mr Clyde, listen.' Alice grabbed her teacher's arm as he tried to pass. 'Sorry, sir, but honestly, I haven't taken anything back to my billet. Other than in my head, by memory. Please. Let me explain.'

'You have five minutes.'

'Thank you, sir. You see, I was so fascinated by your teaching yesterday, I simply couldn't get it out of my head. For the first time in my life, I felt like I was actually living.' She paused, checking to see if Mr Clyde was listening as she bared her soul. He was. He sat in one of the other chairs, leaning forward on his elbows. He nodded for her to continue. 'You see, I've always loved mathematics, have used it is a sort of hiding place. Like when I was lonely at school or when Tom, my brother, left home. Any time I was sad or upset I suppose.

'But I also love words and letters, the patterns they form, the stories they tell. The two — the numbers and the letters — have never gone together, to match. Until yesterday.'

She picked up the pencil from her desk, surprised to see her hands shaking. *I have never felt so passionate about anything before.* She glanced over at her teacher. The anger from earlier had evaporated; he was smiling, his blue eyes dancing with delight. And mischief. He still didn't speak, so Alice continued.

'And then, sir, you stood up with your grid and your code and your numbers and letters. And suddenly it all fits. Everything fits...'

Alice couldn't continue. Horrified, she began to cry, her face crumpling, her cheeks burning. Self-revelation overwhelmed her. *This is what I was made for. This. This is it.*

Mr Clyde was offering her his handkerchief.

'Yes, Miss Stallard. Alice. It does all fit, doesn't it? Compose yourself and then please, let's discuss the work you have in front of you. I take it you spent the evening deciphering our message from yesterday? Am I right?'

Alice nodded. 'I couldn't get it out of my head. All the way home, it went around and around. I even walked past my billet, I was thinking about it so much.'

For the next fifteen minutes Alice showed Mr Clyde her workings, described the process she used to decipher the message, checked and rechecked with him that she was correct. By the time the others arrived, she was calm again. Her new mentor, having retrieved his sodden handkerchief with a grimace, stood at his place next to the blackboard as usual. He began writing as everyone settled into their seats. The tapping of the chalk brought them all to an expectant silence.

'Good morning, class. Before we move onto the next level of encryption and coding, we first need to make sure we can decipher our own messages.'

The students laughed and together worked through the example. By lunchtime they were at the same place Alice had been since the previous evening.

A short break to consume the luncheon meat and overboiled carrots offered by the school canteen, and they returned to the classroom for an afternoon of further practices. Each created their own transposition keys and messages to encode. There was much pencil sucking and a concentrated silence, except for the occasional 'No, that isn't right' or 'I've got the numbers in the wrong order, sir'. Papers were crumpled and thrown on the floor in disgust, new pages begun.

Alice raced through hers. She sat ready for the next part of the exercise — to pass the coded messages on to one another to see if they could be deciphered. Mr Clyde watched her every move, jotting something down on the page in front of him. As they began to try and make sense of one another's scrambled orders, he got up from his seat to pace around the classroom, stopping to look over Alice's shoulder as he reached her desk.

Again, Alice finished before her fellow fledgling coders.

Mr Clyde held her book aloft.

'This, dear people, is how it should be done. Neat, precise and speedy. Congratulations, Miss Stallard, you go to the top of the class.'

Everyone burst into a round of spontaneous applause. Even Bill joined in. He winked at Alice from his place at the other side of the classroom. 'Bravo, Miss Stallard.'

Mr Clyde clapped his hands together to regain the class's attention.

'That's enough, thank you. But before you go on your way, I want you to be aware the exercises we do here are child's play in comparison to those you will encounter on your graduation from this place. Each code group will comprise five letters, not the four we've been working with. There will be indicators included; codes which inform the cryptographer which key words should be used when deciphering the message. Furthermore, there will be security checks which you will need to watch out for — deliberate mistakes, that sort of thing. Then, of course, you need to remember the message sender is unlikely to be creating or transmitting his communication from the comfort of a classroom such as this...' He broke off. His gaze became blank as though focused, not on a group of students, but some experience or memory which Alice couldn't begin to guess at; whatever it was, it was a disturbing nightmare even daylight hours couldn't banish. Mr Clyde licked his lips and refocused his attention on the men and women sitting in silence in front of him. 'That's it for today. Make sure you rest well tonight. Double transposition tomorrow.'

He looked over at Alice who nodded in acknowledgement.

There was the usual bustle as everyone grabbed their things and headed out of the door, eager to escape the confines of the classroom.

Bill caught up with Alice on the stairs.

'Alice, wait up.' He walked beside her the rest of the way down. 'You're rather good at this, aren't you? No, don't be modest — I've seen how quickly you get everything finished. You're always the first to be staring out of the window, waiting for the rest of us to get a move on.'

'Well, you're always a close second, Bill.' She paused. 'It's fun though, isn't it? Aren't you enjoying it?'

'Yes, it is better than I expected. I want to be out in the action though, not messing around with letters and numbers all day. My friends are in France...Africa — not that they can be specific about anything, but you get to hear, don't you?'

He waited for Alice to put on her hat and scarf then together they stepped out into the early evening twilight. Classmates shouted their farewells, walking down the street in small groups.

'Where is your billet? Can I walk you home?'

'Thank you. But I'm further back down St Andrew's Road — isn't it out of your way?'

'No, not really. Besides, I could do with the exercise and the fresh air. And it gives me a chance to get to know you a bit, without all the other chaps hanging around and listening in.' He looked at Alice, a faint blush growing on his cheeks. *Or is it just the cold?*

Alice always thought of boys — men — as she did her brother and his friends; to be tolerated at worst, to be competed with at best. Mavis and Vera were appalled.

'Really, Alice, can't you tell he likes you?' Vera would say, eyes rolling in despair. 'I don't know why you don't realise how pretty you are. All those blonde curls. And big blue eyes. If you just dressed up a bit, you know, used some of this lipstick I keep offering to you, you'd be quite irresistible.'

Alice wasn't sure she wanted to be irresistible, especially not to Bill who took her elbow as they navigated a frozen puddle in the pavement. Not that there was anything wrong with him, he just wasn't her type. *Oh, so you do have a type, then?* Vera would be in hysterics at that.

'Thank you, Bill, it's kind of you to walk with me.' She pulled her arm away, not wanting him to get the wrong impression about her. 'So, where do you want to be for the rest of the war, then? Once you're finished here?'

'I was all set to join the RAF, become a pilot, all that sort of thing. I know, it sounds corny, doesn't it? It's what all the boys want.'

'Ha, yes, and all the girls want to be Wrens. It's the uniform! Sorry, go on.'

'Anyway, so I was all set to join up and do the training and so on, when I got a letter telling me I was needed for some other special duties. And to report here for training. I don't know anything other than that. Oops, careful, the snow here is quite deep.'

He helped Alice over the pile of snow covering the path, then let go of her hand. *Well, at least he's getting the message. I do hope I haven't been rude.*

'The snow does seem to have got worse during the day, doesn't it? I'll be glad to get indoors out of this wind.' Alice hoped a grateful smile would take the sting out of her obvious rejection of Bill's tentative advances. She would like to have him as a friend, at least until the course was over. It did get a bit lonely, spending all her time with only the Minton-Browns. 'I haven't been told anything, about what I'm doing or where I'm going to next. I know it's all terribly hush-hush, but you'd think they could give us some idea, wouldn't you?'

'Yes, you would. Oh well, I suppose all will be revealed.'

They crunched on through the snow, an easy silence between them.

'I say, a few of us are planning on going to the pictures at the weekend. Would you like to join us?'

'That would be lovely. Thank you. Oh, this is me.'

Harry still wasn't back from his visit to London, his parking space empty of all except the freshly fallen snow.

'Good, I'm glad you'll join us. And have a good evening — see you tomorrow. Maybe I'll beat you for once.' Bill gave Alice a mock salute, clicking his heels together for emphasis.

She laughed and resorted to her Brownie salute again in response.

'We shall see about that, sir! Thank you for walking me home, it was kind of you.'

'The pleasure is all mine. Until tomorrow then.' Bill turned and walked back the way they had just walked.

On your way indeed. Alice chuckled. *The girls would be proud of me.* She was still smiling as she entered the house. 'Hello Emily, I'm home.' It had been a good day, what with one thing and another.

Alice

Postings

•⁻ •⁻•• •• ⁻•⁻• •

W inter progressed to Spring in Bedford. Gardens, covered in snow
for what felt like months, were instead carpeted with snowdrops
and the pale purple splash of bluebells. Hedgerows were alive with the
sound of nesting birds. The pervading smell of damp clothes and musty
rooms gave way to the effect of open windows, blossoming flowers and
bright, fresh air. Emily's vegetable patch yielded early peas and beans, a
welcome change from the root vegetables of winter meals.

Alice strolled to the coding school along a street transforming before
her eyes. She was excited for the change in season; not only for the passing
of the bitter cold of the last few weeks or the joy of longer days, but
also for the slow awakening from hibernation she felt within herself. No
longer a lost child pushed from billet to billet, she woke each morning
with a sense of purpose. Of belonging.

Emily and Harry were her parents away from home, loving and kind
without probing or enquiring all the time. The group of students she
went about with at weekends entertained her as much as her university
friends ever had; they went to the pictures, or to dances, or for long walks
in the thawing countryside. They laughed at each other's eccentricities,
or inability to grasp the latest cryptographical challenge. They cried
when telegrams arrived with news of tragedy or loss, cheered when
engagements and births were announced.

The time of training and learning was coming to a close. There was
a new edge to their socialising, a poignancy born out of uncertainty.
Anxiety lurked on the outskirts of every conversation, tinged every

moment. 'Will I ever see you again?' the unspoken question in every laugh, behind every smile.

Alice had excelled in all areas of the course, continuing to beat Bill, now her best friend, in most exercises. Mr Clyde gave her harder and harder messages to encode or decrypt, her mind becoming more supple and capable as her fingers flew faster across the pages of squared grids she produced.

Today they were to be told of their next assignments.

One by one they were called in to the 'headmaster's' office and presented with a sealed envelope of instructions. Alice arranged to meet Bill at the café in town where they would compare notes.

'Bill, there are you, sorry to have kept you waiting. Goodness, Major Masters can go on, can't he?'

Bill didn't answer. He avoided her gaze as Alice took her seat opposite him, withdrew his hand as she reached to give it a squeeze of hello.

'Bill? Whatever is the matter?' Her eyes fell on the brown envelope beside Bill's tea plate. 'Oh...'

She busied herself with the menu while she waited for his reply, blinking away a rush of emotion which took her by surprise. *Good job I know it off by heart.* They both knew they would be sent to do some sort of war work; after all, that was the whole point of them being on the course. Every time they discussed it, despite the tense atmosphere at the cryptography school, they shared one another's excitement and anticipation. They talked of postings and heroics, of high drama and magnificent reunions. Hearing the distress in Bill's continued silence, reality was sinking in.

'What does it say, Bill? Where are you going?' He looked up at her, warning her not to say anything further. 'I know it's secret and you can't tell me exactly. But it's me, Bill, you can tell me something, surely?'

'Let's go for a walk. I don't feel like tea.'

He stood up without waiting for a reply, almost knocking into a waitress passing behind him.

'Oy, watch it.' Her tray of tea things rattled and threatened to fall before she steadied herself.

'Sorry.' Bill was already halfway to the door.

'Sorry, bad news I think.' Alice apologised on his behalf then followed out into the street.

'Let's go to the park. No one will be listening there.'

They found a bench next to the pond. A family of newly-hatched ducklings waddled along the water's edge, shepherded by their mother at the front and father at the back. They plopped into the water and paddled across to the other side, a neat 'V' following in their wake.

'So?' Alice could hear her heart beating in her ears. Her palms were damp and sticky as they rested in her lap. *Please, just tell me.*

'Scotland.'

'Scotland? Why Scotland? Oh...' Understanding spread across Alice's face, her eyes wide.

The students at the cryptography school weren't told much about who ran the facility they attended or what its broader purpose was, but they all picked up bits of conversation and snippets of information which they shared with each other. They knew it was part of a secretive division of the War Office, apparently overseen by Churchill himself. What exactly that division was responsible for, they weren't sure, but they had heard it ran underhand or 'ungentlemanly' tactics in its effort to win the war against the Germans.

The school was one of several specialist training institutions dotted around the country. It was believed there was also one in the Scottish Highlands.

'Well, you wanted to do more than write messages in bottles, dear Bill.' Alice took his hand in hers, trying to reassure herself as much as her friend.

Bill rubbed the back of her hand with his thumb, his mind elsewhere. He sat up straighter on the bench.

'Yes, you're right, of course. It was the shock, I think. I don't know where I expected to end up, but it certainly wasn't Scotland. I hate the cold.'

'I'll knit you some socks.' Alice was as determined as her friend to keep the tone light. Regardless of how false they knew they were being.

Bill twisted in his seat to look at her. 'Thank you, I will wear them with pride. And think of you often.'

Alice swallowed hard. She focused her attention on the returning ducks.

'Anyway, old girl...' He knew she hated the expression. A deliberate attempt to make her smile or react with feigned annoyance. It didn't work; she continued to follow the progress of the ducks. 'Sorry, I know it's not a laughing matter. But as you say, I do want to get involved. You know I do.'

Tears shone bright as she turned to face him. 'Yes, I do. So does everybody.'

He lifted her hand to his lips, grazing a kiss across her fingers.

'Dear Bill. I shall miss you terribly. We shall meet up though, when you have leave?'

'Of course, silly goose. But where shall we meet? You haven't told me where you're to report for duty?'

Alice sniffed, wiping her eyes with her hand. 'London. Well, to start with anyway. I must go for some interview or other. Oh, but you know why I took so long earlier?'

'No, tell me.' They were friends again, chatting about the banality of their day. Nothing sinister.

'So, when I went into the office, there was a woman sitting beside the Major.'

'There wasn't when I was there. Sorry, sorry, I'll stop interrupting.'

Alice frowned then carried on with her account. 'Yes, so there was this woman there. In a brown uniform. Bit like the Auxiliary Territorial Services one, you know?'

Bill nodded but kept quiet.

'So, when I was told about going for an interview in London, she pipes up that I would be asked to join up as a volunteer with the FANY.' Seeing Bill's mystified expression, she translated for him. 'The First Aid Nursing Yeomanry.'

'What? They want you to become a nurse? On horseback?!'

'Well, I'm not sure. I certainly hope not. I'd be very unsuitable — I faint at the sight of blood and can't ride a horse to save my life. I did have an aunt who was in the Calais line back in the Great War. The woman seemed quite impressed when I told her that.' Alice paused, remembering the strange nature of the earlier interview. The woman and the Major kept exchanging looks, or scribbling notes on the papers in front of them. A late afternoon sun dappled the desk with its dancing light and shadows so Alice couldn't make out what they wrote, despite being quite good at upside-down reading. The scene felt staged, as though they were running through a formality, the outcome of which was decided days before. 'She said they do other things now. And that I would be highly suited for involvement with one of those 'other things' once I completed some further training.'

'London could be a bit tricky, if that's where you get to stay. Have you seen it since the Blitz?' Alice shook her head; she hadn't been to London since the war started. 'You'll get a shock when you do go. And when is your interview, by the way?'

'Day after tomorrow. Bill, will you travel down with me? Please. I've just thought of it. We could make a day of it.' Emotion made her voice wobble. 'I'd like your company.'

Rosie

August 1998

•⁻• ⁻⁻⁻ ••• •• •

R osie stretched over to pluck a few beans from amongst the trailing
vines. Gran knelt beside her, searching for the last strawberries of
the summer. Gramps watched them from his seat in the conservatory,
his favourite place to watch whatever was going on. The warmer weather
and longer days, slow walks in the fresh air and afternoon naps in the
shade of an apple tree in the garden had worked together to heal and
restore him from his winter ailments; his skin was tanned and healthy,
the cough a minor irritation when he laughed or if food went down the
wrong way.

Gran was also happier, more relaxed, than the last time they had come
to the farm. Then, she had looked worn and anxious, concerned for the
health and well-being of her husband.

'The slugs have been having a feast down here.' Gran sat back on her
knees, her hands resting on her thighs. She wore a wide straw hat and soft
leather gardening gloves. Damp soil marks were smeared across her face
and upper arms.

'Gran, you do look a sight.' Rosie tried to wipe the worst of the dirt
from her grandmother's face. 'Oops, I think I made it worse. I wish I had
a mirror, and I would show you.'

'Oh dear, occupational hazard of gardening, I suppose.' Gran laughed,
wiping her gloved hands across her nose and making even more of a mess.

'Goodness, you look as though you're off to do some army deep-cover
camouflage exercises down at Dartmoor.'

'Never mind dear, I'm almost finished here. Just want to get
something for these slugs, then I'll go in and clean myself up.' Gran got

to her feet. Rosie put out out a hand to help her, but it was swatted away. 'I might be old, but I can still stand up on my own, you know. You cheeky young thing.'

As if to prove a point, Gran took brisk, firm strides to the garden shed where Rosie could hear her moving pots and tools in search of the home-made slug repellent Gramps concocted every summer. She had no idea what was in it, but it worked a treat; Gran's vegetables and flowers displayed fewer signs of having been munched by the slimy creatures than those at home.

Rosie turned back to the beans. She was grateful Mum and Dad had given their permission for her stay here. A couple of short discussions about how long she could be spared away from the farm, a phone conversation with a delighted Gran and it was all arranged.

Rosie wiped the sweat from her forehead; she couldn't remember having been so hot in all her life. The news reports kept saying it was the warmest summer on record. There were hosepipe bans in place across the country; cars were dusty, and the grass was brown.

She turned at the sound of Gran returning from the shed.

'Here, Gran, let me do that. I've done with these beans. Look — that'll be enough for dinner tonight, don't you think?' She held the bowl out for Gran to peer inside.

'Wonderful. They'll be delicious with the sausages I bought earlier. They've started doing some fancy ones at the farm shop down the road.' Gran took the beans, gave Rosie the slug stuff. There was a faint whiff of creosote. 'Sprinkle it around but be careful not to get it on the actual leaves; it burns holes in them, especially when its dry like this.'

She looked up at the cloudless blue sky. A couple of swallows flitted past, hunting for insects.

'Even the birds look hot. Reminds me of '42 — bitter cold that would cut you in half during the winter, then you'd think you were living in a desert by the summer. Dreadful. The War was bad enough, but the weather on top of it...'

Rosie busied herself with the slugs. If she appeared not to be listening, perhaps Gran would say more about that time. Direct questioning could wait, Rosie had memorised her list and was ready should any suitable opportunity present itself. *A few more days, then I'll give the easy questions a try.*

Gran was talking again, but not about wartime. 'Anyway, your Gramps will be parched and thinking his throat's been cut, if I don't get to making him some tea. We'll have these last strawberries with that pot of cream I bought earlier. Do you want tea or that homemade lemonade again?'

'I honestly don't know how you can drink hot tea, Gran. And don't tell me it's the best way to cool down because I'm certain it isn't. I'll come and pour myself lemonade when I come in. With lots of ice...'

'Alright then, dear. That shouldn't take you a couple of minutes. Can you put the container back in the shed when you're done?'

Rosie nodded

Gran stepped over to the house, a bowl of beans in one hand and a basket of strawberries in the other.

'Coo-eee! Bill, wake up, it's time for tea. Look, the last few strawberries.'

Rosie was tired and sticky by the time she'd finished with the slug poison. Pulling her shoes off before entering through the conservatory, she saw the tea things already laid out on the low table next to Gran's chair.

'I'll just run upstairs and wash my hands and face, Gran, then I'll be with you. I'm so grimy I don't know what to do with myself.' She took the stairs two at a time, singing the chorus of a pop song she'd heard on the radio the previous day.

At the basin in the spare bathroom she splashed water over her face and hands, drying herself off on a pale green hand towel. She ran her fingers through her hair, gave a quick glance in the mirror and, satisfied, started back downstairs.

'Rosie, dear, will you pour the water into the pot when you come down? The kettle's boiled already. I've got everything else.'

'Yes, Gran, I will. On my way.'

A China teapot, decorated with tiny pink roses, stood on the counter next to the kettles. Two or three teaspoons of loose tea leaves covered the bottom of the pot. *So old fashioned. Sweet though.* Rosie flicked the switch on the kettle and poured lemonade for herself while waiting for the water to re-boil. She added a couple of ice cubes to her glass, grabbed a lemon from the fruit bowl and plopped in a thick slice, her lips pursing at the sour aroma.

'Coming, Gran, Gramps. You sure you've got everything else?'

'Yes, dear, we just need the tea. Thank you, put it down on the tray here. I'll pour for us.'

'No, don't get up. I'll do it. Gramps? Are you ready?'

'Am I ready? A man could die of thirst around here, y'know, it takes so long to get a cuppa.' Gramps twisted around in his chair, watching his granddaughter. 'Do you remember when you were a young thing, how you always wanted to play "tea" with me and your Gran? That would keep you busy for hours. Us too, come to that. Hey, Alice? The hours we wasted, pretending to drink soapy water out of thimble-sized doll's tea sets.'

'What do you mean, pretended? You mean you weren't actually slurping it down then? Oh, you hurt me so, Gramps.' Rosie clutched her chest, crumpling her face in mock distress. 'Ha ha, it was fun though wasn't it? Emma always wanted to put petals in hers, but I wouldn't let her. I was worried you might choke or something. Here you are — a proper cup of tea. Promise.'

'Thank you. Yes, those were the days. I can still see you out there in the garden, setting up all your teddies on that old chequered picnic blanket we had, laying everything out so neatly. Bossing your sister around, of course.'

'Not that she ever listened, Gramps — still doesn't. Gran, here's yours. You didn't want me to add any sugar did you? It's not here on the tray, but I can get it if you like?'

'Oo, no, I'm sweet enough.' Gramps and Rosie rolled their eyes at each other; she said it every time. It was all part of the ritual of tea with them.

As were the flowery mugs and the proper tea pot. *I've always wondered about that.* 'Gran, why do you always like to use your best china in the afternoon? I mean, you don't use it at any other time of day, do you?'

'No, you're right, I don't suppose we do. Here, Bill. Do you want cream with these strawberries?'

'No thanks, Al, the strawberries on their own will be enough for me.' Bill took the plate from his wife, putting it on the arm of the chair while he continued to sip his tea.

'What were you saying, Rosie? Oh, the best china. I think that was a wartime thing, if I remember. People I lived with for a while, they always brought out their best tea things in the evening. It must have made an impression on me, that they made the effort to do something nice at the end of each day, no matter what may have passed earlier. Cream, or just the strawberries for you as well?'

'Cream would be lovely. Thank you.' *Maybe it's a good time to try a couple of questions on Gran.* 'So who was that then? Not Great Granny and Grandpa? I don't remember you saying anything about where you lived for most of the war.'

Gran's reply was muffled as she took a mouthful of strawberry. 'No, not my mum and dad. We didn't have "special"; everything was for everyday. No, this was somewhere else...So what do you think of the last of the strawberries, both of you? A good crop this year, despite this dreadful heat, don't you think?'

You've done it again, Gran. Frustrated, Rosie drank her lemonade in silence.

'It was a couple I stayed with in Bedford.'

'What was? Oh, the smart tea thing, you mean?' Rosie put her glass down, tried to pretend she wasn't bursting with interest.

'Yes. They were called...let me think, some double-barrelled name.'

'Brown-something wasn't it?' Gramps replying surprised Rosie. She didn't think they'd known each other until the war was over. That's what Mum told her, anyway.

'Yes, that's right. Clever you.' Gran reached across and patted Gramps on the knee. 'Yes, Milford-Brown. No, that's not right. Milton. Milton-Brown. Emily and Harry.'

She turned a triumphant smile on Rosie. *Oh no you don't, you're not getting off that lightly.* 'What was so special about tea with them then? Were they family or something?'

'No, not family. Just a couple I lived with for a few weeks at the start of the war. They felt like family, by the time I moved on though. Ah, listen, can you hear the cuckoo?'

'But you were too old to be an evacuee in the war, weren't you Gran?' Rosie was determined to keep the conversation on track. 'A child evacuee, I mean. I think it's a bit mean, sending little kiddies off to the middle of nowhere, to stay with a bunch of strangers. And not knowing when they'd get back home to see their own parents.'

'If they ever did.' Gran's voice was quiet. 'They did look so lost, poor lambs. Any time you travelled, especially on the trains, they'd be huddled together in groups. Wide eyes, pale faces, Sunday best clothes. Terribly sad. Necessary, but sad.'

A bee buzzed past the open conservatory door. Gran poured a second cup of tea for herself.

'Bill, do you want another? There's enough in the pot?'

'No thanks, love.' Gramps picked up the newspaper, fiddled with his reading glasses.

'Yes, so it was Emily. She said they liked to use their best china as a special moment in every day, no matter how bad that day might have been. As the war drew on I liked the idea. Of course back then, I didn't have anything nice of my own to use, but I did promise myself that one day, when I did, I would be like Emily and use it to remind myself of the special to be found in every day.'

'Yes, I like that too. Maybe I'll carry on the tradition.' Rosie allowed Gran to sip her tea for a few minutes before she tried out her next question. 'And Bedford — that was a funny place to stay, wasn't it?'

Gran smiled, looked over at the snoozing Gramps, put her cup down on the table in front of her. 'Yes, I suppose it was. I liked it though.'

'What were you doing there then? I can't remember reading about the Germans arriving in Bedford?'

'No, they didn't. I was on a course. Typing. Nothing very interesting.' Gran bent down and picked her knitting up from beside her chair. She click-clacked the needles back and forth.

Conversation closed.
For now.

Over the next couple of days, Rosie settled into the slower routine of her grandparents' lives. Mum was worried she would find it boring, too quiet, over at Gran's. But Rosie loved it. She could sleep in for as long as she liked, no tractor rumbling away under her window to wake her up and remind her that she, too, should be working. Here, only the sound of the Today radio programme disturbed her morning dreams.

However, Rosie found habit and body clocks to be strange things and she often found herself awake earlier than she would like to be. Gran was an early riser, pottering about downstairs and making tea or checking her garden before it got too hot. Mitzy, their golden retriever, paced around after her, begging for a walk along the lanes of the village.

Rosie's bedroom was stuffy and uncomfortable this morning despite the window being wide open. No breeze moved the curtains or rustled the leaves of the trees in the field opposite. Throwing off the thin sheet covering her, Rosie gave up pretending she was asleep. She was pleased Gran had opened up over the tea things the day before. It wasn't much, but it did feel as though the door to further conversation — investigation — was at least open a chink. Wanting to strike while the iron was hot, Rosie decided to get up and offer to go with Gran on her morning walk. The view and the exercise might distract her and prompt her to reminisce some more.

Pulling on her running shorts and a bright orange vest top, Rosie tied her hair up in a messy ponytail, grabbed her shoes from the cupboard and went downstairs in search of Gran. She found her sitting at the kitchen table, an old cardboard box open in front of her which she closed as Rosie entered the room.

'Morning Gran.' Rosie walked over and planted a kiss on her grandmother's cheek. 'What's that you've got there? You sorting out your filing this early in the morning?'

Gran kept her hands folded over the box. Protective. 'Good morning, dear. Did you not sleep so well? You're up early — for a change.' She made a show of looking at the clock on the wall.

'I know, I'm surprised myself. It's too hot to sleep in this morning. I wondered if I could join you and Mitzy on your walk? It would be nice to get out before it gets even hotter.'

'That would be lovely. Do you want a cup of tea before we go?' Rosie nodded, went over to switch the kettle on. 'You can do another for me, while you're at it. Here's my cup.'

Morning tea wasn't nearly as fancy as in the afternoon; a cheery red polka dot teapot and matching mugs, milk from the bottle, sugar from the container in the cupboard. Rosie liked the delicacy of afternoon tea but was more relaxed with the chunky breakfast set.

'I'll pop this out of the way.' Gran lifted the box from the table and carried it through to the dining room. Rosie heard the squeak of a door in the oak dresser.

'Here's your tea, Gran.'

'Smashing. We'll have this and then get going before Mitzy digs up the entire garden.' Gran pointed out of the window. The dog was running around in frantic circles, soil and grass spraying out behind her. 'Do you want a biscuit with your tea? There's some Hobnobs in the tin on the shelf there.'

'Thanks, Gran. You always know my favourite, don't you?'

'I try!'

Twenty minutes later they were out in the lane, Mitzy pulling at her lead in an effort to hurry her owner along. 'Mitzy, stop pulling. You'll choke yourself.'

It was a magnificent morning. Butterflies of every size and colour flitted around the drooping bells of the pink foxgloves. A blackbird hopped along beside them. One or two cotton-wool clouds drifted across the otherwise clear sky. Cows grazed in the field at the end of the lane, the pungent smell of manure heavy in the still air. *This is what summer is all about.*

'You don't like to talk much about the war, do you Gran?' Rosie decided it was time for a more direct approach.

'Well, it's not that so much. There's just nothing much to tell.'

'Nothing to tell? But Gran, you were my age. It must have been so exciting. Like, what about the Blitz? You know, everyone huddling together in the Underground, singing songs and sharing tea.'

'Goodness, I'm not sure it was anything like that. You young people — or Hollywood, more likely — have made it seem far more romantic than it really was.' She paused while Mitzy sniffed around the hedgerow. 'I wasn't in London myself, not during the Blitz. I visited it afterwards though. It was horrible. Smelled of soot and smoke everywhere you went; I suppose the fires got into the bricks or something. So sad, so many homes destroyed. You know, a home isn't just a house — it's a family; it's photographs and heirlooms and treasured sentimental bits and pieces. Stuff that means nothing to some German bomber but everything to the ones who lose it.'

Now she had started speaking, Gran appeared reluctant to stop. 'My first time in London was when I went for an interview. In Baker Street, of all places.'

'Oo, were you going to work for Sherlock Holmes?' Rosie laughed. Gran loved the Arthur Conan Doyle stories as much as she did; she knew the location would have been as significant to Gran as it was to her.

'That's exactly what I thought. I was a bit disappointed to not be knocking on the door of 221B. I quite fancied myself in a deerstalker, smoking a pipe and playing the violin.' This was safer ground, a happier memory. 'It was a block right opposite the Tube station. Owned by Marks and Spencer, apparently. Awful place. All winding corridors and pokey little offices.'

They turned right into the next lane, following the path to a shallow stream. Mitzy, released from the restraint of her lead, was ahead of them and they could hear her barking and splashing around in the shallow water.

'What was the interview for, Gran?'

'Mm? Sorry, miles away there. The interview? For one of the volunteer organisations, the FANY.'

'The fanny? No come on, Gran, that can't have been a real thing.' Rosie suppressed a giggle; she didn't want to offend her grandmother who was looking at her with narrowed eyes.

'The First Aid Women's Yeomanry, I'll have you know. Mind you, that's not much better, is it?' She chuckled. 'Did you study anything about them in your History classes at school?'

'No I don't think so. There was something about women who drove ambulances around? Or was that the First World War?' Rosie was confused. Surely Gran couldn't have been a nurse without their knowing, could she?

'Yes, they did drive ambulances in the first war. Terribly brave young women you know, right in the thick of it at the Front. Drove into danger so they could rescue the broken bodies of so many young men. Boys, lots of the time. Some FANY drove ambulances during the next war too, although they also drove lorries and delivery motorcycles. Whatever was needed, they did it. Mitzy? Mitzy, where have you got to? Oh there you are. What a mess, I'll be giving you a bath the moment we get home, young lady.'

Mitzy, clearly understanding her mistress' intention, raced back into the undergrowth, her tail wagging in sheer delight.

'So is that what you did, Gran? Drove trucks and things?'

'Well, during training, yes I did a bit. I didn't have my licence though so I couldn't do more than practice off-road.' She whistled for Mitzy. 'We'd best be getting back, Rosie. Gramps will be up and about and wondering where we are.'

They retraced their steps. There was no further talk of war or FANY or nurses driving lorries. Rosie tried to be pleased that Gran was at least starting to talk, but it was all so vague and unsatisfactory. *But what* did *you do, Gran?*

As Gran guessed, Gramps was up and waiting by the gate for them. 'Morning, ladies. How was your walk? Lovely morning isn't it?'

Rosie kissed his wrinkled cheek. 'Morning Gramps. You must be starving. Did you think we weren't coming back?' She tucked her arm into his and walked with him around the side of the house and into the kitchen. 'Gran has to give Mitzy a bit of a clean-up so why don't I get breakfast for today? I see the fruit bowl is overflowing; shall I make us a nice fruit salad and then we can have some toast with coffee?'

'That sounds grand, Rosie-Posie. And I'll supervise from that comfy chair over there...' He winked and shuffled over to the armchair kept in the corner of the kitchen especially for him.

After breakfast, Rosie and her grandparents spent the rest of the day relaxing in the shade of the old trees at the end of the garden; the weather was stifling.

They heard the first rumble of thunder at around tea time. Fat drops of rain began to fall.

'I think we'd better get inside. I'll carry in the glasses. Rosie, grab the blanket and pillows and bring them in before the heavens open. We can leave the chairs.'

They weren't a moment too soon. A crash of thunder, sounding loud as it echoed around the hills, sent Mitzy scurrying for her bed in the conservatory. The slow drips of rain increased to a steady flow.

'Well, at least we'll have a cooler night tonight. The weather had to break sometime. It's been so muggy the last few days. Rosie dear, seeing as we're housebound, wouldn't you like to fetch that box I was busy with this morning? It's in the dresser in the dining room?' Gran tried to sound as though she was still talking about nothing more interesting than the weather. But the slight quaver in her voice didn't convince Rosie.

'Gran, please don't feel you have to. I'm sorry for asking so many questions. It's just so interesting and I would love to know what it was really like, you know. Mum doesn't seem to know anything about what the two of you did during the war. She says you never spoke about it when she was growing up.'

'No, I suppose we didn't.' Gran paused. 'But it's alright. You go and fetch that box and we'll look at it together while we have tea. There's no harm in a few old photographs and theatre ticket stubs, is there?' Was Gran trying to convince herself? Or ask permission from someone? Gramps maybe?

Rosie turned the light on in the dining room; the bright sunshine of earlier was hidden behind dense storm clouds and the room was gloomy. The hairs on the back of her neck tingled. *Don't be silly, it's just a cardboard box of photos.* Rosie gave herself a shake and crossed to the dresser. Pulling open the left-hand door, she peered inside the low cupboard. There it was. Pandora's Box holding all her grandmother's secrets? Or a boring collection of mouldy memories?

'Bring it through to the kitchen; the light is better in here.'

Rosie carried the box through. It was dust and cobweb-free — not what she expected. *Do you go through it often, Gran? Why haven't you shared it with us before?*

The delicate afternoon tea set was today replaced with the red dots of breakfast time. Because they were drinking in the kitchen? Or was the break in ritual something more significant?

'Have a custard cream biscuit.' Gran pushed the plate towards Rosie, her eyes on the box rather than her granddaughter. 'Well, go on then, open it.'

'Gran, are you sure? I mean, I'd love to see but if you'd rather not...We can leave it for another day if you want.'

'No let's do it now, before I change my mind. Anyway, like I said, it's just some old photographs, things like that. Happy memories, you know.'

Rosie walked behind Gran's chair and put her arms around her shoulders. 'Thank you, Gran. I know I'm being nosy. It's just I'm so sure there's something you're not telling us. Something exciting.'

'Well, you won't find anything much that's exciting in here. Come, sit next to me here. We'll open it together.'

Rosie hitched her chair around so she was next to her grandmother. She lifted the flap on her side of the box; Gran did the same with the other.

The smell of musty papers was the first thing Rosie noticed. It reminded her of an old library they used to visit as children, with its rows of neat, organised shelves. She took a peak inside. Piles of photographs were stacked in each of the four corners. Rosie picked one from the top. A black and white picture of three girls wearing dated summer dresses and floppy sun hats. Arms draped around one another, laughing into the camera. In the background a blurred impression of a lake surrounded by trees. Sun glinted on the lake's surface.

Gran took the photo from her, held it towards the light.

'That's a fun picture isn't it? That's me, there in the middle. With Vera, the one with her mouth wide open. And on the other side, Mavis. I'm sure I've mentioned the two of them to you, haven't I?' Before Rosie could reply, the kitchen door opened and Gramps ambled in.

'Is there any tea? I must have nodded off, well, rested my eyes I mean. I didn't notice you leave.'

'Look, Bill — you remember this don't you?' Gramps squinted at the picture Gran held towards him.

'Hyde Park! Well, that's going back a bit isn't it? Look at you — always the prettiest girl of any of your friends.'

Rosie watched their exchange. *Surely not?* 'You mean, you knew Gran when she was this young, Gramps? How old are you here anyway, Gran? Nineteen, twenty?'

Gran pulled out the chair on the other side of her, indicated for Gramps to join them. 'Eighteen. Very young. And yes, Gramps knew me back then. He took the photograph with a Box Brownie he carted around everywhere with him. Terribly embarrassing, always taking snaps of me and my friends.'

'You loved it. I couldn't keep her away from posing, let me tell you.' Together they laughed, a shared joke which Rosie wasn't included in.

'Of course, we were just friends at that time. Your Gramps travelled to London with me, for the interview I told you about.'

'Yes, absolutely only friends.' Gramps winked at Rosie. 'Let her believe what she wants to, hey?'

Alice

London

'**C**ome on, Alice. Hurry up. We haven't got all day.'

'Sorry, I had a stone in my shoe'

'Right-o, Bill, we're ready. Smile, girls!' Vera draped herself over her friends, mouth wide in delighted laughter.

'Hold it, hold it. There. Thank you, ladies, you can relax.'

'Thank you, Bill. And thank you, Alice, for bringing Bill to meet us. Wherever did you find him?'

Alice felt her cheeks burn. 'Vera, we're friends, I told you that. We've been at a training school thing since February. But that's over, and we all go our separate ways from here.'

Bill fiddled with his camera a few metres away from the girls. He looked up and smiled at Alice.

'Sorry,' she mouthed.

It wasn't supposed to have been like this. Bill had travelled on the train to London with Alice on the day of her interview in Baker Street. He was going to hang around and wait until she'd finished, then they were going to find a Lyons Tea House for a bit of a treat before returning to Bedford. The following day, Bill was leaving for whatever his posting in Scotland was all about; Alice, accustomed to the abrupt and sudden instructions issued to those trying to help in the war effort, fully expected she too would be leaving Bedford within a day or two.

She rued the day she had written to Vera, telling her of the interview and her planned trip to the Big City. Never one to miss an opportunity for an adventure, Vera replied by return of post that she would gather Mavis from whatever farm she was currently mucking about on —

'Literally, darling. I don't know how these Land Girls put up with it. And the smell. Mr Churchill has a lot to answer for, you know.' — and find a way out of her own commitments as line supervisor in an armaments factory in Birmingham; they would meet Alice in London for the day.

Alice didn't want to tell Vera about Bill. Not that there was anything to tell, of course. But Vera wouldn't understand. She would giggle and assume and embarrass the poor chap who, after all, was being kind to a friend. Mavis, the more sensitive of the two girls, would be more diplomatic, ask fewer questions. Alice dreaded having to respond to Vera's persistent whispers and suggestions.

Against her better judgement, she agreed to meet them by the bandstand in Hyde Park at lunchtime; she was certain her interview would be over by then.

As it happened, her appointment at Baker Street was even more brief than she had anticipated.

Bill escorted her right to the doors of the building, waving goodbye as she walked in through the main entrance.

'See you at the station. I'll wait in the café for you. Take as long you need — I've got my paper.'

'Thanks, Bill. Hopefully, I won't be long.'

Nerves fluttered in her stomach as she gave her name to the austere lady with a tight bun in her hair, at the reception desk. *Why do they always put the most unwelcoming people on the welcome desk?*

'Good morning, I am Miss Stallard. I'm here to see...' she checked the piece of paper she held in her hand. '...a Mrs Peggy Minchin.'

'Take a seat. I'll call one of the Corporals to take you to her office. But first, you'll need this.' The lady held out a badge with VISITOR stamped in prominent letters. 'And sign here. The register.'

Alice bent over and took a deep breath to calm herself before filling in her details.

There were two hard, straight-backed chairs pushed against the wall to her left. Alice perched on one, waiting for her guide to arrive. After an anxious five minutes, during which she was glared at more than once by Reception Lady for her toe-tapping impatience, a man dressed in suit and tie came to collect her. A central parting in his dark hair was Brylcreem-ed into place.

'Miss Stallard. Follow me please.'

Alice was glad to have someone to follow rather than be required to memorise any directions. The place was a maze. They twisted and turned along dark corridors and up a couple of flights of stairs. Doors to left and right were closed, muffled voices the sole indication of activity in the rooms they protected. In one corridor, a door was flung open and a harrassed-looking individual darted out and hurried past them, carrying bundles of papers or files as she went.

'Here we are...' Her guide stopped without warning, Alice crashing into the back of him. He pushed on the door in front of them and announced her arrival.

Seated behind a desk in the centre of the room sat a woman a few years older than Alice. A man's scent lingered, a previous visitor ducking out moments before Alice arrived.

'Thank you, Timothy, please wait outside for a few minutes. I'm sure we won't be taking up much of Miss Stallard's time. You can show her out in a moment.' The door closed behind Alice with a soft click. 'Miss Stallard, do take a seat.'

Alice sat where indicated.

'So, I hear you did well at the school in Bedford. Found your calling, it would seem?'

'I enjoyed learning everything, yes, Ma'am.'

'Well, good. I understand you were encouraged to join the First Aid Nursing Yeomanry before you left?'

Alice nodded. It had somewhat mystified her parents when she had written to ask for their permission to work voluntarily for an organisation she seemed entirely unsuitable for.

"It is wonderful, of course, that you want to dedicate your time and considerable talents to such a worthy cause, my dear, and we are both proud of you for making such a decision. However, your father and I are both a little concerned that those same talents you have exhibited throughout your school career are being wasted, given your choice of organisation to join. After all, I seem to recall you hated the pony gymkhanas we tried to encourage you towards. And nursing? Well, for someone who nearly faints

when the cat brings in a mouse, I'm not sure how well you will manage when dressing the wounds of war."

And so her mother had continued over several concerned and confused pages.

However, her letter ended well.

"Having said all this, we are still both committed to supporting you in this latest scheme. As with Tom, so with you. 'Fight the good fight, etc etc'"

'Yes, Ma'am. And my parents have assured me of their support.'

'Good. Before we can place you where you will be truly useful, here with the Interservices Research Bureau — no, don't ask any questions. Surely you know that? — you will need to undergo the compulsory training course at a place near Banbury. Rather grandly entitled Overthorpe Hall. I can assure you your stay will be less than glamorous, however.'

Oh goodness, more training. When will I be allowed to do something useful? The war will be over by the time I get started. 'Yes, Ma'am, of course.'

'You will receive a telegram in the next day or so with further details. Remain at your billet in Bedford until then.'

The interview was over before Alice knew it began. It wasn't an opportunity to be asked questions, given chance to shine or prove herself; rather, it was the next list of instructions she must again follow.

'Timothy! You can come in. Please help Miss Stallard find her way out of this place. And Miss Stallard — Alice — good luck to you.'

Alice was over the road looking for Bill within minutes. He looked up at her arrival in surprise.

'That was quick. I haven't started the crossword yet.' He put down his newspaper, called a waiter over, and ordered another pot of coffee. 'Well? What did they say? Where are you going? They're not dropping you behind enemy lines, are they?'

He couldn't quite keep the anxiety from his voice. Alice waited for the coffee to arrive before replying. 'Dearest Bill, you are the sweetest friend I have. No, I'm not going anywhere exciting at all. More's the pity. More training, apparently. In Banbury. Stop laughing! You're lucky, you at least get to move further away. Scotland feels like the other side of the world to me.'

'Oh, sorry old girl. That is a rough one. Did they tell you what you're training for?' Alice sipped her coffee, shook her head. 'No, well, we're in the same boat then. More training, more getting ready. Wish we could get on with it, I must admit.'

There was nothing else to say. They both knew they couldn't talk anymore about their respective placements, even if they did have more details. They drank the rest of the coffee in silence, watching the crush of people going in and out of the Baker Street station.

'I say, what time are we meant to be meeting your friends?'

Alice checked the clock on the wall behind her. 'Goodness, we'd best be off. I'd rather not keep them waiting.' She rattled her cup back into the saucer. 'Are you sure you don't mind coming along, Bill? It's bound to be terribly boring for you.'

'It'll be fun. I've been dying to try out my camera on some worthy subjects. Where are we meeting them, did you say?'

'Hyde Park. By the lake or something. I hope it's obvious; we rarely came to London growing up and I don't know anywhere very well. It was Vera's idea to meet there. Somewhere easy and central, she said.'

'Don't worry, I've been here loads of times — I have an uncle who lives down here.'

Bill paid for their drinks, despite Alice's objections.

'I've been sitting here longer than you. Had more to drink.'

They decided to catch a bus for a few stops, then walk the rest of the way to the park. It was too hot for the underground and Alice wanted to see for herself the effects of the Blitz.

'Goodness, it's much worse than it looks in the newspapers, isn't it? I suppose they can't share the smell.' Alice wrinkled her nose. Even from inside the bus, they caught the smell of dust and old smoke and charred, wet wood.

The bus stopped for a group of army boys to climb aboard. They were laughing and joking, showing off without a care in the world.

'They've obviously not seen any action yet, then.' Bill kept his voice low.

'I know. Tom — my brother — was like that when he first signed up. Didn't last long. He hardly said a word when he came home last time. Mum was so worried.'

'Oh well, they'll find out soon enough.' Bill shrugged 'Ours is the next stop.'

They hopped off the bus and turned down a residential side street.

'Shortcut.' Bill took Alice's arm.

Their way was blocked halfway down by a cluster of people gathered around a pile of rubble, the acrid smell of brick dust and smoking embers turning Alice's stomach. A woman stood to one side, shivering despite the heat of the day. She gripped a thin cotton shawl around her shoulders. She wore a dirty yellow dress and a pair of clumpy black shoes. Alice could hear her mumbling to herself. 'Everything. It's all in there. I didn't have time to get anything out.'

Another woman stepped over, laid a gentle arm across the grieving woman's shoulders. 'I know, Mary, I know.'

'I bought a new tablecloth from the market on Saturday. Was going to use it tonight when Fred came off shift.'

A couple of children kicked a misshapen lump of brick around at the edge of the crowd. Three or four women huddled together, nodding in the direction of the woman called Mary. Men shook their heads, waved at the sky, moved on. An air raid warden wrote notes on a clipboard.

'Look, they're still digging through the rubble over there. How awful for people – searching through what was their home or workplace, trying to find anything of value still in one piece.' Alice tugged on Bill's sleeve. 'C'mon. We shouldn't be here. This is private.'

Mavis and Vera were at the bandstand. Vera let out a shriek as soon as she spotted them, waved a hand in frantic welcome.

'Alice. You made it. With your sense of direction, I was beginning to wonder.'

'Don't tease, Vera. We just got here ourselves, Alice. Don't let her get to you already.' Mavis gave Alice a kiss on the cheek.

'Oh, don't be so genteel, Mavis. Bear hugs all round, I'd say.' Vera pulled the other two girls towards her, their sunhats colliding as they drew close.

'Goodness, it is lovely to see you both. Gosh, Mavis, you've picked up quite a tan. And look at your arms — I've never seen such muscles.'

Mavis flexed her arm, showed off the bulging bicep. 'Outdoor work and carting spuds all over the place, that's what this is.'

'So, you joined the Land Girls then, like you said you would?' Alice was impressed. Mavis was the quietest of the three of them, studious and polite. She couldn't imagine her at home on a farm. 'Do you enjoy it, though?'

'I'm not sure "enjoy" is the right word. It's super hard work, and awfully long hours. I've never been up so early in my life before. I'm halfway through my first chore when the dawn chorus breaks out.' She gave a wide yawn. 'All us girls are sharing a big room at the front of the farmhouse. Well, sharing beds. It's a bit of a squash, but we all get along well, so it's fine. The farmer — Mr Havers and his wife Betty — are lovely. They've been happy to teach us our duties rather than throwing us in the deep end. That's not the same everywhere, I can tell you. And of course there's always more than enough to eat — rations don't seem to apply on farms. Or not theirs anyway.'

'You are lucky, Mave.' Vera rubbed her stomach. 'I'm hungry all the time. My billet is perfectly comfortable, and I do at least have a room to myself, but the food is beastly. I think my landlady keeps the extra rations I bring in for herself, and herself only.'

Alice scrutinised her friend. Vera did seem to have lost weight. And she was pale, as though she hadn't seen the sun in weeks.

'So what are you doing, Vera? Are you surviving?' Alice didn't want to sound too concerned; Vera hated a fuss.

'Yes, darling, I am surviving. And of course, I can't tell you what I'm doing. Official Secrets and all that. But it is satisfying to know that me and my team are personally contributing to giving Hitler a hiding...But enough about me. What about you? And who is this you brought along with you?'

'How rude of me. Bill, these are my friends Mavis and Vera. Mavis, Vera — this is Bill.' Alice wafted her hand in the direction of each of them, avoiding their gaze.

Bill swept his cap from his head, bowing low. 'Good afternoon, ladies. I'm pleased to make your acquaintance.'

'And yours too, I'm sure.' Vera extended her hand. Bill clasped it in his free hand, pumping her arm up and down.

He turned to Mavis. Rather than shake her hand, he lifted it to his lips and gave her an old-fashioned kiss.

'Well, I like that. The farm girl gets a kiss, while the factory manager receives a robust handshake.'

Alice, who had been watching the exchanges with some anxiety, laughed. 'He is an excellent judge of character, you know.'

'Now, now, ladies. Let's put our claws away for a photograph, shall we? How about you stand over there, your back to the lake? Alice, you go in the middle.'

Giving each other a series of pushes and shoves, the three girls got into place. Bill fiddled with his camera, looked up, shouted 'Churchill' at them, then snapped the shutter.

The four of them spent the rest of the afternoon wandering around the park or lounging under the shade of the trees. Bill regaled them with stories of his youth — evil initiations at boarding school, cracking scores at cricket and rugby, putting frogs in his sister's bed.

Alice lay back, her arm behind her head. It was the best day she'd had since stepping on the train bound for Bletchley.

'We're going to buy ices.' It was Mavis, standing over Alice and blocking the sun. 'You want one?'

Alice sat up. Vera's eyes were shut. 'Who's going? You and Bill?'

'Yes, if you don't mind sharing him?' Mavis giggled. 'He's awfully nice, isn't he?'

A blush reddened Alice's cheeks. Thank goodness Bill was down on the path and wouldn't have overheard. 'I'd love an ice, if you can find any. It's still scorching, isn't it?'

'Righto. We'll be as quick as we can. Come on, Bill, I think I saw someone selling over this way.'

Alice remained seated, plucking at the grass as she watched them go.

'So, what's the story with Bill, then?'

'Vera! You made me jump. I thought you were asleep.'

'Yes, that was my intention. I wanted to have you all to myself for a few minutes. Selfish of me, do you think?' Vera sat up, stretched her arms above her head. 'Mind you, I think I did nod off for a moment there. But don't change the subject. Bill?'

'Well, there's nothing to tell. He's a classmate, that's all.' Alice avoided looking at her friend.

'Ha, a classmate who travels all the way to London in wartime to sit and wait in a café while his classmate has an interview? Does he do that for everyone in the class? No, I didn't think so. Really, Alice, you are hopeless.'

'Don't be silly. He knew I didn't know my way around, offered to accompany me in case I got lost. Honestly, Vera, we're just friends.' Alice was silent. *And my classmate is about to leave for Scotland, and I'm going to some stupid country house in the middle of nowhere and we probably won't ever see each other again.* She sighed. 'This war is so dreadful, isn't it? Stops us doing all the things we dreamed of. Splits up good friends like the three of us.'

'And we can't talk or write anything of any importance, either. I've never kept a secret in my life, you know; I've always told you and Mavis everything from when we first met. Now I can't even tell you where I live, much less what I do.'

Alice rested her head on Vera's shoulder. 'We must simply find new things to talk about. You know, new ways of being with each other.' She paused. 'Thanks for getting us together today, Vee. I wouldn't have thought of it, and it's been so special.'

'It has, hasn't it? Let's do it again, next time we have a weekend off together. We'll go to one of the big hotels in town and dance the night away. There are some wonderful bands playing, you know, in spite of everything. And lots of dishy men in uniform to dance with. Not that you need one, you're already spoken for.'

'Vera, stop it.' Alice lifted her head from where it rested, thumped Vera in the arm instead. 'Honestly, we're friends.'

'Alright, keep your hair on.' Vera rubbed her arm. 'What have they been teaching you at that school of yours, anyway? Boxing?'

'Look, here they come. It looks as though they've had success, doesn't it? Come on, let's walk to meet them.' Pulling Vera to her feet, Alice linked arms with her and together they strolled towards the path. 'Hello. Did you find something, then?'

'Yes, a drink. All the ices sold out earlier in the day. But it's better than nothing. Homemade lemonade. Here.' Bill handed Alice her cup. 'You'll have to drink that up quickly though — we need to get back to the station soon, or we'll miss the train back.'

'Ah, but it feels like we've had such a short time together.' Vera pouted her Victory-red lips. 'Do you really have to go so soon?'

'I'd better be off as well, I'm afraid.' Mavis drank down the rest of her lemonade in one gulp. 'I've got a lift back up to the farm. Have to be back before "lights out", of course.'

'I think it's been wonderful. And yes, Vera, we will definitely do it again. And next time, with dancing.'

Alice gave her friends a hug. Saying goodbye got harder every time. *Don't be ridiculous, you're only going to Banbury.*

Alice

Overthorpe Hall

.− .−.. .. −.−.. .

Alice lugged her suitcase along yet another unfamiliar road in search of yet another new address. At least this time she wasn't looking for a nondescript house in the middle of an anonymous street; surely Overthorpe Hall would be easy to find.

A farmer gave her a lift part of the way from the station on the back of his trailer. He turned into his farm before reaching her destination, so he helped her and her luggage down and pointed her in the general direction of the Hall.

'Bit further on up there, lass. Sorry can't take you the rest of the way — got to sort out a new bunch of girls who've arrived to help around the place. Not that they're likely to be much useful help, at least not at first.' The farmer looked Alice up and down, assessing her in much the same way he might a prize cart horse. 'I did think you was one of them, when I first saw you at the station. But you're even smaller than the ones I've already got. Wouldn't be much good around here, that's for certain.'

Alice wasn't sure whether to be offended or grateful. *Poor Mavis, no wonder she's got all those muscles, if this is the kind of man she has to work for. Mind you, she does get to eat better than I do.*

'Thank you for the lift this far, anyway.'

'Ah, you're welcome.' He took his cap off and wiped his brow with a handkerchief he pulled from his trouser pocket. 'Glad to have saved you some of the journey on another hot day. We could do with this weather breaking; need some rain. You mind how you go, miss.'

'Thank you, I will.'

Alice was grateful for the shade from the overhanging trees as she walked the rest of the way to the Hall. She plucked a piece of long grass from the hedgerow. Chewing as she went, she sucked in the sweet juice. *Not quite the fresh lemonade from Hyde Park, but good enough.*

For the second time in a few months, Alice was confronted by a set of gates guarded by a sentry.

'Good afternoon. I'm Miss Stallard. I'm supposed to report here for some training...' The last few months had increased her confidence; she no longer blushed every time she spoke to complete strangers.

The sentry pulled out a clipboard from the hut behind him and riffled through several pages.

'Ah, yes, here you are. Welcome to Overthorpe Hall, Miss Stallard.' Replacing the clipboard on the table inside the hut, the guard pushed open the gate and ushered her through. 'On up to the main entrance, over there see? And someone will be there to greet you. Have fun.'

The bark of laughter which accompanied this last remark caused Alice to wonder. *What am I getting myself into? Gosh, I do wish people would tell us what's going on and what to expect. We're like pawns in a giant game of chess.*

Alice followed the path across the park towards the entrance to the Hall. The sweeping grass lawns and ornamental flowerbeds were transformed into functional vegetable plots. Alice identified cabbages and the leafy tops of carrots and potatoes. Two or three women about her age were hard at work, weeding and hoeing. One straightened up and pushed her hair out of her face.

'Hello. Are you one of the new recruits? Good-oh! We could do with some more help around here. Backbreaking work, honestly.' She pulled her gardening gloves off and advanced towards Alice, hand outstretched in greeting. 'I'm Gertie — you can guess what that's short for, can't you? Dreadful name — nice to meet you. Best you get on in and stow your things. We'll meet up again at tea, find out all about each other.'

'I'm Alice. And thank you, I'd like that.'

Relieved that her first encounter with the other girls was a friendly one, Alice continued past the garden and on up to the front door. The entrance was flanked by a pair of clipped miniature fir trees. The Hall was as grand as the one at Bletchley, although a bit more conventional and better proportioned. Sandstone walls glowed yellow in the summer sun; the windows, both upstairs and down, were propped wide open. A woman in khaki tunic, skirt and peaked cap introduced herself to Alice. 'Good afternoon, Miss Stallard. I am Mrs Burnley-Smith and I will be responsible for you during your stay with us. Audrey here will show you up to your billet where you can get settled. Tea will be served in the dining room over there —' she indicated with a wave of her hand — 'in half an hour. Please don't be late.'

Audrey stepped forward and greeted Alice with a smile.

'You're sharing with me and four other girls. It's a bit of a squash but we have a laugh. We're in the old nursery at the back of the house.'

A grand staircase with polished oak bannisters swept upwards from the entrance hall. At the top Audrey directed Alice down to the right and then led her through a series of narrow, winding corridors; Alice wasn't sure if she would find her way out by teatime.

'Don't worry, you'll soon get used to it. We were all the same when we first got here.' Audrey stopped outside a door on the left and flung it open. 'Ta-da. Your home for the next three weeks.'

Alice squeezed past her guide. The room was furnished with three metal bunk beds. The bottom bunk furthest from the door was the only one free of the paraphernalia of a girl's bedroom; stockings were draped over the frame of one bunk; a make-up bag spilled its contents over the top bed of another. A stuffed teddy sat, out of place, on the pillow of a third. Varying perfumes competed to scent the room.

'I suppose it's pretty obvious which is yours. Sorry, it does tend to get somewhat untidy in here, despite the spot inspections they do.' She walked over to a chest of drawers and pulled out the bottom drawer. 'I hope this will be big enough for you. It's the only one left. You can shove your suitcase under the bed and use that for extra storage.'

'I'm sure I'll be fine.' Alice hefted the suitcase onto her bed. 'Please don't worry about me. I'm sure you need to get back, don't you?'

'Well, yes, if you don't mind? I'm on tea duty, have to get all the dratted cups and saucers laid out as though it's the King's garden party. Ridiculous but there you are. "We have standards to maintain, gals!" as Mrs Burnley-Smith always drums into us.' She rolled her eyes, mimed drinking a cup of tea, her little finger extended at a perfect angle. 'Are you sure you'll be able to find your way back to the staircase? It is a bit confusing at first.'

Alice nodded. 'Yes, I should be able to.'

'I'll send out a search party if I don't see you at tea. Toodle-oo.'

Alice perched on the edge of her bed, leaning forward at an uncomfortable angle on account of the upper bunk, and took stock of her latest sleeping quarters. The faded wallpaper was decorated with circus elephants and clowns for the children's room it once was. In the corner above where Alice sat, a damp stain spread across the ceiling and down the wall, the wallpaper curled and peeling. An old fireplace occupied much of the far wall, its iron grate rusting and bare. Photographs in silver and gold frames were arranged in groups on the wide mantelpiece — mothers and fathers, brothers, sweethearts. Alice didn't have any pictures with her; she hadn't thought there would be anywhere to put them.

The window, wide open here as at the front, looked out over the back of the house where more girls were working on what must have been an old vehicle of some kind. Alice could hear the clank of metal on metal as they hammered away at something.

'Ow, watch it. That was my thumb.'

'Oo, sorry. Good job we did the First Aid practice yesterday. Here, let me look.'

Hammers, First Aid? Have I been sent to the wrong place? I thought I was going to do more coding.

Deciding to leave unpacking her things until later, Alice got up to prepare for tea. Careful to avoid catching herself on the metal bed frame, she smoothed her skirt and finger-brushed her hair. She checked herself in the mirror above the fireplace. Satisfied she didn't look too bad despite the day spent travelling, she turned to navigate her way downstairs for tea.

After one or two false turns, Alice arrived at the dining hall where tea was in full swing. Gertie was true to her word and sought Alice's company while they ate. She introduced her to the rest of the girls — Alice wished they could all wear name badges or something so she could keep track of everyone — then proceeded to regale them all with a variety of tall tales of life on her country estate somewhere in the north of England.

By the time tea was finished, Alice couldn't keep her eyes open.

'Oh you poor dear. You must be exhausted. Travelling in this heat is dreadful, isn't it?' Alice's stifled yawn didn't escape Gertie's sharp notice. 'You get started on everything tomorrow, so you might as well go on up to bed and get an early night. Will be your last for a while. Breakfast is at half past six, back here in the dining room.'

Alice excused herself and returned to her nursery bedroom. She pulled her nightdress out from her suitcase, changed and folded her skirt and blouse on top of her other clothes. Closing the lid of the suitcase, she shoved it under her bed.

Tomorrow is another day. I'll unpack properly then.

Alice climbed under the thin blanket and rolled onto her side, her back to the room. Falling into a deep sleep, she didn't hear when the others came clattering to bed an hour or so later.

She did hear them all getting up the next morning. Rubbing her eyes and stretching as best she could in the cramped quarters, she watched in amusement as the other girls scurried around getting ready for their day.

'It's Alice isn't it? Good morning, I'm Pam. I sleep above you.' A girl with unruly red hair and freckles peered at Alice. 'Hope we didn't wake you last night when we came to bed? No? That's good then. Best you look lively and get up. It's after six already. You don't want to be late to breakfast. There's nothing left if you're even five minutes delayed.'

Alice did as Pam suggested and was down in the dining room as the first dishes of egg and toast were carried out. Steaming pots of tea were placed in the centre of each table with jugs of watery milk. There wasn't any sugar. Other girls wandered in as Alice ate, taking their places and reaching for their tea or some toast. Gertie spotted Alice and made her way over.

She plopped down in the seat next to Alice. 'Morning, Alice. Pass the tea won't you. Oh, no sugar again? Good for the figure, I suppose.' She poured tea into the cup in front of her. 'No, nothing for me thanks — I can never face eating when I've just woken up. Especially when they always burn the toast. Did you sleep alright? I hear you're in the nursery?'

Alice swallowed her last mouthful of the offending toast and washed it down with the rest of her tea. 'Yes, I am in the nursery — with Audrey. And yes, I slept like a log. Didn't even hear the others come to bed.'

'I'm not surprised — you looked shattered last night. Anyway, the first day is always a good one — lots of history lectures, that sort of thing. The real work starts tomorrow.' She winked at Alice. 'It's not all fun and games with the FANY, you know.'

Alice suspected she was about to have a rude introduction to her work as a volunteer. It was a far cry from the academic atmosphere of Bedford. *I wonder what Bill's up to?*

The rest of the day was spent, as Gertie predicted, in a series of lectures. Mrs Burnley-Smith from the day before called all the new recruits through to what must once have been a fine drawing room; it was cluttered with old school desks and rickety chairs and smelt of beeswax polish. They started with a brief history of the Corps from its inception in 1903, the brainchild of the eccentric Edward Baker. Alice envisioned him lying wounded on the battlefields of Sudan and deciding he needed a 'nurse on horseback' to administer much needed aid. It was such an incongruous picture of war. And yet, his idea became reality within a few years and a group of upper-class ladies became the founder members of the First Aid Nursing Yeomanry.

As with most of the students, Alice yawned her way through the years between the group's formation and its eventual useful service in the Great War. *Who cares who was running it or why they told Mr Baker not to?* But the accounts of women tending wounded soldiers in Belgium and later in France stirred her interest. Women who, with no care for their own safety, carted around tea stations and set up mobile cinemas; who rushed in to collect the wounded from the front lines, themselves enduring bombings and gas attacks. Alice pored over grainy black and white photographs of the Calais Convoy to see if she could find her Aunt Hazel in any of them. She thought she found one, with her aunt at the back of a group of women clustered around a battered ambulance, smiling at the camera as though they weren't witness to some of the worst atrocities of a terrible war.

Aunt Hazel hadn't spoken much to Alice about her time with the FANY during the First War, but perhaps that was more because Alice hadn't bothered to ask about it. Now, sitting in a dusty drawing room with a dozen other young women the same age that her aunt had been when she ferried the wounded to the field hospitals in Calais, Alice was ashamed of her disinterest. The bravery of her aunt and the other women with her, their courage and determination to help and serve, no matter the cost, stirred uncomfortable questions in Alice. *What am I doing, in this war, that is brave or noble? Who am I helping or serving?*

Her frustration increased the further through the course she progressed. The history lectures were replaced by a day of First Aid training. Alice hated it. She was paired with Eve, a girl from Northumberland who spent her childhood 'doctoring' all her nursery dolls; she could bandage the 'injured' Alice in a matter of minutes, symmetrical bands of cloth wrapped around any 'wound' no matter where it was situated. Alice, on the other hand, was hopeless. The bandage became tangled before she was even half way through the task. Eve tried her best to coach and encourage a neater way of working, not understanding why her partner was finding it so difficult. By the end of each session, Alice wasn't sure whether to laugh or sob.

'Alice, don't be upset. You'll get the hang of it, honestly you will.' Eve tried to comfort her new friend.

'Eve, you know I won't. And to be honest, I'm not sure I want to. I don't want to do nursing. Or horseriding, come to that.' Alice threw the dishevelled bandage down in despair. 'Sorry, Eve, but really. What am I doing here? I like numbers and letters and puzzles and things like that.'

Alice fared better in the practical mechanics sessions. Now it was Eve's turn to struggle.

'I think I'm not strong enough. Or something. I can't get anything to budge, no matter what I try.'

'Here, let me look.' Alice took the spanner from her partner. She gave the stubborn nut a couple of determined thumps with the end of the tool, earning them a sharp look of enquiry from the instructor. 'That should do it. Let's try.' Grunting, with her tongue sticking out and her forearms bulging, she managed to loosen the nut.

Eve gave a little clap. 'Well done, Alice. Thank you. My wounded soldiers would have died of their injuries if this was a real ambulance in a real war and I was on my own.'

The next lesson for the girls was advanced map reading skills which took up the entire day. The girls were relieved when the dinner bell rang. They folded up their papers, chatting and laughing. Only after they stood to leave did they notice their instructor still stood at the desk in front of them. A pile of unopened documents — maps? — sat in the middle of her desk.

'Right then girls. Leave your papers on your desk and make your way outside in as orderly a fashion as you can manage. You have five minutes to assemble on the front lawn outside.'

Alice looked over at Eve, one eyebrow raised in question. Eve shrugged, shook her head.

'Do you think they're giving us a picnic or something?' Eve whispered as they filed into the hallway.

'Doubt it. Did you see that pile of paper on Mrs Wilkinson's desk? Doesn't look like a picnic menu to me.'

Parked outside the door were two trucks, their tail gates hanging down. A FANY driver stood beside each one; Alice noticed one of them was Gertie.

Once they were gathered on the lawn, Mrs Wilkinson appeared in the doorway behind them. The pile of papers was with her.

'Now then, ladies. We all know the FANY motto — "I'll cope". Well, tonight we're going to see how well you can. Alice, could you hand these out to each pair of girls.' Alice stepped forward and took the papers. Mystified as to what was going on, she handed them out as requested. 'Thank you, Alice. In your hands, girls, is a map. A map of an area of woodland located a few miles from us at Overthorpe Hall. Our drivers here will escort you to that piece of woodland. You will be dropped off, and then, in your pairs, you will find your way back here to 'base camp'.'

There was a shuffling of paper and feet, a muttered grumble from a few of the girls at the back. One girl — her name was Lynette, Alice thought — burst into tears. Her partner gave her a couple of awkward pats on the back then handed her a handkerchief. Lynette sniffled for a few seconds longer before managing to regain her composure.

'Of course, you won't be able to see where you're going from the back of the vehicles, so you really will have to rely on your mapwork skills.' Mrs Wilkinson beamed at her trainees.

'You'd think we were being treated to a picnic, the way she keeps smiling.' Alice was hungry and tired. She wanted nothing more than to return to the dining hall, grab some supper and head up to bed.

'You never know, it could be fun. Better than nursing, I should think.' Eve winked at Alice.

'Mm, that's true. Every cloud has a silver lining I suppose.'

'You need to go and collect your torches and compasses. Two minutes ladies, then we'll be leaving. There's a canteen of water for each of you in the dining hall. Collect that as well.'

Alice and Eve decided to split the tasks between them, Alice running back to the classroom to fetch the extra equipment needed for the night's excursion; Eve made straight for the dining hall and the containers of water. As it was still light, Alice hoped they would be back long before it got dark but grabbed the torches anyway.

The two of them clambered into the back of the second truck and settled themselves on the hard wooden bench pushed against the side. Lynette and her partner, Ruth, climbed in next to them. Lynette appeared to have recovered from her earlier outburst, although she still fidgeted with nerves.

Alice tried to keep track of the twists and turns in the road as they trundled along to their destination. She closed her eyes, trying to picture where they were going, but realised after the first couple of stops and corners that she didn't know the area well enough to be able to navigate their way back from memory. There would be nothing for it but to rely on their combined ability to read a map.

The truck jolted to a halt after about twenty minutes of driving. *Not too far away then. But quite a hike still.* The girls jumped out of the back and surveyed their surroundings. They were in a small clearing surrounded by tall trees. Beyond where they stood, the evening light filtered through the thick leaf canopy of the trees. A narrow pathway led off to the left. Everywhere else was dense undergrowth. The alternative way out was the uneven track they drove up.

Any idea of following that back to the road and so finding an easy route home was soon abandoned. Mrs Wilkinson called the group to order with a shrill whistle.

'Quiet please, ladies. There are few last minute instructions for you. Firstly, no, you can't follow the trucks back to the road. That would be cheating. And in a real life situation, would be certain to get you noticed and probably arrested.

'You may take the path over there or forge your own way through the woods. It is entirely up to you and your partner and your joint interpretation of the map.

'Secondly, should you meet anyone on your journey back, you are not, may I repeat, NOT, to ask for directions. In fact, you should rather remain hidden from sight. After all, he or she may be the enemy.

'Thirdly, we know how long it should take you to return to base. If you have not arrived within a certain time, we can send out a search party for you. However, I'm sure you would rather be saved the embarrassment—and further punishment — by reading your maps correctly and finding your way.

'Fourthly, and finally — have fun! Remember, you are FANY, you cope. Dinner will be waiting for your arrival.

'Good luck, my dears. See you in a while.' With that, she climbed into the passenger seat of the first truck. The vehicles revved their engines and bumped back down the track to the road. Within minutes, they were out of sight and beyond earshot.

'Well Eve, let's get that map open and see what's what. I'm hungry so we need to find the quickest route back.' Together they knelt on the damp earth and spread the map out between them. Around them murmurs of focused discussion disturbed the stillness of the glade.

After a few minutes of fumbling with the compass and pointing out various possible routes, Alice and Eve were ready. They were one of the last groups to leave.

'Don't worry, more haste less speed, as my Gran used to say.' Alice was concerned at how long their planning took, her anxiety communicating itself to the ever-sensitive Eve. 'We've planned where we're going, so we're less likely to get lost on the way. The others have gone off too quickly. You'll see — we'll be back before them.'

She was right.

They cut through the woods in the opposite direction to the path, pushing through brambles and ferns and scratching arms and legs as they went. Midges and gnats swarmed around their heads, biting the exposed flesh on their faces. A wood warbler, disturbed on her nest, flew away in a rush of twittering fury.

Within a few minutes they reached the edge of the wood. Ahead was a meadow of long waving grass, dotted here and there with bright yellow buttercups and clumps of white clover. Sheep grazed, unconcerned by their sudden appearance. The loamy smell of the woodland was replaced by the fresher scent of fields and flowers.

'Right, straight down that hill. Then we should find ourselves on the outskirts of Banbury. And nearly there.' Alice was kneeling down, looking at the map again. 'We might make it before the sun goes down, but I'm not sure.'

'Well, it will still be light enough for a while after that. Let's get going and see how we get on. Do you want some water before we start?'

'Good idea. Might stop my stomach rumbling for five minutes.' Alice opened her canteen and gulped a few mouthfuls of water. Wiping her lips with the back of her hand, she replaced the lid and slung the strap over her shoulder. Pulling her cap lower to shield her eyes from the sun, she paused to take in the view. 'It is pretty though, isn't it?'

'Extremely. Don't you love how the light catches that church tower over there? As though it's being kissed by God.'

'Goodness, Eve, that's very poetical of you. But yes, it does, doesn't it? I hope God is kissing our world, you know. It doesn't seem like it at times, does it?'

Alice

The Telegram

•▬ •▬•• •• ▬•▬•• •

T he rest of the hike back was easy, their chosen route perfect. The
meadow rolled downhill until ending at a small stream where Alice
and Eve wasted a few minutes splashing and giggling in the water before
crossing to the far bank. They climbed over a stile in the fence and into
the lane beyond before checking the map again to be certain which way
to go. Turning left, they were soon walking around the edge of Banbury.

'"Ride a cock horse, to Banbury Cross." Never thought I'd be living in
a nursery rhyme, I must say.' Eve linked arms with Alice as they marched
along the road. 'What do you want to do when this is over? You know,
the course. Not nursing obviously.'

'Oi, that's rude. No, but you're right, definitely not nursing. I have no
idea — I was sent here rather than chose to come. I was told I have to
go through the course to become a proper FANY, then when I'm done
they'll tell me where to go next.' Alice sighed. It was too frustrating for
words. 'What about you? Where do you think you'll end up?'

'I do like the nursing side of it. So maybe one of the hospitals that
they're setting up in the country. You know, convalescent homes or
whatever, like in the other war. But I'm happy going anywhere that's
useful, I suppose. I'm sure they know better than me where I'm needed.'

'You're a contented soul, aren't you?'

'Yes, I suppose so.' Eve sounded surprised. 'I've never thought about
it like that. I just, I don't know, feel like there's a bigger purpose to
it all, a "guiding hand" behind whatever I'm doing and wherever I'm
going...Sorry, I sound daft.'

'No, you don't. I had a similar thought when I first went to, er — ' a vision of the Commander at Bletchley Park exhorting secrecy at all times, no matter who you were talking to, floated into Alice's mind.' — um, a place I was at before. But since getting here? I don't know. This doesn't seem to fit. Or something...Now I'm the one who sounds daft.'

Eve gave her arm a squeeze. 'It'll become clear, don't you worry. Look, there's the Hall.'

The light was fading but they could just make out the hulk of building a little way ahead.

'I wonder how the others have got on? Funny we haven't seen any of them.'

'Well, they all went haring off in the other direction to us. I'm not surprised our paths didn't cross.'

As they spoke, a car turned out of the lane in front of them, a slit of headlamp shining on the road.

'Oops, quick, hide behind this wall.'

'What do you mean, hide? We're not in any trouble or anything.' Alice crouched next to Eve, their faces so close she could feel Eve's breath on her cheek.

'Ssh, he might have seen us, be looking for us.'

The car crunched past them. No-one stopped to look for them. Straightening up, Alice swatted her partner on the arm.

'Good grief, you do take these things seriously, don't you? Can we get on now? I really do need my supper.'

'You'd be glad I took it seriously if we were running for our lives in France or somewhere.'

Alice rolled her eyes and grabbed Eve by the hand. 'Come on. Let's run the rest of the way.'

Breathless from exertion and laughter, they ran along the lane and up the sweep of driveway to the Hall's front door. To Alice's surprise, Mrs Burnley-Smith was there to greet them.

'Well done, girls, you're the second couple to return so far. You chose a good route. Top marks for mapwork skills.'

'See, what did I tell you?' Eve was triumphant.

'Eve dear, you hurry along to dinner. I want a quick word with Alice here.'

Alice looked at Mrs Burnley-Smith. Was that concern showing on her face? *What now? Another move?*

'Alice, come inside. Here, to the office. Yes, take a seat.' Mrs Burnley-Smith busied herself with cups and a teapot. 'Here, some tea for you. I've added a bit of sugar.'

Bewildered, Alice took the offered cup and saucer but waited before drinking any. 'Have I done something wrong, Mrs Burnley-Smith? Did I forget to finish one of my duties earlier?'

'No, no, nothing like that.' She cleared her throat, took a sip of her own tea. 'I have news from home for you, Alice. A telegram from your father.'

Alice replaced her cup in its saucer, sloshing tea over the side. Her hands were clammy and damp. 'News? What news? What about?'

'Here you are, read it for yourself. Unless you would like me to?' She held out a piece of paper.

Alice put her tea down on the floor beside her chair and reached for the telegram, her hands shaking. She glanced at the words, but they jumped around, black shapes with a life of their own. Taking a deep breath, she tried again.

BROTHER TOM STOP MISSING IN ACTION STOP LOVE DAD

Was that it? She turned the page over, held it to the light. Surely there was more, some other vital piece of information she hadn't seen the first time. Nothing. She read it again.

MISSING IN ACTION.

Alice looked up at Mrs Burnley-Smith, tears filling her eyes. 'What? I don't understand...Does that mean...?' She couldn't finish the sentence. Crumpling the telegram into a ball, she pushed out of her chair. 'Excuse me. I, I, need to...'

Mrs Burnley-Smith was already by her side, helping her to the door. 'Come, let me take you to your room. I'll make sure the others leave you alone for a while.'

The kindness was more than Alice could bear. Her face crumpled like the piece of paper in her hand. She doubled over, a stab of physical pain winding her. Mrs Burnley-Smith caught her and helped her back to her chair. She pulled a second chair close, reached for Alice's hand.

The older woman remained silent. A clock ticked on her desk. The girls returned from their map-reading adventure, feet clumping backwards and forwards outside the closed door — oblivious to Alice's distress.

'Where's Mrs Burnley-Smith? Doesn't she need to be here to sign us all back in again? I want to get on with supper.' Someone tired and hungry made their displeasure at being held up clear.

A knock on the door. 'Mrs Burnley-Smith, are you there? The girls are all returning.'

'You see to it, Mrs Wilkinson. I am otherwise engaged at the moment.' She returned her attention to Alice. Untangling her hands, she reached up and stroked the hair from Alice's forehead. 'There now, a good cry is what you needed. And now for bed and tea. In that order. You sit here while I get everything organised.'

Mrs Burnley-Smith straightened up, squeezed Alice's shoulder and opened the door into the hallway. 'Audrey, could you come here a moment please. I have a job...' The rest of the instruction was muffled by the closing of the door.

Alice was alone. She rocked backwards and forwards in her chair; a small movement, but one that comforted in the way the old rocker in the kitchen at home did any time she had fallen and hurt herself as a child.

'Tom...' It was barely a word, barely a name. A low moan repeated over and over.

She was unaware of the door reopening until Mrs Burnley-Smith and another figure were at her side.

'Alice? Audrey here will take you to your room and get you settled. She'll make sure the others don't disturb you until bedtime.' The voice was gentle and quiet, so different from the usual tone of their Principal and Commanding Officer.

Alice nodded without speaking. She allowed herself to be lifted to her feet by the two women. Audrey slipped one arm around her waist and half shuffled, half dragged her charge towards the door. Mrs Burnley-Smith pulled open the door, checking to make sure everyone was busy at their places in the dining room.

'There you are, dear, Audrey will take good care of you. Audrey, take it easy with her. She hasn't had anything to eat or drink since the excursion. I should have thought of that before I showed the poor child the telegram, but I felt it important to break the news sooner rather than later.'

'Yes, Ma'am. Don't worry. I'll make some tea and a piece of toast or find a biscuit.' Mrs Burnley-Smith allowed her to pass, watched the girls' progress across the hallway and up the stairs.

Alice remembered nothing of how she got into bed. But, here she was in her nightdress, a cup of tea untouched on the table beside her. A plate with a piece of toast, the once-melted butter now congealing in yellow pools, sat abandoned next to it. The room was dark on account of the blackout curtains, the light not yet having been switched on. The door was closed. Only the squeals and laughter of a group of girls playing a last game of rounders, or something, were heard through the open window.

Alice rolled over, her back to the room. Curling into a tight ball, hot tears dripped from her face onto the pillow. There was no sound of crying to accompany them; there was no sound left.

She must have dozed off, exhaustion combining with misery and shock to bring some relief. She woke as the others crept in, trying not to disturb their friend. Unlike most nights, when they chatted to one another, sharing stories from their day or simply teasing one another, no one spoke or giggled.

'Goodnight Alice. We're all so sorry.' It was Audrey, ducking under the top bunk and leaning over Alice. 'Please let us know if we can do anything. Wake us, please, if you need to.'

She kissed Alice on her damp forehead. Alice didn't move, wanting to let them all think she was fast asleep and not able to hear their concern. Their sympathy.

Once the room was filled with rhythmic breathing and occasional snuffles and snorts, Alice knew they were all asleep. She uncurled from her position, throwing off the covers as she did so. Anger was replacing her earlier grief. *I can't lie here any longer. I have to get up, to walk, to think.*

Ignoring the stiffness of her thighs and calves thanks to the earlier hike, Alice tiptoed over to the door and out of the bedroom. The hallway was lit by a night light at the top of the stairs. *I need to get outside. Feel the fresh air.* Pausing at the bottom of the staircase to make sure no one was following, Alice made for the main front door.

She half hoped she was to be thwarted in her escape attempt, but to her surprise the door was unlocked. She opened it a crack and slipped out into the cool night air. The stone steps were cold on the soles of her feet. *Should've brought slippers. How can you be so self-centred, Alice? This isn't about your comfort. When Tom is...Tom is...*

Alice stuffed a fist into her mouth to prevent her crying again. She bit down on the knuckles, physical discomfort preferable to waves of heart-pain threatening to overwhelm her. She stepped onto the gravel driveway, taking notice of each sharp stone as it dug into her cold flesh. She paced along the front of the hall. Its darkened windows followed her progress with blank, uncaring stares.

Allowing her fist to fall to her side, Alice muttered to herself.

'Go and join the FANY. You'll be helping the war effort if you do. How is hiking through woods on pleasant summer evenings, helping the war? How is it helping...helping Tom? Or his friends? Or Mum and Dad?' She stopped walking, hugged herself as she gazed out over the vegetable garden and the gate beyond. 'I could leave. I'm only a volunteer — they can't stop me. Go and do something useful. I could find Mavis and work on the farm with her. No, that wouldn't work, would it? One of the munitions factories? Yes, that's the answer. I can build bombs and bullets and fight back. Better than sitting here, learning how to tie bandages or fix tractors.'

The idea solidified in Alice's mind. She would get up early and pack, before anyone persuaded her to stay. She would ask Gertie for a lift to the station. If she refused then Alice would walk and hitch a lift as she had on her arrival. Where to go from there? London? Maybe Birmingham. The munitions factories are there, aren't they? Alice resumed her pacing. Should I visit home first? No. They'll try to stop me. Say I should finish what I've started, something like that. Dad will tell me it's a waste of my brain. What use is a clever brain in stopping a war?

Alice didn't hear the door open behind her, nor the crunch of gravel as someone walked towards her.

'Alice? It's Eve. No, don't walk away. Sorry if I startled you.' Eve was beside Alice before the grieving girl could stop her. Eve wrapped her arms around her friend, held her close. 'Alice! You're shivering. You must be frozen out here in just a nightdress. Here, I brought you your dressing gown.'

Alice tried to pull away, tell Eve to go and leave her alone. Eve held up the cotton fabric and draped it over Alice's shoulders.

'I'm sorry to hear about your brother. About Tom.'

Alice lifted her head. 'How...?'

'Mrs Burnley-Smith called me aside after dinner. Told me to keep an eye on you. Good job I did. I heard someone leave your room so went to check who it was. I thought maybe you were going to the bathroom. But then when you didn't come back, I knew you'd come out here. I'd have done the same.'

Alice didn't reply. She leant against her friend and sobbed. Eve steered her towards a garden bench at the side of the path. She waited until Alice stopped crying, her shaky breaths and heaving shoulders subsiding.

'I'm going to leave, you know. I'm not staying here, growing vegetables and being all "gentlewomanly" while the war goes on without me.'

Eve didn't respond. Alice appreciated her silence. *Thank you for not trying to dissuade me.*

Rosie

The Photograph

•⁻• ⁻⁻⁻ ••• •• •

'What on earth are you wearing, Gran? Did you join the Army or something? I thought women were either in the Navy or the Air Force?' Rosie held aloft another photograph of a group of women gathered on the steps of a grand mansion. She recognised Gran as one of those in the back row. She was staring straight at the camera, her chin lifted in what may be interpreted as defiance. 'You look quite angry here.'

'Let me see that.' Gran took the photograph from Rosie, squinting at each of the faces. She tapped the paper with a finger bent with arthritis. 'Yes, I was angry here. I remember that. My friend —' she pointed to a pretty girl standing in the front row. '—what was her name? Evelyn? Evie? No, just Eve. That's right — Eve...' She stopped talking, lost in memories and other conversations.

'Yes?' Rosie was fascinated. *Are you finally going to tell me, Gran, what you were doing?* 'Eve? Who was she? And where is this photo taken? It looks like a real stately home, that.'

'What? Oh yes, it must have been fancy once. It wasn't by the time I got there, though. All converted rooms and rattling windows. And the lawn and flowerbeds all but destroyed — made into a vegetable patch to help the War Effort.'

Rosie tried to hide her disappointment. 'Oh, you were one of the Land Girls, were you?'

'Land Girl? Oh, goodness no, I couldn't have done that. I like gardening now, but back then? Definitely not. Mavis was the Land Girl. Loved it. Married the son of the farmer of the place they sent her to. Ended up owning the whole farm after the old folk passed on. Only stopped active farming about two or three years ago. I must give her a ring; see how she's coping with having to take a back seat. Knowing Mavis, not so well.' She chuckled. 'Stop fidgeting, dear. You'll distract me even more and then you'll never know about that photo.'

'Sorry, Gran. Carry on.'

'Anyway, no that isn't Army. That's the FANY uniform. You know, the Corps I was telling you about earlier? And I'll have you know, the Queen herself wore a uniform almost identical to this one — except for the cap. She was ATS — Auxiliary Transport Services. They're the group you've probably heard of. Her Majesty drove trucks around the place, would you believe? And if that uniform was good enough for her, it was certainly good enough for the likes of me.' Rosie choked down another giggle. *I'm not sure I'll ever get used to that name.* 'Eve and I were as thick as thieves for a while. It was Eve who stopped me packing the whole thing in.'

'Really? But Gran, you've always told Emma and me we should never give up, no matter how hard it gets.'

'Yes, I have, and that's right. But in some ways, this wasn't because it was too hard. I think I felt it wasn't hard enough. I didn't think I was helping with the war at all, playing nurses and mechanics and so on. I wanted to do something that mattered, something that would change things.'

'And did you? Where did you go after this house place?'

Gran returned the photo to the box, closing the lid and sliding it towards her as though getting ready to return it to the cupboard in the dining room. 'Oh, to London again. For a bit. Anyway, enough chat. I need to give this silly dog a bath before she trails mud all through the house. Could you pack away the tea things? Come here, Mitzy.'

'Yes, Gran, sure.' Rosie gathered the cups and saucers, rattling them together, irritated. Gramps touched her arm as she passed his chair.

'Don't push her too hard. There's things she doesn't talk about. Not even to me. It's not against you, so don't fret.'

'Thank you, Gramps. I just want to know her story, I suppose. And yours, of course,' she added, not wanting to offend her grandfather.

He lifted one bushy eyebrow at her. 'Mm, that will be a story, when you get to it.' He laughed and let go of her arm.

Rosie squirted washing-up liquid into the bowl and turned on the tap. She wiggled her fingers; the bubbles billowed up and overflowed into the sink. Through the window she watched as Gran continued a dignified chase of Mitzy around the garden. The dog was determined not to be given a bath, burrowing deeper into the hedge on the other side of the lawn. Some dramatic yelping and then Gran caught her, dragging her over to the tin bath brought out from the shed.

'In you go. And stop whining. It won't kill you.'

Rosie returned her attention to the washing up, soaping the cups and saucers, then rinsing them under a trickle of water from the barely open tap. Leaving everything piled up on the rack to drip-dry, Rosie leant out of the window. 'Gran, it looks like you need a hand. I've finished the washing up. Hold on to Mitzy and I'll come out.'

Nothing more was said about Gran's war experiences for the next few days. Try as she might, Rosie couldn't turn the conversation in that direction, and the box of mementoes and photographs remained hidden away.

Besides, there was no spare time for delving into the past; it was the week of the local church summer garden fête, and Gran was preoccupied with shopping and baking and collecting items for the 'white elephant' stall. She roped Rosie in to help.

'Rosie dear, please pass me that vase over there. Isn't it perfectly dreadful?' Rosie couldn't disagree. The vase was brown ceramic, with wavy edges. Several of the waves were chipped. 'Old Mrs Finley dropped it off. I couldn't say no, but honestly, how am I going to sell it?'

'Call it vintage, Gran. That'll work. Maybe.' Rosie was doubtful, but wanted to encourage her grandmother. Some of her more arty friends at home might like it. Laura, or maybe Claire. 'I tell you what, if it doesn't sell, I'll buy it. One of my friends might like it. For uni, you know.'

'Well, that's kind of you. I'll make sure to give you a discount.' She winked, then took the vase from Rosie. She wrapped it in a few sheets of old newspaper. 'Just because it's not a treasure to us, doesn't mean it wasn't a treasure to Mrs Finley. Or to its new owner, for that matter.'

Boxes of *bric-à-brac* cluttered the hallway.

'Let's get these all into the boot of the car, out of the way. Then we can concentrate on the baking. Much more fun.' Gran passed the car keys to Rosie. 'Here, you take that one out and I'll bring this. Gramps helps most years but, with you here, he doesn't have to this time. He's not as strong as he was, after that cough over the winter.'

Rosie carried the heavier boxes to the car. She helped fit the smaller boxes and bags into the boot, slamming the lid before anything fell out. 'No more collecting for the stall now, Gran. We won't be able to fit anything else into the car.'

For the rest of that day and the morning of the next, Rosie mixed and rolled, and baked and packed, and washed up. Gran stood beaming at all the containers full of scones, biscuits, and homemade sausage rolls. The kitchen hadn't quite lost the aromas of warm pastry and melted sugar. Rosie gave an exhausted smile.

'Lovely. Thank you, dear, you've been such a help. The tea will be a big success this year, thanks to you.' Gran pulled the lid off the tin closest to her. 'I think we deserve a reward, don't you?'

You can look just like a naughty child sometimes, Gran. 'That sounds like a good idea. I'll tell Gramps...'

'But he didn't help. You know the story of the Little Red Hen, don't you? No one wants to help until it's time to eat the fresh bread she makes.' But she took three biscuits out, anyway. 'Well, he can be our official 'taste tester' then.'

Rosie went in search of Gramps. She found him in his usual chair in the conservatory, the doors to the garden open, and Mitzy dozing at his feet. He waved the newspaper in her direction, a broad smile of triumph on his face. 'I've just finished the crossword — been battling with it all day. I try to do it before your Gran gets it. With all this baking, she hasn't had a chance to look yet. So, I beat her.' He gave a wheezy chuckle. 'Did your Gran ever tell you about the crossword competition she won? Oh no, don't ask me — she tells the story much better. Oh, and tell her, yes please, I'd love a cup of tea and one — or two — of whatever you've made. I'm not fussy!'

Rosie relayed the message. 'Gramps says yes, please, he would like tea and whatever you can spare.' She picked out a selection of goodies to add to the biscuits and stacked them on the plate Gran handed to her. 'He was saying you won a crossword competition once?'

Distracted with the tea making, Rosie wasn't sure if Gran heard the question. Or if she was ignoring it. As usual.

'Well, he would want a free sample, wouldn't he?' She rolled her eyes. 'What's he been doing all day, do you know? I've been so busy with everything for the fête, I've hardly said two words to him since breakfast.'

'He was finishing the crossword. Said it took him all day. Said he was glad you were too busy to look at it, so he could still beat you.'

'Oh, don't let him fool you. He's quite a crossword whizz himself. I lose as many of our 'races' as I win.' She set the teapot on the tray. 'We just need the milk and sugar. There. That's everything.'

'So, what was the competition you won?' Rosie followed Gran through to the conservatory.

'Here you are, Bill, dear.' She put the plate down on the coffee table, picked up the newspaper from next to Gramps. 'Goodness, you have made a dog's breakfast of this, haven't you?'

Gramps snorted. 'I'd like to see you do any better. It's by Chifonie...I told Rosie here you've won a crossword puzzle before. Quite an important one.'

A look passed between her grandparents which Rosie couldn't interpret. Gramps looked so proud, like a father given a glowing report of his child's progress at school. Gran, however, frowned, shaking her head.

Gramps took the newspaper from Gran. He gave his wife's fingers a squeeze as he did so. 'Oh, go on with you. It's before all the other thing...'

'Please, Gran, I'd love to know. I've never won a competition for anything.'

'Well, it was at the start of the war. And I didn't actually win it. It was just I finished it quicker than most people. And Vera and Mavis sent in the completed puzzle to the editor — or persuaded me to, I can't remember now — and told him how speedy I was.' She bit into a flapjack, oat crumbs cascading onto her plate. 'Mm, these are good, although I do say so myself. So yes, the editor of *The Daily Telegraph* was — impressed although, I think he didn't believe my time. He contacted my Professor at Cambridge.'

Rosie choked on her tea. 'Cambridge? You were at Cambridge during the war? Wasn't that quite unusual? For women to go, I mean?'

'Yes, it was. I think Father — your great-grandfather — put in a word for me. He was quite well connected for a village parson. That's where I met Vera and Mavis.' She took a sip of tea. 'But then the war wasn't ending as quickly as everyone thought it would, and they needed everyone to help in whatever way possible. So, plans changed. That's when Mavis went off and became a Land Girl.'

'And the crossword — ?' Rosie prompted.

'Well, my professor called me in, asked about it. I told him that was how long it took me and that, of course, it was the truth. No, I have no idea how long it took me, far too long ago. They just said it was one of the quickest times by a girl of my age.'

'And? What did you win?'

'Nothing, I don't think. I left Cambridge after that. Joined those FANY you find so funny...Anyway, enough of this sitting around and chatting. If I sit here any longer, I'll doze off. We still need to make sure everything's ready for tomorrow. I need to ring Joan and check there are enough people available to serve the teas. Let me do that now, before I forget.'

That evening, Rosie asked to use her grandparents' computer, kept in the room she was sleeping in. The conversation about the crossword had made her think. Weren't they told in History about a puzzle of sorts being used to recruit people? She booted up the modem and waited for the connection to go through, tapping her fingers on the desk while she waited. Once it was ready, she opened up the web browser, entering a couple of search words she thought might work. And there it was — *The Daily Telegraph* crossword puzzle published in January 1942.

Rosie skimmed the newspaper articles associated with her search. Several mentioned Bletchley Park, the home of the Government Code and Cypher School. Photographs of something like a typewriter accompanied most of the stories; an Enigma machine, so the captions said. After half an hour of searching, Rosie found some photographs of Park personnel. Men in loose-fitting trousers and cardigans, smoking pipes or playing bowls, were common. The Park also employed a lot of women, but they wore smart uniforms, unlike the sack-like FANY uniform Gran wore in her picture.

Rosie did another quick search to see if there were any FANY working at Bletchley during the war. It didn't seem so. Confused, Rosie logged out and turned off the computer. Although past 9 o'clock, it was still light. Outside, swallows darted and swooped, catching their last meal of the day. A fly buzzed against the window pane, irritating Rosie. She opened the window and wafted her hand to encourage the fly outside where it belonged. Free at last, the fly disappeared into the evening sky.

The woods at the top of the hill beyond the lane were silhouetted against a sky turning a delicate candyfloss pink. Brush strokes of white clouds streaked the horizon. Someone further along the lane was doing some late-evening lawn mowing; Rosie heard the clatter of the machine's engine, smelled the sweet, freshly cut grass.

Does it matter if I don't know Gran's story? Will it change who she is to me? No, it won't. But it's important, I know it is.

Alice

Grief

•‾ •‾•• •• ‾•‾• •

A lice sat alone in the lounge. The fire had long since gone out; cold, slate-grey ashes piled in the grate. She had insisted that Eve return to her room, assuring her she would be fine on her own. She heard the creaks of the old house, settling for the night. Alice was far from settling. She was grubby from the trek through woods and across fields, too fraught with grief or anger, or whatever she felt, to be bothered with the effort of cleaning herself. A couple of scratches on her legs oozed blood. She couldn't remember having hurt herself. Her whole body ached. She was heavy and listless, like a young child coming down with a fever. Only now, there was no mother to comfort and carry her to bed; no warm, soothing hot water bottle to tuck under the blankets and keep the shivers at bay. Here there was nothing but the empty numbness of loss.

The telegram was scrunched in her hand; and despite Eve's efforts to prise Alice's fingers open and take it from her, they remained frozen in place. Flesh turned to stone. Cajoled back inside by the soft gentleness of Eve's entreaties, Alice thought she may never move again. She would remain here, in this lounge, covered in cobwebs and memories. Like Great Expectation's Miss Haversham. But there would be no Pip to discover her. No Tom to rescue her.

Eve knelt at Alice's feet, cradling ice-cold fingers in her own warm hands.

'May I pray for you, dear Alice? Before I leave you to your own thoughts?'

Alice gave the slightest of shrugs. Even in her distress, she couldn't quite bring herself to be rude to her friend. *What good will prayer do?*

'Dear Lord and Saviour Jesus. Thank you that your promise is to always be with us, even in the valley of the shadow of death. I ask that you would be near to Alice and stay with her throughout the night. Let her know you are here. Thank you, heavenly Father. Amen.'

Alice felt the warmth of tears dripping onto her clenched palms, unexpected droplets of love. She needed Eve to leave her now, though; to take her compassion and prayers. Her friend stood, and still holding Alice's hands, she leant forward and kissed her on the forehead.

'I'm here when you need me. You can wake me later, if you want. Not to talk. Just to be with you. You know...'

Alice nodded, unable to speak as her throat closed up. She swallowed hard. Pulling her hands free from Eve's grip, she turned her head in dismissal. Eve, tugging a handkerchief from her pocket to wipe away tears of her own, stepped away. Leaving Alice alone.

Mrs Burnley-Smith gave Alice two days off duty. She remained in her room, rolling to face the wall each time the other girls came in. Eve brought food on a tray, often returning it to the kitchen untouched, hours later. The telegram was stuck to the wall beside Alice's pillow; the wrinkles smoothed over and over by her restless fingers.

During the day, Alice kept the curtains drawn, and the windows closed, despite the stuffiness. She couldn't bear the sounds of life continuing as though nothing had happened; one of the girls laughing and joking each time she dropped something or made a mistake; Mrs Burnley-Smith welcoming a steady arrival of newcomers with her false cheeriness. *Don't they know there's a war on? That there are bombs and torpedoes, and people are dying?*

At night, Alice was afraid of the dark, of the nightmares she knew would come if she closed her eyes. Then she would get up, tiptoeing to the window to peer around the blackouts to catch a glimpse of moonlight. She wasn't sure if she woke anyone; no one questioned her or complained. But maybe she had made it clear enough — she wasn't going to listen to them, anyway.

On the third morning, the other girls got up and left the room as usual. Alice settled back on the pillow, glad of the peace. The door opened and Mrs Burnley-Smith advanced in all her uniformed glory. She glared at Alice.

'Miss Stallard. While I understand — and sympathise — with the shock you have received on the news of your brother's disappearance — ' she glanced at the telegram pinned behind Alice's head, paused in her tirade — 'there is a war on. And you have a place in it. No, don't interrupt. I know you have not been eating and you will no doubt be feeling weak and woeful. I have therefore ordered a bowl of soup to be brought up to you. You will, whilst you wait for your meal, get up and clean yourself up. I think you have not washed effectively since your orienteering exercise. It certainly smells that way.' Mrs Burnley-Smith strode across the room and flung open the curtains. She unlatched the window, opening it wide. A blast of cold, wet air made Alice gasp.

'As you see, the seasons have changed in your absence. Now, where was I?' She turned from the window and looked down at Alice. Her eyes softened; her tone gentle. 'Miss Stallard, there really is work to be done, and you are the one to do it. The best way you can help your brother and his friends is to apply that mind of yours to the matter at hand. Your posting has come through. I can't give you the precise details, but you'll be based at a top-secret station a few miles from us here at Overthorpe House. You need to get packed and they will collect you later this afternoon. I have allowed Miss Millington — Eve — to assist you in getting ready.'

She leant over Alice, stroking a lock of hair from her forehead, much to Alice's surprise and embarrassment.

'Child, you will find your way. Take each day as it comes, one step after another. May the Lord bless you...It's time to get up and get going.' Mrs Burnley-Smith straightened, smoothed her skirt. She gave a last glance around the room before hurrying away, uttering a slight tut of disapproval at the clothes and hair accessories strewn across every available surface. She left the door open.

'Well!' Alice, stunned by the encounter, was shocked into speech and action. She pushed the blankets from the bed, wrinkling her nose. 'Mm, I think I do need a wash...'

'I'll say. You haven't moved from that flea-pit of yours for the whole week. Well, the last couple of days, anyway.' Eve shuffled into the room, laden down with a tray of steaming cups and bowls. 'Goodness, you girls are much untidier than we are in our room. Where on earth can I put this?'

Alice rose from the bed, her head missing the frame of the top bunk by little more than an inch. She shoved aside a couple of hairnets, half a dozen curlers, three lipsticks and a lidless pot of face cream from the table below the window, and made space for the tray. Eve placed her load on the cleared surface and turned to her friend.

'It is good to see you up.' She advanced, arms open for a hug.

'Maybe I should bath first?' Alice grimaced. 'Sorry, have I been beastly?'

'No, dearest Alice, you could never be beastly. Just sad and a little lost.'

Eve's kind words stabbed through the fog of Alice's grief. She crumpled back on the bed, her shoulders heaving with silent sobs. Eve plopped down onto the bed beside her friend, pulling her close while the waves of sadness formed and broke. After several minutes, Alice pulled herself free, gulping air into her lungs.

She wiped her hands over her face. 'Goodness, I must look a real sight.' Her voice wobbled as she spoke. 'Thank you...'

'Go and have your bath. Then we can eat. I'm starving, even if you aren't.'

Alice gathered up her things and made her way to the bathroom. Her legs were like jelly and her stomach growled. Standing in front of the mirror, Alice surveyed the damp clumps of hair, the red and swollen eyes, the ugly blotched skin.

'Yes, I am a sight...'

Ten minutes later, she was back in her room, clean and fresh. She sniffed back a few last tears.

'Ta-da. That looks better.' Eve greeted her return with a clap of delight, as though seeing a friend for the first time in months. 'Now, let's eat.'

Alice threw her wet sponge at Eve, laughing. It felt good.

The soup was delicious, full of carrots and turnips and a bone or two. There was tea and even a few biscuits. Once finished, Eve piled everything back on the tray, then reached for a small, wrapped parcel Alice hadn't noticed.

'This is for you, Alice. To take with you, wherever you go. May it bring some comfort and lighten the load you will no doubt have to carry.'

Alice took the parcel. The paper was exquisite — delicate flowers and birds entwined together. It was hand-painted. Alice stared at Eve. 'You did this, didn't you? I'd heard from the others you were good at art, but not like this. This is beautiful. Maybe you should sell this? Oh, you probably do, don't you?' Alice noticed the blush advancing up Eve's neck. 'Sorry, didn't mean to embarrass you. You are really the most talented, generous, kind, and caring girl I know. And yes, I do mean to embarrass you now.'

She untied the string around the parcel. *I do hope this isn't a Bible. I don't want to have to pretend to be pleased. Not that I don't like the Bible, but it's not the kind of gift I want right now.* The wrapping paper parted to reveal a cream book. 'The Screwtape Letters' by C S Lewis, fellow of Magdalen College, Oxford. A central block outlined the contents: "These brilliant, challenging letters from an elderly devil in hell to his junior on earth are the most vital and original restatement of religious truths produced in our time — a profound, hard-hitting, provoking, yet truly reverent book."

Alice looked up at Eve in surprise. This was not what she would have expected from her serious, gentle friend. Eve smiled.

'I thought you'd like it. Not at all stuffy and churchy. You know who he is, don't you?' Alice shook her head. 'He's on the wireless from time to time, talking about faith and religion, and all sorts. This has just come out. It's so different from anything I've ever read, but so inspiring.'

'Thank you. I can tell you like him.' She picked up the book, read the inscription inside.

Dearest Alice,
May you find the dreams of your heart and the purpose of your life.
All my love

Eve.

Alice blinked, tears threatening to spill over again. 'Eve, you are the dearest, most precious friend I will ever have. No matter where this war takes us — takes you — I will never forget your kindness. And this — ' she stroked the book — 'I will treasure forever.'

'And I'll treasure the memory of our time together each time I read my copy.'

A sharp knock on the door which surprised both girls prevented further conversation. Audrey peered in.

'Alice? Oh good, you're up. You look better. I am glad. And we're all so sorry about your brother.' She rushed on before Alice had a chance to comment or start crying again. 'They sent me up to help you pack. You're to be downstairs as soon as we're done. Transport will be picking you up and moving you to your next billet. Lucky you! I'm so fed up with gardening and fixing cars. I could have stayed at home and done that.'

The three girls spent the next few minutes collecting Alice's belongings. It was chaos in the small room; all 'scuse me's' and 'ouch, that was my toe', and unfolded clothes shoved into the suitcase. Alice was given no time to wonder about her next assignment, or even think much about the friends she was about to leave behind. A fluttering of nerves made her laugh rather than cry, her eyes bright and wide. At last, everything was packed. Alice picked up the copy of 'Screwtape' from where it lay on her pillow. She stroked the cover, then placed it on top of the rest of her belongings. She glanced over at Eve. No words were necessary. It was time to go.

Rosie

Message in a Book

•⁻• ⁻⁻⁻ ••• •• •

R osie woke the next morning to a persistent clattering of dishes and pots and pans in the kitchen below her. The sun streamed in through her curtains. *It's the fête! Oh goodness, have I overslept?* She checked her watch on the bedside table. *Phew, no. Gran must have been up with the larks this morning.*

A knock on her door confirmed it was Gran who was already up and about.

'Rosie, are you awake? I've brought you some tea...'

'Yes, Gran, I'm awake.' The door creaked open. A mug of tea led the way into the room. 'Good morning. Thank you for bringing tea. You didn't have to. I'm happy to come down and help. Have you been up for hours already?'

Gran passed her the tea. 'Well, yes, I do feel as though half the day is behind me already.' She perched on the edge of Rosie's bed. 'I've just had a call from Joan. A couple of the girls who were supposed to be helping with the tea have come down with a stomach bug. They won't be able to make it...Would you...?'

Rosie interrupted her. 'Yes, Gran, of course I'll help. What would you like me to do? Serve tea, or run the white elephant stall?'

'There's a thought. I can help Joan with the teas. I know more people than you do, so it'll be easier for me to chat to them. And I'm sure you'll do a better job of selling some of those, well, 'treasures' than I will. You'll find a way to make them appeal to the young folk.'

Rosie grimaced. 'I'm not sure about that. But I'll give it a go.' She looked at her watch again. 'When do you want to leave? Have I got time for a shower?'

'Yes, yes, of course. I thought about making us a bit of a fry-up before we go. You know, keep us going through the day. Here, I'll take your cup if you've finished.'

Rosie handed her the empty mug. She flung her arms around Gran. 'You are wonderful, Gran. Bacon and eggs for breakfast. What a treat.'

Gran wriggled free. 'There won't be anything more than a dry crust of toast if you don't let me get on with it. Come down when you're ready. Gramps is doing a tour of the garden.'

The three of them ate breakfast together at the kitchen table. Gran kept getting up and down to pack some last-minute things— an extra spoon for the jam, some ice to keep the cream cold. Rosie gathered up the breakfast dishes, took them to the sink, and rinsed them under the running water.

'Leave those, Rosie. Gramps can finish them later. Can't you, Bill?' Gramps nodded, pouring himself a second cup of tea. 'Come on then, Rosie, let's get off. See you in a bit, Bill. Penny said she'd call around at about 12ish, if you want a lift.'

'I think I'll take a stroll down. It's a lovely day again, not too hot. Go on with you, or you'll be late. I'll see you at about lunchtime.'

Gran drove the short distance to the church hall at a snail's pace, trying to stop the boxes in the back from sliding around too much. Rosie sat with a basket on her lap. Turning in at the entrance to the car park, Gran found a space as close to the hall as possible.

'I'm sure we've got more to carry than anyone else. The white elephant stall will be outside; we'll serve the tea inside the hall. Maybe you can start offloading the boxes and carrying them around. I'll go see who else is here, and get someone to help.'

Rosie handed the basket to her grandmother, who then bustled off into the hall. She heard Gran greet all her friends as she walked in. 'Coo-eee everyone. Isn't it a beautiful day? Gladys, I've got those tablecloths you asked me for...'

Rosie hefted the first of the boxes and followed the path around the side of the building, to the garden beyond. It was organised chaos. A couple of older men were trying to string bunting between the trees while their wives issued shrill instructions. 'No, higher at your side, Dave. Not that high. Yes, that's about right. You'll need to tie it tightly. You never know, the wind might pick up later.'

Rosie glanced at the unmoving leaves on the tree, the cloudless blue sky overhead. *Doesn't look much like a gale is on its way.*

Trestle tables were assembled on every spare patch of grass. Loudspeakers were rigged up, cables running behind her into the hall. Music played in fits and starts as someone fiddled with levels and volume. The vicar tried out the microphone.

'One, two. One, two. Oo, that feedback is terrible. Do we need to move around a bit?'

Rosie searched for the tombola stand; Gran said they always set up the white elephant stall next to it. She spotted Gran's friend, Mrs Lorrimer, bending down over a large tea chest. *That must be it.*

'Hi, Mrs Lorrimer. It's Rosie, Alice's granddaughter. Is this where the white elephant table will be?'

Mrs Lorrimer paused in filling the chest with bags of sawdust and looked up. 'Oh, hello, Rosie. It is lovely to see you again. My, but you young things do grow...Yes, you can put everything out on that table there. Jim has just managed to get it up. Think a leg broke, or something. Hope it doesn't collapse during the fête.'

Rosie hoped so, too. She would hate for any of the 'treasures' to get broken before they found new homes. Putting her box down on the grass, she gave the table a firm shake. 'It seems fine. I'll just have to be careful when I'm laying everything out.'

'Yes, that'll be best. Where's Alice — your Gran?'

'She's inside with the tea things. A few girls couldn't come, so I'm doing the stall and she'll help with the tea instead.'

'Right you are. Let me finish with this tombola. I hope we have enough prizes for everyone.' She pointed to a pile of wrapped-up toys and trinkets.

'I'm sure you do. You can always use something from our stall if you need to.'

Mrs Lorrimer laughed. 'Well, it wouldn't be the first time we've done that. Oh, there you are, Jim. Please help Rosie here — you know, Alice's granddaughter — with bringing everything over for the white elephant stall.'

'Sure. Hello Rosie, good to see you again. I won't tell you that you've grown — even though you have.'

Rosie groaned. It was going to be a long day.

'Thanks Mr Lorrimer. Gran parked over there, by the entrance to the hall.'

The rest of the day was a blur. Gramps arrived at some point, settling himself on the chair behind Rosie's table. Much to her embarrassment, he cheered or clapped every time she made a sale. The tombola did run out of prizes. Mrs Lorrimer and Rosie spent a frantic half an hour scrabbling through the smaller bits and pieces of the white elephant table and wrapping them in paper discarded from the already-claimed prizes. Later winners of the game were happy enough. Mrs Lorrimer and Rosie grinned.

'Why don't you go and have a browse around the other stalls, Rosie? I can manage here for you.'

'Are you sure? Thank you. I'll bring you back tea and a piece of cake, or some biscuits.'

'That would be lovely. 10 pence a try, young man...'

Rosie left Mrs Lorrimer with her customer. She wandered around the tables, tasting a bit of fudge from one, trying on a summer hat at another until she reached the stall she really wanted to browse; the secondhand books.

Twisting her head to read the book spines, Rosie hunted for her favourite authors. There were a couple of Wilbur Smith's, but she'd read those. A book of old maps was interesting. She flicked through the pages, delighted by the artwork, the vibrancy of colours. They were so intricate. She could buy it, then cut out her favourites to put in frames. They would make lovely gifts.

She put the book to one side and continued browsing. There was a pile of C S Lewis books, and not just the Chronicles of Narnia. Rosie hadn't known he wrote anything other than the popular children's series. She picked up the topmost book. 'The Screwtape Letters'. *Sounds intriguing.*

'Oh, that's a marvellous book.' It was Gran, released from tea-making duties. 'I have it at home somewhere. An original, probably. I got it during the war.'

'Ugh, you made me jump, Gran. I didn't hear you coming.' Rosie replaced the book on the pile and turned to give her grandmother a hug. 'How are you getting on with the tea? It must be so hot in there.'

'The windows are all open, so it's not too bad. And yes, we're almost sold out of most things. There are quite a few biscuits still left. And a few slices of cake. Do you want some?'

'Not tea, thanks, but a biscuit would be nice. I'm starving — breakfast seems ages ago.' She paid for the book of maps and followed Gran back to the tea room.

'It does, doesn't it? Let's get fish and chips for tea later. We can get them on our way home, from the chippy on the corner. Bit of a treat after all this hard work. What do you say?'

'I say yes please.' Rosie could already taste the lashings of vinegar she would pour over her chips. 'I need to get Mrs Lorrimer some tea while we're here. She's looking after the elephants for me.'

Gran chuckled. 'The elephants indeed. Wait here a minute — I'll go ask Peggy to get one of her girls to bring us some tea to the stall. It will be cooler there, under the trees.'

Rosie waited while Gran organised their tea. A few people recognised her, said a friendly hello. The fête was quietening down, the car park slowly emptying of cars. She was relieved. She was getting bored and hungry.

Gran strode back to where Rosie waited. *Do you never get tired, Gran?* She tucked her arm into Rosie's, and together they strolled back to their corner. Gramps was asleep in the chair. Mrs Lorrimer tidied things away.

'Hello there, Alice. How have you got on? I think it's been a great success again this year, don't you? The weather has been perfect. Rosie, I sold a couple of things for you. A chipped old brown vase was one of them, surprisingly enough.'

Rosie and Gran burst out laughing. 'Sorry, Gwen, it's not you. It's that vase. It's so dreadful, we really didn't think it would sell. But I hadn't the heart not to include it. Who bought it out of curiosity?'

'I know what you mean. It's not a beautiful piece, is it? It was that new couple who recently moved into the village. You know, the ones doing up old Mr Fletcher's place? Said it had exactly the right 'retro' image they were looking for.' She shrugged. 'It takes all sorts, I suppose. Is that my tea? Thank you, dear — I'm quite parched!'

Peggy's 'girls' arrived, laden down with trays of tea things. They all lazed in the tree's shade for a while, before declaring it time to go home. Rosie packed the few unsold items into a couple of boxes.

'We'll take those home, Rosie. I'll chat to Dorothy at the next PCC meeting, see what they want to do with them. Keep them for next year, maybe, or donate to the Oxfam shop in town.'

Handing the keys over to Gramps so he could unlock the car, Rosie carried the two small boxes that were left. Gran kissed the Lorrimers goodbye, going via the tea hall to retrieve her basket.

True to her word, they stopped at the 'chippy' on the way home. Rosie's stomach rumbled as the smell of vinegar, fish and fried batter filled the car.

'Leave everything in the car. We'll unpack later. Or tomorrow. Let's eat these while they're fresh. From the paper, I think, don't you?'

Gramps and Rosie nodded their agreement and carried the fragrant parcels to the conservatory while Gran clattered around in the kitchen pouring glasses of cold juice.

'Before I sit down — I'll never get back up again once I do — let me find you that book we were talking about. The 'Screwtape Letters'. You can start reading it once we've cleared up after dinner.'

She disappeared to the lounge, returning a few minutes later with a well-read copy of the same book Rosie had seen at the fête. The corners of the cover were a bit bent, the colours faded, but otherwise it was in good condition.

Rosie took it from Gran and put it down next to her chair. 'Thank you. I'll look at it as soon as I've eaten. I can't smell these chips any longer without eating them.'

They each unwrapped their food, as excited as children at Mrs Lorrimer's tombola. None of them spoke as they broke off chunks of soft, battered fish and ate with their fingers.

Rosie swallowed the last chip with a sigh of satisfaction. Gran smiled.

'It is good, isn't it? I'll leave these scraps for Mitzy — I couldn't eat another thing. You, Bill? Are you done?'

'Yes, thanks.' Gramps folded up the paper, handed it to Rosie. 'Thank you, love. Shall we have some ice cream?'

'I couldn't, Gramps. Not yet anyway. Maybe later. Let me clear this away — no Gran, you sit, you must be exhausted. I'll take this through to the kitchen, then come back and look at your book.'

Flopping back into her chair, Rosie retrieved the book from where she had dropped it. Gran and Gramps were listening to the radio, an evening concert on Radio Three about to start. Flipping to the first page, Rosie gasped. Gran was right — this was a first edition. Published in London in February 1942.

'Gran, this must be worth a fortune. A first edition, and in such good condition.'

'Mm? Oh yes, maybe.' She smiled at Rosie. 'But I'd never sell it. Far too precious.'

Rosie wondered why. She turned to the next page.

Dearest Alice,

May you find the dreams of your heart and the purpose of your life.

All my love

Eve.

Eve? Wasn't that the FANY friend, the one whose name Gran couldn't remember? Or pretended not to remember?

'It says it's from your friend Eve.'

Gran was watching Rosie. 'Yes, it is.' Her voice was quiet. *Sad?* 'And of course I knew her name as soon as you found the photograph the other day. I'm sorry I pretended not to. I think it was the shock of seeing her face again, after all these years. I hadn't seen that picture in ages ...'

'You don't have to tell me, Gran. I'm happy to read. I'm just a bit scared to be holding something so valuable. I'm glad I washed my hands first.'

'No, it's alright, we can chat. I'm too tired to do much else this evening, anyway.' Notes from Elgar's cello concerto filled her pause. Mitzy wandered in from the garden. 'I didn't know Eve for long. About three weeks. We were at the FANY training college together.' More Elgar. 'I was going to leave. Pack it all in, and work at a factory somewhere. I wanted to punish the Germans so much, it hurt.'

Gramps was listening, enquiring eyes on his wife, the bushy eyebrows raised in surprise. 'I didn't know that.'

More secrets...

'It was when I first heard about Tom. Your great uncle, Rosie. His ship went down in the Atlantic. They thought there were no survivors. We received telegrams. Turned out, a merchant navy ship picked up most of the men, but for some reason, the message didn't get through for weeks.

'Anyway, I was so fed up with doing stupid things like growing vegetables and playing at nurses. I wanted to find something more — useful — to do. More directly related to winning the war, I suppose.'

I think I would feel the same. Rosie kept quiet, not wanting to disrupt the flow of words.

'It was Eve who persuaded me to stay. Well, Eve and her prayers. I'd grown up in a vicarage, knew the Prayer Book off by heart, went to church at least twice every Sunday. But I never prayed the way she did. It was like she knew who she was talking to...' Gran paused, lost in thought.

With a small shake of her head, as though admonishing herself for wandering down a particular — forbidden — path, Gran pushed out of her chair.

'Goodness, I am suddenly tired . I think it's time for me to head up to bed.' She smiled through a yawn. 'Bill, are you staying here a bit longer? I'll close the window if you like, so you're not sitting in a draught?'

'No love, I'll come up too. It's been quite an eventful day.' Gramps groaned as he straightened. 'Oof, I'm stiff from all that walking at the fête today. Or else I'm getting old.' He winked at Rosie.

'Good night, both of you. I think I'll stay down here for a bit longer if you don't mind? Before I go up, I'll close all the windows. I fancy getting started with your book, Gran.'

'Right you are. I hope you don't find it too dull. The language is a bit old-fashioned now.' Gran reached over, gave Rosie's shoulder a squeeze. 'Good night, dear, thank you for all your help today. It's lovely having you here, you know.'

They left the room. Gran blew an exaggerated, pantomime kiss in Rosie's direction.

Rosie laughed. Tucking her legs beneath her, she picked up the copy of 'The Screwtape Letters' and turned to Eve's handwritten inscription again. Here was someone — well, the handwriting of someone — who knew more about Gran's wartime life than even Gramps did. Rosie wasn't sure how she felt about that.

The stories she had grown up with, listened to over and over, now rang false, as though made up for the benefit of an easily entertained audience. Here, in her hands, was the authentic story. Eve's brief note contained entire chapters of missing pieces, of questions not yet asked. *What were your dreams Gran? Did you find them? And purpose? Did people even talk about 'purpose' back then?* Rosie had vague recollections from History lessons about duty and sacrifice, the common good being the greatest aim. But never about purpose. And why was this book, by the writer of children's fantasy novels, so important?

Rosie twisted a strand of hair in her fingers. She was cross, put out — like when her friends went off to the bathroom together at school or at a party, and didn't ask her to join them. Her parents — and grandparents — had taught her that honesty was one of the highest virtues. But, here she was confronted with the fact that her grandmother hadn't told the truth about something as significant as her own life.

Maybe there were reasons Rosie had no idea about. It was during the war, after all. Wars were strange like that; people either wanted to tell everything in minute detail, or tell nothing at all. Did Gran fall into the 'nothing at all' category? But she had pulled out the box of mementoes, and shown the book to Rosie, allowed her to read it. That had to count for something, didn't it?

Trying to keep an open mind and give Gran the benefit of the doubt, at least until she'd finished reading, Rosie turned the pages of the book. They were yellow and smelt of dust. Little spots of dark mildew stained the corners, speckled like a hen's egg. The typeface was smaller than

Rosie expected. The cramped writing made the text hard to read. She sighed. *Maybe I should leave this for tomorrow, when I'm less tired.* She stared out of the open window, watched as a flock of starlings flew overhead, bustling their way back to their nests for the night. The stillness of evening was descending on the garden, dust motes dancing in the last rays of golden sunshine.

She returned her attention to Screwtape. *It's not a thick book; I can probably finish it before going to bed.*

Alice

Station 53a

.- .-.. .. -.-. .

A lice's bones ached by the time the rattling transport reached its final destination. She'd been helped into the back of an ancient army truck where she took her place next to four other girls seated on the wooden bench inside. They smiled at each other and exchanged 'hellos', but nothing more; it didn't seem worth the effort, knowing they would likely be dropped at different locations and never see each other again.

Alice was alone for the last few miles. She peered out of the end flaps of the truck. A church slid past on the right, a row of neat red-brick cottages on the left. The truck slowed, brakes squealing in the quiet of the country afternoon. The driver twisted in his seat to face Alice.

'This is you then, Miss. Hurry along — I need to be back at base by nightfall.' Without offering to help Alice, he turned back to do battle with the gear lever of the idling vehicle.

Alice clambered down from the truck, heaving her suitcase behind her. House martins and swallows whirled and swooped overhead; calling and whistling as they darted through the air. The truck lumbered away in a cloud of exhaust fumes. Alice was at the grand entrance of yet another large, stately home. Red brick pillars held a black wrought-iron gate in place. Closed. Through the ornate swirls, a long sweep of gravelled drive ran uphill. Dried up, dusty lawns of yellowing grass sprawled on either side. The house itself was beyond her view, hidden behind a clump of dense trees.

Sighing, Alice picked up her suitcase. *I'm so tired of being moved from pillar to post. My fourth home in nearly as many months. How I envy Mavis her farm, and Vera her factory. They aren't constantly being relocated.* She straightened her skirt and tunic with her free hand, and patted her hat. Mrs Burnley-Smith insisted she travel in uniform, despite the heat of the day. *At least now it's a little cooler.*

A young corporal in an olive-green uniform appeared from behind the pillar. So many gates, so many young men standing guard. Surely they wanted to do something more with their war?

'Miss Stallard? We've been expecting you. Welcome to Grendon Hall.' His smile was broad, friendlier than the entrance he guarded. He swung the right-hand gate open and moved towards Alice, his hand outstretched. 'Here, let me take that. You're just in time for dinner. I'll lead the way.'

Alice stepped through the opening. *Will this be my Wonderland?*

The corporal set off up the driveway, not waiting to see if Alice was following. She hitched her handbag and gas mask onto her shoulder, catching up to him within a few strides. To the right of the driveway, a series of low wooden huts were ranged in neat rows, windows flung wide to encourage the cooler air to enter. Big band music spilled from one, its frenetic energy in contrast to the surrounding stillness.

'You'll be billeted in one of those, with the other girls. They're not too bad. Boiling hot in summer, and freezing in winter, of course, but you'll get used to that. They serve meals in the dining hall — breakfast, lunch and dinner for both day and night shift.'

Night shift? No one had said anything about that. Mind you, no one had said anything about much.

'So, what exactly is this place, then? Some kind of field training centre?' They were at the brow of the hill, the Hall in full view. *It's as beautiful as Bletchley Park was ugly.* She stopped walking, transfixed. Gables extended outwards on either side, arms open in a welcome embrace, the panes of glass in the bay windows winking in the sun.

Realising the corporal was continuing without her, Alice hurried to catch up with him again.

'Training centre? No! There's some training done here of new recruits before they head off out into the field, but for the likes of you and me — this is all work. Radio transmissions mostly.' The corporal waved at some tall masts Alice hadn't noticed before. 'Anyway, here we are. I'll leave your case at the entrance, then take you through to the dining hall. Someone will show you to your billet after dinner.'

'Wonderful, thank you. I'm starving. This way you say?' She followed across a scuffed parquet floor towards a door, from which came the noise of chatter, the rattle of crockery and cutlery, and the distinct smell of overcooked cabbage. Alice wrinkled her nose. 'I'll be glad when this war is over, even if it's just so I never have to eat cabbage again.'

The corporal laughed his agreement and pushed forward into the queue of people waiting to be served. He grabbed a plate for Alice, passed it back to her. 'Here you go. Help yourself. There's not much choice, but it's good enough. I need to get back to the gate. Hope to see you around, Miss Alice Stallard.' He winked and turned to go. Alice watched his progress to the door. He waved and greeted everyone he passed — a punch on the shoulder here, a kiss on the cheek there, a smile and a word of hello. *I'm glad he was on duty today.*

Alice filled her plate with a slice of cold ham, a spoon of mashed potato, and a portion of watery-looking cabbage. She found a free table in the corner from where she surveyed the room as she ate. The evening was a blur of men and women in uniforms and *mufti,* some lingering over their meals, others rushing off to attend to something important. Underlying the easy chat and friendship was an edge of seriousness; this was a place of work, not play.

One woman, dressed in the same FANY uniform as Alice, sat at a table apart from the others. Dark rings under her eyes, and stifled yawns indicated exhaustion. She pushed the food around her plate. After a while, she gave up altogether, letting her fork fall onto the china with a clatter. She held a pencil in her other hand, twisting it through her fingers while staring into space for several seconds, then scribbling in a notebook at her elbow. Alice wondered who she was. She found out later that evening on returning to the hut assigned to her; the girl was Alice's room-mate.

'Howdo? I'm Rita. Hope you don't mind, I need to turn in. Been a dreadful day. That's your bed, on the far side. Goodnight!'

Alice, unsure whether to be offended or grateful that she wouldn't have to stay up all night getting better acquainted with the girl, extended her hand. 'Hello, Rita. Pleased to meet you. I'm Alice. Sleep well yourself.'

Alice

Mr Marks

•‒ •‒•.. .. ‒•‒•. •

Rita, already up and dressed, ready for the day ahead, woke Alice with a rough shake of her shoulder.

'Morning. Alice, wasn't it? Sorry, I think I was awfully rude last night. Long shift, bad day. But anyway, here we are. And you'd better hurry. I've got to take you to breakfast, then drop you off at the lecture with Mr Marks. You'll enjoy that.' She grinned at a bewildered Alice.

'Morning, Rita. Thank you for waking me. What time is it?' Blackouts blurred the distinction between night and day, sunset and sunrise.

'Five o'clock. We start at six.'

Alice groaned and shoved back the starched cotton sheet. Picking up clothes and a toiletry bag from the end of the bed where she'd dumped them the night before, she scurried off to the bathroom at the back of the hut.

By half-past five, the two girls were hastening up the driveway to the Hall.

'I hear you're good with numbers and letters, anagrams, that sort of thing?'

It surprised Alice that Rita had heard anything about her. 'Yes, I suppose so. I did well at a course in Bedford...'

Rita chuckled. 'Don't worry, you don't have to pretend anything. We all did that course. And they send only the ones with top marks here. So, you must be good. And how did you find Overthorpe? Boring as blazes, didn't you think? How's old Mrs Burnley-Smith? She was quite the battle-axe when I was there. Has she mellowed?'

They swapped stories over a breakfast of cold toast, powdered eggs and overly-sweet tea. No problems with rationing here, or so it appeared. Downing the last dregs of liquid, Rita looked at her watch. 'We'd best be off. I need to drop you with your new boss. She'll explain your duties and so on.'

'At last. I have no idea why I'm here, or what I'm supposed to be doing. So much for being vital to the winning of the war.' Alice sounded more bitter than she intended. 'Sorry, it's been a frustrating few weeks.'

'No, no, don't apologise. It's dreadful, isn't it? All the training and waiting and being kept in the dark. Don't worry, you'll be right in the thick of it before you know what's hit you.'

Alice wasn't so sure. Especially when Rita deposited her at the door of yet another sitting-room-turned-classroom, with a, 'Bye, must dash, will be late for my shift,' and a cheery wave. Pushing through the door, Alice sighed at the sight of a blackboard facing neat rows of desks and chairs. *More training. More learning. More time-wasting.* Worse still, she was the first to arrive. *So much for being late.* She was about to stamp her foot and fling her bag onto a waiting table, when she noticed the man. He stood with his back to the room, his attention fixed on the window and whatever lay beyond.

Phew, that was close. Grateful to have seen him before she embarrassed herself with a tantrum, Alice settled into a chair. She pulled a notebook and pen out of her bag, doodling swirls and loops on the front cover while she waited for others to arrive. The pattern of order and symmetry spreading across the page calmed her agitation. Mrs Burnley-Smith's parting words floated into her mind. 'The best way you can help...is with that brain of yours...'

The door creaked open and two girls entered. They exchanged greetings and sat at the next desks. A few seconds later they were followed by an older woman dressed in the familiar olive uniform of the Corps. Her hair was pinned in a thick roll at her nape. She strode to the front of the room and waited beside the blackboard. She checked her watch. 'We'll hang on another couple of minutes for those still finishing their breakfast before we get properly started. In the meantime, good morning, ladies. Mr Marks, when you're ready —'

The man at the window turned, startled. He looked around the room, blinking as though to clear his eyesight of the outdoor light . Hadn't he heard them filling the room? He looked just a few years older than Alice and the other girls, although his eyes showed a weariness that surprised her. *He looks as though he's been up all night. Or slept in his suit.* There were dark smudges under his eyes, and his blue suit was faded and crumpled. He licked his lips, lifting his hand to run it through his hair, then dropped it back to his side

He weaved between the desks and stood beside the FANY officer. Rubbing his hands together, he started speaking but was interrupted by the door opening and six girls bursting into the room. Their giggling stuttered to a stop, and a couple of them muttered words of apology as they slid behind the remaining desks.

Mr Marks tried again. He gave a dry cough and reached for the glass of water standing on the table in front of him. Taking a sip, he returned the glass and spoke.

'Girls — ladies — you are about to embark on what could be considered the most important job of your young lives; the most important job of your whole life. Others are relying on you doing that job to the best of your ability. Their lives are in your hands. Their lives are in the quickness of your minds. Their lives are in your ability to solve a puzzle no one but you can solve.'

He was warming to his subject. The transformation fascinated Alice. He was so timid, so unsure of himself when he first started speaking. Now the words fell over themselves in the rush to be aired, to be heard. He was pacing backwards and forwards, punctuating each sentence with a change in direction. Then he was in front of the blackboard.

He picked up a piece of chalk, tapping out a message like a woodpecker searching for grubs. As he did so, he spoke in short bursts, his mind able to perform only one task at a time. 'When I was here on a previous *tap-tap* occasion, I told the girls *tap-tap-tap* of a telegram I had recently *tap-tap* received. About a young man *tap-tap* from Yugoslavia, eighteen years old, who was transmitting a message on behalf of an agent — '

He finished writing on the board. Popping the chalk into his jacket pocket, he turned back to face his now enthralled audience. They held their breath while he clapped his hands together, creating a cloud of chalk dust. They waited for his cough to subside. 'His first message hadn't come through correctly and he was sending it again. This time, though, he was discovered while operating the wireless transmitter.'

Marks clamped his mouth shut, fixing his gaze at a place somewhere behind the girls' heads. Alice resisted turning to check if there was anything there. No one moved. Alice chewed her lip, waiting. She nearly didn't hear his next remark, his voice was so quiet.

'He was eventually found in the town's mortuary. "No longer recognisable as a human being," so the report said.'

'Oh...' the girl on Alice's right gasped, her hand to her mouth.

Marks gestured towards the board. 'Messages and codes, ladies. This is your role, your task, your responsibility for the duration of the war. You will never meet those whose messages you receive. You will never know their names, or their stories, or their missions. But you will know their messages. You will recognise their 'accent', you will spot their Morse stutters as easily as a mother knows the voice of her child. And you will decipher what is indecipherable. So now, to work.'

Alice struggled to hold back tears. *I am going to fight this war, and I'm going to use my brain to do it.* Images of the Bedford classroom flashed through her mind; the hours spent working through a new code, learning to unravel its mysteries and patterns; the delight on Mr Clyde's face when she was the first to figure it out; Bill, sucking on his pencil as he anagrammed his way through the puzzle. *Dear Bill, I wonder what you're doing right now? Are you using those codes we learnt, fighting with your mind and your imagination? Or are you marching across a continent, brandishing a rifle, and praying you're not the next one caught?*

Mr Marks was speaking again. Was he preparing to leave? Was that it? What about the letters on the board? 'Miss Rivers here will work through this with you for the rest of the day. You can send me the decrypted message when you've cracked it. And then, tomorrow, you'll be breaking codes for real. No more playing games. This is war.'

Marks ducked his head. Was he embarrassed by the melodramatic end to his speech? He was again the nervous civil servant, avoiding eye contact, and shuffling from the room. The girls watched him go, returning their attention to the front of the classroom after the door closed with a click.

Miss Rivers took her place beside the blackboard. 'Humph, he took the chalk.' She grinned. 'Mr Marks is the most intelligent, clever man you will ever meet. He is also one of the most awkward.'

They all laughed, the tension from the previous lecture released.

Miss Rivers looked at her watch for the second time that morning. 'It'll be time for lunch soon, ladies. We'll work on this —' she waved toward the ranks of letters on the board — 'this afternoon. But for now, I'd like to welcome you to Station 53a. You've all come here through different routes and along different paths. Many of you are confused and frustrated at not knowing what is going on. I know I was.'

Alice looked up, surprised. She raised her hand an inch, not sure if questions were permitted.

'Yes? A question — good. And you are...? Would you care to introduce yourself?'

Alice rose to her feet, a furious blush of embarrassment rising up her neck and across her face. Everyone turned to look at her. The girl in front smiled. 'I — I am Miss Stallard. Miss Alice Stallard. Alice.'

'Hi Alice!' A chorus of welcome helped settle her nerves.

'Miss Rivers, I was wondering. The last few weeks, well months, I suppose, have been surrounded by secrecy. I really don't feel I know anything at all about why I am here, or even where in fact I am. Are you able to, um, tell us anything? Seeing as it seems we're to be working here. What exactly is Station 53a? Who is Mr Marks? What agents is he talking about?'

'Yes, and what messages are we meant to be reading and translating? Who are they for?'

'And what happens if we can't do it?' The Gasping Girl was near to tears, her voice trembling as she spoke.

Alice had burst the dam of unspoken questions all the girls wanted answers to. She dropped back into her seat, wiping damp palms on her skirt, unsure whether Miss Rivers was pleased or angry.

'Girls, girls! Wait a moment. I understand, really I do.' Miss Rivers stepped in front of the desk. She leant back, gripping its edges with her hands behind her. 'You have all signed the Official Secrets Act, haven't you?' They nodded. 'You know, then, that some information simply isn't allowed to be shared with you. I'm sorry, I know that sounds like an excuse. But it is true.'

There were groans of dismay, a slight murmur of disapproval from the girls as they expected to be kept in the dark, yet again.

'However, now that you are here, you do have a right to some of that information.' Claps and cheers from the girls interrupted her. 'Don't get too excited, it's still only what you're allowed to know, and nothing more.

'Station 53a is one of over 50 stations positioned around the country — with more beyond our borders — run by the Special Operations Executive, or SOE. This is a branch of the War Office set up on the express instruction of Mr Churchill himself, and it reports directly to the Prime Minister on certain issues. The role of the SOE is to help win this war in whatever way is possible — gentlemanly or otherwise. Agents are trained by SOE in various acts of sabotage that will best disrupt the Third Reich in its efforts at expansion across Europe.'

So the rumours at Bedford were right.

'An essential element of that sabotage is information. Agents observe what is happening, and report back to London with details of troop movements, actions taken by local police forces, or whatever else might be considered of interest and importance to those co-ordinating the fight back home.'

'You mean spies?' A girl at the back asked, her voice breathless with excitement. 'We're going to be spies?'

'Well, no dear, not quite. You're going to be the backup for the spies. The safety net. Their voice in London, if you like.' Miss Rivers paused, pushed herself away from the desk. 'Mr Marks is based in London. At Baker Street. Some of you may have visited there.' Alice nodded. The pieces of a puzzle, which characterised the last few months, were falling into place. 'He is in charge of all codes and related issues when they involve our agents in the field. In effect, he is your boss.

'As he explained earlier, these communications are literally a matter of life and death for the agents sending them. Each time we can't read or decode a message accurately, their superiors ask them to resend their message. Imagine that. They have to find a secure location again; they have to power up their wireless sets; they have to re-input the message they believed was right the first time. The longer and more frequently their radio sets are in use, the more likely it is that the Germans will find those radios. And their operators.'

Miss Rivers allowed the silence to lengthen.

There was a sudden clatter of footsteps out in the corridor, people chatting and laughing as they walked past. Normality replacing imagined horrors.

'Lunchtime, girls. Let's make it quick today if you don't mind — half an hour. Don't be late, please — we have a lot to get through.'

Alice

The Promise

●▬ ●▬●● ●● ▬●▬● ●

L unch was a bustling, noisy affair. Alice couldn't wait to get back
to the peace of the classroom, to get started on the code written
up on the blackboard. For she was certain it was a code. That's what
Mr Marks implied when he spoke about them using their brains for the
war effort. Miss Rivers' introduction to Station 53a also piqued Alice's
interest. Spies and codes and secret messages. This was more like it.She
was the first back to her desk, already sucking on a pencil and jotting
ideas into her notebook by the time the others returned. Miss Rivers was
the last to arrive.

'Sorry, girls, it's me who's late this time. Bit of an emergency in
the code room. Anyway, let's get on shall we?' Without waiting for a
response, Miss Rivers picked up a new piece of chalk and turned towards
the board. 'Right, a simple little decoding exercise to get you warmed
up before you take your turn in the code room. Where do you think we
should start?'

There was an awkward shuffling of chairs, and a nervous tapping of
a pencil or two. Alice knew they must have all had some experience
of coding and cryptanalysis or they wouldn't be here. She wondered if
she had more than most. She didn't know any of the other girls seated
alongside her; she hadn't come across them either in Bedford — despite
Rita's assurance that everyone had gone through the coding school — or
Overthorpe Hall. Or even Bletchley.

She raised a hand, less nervous to contribute than the first time. *Might
as well get the ball rolling.* 'Shouldn't we start by identifying any patterns

in the letter groups? You know, if there are any common letters we can work from, work out their frequency and so on?'

Miss Rivers beamed. 'Yes, Alice, you are quite right. Mr Marks wanted you to approach this exercise from the perspective of a member of the Gestapo. One who has intercepted a message on its way to us here at Station 53a. What would he be looking for? How would he untangle the letters in front of him and so discover their contents, to the detriment of our safety? And, more especially to the detriment of the safety of the agent who sent it...'

Another hand shot up. 'Well, he'd know that 'e' is the most common letter in the English language, wouldn't he? So he might guess all those 'h's' translate to 'e's'. And it's Lucy, Miss.'

'Thank you, Lucy. And yes, that would be a good place to start. So, let's assume we have a lot of 'e's' in our message. Once we fill those in...' she scraped away at the board. 'What's next? Anyone like to guess what some other letters might be? Or even try testing a few words out?'

The rest of the afternoon was spent in the best way imaginable for Alice. Together they anagrammed and guessed and gave up and started again. The girls soon lost their initial shyness, delighted to be doing the kind of puzzles they loved, in the company of like-minded young women. Lucy was almost as quick as Alice at working out what words fitted where. An older, dark-haired girl called Bridget, sitting near the back, was slower but more deliberate in her responses; she didn't rush to shout out her answer, but listened and took notes, before offering her thoughts.

'Girls, you need to learn to be a bit more like Bridget. Take the time to check what you've already got; what you've already tried. Remember, these are messages being sent from behind enemy lines, for strategic purposes. They will not be talking about picnics and late-night parties. You should look for references to the weather, or a location you've heard mentioned before. And don't forget, in the panic of the moment, spelling mistakes will creep in. The agent's finger may 'stutter' and the Morse code may not come through correctly. You must use your imagination, as well as your knowledge.'

By the time they cracked the code, Alice felt a headache lurking. They were all exhausted but elated. They congratulated themselves with little cheers and pats on the back.

The clear text, written in Miss Rivers' firm hand, read, 'From the coders of Grendon to the agents of SOE. THERE SHALL BE NO SUCH THING AS AN INDECIPHERABLE MESSAGE.'

Miss Rivers was looking at her watch, yet again. 'Well done, ladies, you got there, eventually. This is our motto here at Grendon — we will work to the best of our ability, for as long as it takes, to ensure no agent has to resend his message. No matter how terribly it is mangled by the time it reaches us!' The girls laughed, although the weight of their instructor's words wasn't lost on them. 'But you will need to be a lot quicker. Time is of the essence. Many of the messages contain instructions for imminent supply drops, or details of upcoming events, where timing is everything. You will get there, but your first few days on the job will test you to your limits.'

Alice straightened her shoulders, sat taller in her chair. She noticed a few of the other girls do likewise. *I will rise to the challenge. I will work my fingers to the bone. I will do it for you, Tom. And you, Bill.* She picked up her pencil and turned to a clean page of her notebook. In big bold letters, she wrote 'THERE SHALL BE NO INDECIPHERABLES ON MY WATCH'. She tipped her head to one side, assessing the words she had written. A bit melodramatic? *Maybe, but I mean it.*

Miss Rivers was speaking again. 'From tomorrow, you will be on shift in the main code room. There are two sections to the code room. The first is where the radio operators work. They receive the Morse code transmissions from the agents. They will also receive telegrams from time to time from Mr Marks in London. Transcripts will be sent to your section, where you'll be responsible for their decryption. Write the message in clear and pass it to the Code Room Supervisor. What happens to it after that is none of your concern. A few of you —' here she looked at Alice, Lucy and Bridget — 'will work entirely with those messages which others have failed to decode. Mr Marks has developed a few tools to help you in your task and there are several other girls with whom you will work closely, but be under no illusions — it can take several thousand attempts before you have anything which makes sense.'

The girls turned to acknowledge each other; an elite team of three.

Miss Rivers paused for a moment, then continued. Her earlier tone of easy congratulations was gone, replaced with a voice of urgent authority. 'Girls. Before you leave this room, I need to remind you once again about the nature of the work we do here. The SECRET nature of our work. As we said earlier, you've all signed the Official Secrets Act. Now is the time to revisit and reinforce your commitment to keep everything to yourself — and I do mean everything — that you see and hear during your stay here at Grendon Hall. It is not to be discussed outside the gates of this establishment. You are not to write home or write to your sweethearts, giving any details of what you are doing here. You won't know the names of the agents you interact with, only their codenames. Even these are not to be discussed. No guessing who they might be, where they are stationed, what the messages they send through meant. Your role is to interpret the codes, unravel the messages, and pass them on. Nothing more. Are we clear?'

No one spoke. They hardly moved. The fun of the day, the solving of the puzzle, was no longer a game.

'Right then, I think you need to get off to dinner before you miss out on the potatoes.' Miss Rivers' lighter tone broke the spell. Alice noticed sounds coming through the open window — a couple of birds squabbling in the branches of a nearby tree; a vehicle revving its engine; men's voices calling to one another.

Lucy was already out of her seat, gathering her belongings together. 'Thank goodness, all this brain work makes me hungry. I'm starving. Come on, Alice, I'll sit with you.'

'I was thinking of skipping dinner tonight. I'm so tired after travelling yesterday, and then all this. But you're right — I'm hungrier than I thought I was. Bridget, you'll join us, won't you?'

'I'd like that. So long as it's not Spam and carrots. I can't eat any more of that. Not this week, anyway.'

They wandered out into the hallway and along towards the dining room. The other girls were ahead of them, the morning's latecomers already a self-contained, self-absorbed gang. It reminded Alice of herself when she was with Mavis and Vera. *Are we like that? I do hope not. Poor Bill, he must have hated that outing to London, if that's the case.*

So lost in thoughts of Bill — *Where is he? What is he doing? Does he ever think about me?* — Alice didn't hear her name being called.

'Hey, Alice! A penny for them.' It was Rita. 'You were miles away. Anyone we know?' She winked at the other two girls and extended a hand in formal greeting. 'Hi ladies. I'm Rita. I take it you've all finished your training course? Get ready for the proper work tomorrow. It's not all fun and laughter then, I can assure you.'

She yawned. Draping an arm around Alice's shoulders, she steered her roommate over to the serving hatch. Lucy and Bridget followed in their wake.

'Dash it, Spam and carrots. I should have known, shouldn't I? Oh, for a piece of real meat. Roast beef maybe. Or a side of lamb.'

Lucy rolled her eyes. 'A side of lamb. Listen to you. You'd think you were a member of the aristos, talking like that. You'll be begging for Kedgeree and kippers for breakfast next.'

'That would be nice, wouldn't it? And yes, I do sound like that, don't I? I suppose I would really...' She laughed as Lucy's pale features turned a deep shade of red embarrassment. 'You can call me Lady Bridge, Lucy dear.'

'I shall do no such thing. Here, pass me a plate so I can pretend I'm eating my 'side of lamb' with you.'

Rita stayed with the three new girls for the rest of the meal. After a last sip of her lukewarm tea, she scraped her chair back on the parquet floor. Bridget winced.

'I'm off. Up early again tomorrow. They're expecting messages from a particular section.' They all looked at her, waiting for an explanation. Rita sighed. 'Well, of course I can't tell you which one it is. Secrets and all that, you know. But I will tell you, they have one or two of the worst coders on their team, and we get the dubious pleasure of trying to figure out what on earth they are trying to communicate before it's too late for all concerned. You're in for a fun day, darlings! Alice, I'll see you back at the hut. You'll be alright walking down on your own?'

Alice nodded. 'Yes, of course. Thank you for all your kindness to me — to us — today. Please don't wait up for me. Although I shouldn't be much longer myself.'

'Don't worry, I won't. Night Lucy, Bridget. *Lady Bridget,* sorry.'
Rita gave Bridget a playful punch. 'Nice to meet you both. Good luck
tomorrow.' She moved away; her dirty dishes left for the others to clear
away . Alice didn't mind; Rita was kind to take them under her wing,
even if only for today.

'She's a good sort, isn't she? You're lucky to have her as your
roommate. She seems popular.' Bridget was right. Rita was making
slow progress across the room as each table of diners waylaid her with
greetings and shouts of welcome. She had made it as far as a table of
young men, all hanging on her every word. She was leaning forward
between two of them, her hands resting on their shoulders. One of them
said something which made her laugh — not the polite giggle of the girls
Alice was used to, but rather a deep, throaty laugh. Head thrown back in
delight, no one could miss Rita.

Alice smiled. She was lucky. *And I'm the one who gets to share a billet
with you. I wonder what you're like when the lights are out, though?*

'I can't stay awake any longer. I'm going back as well. You two? Who
are you sharing with?'

'Each other.' Lucy beamed. 'We arrived on the same bus, and they
said we could stay together, at least for the time being. I'm so glad. I
was dreading getting someone awful, you know, an old spinster lady or
someone like that.'

'How do you know I'm not an old spinster lady? Maybe I'm in
disguise. After all, this is the place for spies and agents and so on.'

'You are daft, m'lady. Come on, let's clear up and get an early night for
once. I think we're in for a difficult day tomorrow.'

Together they gathered the plates and dishes, taking them to the
serving hatch where a lady in a black apron received them with a brief,
'Thank you dears,' before turning back into the kitchen.

Out in the cool of the evening air, the girls parted company. Alice's hut
was further down the driveway.

'Good night, girls. I do hope we're working together tomorrow. I
don't fancy trying to sort out those messages Rita spoke of — whatever
they are — on my own. Sleep well — sweet dreams.'

'Goodnight Alice. See you in the morning. It's lovely to have met you.'
Lucy squeezed Alice's hand.

'Night! Don't let the bed bugs bite...' Bridget blew Alice a kiss. The two girls turned onto a narrow pathway to their left and made their way down the row of huts until they reached the second last one on the far end. They waved back at Alice before disappearing in through the doorway.

Alice was on her own for the first time that day. She stood still, relishing the slight breeze as it ruffled her now untidy hair. The last rays of sunshine filtered through the leaves of the trees above her, casting long, dancing shadows. The gates at the bottom of the driveway were closed for the night, the road beyond them quiet. Alice watched a young woman emerge from a hut further down. She straightened her cap, then started up the driveway towards Alice. Her heavy shoes crunched as she strode up the hill. She greeted Alice with a brief 'good evening' but didn't stop to talk; the night shift was starting.

The spell of silence broken by the other woman, Alice continued towards her hut. There were a couple of girls sharing the second bedroom; she didn't want to disturb them, if they were already in bed. She opened the door with a care Mrs Anderson would be proud of and then closed it with a gentle push. She paused for a few minutes in the narrow hallway between the two bedrooms, waiting for her eyes to adjust to the dim interior. No light shone out from under either bedroom door. The others must either be asleep, or out manning the radios and translating Morse.

Alice bent down to untie her laces. Removing the clumpy shoes, she tiptoed to her own room and pushed the door open enough to allow her to squeeze through the gap. Inside, the window was pushed open, the blackout curtains abandoned in favour of fresh air. Rita lay curled in a ball under her blanket, facing the wall, her breath even with deep sleep. Her heaped clothes were discarded on the floor at the end of the bed. Alice placed her shoes under her bed and her bag next to her pillow. She reached down for Rita's things, which she folded and placed on the only chair in the room. An appropriate way to thank her new friend.

Sighing, Alice pulled the cap off her head and undid the clips holding her hair in place. Her blonde curls had been escaping all day and now they tumbled down her shoulders. She rubbed her head, easing the pain where the pins caught and pulled. Ready for bed, she slid under the sheets.

Before it got too dark, there was something she wanted to do. Opening the bag beside her, she took out her notebook. She turned to the last page and tore it out. Checking that the sound of ripping paper wasn't disturbing Rita, Alice held the page in her hand. Returning her notebook to its place inside her bag, she re-read the message she had written to herself.

THERE SHALL BE NO INDECIPHERABLES ON MY WATCH.

Alice closed her eyes for a moment. She pictured Eve kneeling beside her, holding her hand, encouraging her to whisper the words of her heart in prayer. *Heavenly Father, I don't know how to talk to you the way Eve does, but I want to ask you to help me with this work. I feel it's important to get it right. From tomorrow and always. Amen.*

The room was a shade darker when she opened her eyes. Alice reached over to the table under the window and felt around for the hard cover of The Screwtape Letters. She picked up the book, opening it at a random, unseen page. Taking the torn page of her notebook, now folded in half, she placed her promise — and her prayer — into the book and replaced it on the nightstand. Satisfied at last, Alice snuggled under the sheet, and watched as the light at the window faded from pale blue to the deep purple of night.

Rosie

The Note

• ‑ •   ‑ ‑ ‑   •••   ••   •

R osie woke to a gentle tapping on her door.

'Rosie, are you awake? I've brought you a cup of tea.'

Rosie stretched, opening sleepy eyes to a room bright with mid-morning sunshine. It had been a late night; she was sure she'd heard the first strains of the dawn chorus as she fell asleep.

Reading The Screwtape Letters had taken longer than expected. She managed to get about halfway through, despite pausing for the first time to make another cup of tea at around midnight. It was more than the cramped typeface and the old-fashioned language that made progress slow; Rosie kept trying to imagine how the book must have impacted Gran when she first read it. It was so different from anything Rosie read during English lessons from that period. At first glance, it was an upside-down comedy about devils and hell. But as she read and re-read 'letter' after 'letter', Rosie caught a glimpse of something deeper; as though what she thought was a puddle in front of her was, in fact, a lake of bottomless depths.

It wasn't only the words of C S Lewis that kept Rosie up until near dawn. It was a discovery of words written in another, more familiar hand.

About to give up for the night, Rosie flipped forward a few pages to see if there was a natural break coming up soon. She didn't want to leave a 'letter' halfway through, but her eyes were stinging with the effort of reading in the shaded light of the table lamp beside her. There were brighter lights in the sitting room or even her bedroom, but she didn't want to move from the comfort of the chair she already occupied.

At first, she thought she'd found a bookmark, a scrap of paper like the one Mum tucked in whatever novel was currently on the go. But this was too large to be a receipt or a bit of an old envelope. It was a folded piece of notepaper wedged firmly between two of the pages. Placed with care. Of importance? And value?

Should I look? It's been here for so long, Gran must have forgotten about it. So, it wouldn't matter if I read it. It is a long time ago...

Rosie chewed the skin around her thumbnail, a childhood habit returned to when puzzling through tough questions. After a few minutes of staring out at the silent garden beyond the conservatory window, Rosie reached a decision: she would leave the note where it was, undisturbed. *I think I'll ask Gran about it tomorrow. Yes, that would be better. After all, I'd hate for Mum to go through my diary if ever she found it in my room. That would be embarrassing, and an invasion of my privacy.*

Removing her soggy thumb from her mouth, Rosie picked up the book again. She closed it, a satisfying thud of self-congratulation. She reached over and turned off the lamp next to her, summoning the energy to stir herself and head up to bed. Darkness enveloped her. She blinked, dancing spots of light obscuring her vision. Gradually they cleared. Rosie made out the dark shadow of the tree at the end of the garden, saw the stretch of lawn pale in comparison. She heard the fridge in the kitchen, its on-off whirring disturbing the otherwise silent house.

Rather than push herself out of her chair and make her way to bed as she should, Rosie stretched out her hand and felt for the lamp's switch. Hesitating for a moment, she flicked it back on, blinking in the brightness. The garden disappeared behind the room's reflection. Rosie dropped her gaze. She didn't want to watch herself doing something she knew was dishonest. And cowardly. She wasn't brave enough to ask Gran outright, to risk her saying 'no', and then never finding out what was written on that folded piece of paper.

Perhaps it was nothing. Just an ancient shopping list. Or directions to the nearest post office. It would all turn out to be the biggest anti-climax, and Rosie would go to bed feeling silly. And Gran needn't know she'd read it.

She pulled the book towards her. *Maybe I won't be able to find it again. Then it won't matter, and I'll give up and leave it.* But the book fell open where the note lay undisturbed. A sign that it was supposed to be read?

Before she changed her mind again, Rosie lifted out the piece of paper. It was thin and delicate, like a pressed flower — dried and preserved. Taking a deep breath, she unfolded it. Gran's unmistakable handwriting — less spidery, more confident, but definitely Gran's — covered the top half of the paper.

THERE SHALL BE NO INDECIPHERABLES ON MY WATCH.

Rosie let out a huff of disappointment. It wasn't quite a shopping list, but it might as well have been, for all the sense it made. She yawned, too tired to figure it out. If there even was anything to figure out, which she doubted. She stood, reached around to turn the light off again. Her legs were stiff from sitting in a curled-up position for too long. She bumped into the low coffee table as she made her way to the door, biting her lip to cut off her cry.

The stairs squeaked as Rosie climbed up to the bedrooms. She stopped, listening to make sure she hadn't woken Gran or Gramps. Gramps continued to snore, a whistling grunt that would drive her mad if she was Gran. Once in her room, she put down the book and note on her bedside table, not bothering to turn the light on; she could see well enough with the curtains open. She pulled off her shorts and T-shirt, swapping them for the old T-shirt she wore in bed.

Moments later, it seemed to Rosie, Gran's knock at the door dragged her from slumber. She rolled over and squinted at the clock on her bedside table. Nine thirty! She slept this late only when she was sick. No wonder Gran was coming up with tea, and concern.

'Yes, Gran. Come in.' She sat up, taking the mug of tea from her grandmother. 'Thank you for tea, Gran. That's lovely. I can't believe it's so late. Sorry.'

'Oh, don't worry, child. Gramps and I were just getting a little worried, wondering if you were alright. We left you for as long as we thought sensible, but then we both decided I should come and make sure. Silly us, fussing over nothing. I know you teenagers are night owls and you get up at about lunchtime, more often than not. It's just, that's not really what you're like.'

Rosie sipped her tea, enjoying the hot drink. 'Gran, you really do make a good cup of tea. Especially when it's the first one of the day. I think I lost track of time while I was reading last night.'

Gran was busy with the window catch. 'And you didn't open your window? You must have been tired.' She gave the window a push. Fresh morning air rushed into the room. Birdsong drifted in on the breeze. 'There, that's better. Your Gramps and I were wondering what you'd like to do today...? Do you mind if I sit here, dear?'

'No, of course not. Makes me feel like a little girl again, you perching on the end of my bed while I sit and drink tea. Or milk, as it probably was back then.'

'Oh, listen to you, so old and grown up.' The pair laughed, shared memories creating a bond between them Rosie hoped would never break.

'Anyway, to today. Have you finished? Here, let me take that.' Gran took the mug from Rosie, even though the girl was closer to the bedside table than she was. She leant over, clearing the surface of clutter. As she did so, the notepaper rescued from Screwtape fluttered to the floor. 'Oh, sorry, look at that. Clumsy me. I go to help and I make more mess.'

'Oh no, leave it Gran, I'll tidy up later.' Rosie watched as Gran stretched to reach for the piece of paper. She picked it up, unfolding it as she did so. Then sat motionless. 'Gran, what is it? Are you alright?'

Gran didn't reply. She refolded the paper and pushed it deep into the front pocket of her apron. Still without speaking, or even looking at her granddaughter, she pushed herself up from the bed. She turned to leave the room, then paused.

'Where did you get this?' Her voice absent of any trace of the earlier intimacy.

'Um. It was in that book you gave me. The Screwtape Letters. But it's just some old note, I'm sure. Does it matter?' Heat flooded Rosie's face. 'I don't even know what it means. Do you?' She tried to keep her voice light, draw Gran back to her; partners in a puzzle to be solved.

Gran turned away. 'Breakfast is ready downstairs.'

Rosie threw back the bed covers. She wanted to explain, to apologise. But most of all, she wanted to ask more questions. What did the note mean? Who was it for? Why had Gran written it, then left it wedged inside a book for over fifty years? And why was she so upset that Rosie had found it?

Rosie stretched for the door handle, listening for the sound of Gran returning to explain to her. To say 'it was the shock, and of course there was nothing wrong, dear, it's just an old piece of paper I'd forgotten about'. Instead, Rosie heard Gran on the other side of the upstairs hallway, walking towards her own room. The door creaked open, then was closed with a definite click.

'Huh. What's all that about, then?' Rosie took the two or three steps over to the open window, muttering. 'Honestly, you'd think I'd uncovered the crime of the century.'

She wrapped her arms around herself, looking down at the lane below. Clouds formed behind the hill, piling up in heaps of fluffy white and grey. A gust of wind shook the branches of the tree, lifted a patch of dry soil in a swirl of dancing dirt. The weather was changing. Rosie's defiance was changing with it. Clouds of doubt rolled across her mind, and a gust of suspicion disturbed the comfortable peace of her friendship with Gran. That is what they shared — a friendship. Gran knew how to calm her in a thunderstorm, how to make her laugh when she was scared. It was Gran who nursed her through chickenpox, Gran who listened to the story of some best friend or other person being mean to her.

What have I done?

Tears obscured Rosie's view as the first raindrop hit the window pane. She turned away. The curtains billowed into the room, lifted like sails caught in a sudden squall. Downstairs, a door banged. Mitzy barked. The room filled with shadows as the storm darkened the sky, the scent of approaching rain distinctive. Rosie flung herself onto the bed, burying her head into the pillow. Her shoulders shook with soundless sobs.

She rolled over to find the sun again shining into her room, the storm passing on to the next village as quickly as it had arrived over theirs. *I must have dozed off to sleep.* The curtains hung limp and damp against the still-open window. A puddle of water glistened on the window sill. *Fairy ponds, as Gran calls them.*

It dawned on Rosie that Gran hadn't been back, hadn't checked on her. Thinking she must have cried for hours, and wondering why her absence hadn't been noticed, it surprised Rosie to discover it was only twenty minutes since Gran left. *A proper summer storm.* Her stomach rumbled. *I must go have some breakfast. And find Gran.*

There was no one in the kitchen. A bowl and plate were next to the kettle, together with her dirty tea cup from earlier. A box of cornflakes was the only breakfast cereal left out.

She put the kettle on to boil and poured a heap of cornflakes into the bowl. While waiting for the water to heat, she wandered through to the conservatory, munching as she went. She couldn't hear the familiar sound of the radio, but maybe Gran and Gramps kept the volume low, not wanting to disturb her. Or it was possible that their shows weren't on, and they were reading instead. But the room was empty. Condensation misted the windows, closed against the earlier rain. Two newspapers lay crumpled on the coffee table, as though discarded in a hurry. Had they been called away to some emergency or other? Someone from the church? Rosie wasn't sure she'd heard the phone ring, but in her distress, she doubted she would have heard much.

The unfamiliar silence was disconcerting. There was always a background noise of some sort, whether it was the radio or the snuffle of Gramps snoozing in the chair. Mitzy! That's what it was. Mitzy wasn't here. They must have gone out for a walk after the rain stopped. Catching a quick stroll down the lane in case another storm surprised them later.

Rosie went back to the kitchen. Dad always told her she should take more control of her vivid imagination. He was probably right.

The scrape of the key in the front door confirmed Rosie's eventual conclusion. Mitzy scratched at the door, always in a hurry to get back inside.

'Hold on, you silly animal. Let me at least get the door open.' Gran's voice sounded normal, much to Rosie's relief. No sign of the earlier upset. Whatever that upset had been.

'Hello! I hope you didn't get wet? Can I make you a cup of tea?' Rosie called out, wanting to reassure them both she was up and about. The front door opened a crack. Mitzy pushed her way through, hurtling down the hallway towards the kitchen. Her muddy paws left a pattern of wet dirt along the hallway and across the linoleum until she skidded to a stop beside Rosie. Mitzy wagged her tail so hard she nearly toppled over. Rosie bent down to ruffle her fur. 'Ugh, you are a dirty dog, Mitzy. I'm surprised they let you in.'

Gran and Gramps were still at the other end of the hallway, removing their coats and hats. Gran pulled off her walking shoes, head down.

'Tea?' Rosie called out again, not sure if they'd heard her earlier.

'Lovely.' Gramps replied. 'We missed the worst of the weather, but I still feel chilled to the bone. That wind.'

Gran didn't respond. She finished tidying the coats, placing muddy boots on the sheets of old newspaper kept inside the door, then stepped towards the staircase.

'I'll get out of these damp clothes...' She spoke to Gramps, then disappeared upstairs.

Gramps clumped down the hallway towards Rosie. He clumped even when wearing only a pair of thick socks. 'Flat feet,' Gran always said.

'Right then, where's that tea you were talking about?' His smile was broad, but he didn't look Rosie in the eye. His voice was loud. Too loud for the quiet house. Mitzy lay in her bed beside the table, unconcerned by the smell of damp that clung to her. 'Have we any biscuits? I'm sure your Gran hid some in here the other day...'

He rummaged in the tall grocery cupboard, emerging with a packet of custard creams, which he held aloft in triumph. 'See, I knew there would be some.'

'Should I make for Gran? Or...?' Rosie let the question hang in the air.

'Why don't you make her one? Then I'll take it up and see if she fancies it. I'll take her a biscuit as well.' Gramps busied himself with the biscuit wrapper. He offered no explanation as to why Gran was back upstairs in her room, nor why he would take her tea up to her, rather than urging her to join them here in the kitchen, or in the conservatory. 'Ah ha, done it. These things are always such a fiddle, don't you find? And would you look at that — the first one is all broken into bits. I'll just have to tidy it away...'

He grinned at Rosie as he picked crumbs and cream filling from the counter. Rosie laughed, tried to ignore the growing unease stirring at the edges of her mind. She grabbed the dishcloth from beside the sink and threw it to Gramps. It landed with a wet slop next to his hand.

'Gramps! You can clean that mess up.' Their exchange was false, forced. 'I'll make the tea while you put those on a plate.'

Rosie took a small tray from the cupboard. She lay an embroidered cloth down, placing Gran's favourite cup and saucer on one side and a plate of custard creams on the other.

'Wait a minute, Gramps —' Rosie dashed out into the garden and plucked a sprig of fragrant lavender from the pot beside the door. She lay it over the biscuits. 'There. You can take it. Or do you think I should?'

Gramps squeezed Rosie's hand as he stretched over for the tray. 'Best not, just this once. Your Gran will be fine again by suppertime, don't you worry.' He didn't sound as convinced as Rosie would have liked.

Rosie

Storms

●⁻● ⁻⁻⁻ ●●● ●● ●

R osie tried to keep busy for the rest of the day. She took Mitzy outside and gave her a bath. She checked the berry bushes at the end of the garden for any sign of damage from the earlier storm, then dashed back inside as another shower passed overhead. She made endless cups of tea for Gramps. By the end of the day, she was exhausted. She slumped sideways in the armchair in the conservatory, kicking her legs backwards and forwards, bumping her feet against the wooden frame hidden under the flowery fabric. Gramps was snoozing next to her. His head hung forward, heavy for his old shoulders.

Rosie yawned. *I should go fetch a book. Or something. But not that stupid Screwtape thing. If it wasn't for that, today wouldn't be like this.*

She was about to get up when she heard a step on the stairs. Her heart danced a jig. *Gran.* Rosie straightened in her seat, not wanting to give Gran something else to be cross about. She heard Gran moving around in the kitchen; the gush of water as she turned the tap; the fridge door being opened.

I'll go help. Rosie jumped up from the chair, all the energy of a day spent doing nothing but worrying returning to her limbs. *Gramps was right. Gran will be fine.*

'Hello Gran —'

Her grandmother continued rummaging in the fridge.

Perhaps she didn't hear me. 'Can I help, Gran? What are you looking for?'

Gran straightened up. She held a box of eggs and a carton of milk. Placing them on the counter at her side, she closed the fridge door. Only then did she glance up at Rosie.

Dark smudges ringed her eyes. New lines appeared on her brow, around her mouth. She reminded Rosie of a piece of old parchment she'd seen in a museum once. Dried out and crumpled. Wisps of hair escaped from the misshapen bun pinned on top of her head. Her hands rested on the egg box, smoothing an unseen wrinkle from the dull cardboard.

Rosie took a step toward her. Her mouth formed a silent cry of distress. Gran raised her fingers a few millimetres from the box lid. Warning Rosie to stay back.

'Scrambled eggs for supper...' the cracked voice was as dry as parchment paper. Gran coughed. She moved over to the bread bin, away from Rosie again. 'It would be best if you went home tomorrow. You can phone Mum later. Make the arrangements.'

'Gran, no!' Rosie was shaking her head, clenching and unclenching her fists. 'You can't send me away. Not over a piece of paper.'

Gran spun around. 'This is more than a piece of paper.' Her voice was no longer dry and scratchy. Two spots of pink flushed her cheeks. Her eyes unforgiving. Rosie shrank away.

'I don't know what any of it is, Gran. You won't tell me.' Rosie's voice rose, loud with confusion and shock. 'Why won't you? What's the big deal?'

She was shouting. She sensed movement behind her and turned. Gramps stood in the doorway, his face pale and taut.

'That's enough, young lady.'

Rosie ran from the kitchen. She pushed past Gramps, rough and uncaring. Flinging herself against the front door, she yanked it open. It flew back, banging against the wall. She slammed the door, the letter box rattling with the force, and ran out into the lane. She turned left, past the other cottages.

The grassy edge of the road was muddy, and she slipped and skidded. She reached out to steady herself. Her hand caught in a tussle of brambles, thorns hooking into her flesh. She pulled her hand back, sucking at her bleeding fingers as she stumbled onwards. She didn't know where she was going, but she knew that she wanted to get as far away from Gran's hard look, the hurt appeal of Gramps. Away from the unidentified spiral of emotion, which was swirling around the usually peaceful home of her grandparents.

Out of breath, Rosie stopped at the corner of the road. To the left, the main village centre — the church and its gardens, the recent host of the annual fête; the post office where pensioners collected their retirement payouts each week; the pub with the playroom Rosie and sister Emma always visited when they came on holiday. All familiar, all part of the essence of Gran and Gramps. All now called into question, all tainted. By a simple piece of paper.

Rosie chose to go right, away from the village and down the hill towards the narrow stream bordering the hamlet. Slowing to a walk, her breathing, and her racing thoughts calmed. *What had Gran meant — it's more than a piece of paper? It means nothing to me. I've never heard of an 'indecipherable'. If that's even a word? But what a reaction. Gran, you're definitely hiding something, aren't you?*

A crow flew low over her head, its raucous cawing disturbing the ideas that were forming, shifting, settling in Rosie's mind She was oblivious to her surroundings until she reached the stone bridge arching over the stream. The water rushed and churned below where she stood. White-topped ripples danced and twirled through the reed beds. Pebbles and small pieces of loose rock were thrown against the side of the bridge. The sharp clacking sounds of impact echoed below. A moorhen huddled on the side bank.

The sun fought through from behind a cloud, dazzling Rosie with a burst of gold reflected off the dripping leaves and racing waters. She leant on the parapet; her cardigan sleeves absorbing the film of rainwater coating the stonework. The damp seeped through the fabric, but Rosie ignored it.

The water below hurried through the narrow span of the bridge, eager to reach the wider flood plains beyond. Two or three days ago, barely a trickle of sluggish water flowed. Then Mitzy had raced down the bank, hoping to catch the heron as it stood sentry on the dry, cracked earth. The dog's wild barking alerted the heron to her approach long before she reached it. It flapped away, out of reach of the mad creature running around in circles of desperation. Rosie and Gran had laughed, pitying the poor dog, but decrying her ability to stalk or surprise.

'Daft thing. She'll never be a hunting dog, will she?' Gran had whistled for Mitzy to come back to their position on the bridge.

How a few days, a few hours, changed everything. The heron was nowhere to be seen; the stream was now a river pulsating with rage and energy. All because of a summer shower or two.

Is that what's happened with Gran? A summer shower which has overflowed the banks and left anger in its wake? Rosie liked the analogy. Gran couldn't be angry forever. Something about that note was like a sudden storm, a flash of lightning across a cloudless sky. Everything would calm down, return to normal, given time. *And a little care on my part.*

She noticed a stick lodged against the wall she leant against. She picked it up and hurled it over the side into the torrent of water below. Racing over to the other side, she peered over the edge, waiting for it to reappear. Would it make it? Or would it get stuck on the rest of the debris caught in the confines of the stone archway? Just as she was about to give up, she spotted it. It bobbed and dipped, disappeared from view, then resurfaced further along. *I win! And I should probably head back. They'll be getting worried about me.*

The first fat drops of rain fell unnoticed on Rosie. Branches clacked together as the wind gathered strength. A dark swathe of dull grey blanketed the sky. Velvet curtains streaked the landscape with rain. Rosie's sodden clothes embraced her body with icy fingers.

Her legs and back ached by the time she reached her grandparents' home. The late night; the shock at Gran's reaction — *overreaction?* —; the walk from the river and up the lane; the growing anxiety at the reception once she arrived back; Rosie carried the day like a burden. A hiking backpack too full of unwanted weight. A wet backpack, thanks to the evening squall. She knocked on the door. And sneezed.

She was about to knock a second time when the door jerked open. Gran enveloped her without a word. The fluff from her soft, pale blue cardigan tickled Rosie's nose, and she sneezed a second time.

'Gran, I'm so sorry. I...I...' She swallowed the words in a heave of distress.

'Shush, child. It's me who should be sorry. Come on, let's get you inside and out of those wet clothes.' Gran's voice was its own hug. Pulling Rosie into the hallway, she reached around her to shut the door, calling out to Gramps as she did so. 'Bill, she's here. The poor thing is soaking wet. She looks worn out. Could you...?'

'I'll put the kettle on, shall I?' Gramps was in the kitchen, clattering about, and whistling.

'Let's get you in a hot bath. Then you can have some tea, and maybe a piece of toast before bed. Or do you want something more than that? Cake maybe?'

Rosie lifted her head from Gran's shoulder. She couldn't look her grandmother in the eye.

She shook her head. 'Just tea and toast, thanks. Gran...'

Gran ushered Rosie up the stairs and into her bedroom. Leaving her to get undressed, she went through to the bathroom and began to run water into the bath.

'Ready when you are, dear. I added a few sprigs of lavender to the water. You know, like the one you gave me this morning.' Gran was back in the bedroom, arms full of towels.

Rosie risked a glance. Kind eyes regarded her with compassion. And love. 'You noticed?' Fresh tears welled up.

'Of course I did. I was too upset — no, too selfish — to thank you.'

She steered Rosie towards the bathroom. Clouds of sweet-smelling steam rose from the water; condensation misted the window and the mirror. Gran hung the fresh towels on the rail. Before leaving, she kissed Rosie on each cheek. Catching more tears as she did so.

'I'll go and see to that tea. And the toast. Call when you're ready. Dearest Rosie.'

The door closed behind her. Rosie stepped into the bath and lowered herself into its steaming depths. Her head rested against the back of the tub, the warmth of the water prickling her cold skin. She breathed the smell of lavender deep into her lungs, felt the tension ease in her shoulders as she closed her eyes. She slid under the water, hair billowing and swirling around her; a mermaid swimming in hidden depths. Alone.

An urgent need to cough propelled Rosie upwards. The bathwater lurched and splashed around her, sloshing onto the floor. She coughed until her eyes watered. She heard Gran hurrying across the hallway, asking if everything was alright. There was no spare breath to answer with. After what felt like five minutes, but was probably less than half that, Rosie managed a weak 'Yes, Gran. Fine. Coming now.'

Wrapped in the softness of a towel, another wound around her hair like a turban, Rosie emerged from the bathroom. Gran stood waiting, frowning with concern. 'Goodness, Rosie, that was quite the coughing fit you had there. Let's get you to bed.'

Rosie nodded. Her throat was burning, too sore after the violence of the cough to speak. Gran pressed a cool hand on the back of her exposed neck. Rosie winced at the touch.

'Well, that's a temperature right there. I'll bring you the tea and whatever in bed. Give you an Asprin as well. Then I think you should sleep, and we'll see how you are in the morning. I might need to call Dr Painter if you've still got that fever.' Gran pulled back the bedcovers and plumped the pillows while Rosie changed into her pyjamas. Shivering, she struggled with the buttons. 'Here, dear, let me do that...'

Rosie eased herself onto the bed and leant back against the pillows. After the warmth of the bath, her teeth were chattering. 'Thank you, Gran.'

'I'll bring you a hot water bottle, too. Rest those old aching joints of yours.' Gran patted her shoulder. Rosie rolled her eyes and waved her away — the sun returned to their friendship.

Alice

An Indecipherable

● ▬ ● ▬ ● ● ● ● ▬ ● ▬ ● ●

A lice put down her pencil and stretched. Her shoulders ached from hours of hunching over the desk. The lighting was poor, making her eyes burn. Rubbing a hand across her brow, she tried to ignore the onset of a headache. Rita sat at the next desk, engrossed in marking up the paper in front of her. She glanced over at Alice and gave her a quick grin.

'Not having much luck there, old girl? You always get the hard ones.' Without waiting for a reply, she returned to her task. She squinted at the rows of letters arrayed across the page, her head tilted to one side. 'Aha, I've got you! You little —'

Alice laughed. She didn't hear the rest of the sentence as Rita dipped her head forward, her hair cascading around her face. But she knew it would contain words her father wouldn't approve of. Rita was quite shocking like that. Alice wasn't sure where Rita learned such language — perhaps her brothers brought it back from Officer Training or something — but it endeared her towards her friend even more. Rita was everything Alice wasn't: vibrant, loud, pushy, raucous. And great fun. She was also clever; a point of commonality between the two girls. Maybe that was why their friendship blossomed, despite the differences.

Alice loved her fashionable, ditsy friends Vera and Mavis. She adored the gentle wisdom of Eve. But Rita was the one who inspired her with her intelligence. Well, the only girl, anyway; Bill had always kept Alice on her toes during the Bedford training stint. *How long ago that felt.*

Pushing all thoughts of Bill and her other friends from her mind, Alice picked up her pencil and shuffled the papers in front of her into a neat pile. *Let me tidy up, pretend I'm starting from scratch, then I may see it.*

The message had come in with the afternoon skeds. The radio girl — a new arrival whose name Alice couldn't remember — assured the head of the cryptanalysts that the Morse she transcribed was correct. Yes, she knew it didn't make much sense, but that's what the agent had tapped out. Being new, she didn't yet recognise the telltale signs of slurred dots and dashes, or long pauses, that the more experienced girls used for identifying agents.

Of course, they never knew the real names of those they conversed with on a near-daily basis. There were funny code names, like Broccoli or Carrot and the more general area titles, such as N or A section. But the 'old hands' always knew who they were speaking to.

'I'm sure he has dark hair. And a moustache. Of course, he's frightfully handsome.' One girl, Clarissa, had the best imagination of them all. 'I think he comes from, let's see, Northumberland. His father has a castle there. And his mother wears nothing but pearls unless they have guests.'

'No, no, he's a farmer from Norfolk. Pigs probably...' The histories of these poor, brave agents became more outlandish — or dull — with every telling.

Until nothing came over the radio. The skeds were missed and went quiet. The messages stopped.

'Oh poor Lord Dewsbury. He will have come home. It is grouse season, after all.' No one was fooled by the light tone, the too-wide smile. Clarissa twisted the handkerchief she held, avoiding eye contact with everyone. Her roommate whispered about sobs in the night.

Lucy and Bridget were paired up on day-shift that week. Alice hardly saw them. They were both waiting for her today, though.

'Hi! Sorry, am I late?' Alice glanced at her watch, sure she hadn't taken too long at dinner.

'No, no, you're not late. We wanted to warn you, that's all.' Lucy looked worried. Her cheeks were pink and her lips were raw and swollen.

'Yes, to tell you, you've got a hard one tonight. Norway...' Bridget tried to keep her voice positive. Upbeat. Alice grimaced. One of the agents in Norway — of course she didn't know who, just the area section he worked from — was notorious for sending unreadable messages; they were often so bad they were left for Mr Marks himself to interpret. But tonight, this one was on her desk to solve. 'I'm sure you'll crack it. You know, best in class and all that.'

Lucy and Bridget were inseparable. They shared a hut and were often on duty together. Alice wondered how it didn't drive them mad, being with each other almost all day and night, every day and night. *Mind you, look at me and Rita. We're practically joined at the hip.*

She blushed. She hated being the class swot, but she always managed to get the top marks when they were tested. Either her or Rita, anyway. They were the quickest at solving the puzzles that passed through their hands. The 'indecipherables' soon gave up their secrets under their scrutiny. The four girls ran a little bet to see who broke the most codes by the end of each week. Alice thrived on the competition, but shunned the praise.

She focused her attention on her two friends and what they were telling her. She frowned. 'Too hard for the two of you to work out together? Are you sure the message was transcribed properly? You know what the newer girls can be like. It's hard going when they first get here.' The three girls shared the conspiratorial superiority of 'old hands' — even though they arrived at the station just a few weeks ago.

Lucy and Bridget shook their heads. Twins in action, and in thought. 'No, we checked with Miss Rivers. She was on duty with us. The new batch coming in are better trained than our group were. They're more ready. So they get it right.' Lucy pushed a lock of lank hair back from her forehead. The afternoon sun shone into the room where the cryptanalysts worked, making it hot and stuffy. Most of the girls were exhausted by the end of a shift, desperate to get back to their huts for a wash, and then return to the Hall for a few drinks and dinner. And to let off steam. Some evenings there would be music and dancing, although more often than not, no one was able to summon the energy.

Alice squeezed Lucy's shoulder. 'You look done in. Go on, both of you, or you'll miss dinner. It's pie tonight. Thanks for the heads up with the message. I'll look and see what's going on. And don't worry.' Alice knew that last instruction was impossible. All the girls worried, almost all the time. If they didn't manage to interpret the message in time, the agent would receive instructions to resend it. Each extra minute on the air was an extra minute in which the enemy might find and capture them. She smiled and pushed the girls away from her. 'Go! I'll see you in the morning.'

Bridget gave a little wave as she hurried away, Lucy following close behind. 'Thanks, Al, you're a brick. Have a good night.'

A brick. What a silly expression. Alice strode into the room and over to her desk, confident she'd have everything under control by ten-ish; midnight at the latest.

It was two in the morning. There was no confidence left in Alice. She looked over at Rita again. She was still busy scratching away on a blank sheet of paper. Her eureka moment must have been correct. Frustrated, Alice tucked the pencil behind her ear and got to her feet, banging her elbow as she did so. 'Ow!' One or two of the others looked up, annoyed at being disturbed. Alice didn't care.

She retreated along the darkened corridor to the main entrance of the Hall. *I need some fresh air.*

Outside, Alice filled her lungs with the cool night air. She strolled around to the side of the building, swinging her arms in the hopes that restored circulation would stir her brain into similar action. The lights of the 'runway' shone below her, garish and bright in the otherwise dark countryside.

Alice remembered the first time she'd seen the two straight rows of night lights. It was in her first week of nightshift. She was put on the same shift pattern as Rita; it was easier for roommates to get their sleep if they weren't on alternating waking and sleeping hours. Rita had pulled her from her desk during a quiet moment.

'Here, there's something you need to see.'

'But Rita, I need to get this message finished. I'm so close. Can't it wait a minute? Or until the morning?' Alice was reluctant to leave something half-finished, worried she might forget her train of thought and have to start picking her way through the code from the beginning again.

'It won't take a minute, I promise. Come on, you must be wanting to stretch your legs by now? We've been at it for half the night already.'

Alice shrugged. There was truth in Rita's words. Her back and neck were aching from leaning forward, and she was starting to fidget. 'Alright, then. But only a minute.'

Rita led the way to the same spot where Alice now stood. She reached up and covered Alice's eyes with her hands for the last couple of yards. 'It's a surprise...Ta-da!' She whipped her hands away. Alice blinked, dazzled by the sudden glare of white light after the impenetrable darkness of night, when even indoor lamps were hidden behind blackout curtains. She closed her eyes; the lights continued to flash and dance on the inside of her closed lids.

Opening her eyes again, she turned to Rita. 'There's an airfield here? I didn't know that?'

'It's wonderful, isn't it? It's not real, you know. They turn all the lights on every night. The Hun think it's a real airfield and fly around and around for ages, trying to work out where they are. Their maps don't show an airfield here, so they think they've gone off course. They eventually give up and fly back to base, convinced they were sent on an impossible mission. I have a pilot friend who told me about it. You know, thinking you're lost and all that sort of thing.'

Alice was amazed. 'They really are doing things differently, this war, aren't they? What fun!'

The girls giggled their way back to their desks.

Now it didn't seem so much fun, though. Alice may have been stationed at Grendon for only a few weeks, but she knew more than she had ever wanted to about the 'unfun' nature of war. It wasn't all tricks and games. With a sigh, she retraced her steps towards the entrance. *Come on, old girl, let's try again. Someone really needs that message to get through. Tonight.*

There was a tea table set up in the corner of the decoding room. Alice made a beeline for it. Putting off the inevitable return to the task at hand. The urn of hot water bubbled and hissed throughout the night. A clumsy pile of clean cups and saucers was stacked alongside two brown teapots, and the coffee and sugar cannisters. Occasionally, there was a plate of biscuits. Alice lifted the lid of the sugar tin, peering inside in hope of something sweet. There were a few grains left at the bottom. Smiling at her discovery, she reached for a cup and saucer. No biscuits tonight, but no matter; a knot of anxiety in her stomach made the idea of eating impossible, anyway.

Nothing I've tried has worked. Nothing. What am I missing? Alice lifted the first of the two teapots and swirled it around. She heard the water sloshing inside. *Hope it's still hot.* She was gratified to see steam curling upwards as she poured the pungent liquid into her cup. Even with the milk added, the brew was so strong it looked like cocoa, but Alice didn't mind. *Maybe it will sharpen my sluggish brain.*

After some noisy poking around in the sugar container, a decent teaspoonful joined the murky contents of the cup. Alice cradled her cup and turned to make her way back to her desk, just avoiding bumping into the duty officer for that night's shift.

'Oh gosh, sorry Miss Needham. I didn't hear you walk over.' Miss Needham was older than the other officers. No one knew her well. There were rumours that she once worked as an agent in the field. In France, someone said. But then another girl said no, it was Belgium. Either way, her presence intimidated most of them.

'Is everything alright? You don't seem your usual, calm self?' Miss Needham indicated Alice's desk. 'You've packed your papers away. And you popped out. Are you finished?' There was more than a hint of disapproval in the question.

'No. That's the problem. I'm not finished. And I don't know what to try next.' Her voice sounded loud and panicky in the studious quiet of the room. Alice gulped, trying to regain control. One of the girls on the far side of the room looked up, frowning at more disruption to her work. Alice raised a hand in silent apology.

'Let me take a look.' Miss Needham led the way over to Alice's desk. Motioning for Alice to sit, she reached over the girl's shoulder for the pile of papers and peered at the first page. She sighed. 'You recognise the agent, don't you? Has he ever been this bad? Made so many errors?'

Alice shook her head. 'No, not when I've worked on his messages, anyway. Maybe his machine is faulty?' Miss Needham shook her head. 'No, I didn't really think that, either. What about the weather? You know how sometimes the Morse gets mangled when it's cloudy. Or raining.'

Miss Needham pulled a pencil out from the top pocket of her tunic. Resting the page in her left hand, she began marking a few of the letters.

Satisfied, she returned the page to Alice and turned her attention to the second, again annotating it as she read. Midway through, Miss Needham gave a 'huh' of frustration and tossed everything back onto Alice's desk. The pencil landed with a soft thud and rolled towards the edge. Alice caught it before it fell to the floor.

'No, it's not static or anything. Looks more like he's in a terrible hurry. Or panicking ...'

Alice handed back the pencil. Her boss took it without comment, preoccupied.

'There is one more thing we can try. Hold on.' The older woman strode from the room.

Her sudden burst of enthusiasm encouraged Alice. *Did she see something I missed? Or has she gone to fetch someone who will?* While waiting to see what would happen next, Alice took up the first page of her notes, eager to check the comments added by Miss Needham. They were punctuation marks of exclamation or irritation. Disappointed to find nothing new to add to any of her own scribblings, Alice let the paper flutter to the floor. She folded her arms and closed her eyes, hoping to eliminate the distraction of the room, and put herself in the place of the agent. *Maybe that way, I'll figure out what he meant.*

Shortly after arriving at Station 53a, SOE code name for the grand Grendon Hall, Alice joined a few of the lectures given to new agents before they were sent off on their secret missions. The girls weren't officially allowed to be present, but many of those in charge thought it would help the radio operators and analysts to have at least a cursory knowledge of what was being asked of those about to be parachuted into enemy territory. Most of the lectures reminded Alice of the comic books her brother, Tom, used to read. There was lots of talk about dressing up like a local to blend in, or how to send messages using different types of invisible ink; lemon juice was Tom's favourite, Alice recalled.

Then there was the boring matter of paperwork and permissions to travel, the sort of thing which Alice was sure would be of vital importance if she were ever to be asked to travel around France, but was otherwise an utter waste of time.

The best session she attended was a demonstration by an experienced radio operator. Fascinated, she watched him assemble his radio, running aerial and earth wires in all directions. He explained how he chose which crystals to use, depending on the frequency he wanted to transmit on. 'The more crystals I have and the more often I can change them, the safer I am from detection.' He paused, held the crystal to the light as though it was a glass filled with fine wine. 'Of course, in the anxiety of the moment, few agents have the wherewithal to remember that bit of the training...'

He held the headset close to his left ear and fiddled with a couple of the dials with his other hand, his students forgotten. With half-closed eyes, he swayed from side to side as though moving to the music of a secret dance. Alice wondered if all the agents were like this. Was the radio set an extension of them, an expression of a life lived under cover? Or was it a tool of work, used simply as a means of communication with distant listeners?

The radio operator stopped swaying and opened his eyes, fixing his attention on his audience. With a broad smile, he announced himself ready to send a test message. He pulled a small brass object from the case at his side and plugged it into the radio set. 'This,' he explained, holding the object aloft, so it glinted in the afternoon sunshine, 'is the Morse key. I press down here, either for a short — dot — or longer — dash — pulse. The trick is keeping the dots and dashes distinguishable from one another. And making sure the pauses between letters are long enough that the radio operator listening in knows it is a proper break, rather than a stutter.'

Alice and a few of the girls exchanged glances. They all knew the smudged and unclear dots and dashes, the nervous stutters. They were the bread and butter of decryption. Agents unable to eliminate certain idiosyncrasies from their transmissions gave a recognisable 'accent' to their communications. Deciphering messages into clear text sometimes involved nothing more than tidying up. Of course, if the styles and coding habits were known to the girls here in Grendon Underwood, presumably they were just as familiar to any enemy listeners as well. The thought sent a shiver up Alice's spine, despite the warmth of the day.

Now she imagined an agent kneeling on the dusty floor of an abandoned out-building. Or perched on the edge of his bed in some dingy lodgings. First, he would have composed his message, keeping it as brief as possible while making sure it contained all the necessary information. His next task would be to encode his message, using words from the poem memorised before leaving England. Alice imagined the stub of a pencil held between shaking fingers, letters traced out in batches of five. Maybe a D becomes an O, or a word from the poem is used in the wrong order. Sweat breaks out on the agent's brow, trickles into his straining eyes. The letters become increasingly illegible. Alice's imaginary agent reaches for the Morse key, taps out his call sign, waits for acknowledgment from HQ. He listens for the sound of a car driving over rough gravel or a knock at the door, heart pounding in his chest, suffocating all other noise. He gets the go-ahead to start transmission. He forgets how long to hold a dash, how short to tap out a dot. The spaces between letters become erratic, making it hard to distinguish between individual letters and groups. He gets halfway through when he is aware of the sound of voices. Of boots clumping up uncarpeted stairs. A hand reaches out and grips his shoulder...

'Alice! Alice, wake up. Miss Needham's coming back.' Rita shook Alice a second time.

'What? No, I didn't fall asleep, did I?' Alice hissed back. 'Ah, Miss Needham, I was just...'

'Never mind what you were just. Rita, don't you have your own work to attend to? Alice, let's see if these can help.' She dragged a chair over from the edge of the room. 'Sorry. Didn't mean to disturb you all. Alice, make some room.'

Alice moved her chair across, trying not to crowd Rita. She turned her back, blocking Rita's view and avoiding eye contact; they wouldn't be able to control their mirth if she didn't.

'These came through from Mr Marks earlier today. No one has tried them out yet. They're crib sheets, charts of possible combinations, that sort of thing. He thought they might be useful with the more tricky messages. Like this one. Shall we give it a go?' She pulled over the notes Alice had been puzzling over. 'Where's the top page? The one I wrote on a minute ago? Oh, there it is, on the floor. Well, reach it, girl.'

Alice bent to collect the paper and passed it over to Miss Needham, who placed it back on the desk. Brushing off the dust with a grimace, she began comparing her notes with the charts from London.

'Look, you see, here? That works, doesn't it?' Alice looked at where Miss Needham was pointing her pencil.

'Yes, I do believe it does.' Alice couldn't hide the relief from her voice. Maybe they would be able to get this message written up in clear before the end of the night after all. Another agent's mission saved. *Another agent's life saved, maybe?*

The two women worked side by side, the older one as determined to solve the puzzle as the younger. Dawn sketched a line of pale light around the edge of the blackouts. The other girls yawned, stretched, packed away their belongings, ready to head out for breakfast and then to crash into bed for a few hours. Rita hung around the longest, concern for her friend clear. Alice blew her kiss of farewell. 'Don't stay, really. You go. Get some rest...'

The next shift banged into the room, wide awake and noisy. Until they saw Miss Needham and Alice. Their voices dropped to a muted whisper. One of them went to the windows and pulled down the dark fabric of night, pushed the windows open. Alice winced as a splash of sunshine fell across her desk. She became aware of her surroundings for the first time in what felt like hours. The fresh breeze lifted her hair. A blackbird sang his morning song, loud and insistent. She picked up her page of notes.

'I think we've done it.' Miss Needham held the sheet of paper aloft. She was triumphant, the victor raising the spoils. Alice's heartbeat returned to a normal pace. 'Well done, Alice. Your perseverance and determination do you great credit. Really, they do. Oh, don't be silly and get all weepy on me. Mind you, this does deserve a touch of emotion; who knows what would have happened if this communication didn't get through? Breakfast and bed for you, my girl, while I get this sent to the Norway section.'

Miss Needham nudged Alice from her chair, but remained seated while she watched the girl leave. Alice stumbled her way across the room. Her head pounded, her eyes stung from the strain of the night. The raucous breakfast service in the dining room held all the appeal of an afternoon at the zoo. Alice walked away, preferring to retreat to the peace and quiet of her hut.

Although exhausted, Alice took her time wandering down the hill. The sky was a glorious blue, the colour of the forget-me-nots growing in the garden at home. Hollyhocks, deep reds and gentle pinks, framed the doorway of the Hall. A lark sang, hovering high above the field of yellowing barley opposite the gate at the bottom of the hill. *What a night. Thank heavens for Miss Needham and Mr Marks. I wonder who we saved tonight?*

Alice

'Friends'

•⁻ •⁻•• •• ⁻•⁻• •

A lice woke with a groan. Her stomach ached, a dull throb like toothache. Rita watched her from the other bed.

'You too? Time of the month?'

'Mm. "Your friend," Mum always calls it. Goodness knows why.' Alice groaned again.

'Funny how we get them at the same time, now that we're sharing here, don't you think?'

'I hadn't noticed. Ugh, I'd better get up and go to the bathroom.' Alice threw back the wrinkled sheet, the weather too warm for blankets. 'You ready for breakfast? You don't have to wait...'

'No, I'll wait. Another five minutes of trying to gather myself won't hurt.'

The girls, late for breakfast, had little choice for their morning meal. Alice grabbed a lukewarm cup of tea and drank it with a grimace. 'That'll do for now. Can't stomach anything else, anyway.'

'No, me neither. Right, let's get on with it, shall we? I really hope we don't get any Cabbage messages today...'

Alice giggled. 'Oh yes, I wouldn't be able to solve any of his puzzles, not today. My head feels as though it's full of cotton wool this morning.'

They settled into their places, pulling the day's messages towards them.

It was an awful day. Alice longed to be back in her bed, a hot water bottle clutched to her cramping stomach. It was impossible to concentrate. Rita seemed to be finding it as hard to focus. Each time Alice glanced over at her friend, she was either staring out of the window or doodling random shapes and patterns on her sheet of paper. *This is hopeless. There'd better not be anything of vital importance in these messages. I'm not sure either of us would notice if there were.* Miss Rivers was on duty with them. She paced around the room, stopping now and then to check Alice's work. Then she moved on to Rita, frowning.

'Alice, Rita. Are you sick? You are taking an age to get through those today. Even with Mr Marks' new crib sheets.'

After Alice and Miss Needham's breakthrough with the Norway message from the previous week, the crib sheets were now in common use, saving hours on decrypting communications.

Miss Rivers had a point. Alice checked through her pile. Just one message was written out in clear text, neat and ready to forward on to whoever needed it. It was already lunchtime. She should have finished the night's skeds by now, ready to receive the new batch hot off the radio as soon as they came in. Rita and her were the quickest of all the girls. Partly because they'd been there the longest and knew what to look for; partly because they were exceptional at anagrams and puzzles. They raced each other to finish the crosswords in *The Times* and *The Telegraph* every day. Their little competition was becoming a bit of a legend around the station; Alice heard there was a regular sweepstake running on who would have won the most by the end of each week.

Alice handed Miss Rivers the one completed note. 'Sorry, Miss Rivers. I'll be better this afternoon, I'm sure.'

She wasn't. Neither was Rita. By the time the night-shift girls arrived, there were more papers to work through than when they arrived in the morning. Both girls prided themselves on leaving an empty desk at the end of their shift. Not today.

'What a dreadful day.' Rita linked arms with her friend as they hurried along to the dining hall. 'Let's get dinner and hope Luce and Marj have better luck.'

Bridget, the fourth member of their gang, was relocated to Egypt a month after arriving at Grendon. She sent regular letters describing decadent parties and horrendous heat. She never mentioned work. Marj, a girl from Northumberland, shared with Lucy now. She was homesick, always telling the others about walking along wild beaches and across heather-dotted moors. She kept telling them how she hated the never-ending flat fields or the dry, dusty air. But when not complaining, she was the greatest fun to be with, inventing stories about highland fairies and goblins, handsome shepherds and lonely princesses. And she could sing; she soon became the leading lady of Station 53a's dramatic society. Marj was even good at code decryption.

Alice was better the next morning. The stomach cramps had eased during the night and her head was less stuffy, her thoughts less muddled. Rita was more her breezy self, too. She was up and dressed when Alice woke, whistling through her teeth as she brushed out her long dark hair.

'Morning! You slept well, darling. You even snored, you know.'

'As though you'd know. You were asleep the second we turned the lights out last night.'

Rita threw her brush at her friend. It fell short, landing with a clatter on the floor. 'Now look what you made me do. It'll be all full of dust and stuff.' She scrabbled around on the floor, reaching to retrieve it from where it had shot under Alice's bed. Alice laughed. 'I don't know what you're laughing at, sleepy head. Have you seen the time?'

With a screech, Alice checked her alarm clock. 'Argh, why did you let me sleep so long? We're going to miss breakfast — again.'

'Not *we*, darling — *you*. I'm off. I'm starving after hardly eating anything yesterday.' Rita gave a little wave as she left the room.

Alice rushed around, pulling on clothes. She smoothed and patted her hair into place while grabbing her bag from the end of the bed. 'Hang on, I'm coming.'

Rita must have run up the hill, as there was no sign of her in the driveway. Alice hurried to find her. After their dismal performance the day before, she didn't want to make it worse by arriving for the next shift hungry and late.

She found Rita as soon as she entered the main house. Or rather, Rita found her.

'Alice. Over here.' The unlit hallway was dark; Alice strained to see where Rita was after the bright sunshine of yet another glorious day. 'I'm here, by the sitting room. No, don't go in for breakfast — '

'Rita, what on earth are you doing? Aren't we late? We don't have time to play games.'

'No game, Alice. Miss Rivers wants to see us. With Miss Needham as well. Mr Marks has been.'

'What? All the way from London? Why? Oh no...' Alice pressed a hand to her mouth, holding back the squeal of dismay as it rushed up her throat. 'Not because of yesterday?' Her voice through her fingers was a muffled whisper.

'I don't know.' Now that her eyes had adjusted to the hallway shadows, Alice noticed Rita hovering by the sitting room door. Her fingers formed an invisible cat's cradle of anxiety as she twisted and turned them together. She stepped further into the open. 'Miss Rivers was waiting for me when I walked in. Called me over, told me to stay here until you turned up, then for both of us to go straight to the library. Ooohh, it's school all over again, isn't it? You know, being called in to see the headmistress to be given the ruler across the knuckles?'

Although not haunted by such an experience, Alice knew what Rita meant. Her own stomach was flittering and flapping — summer butterflies caught in a jar. She licked her lips, trying to moisten the sudden dryness. *Wish I'd put lipstick on this morning.* It was an inconsequential thought.

'The library? Really? Why the library and not the office? Or the code room? And how do you know Mr Marks was here, though?' She took a step or two towards Rita and kept her voice low.

'I saw him. He was saying cheerio to Miss Rivers. Said something about 'leave it with you' or something. I must say, he looked terribly embarrassed. When he spotted me standing there, he blushed like a beetroot. Don't think I've ever seen him leave so fast.'

The girls were making their way towards the library as they spoke. The door was closed. *Is anyone even inside?* Alice knocked. It sounded feeble, intimidated. She tried again, folding her hand into a fist and rapping with her knuckles.

'Come!' It was Miss Needham's voice. Alice grasped the handle and pushed open the door, leading the way. Rita hurried in behind her. 'Ah, Alice, Rita. Close the door, please. And take a seat for a moment.'

Miss Needham sat behind a huge antique desk. *Mahogany?* There was a tray of tea things in front of her. Miss Rivers was fussing with cups and saucers, pouring milk and stirring the pot. She avoided eye contact with either of the girls perching on the edge of the two seats opposite.

Behind Miss Needham, dusty red velvet curtains shaded the window. Worn and faded, with patches rubbed bare through decades of opening and closing. Decorative pompoms fringed the outer edges — several were missing, Alice noticed. The library was often an informal party room. This morning it reeked of last night's cigarette smoke. Gramophone records lay discarded across the settee and the floor. Half a dozen empty beer bottles lined the mantelpiece above the unused fireplace. The book shelves, stripped of their contents long before the War Office took occupation, were vacant and bare. Through the window, Alice watched a truck pull up on the gravel. A dozen lads in civilian clothes hopped out of the back. They were stretching and yawning. One punched another in the arm. It was like a silent movie, only without the piano accompaniment. *So many new recruits in one day; something is up. I wonder what?*

Miss Needham cleared her throat. Alice refocused her attention on her superior. 'Girls, we need a little chat before you get started with your work for today. I understand yesterday wasn't a good one. Am I right?'

Alice picked at a piece of skin on her left thumb. 'No, not really, Miss Needham.' She didn't look up. Rita remained silent.

'Tea?' Miss Rivers handed them both a cup. She settled herself into the chair beside her colleague. Miss Needham indicated she should continue the conversation. 'Girls, I'm afraid we've decided to split you up. Put you on different shifts to each other. For some of the time, anyway.'

Rita sloshed tea into her saucer as she replaced the cup, clumsy with surprise. 'Why? But Miss Rivers, Miss Needham — it was just that one day. We won't let it happen again, honestly we won't. Will we, Al?'

Alice was too shocked to reply.

Miss Needham took over. 'Mr Marks has made the request. He realised yesterday wasn't the first time that it has happened. You know, where you've not been at your best?' She looked from one girl to the other, waiting for them to understand. They remained silent. With a sigh, she continued, 'It seems to happen every month. Or thereabouts...'

A blush of horror and shame rushed up Alice's neck and across her cheeks. 'You mean, um, you know, um...' She couldn't finish.

'Yes dear. It seems your Monthlies are affecting your work. Mr Marks noticed a pattern, but being a young and, well, apparently inexperienced, young man, he didn't know what it meant. He spoke with Corporal Henderson — the personnel officer, not sure if you know her? — in London about it and she explained the basics. He then rushed up here, all set to confront you. Thankfully, he spoke to me first.'

'Thankfully indeed.' Miss Rivers continued the story. 'Mr Marks knows that you are two of our best cryptanalysts. No, don't deny it. You know it's true. And he was concerned that our poor agents are struggling to get their communications through every month because of your lack of ability to concentrate. Of course, yesterday was particularly bad, hence his sudden appearance.'

'So,' — it was Miss Needham again — 'we decided the best course of action is to make sure you are on different shifts, at least for those one or two days that you are thus affected. Mr Marks wanted to put you on light duties, rather. But we felt, to start with at least, it would be better to alter your shifts.' She picked up her teacup and took a delicate sip. 'That way, we don't lose two of our best at the same time on the same shift. There'll be others who can help cover for you. Not as good as you, of course, but better than the nothing we had yesterday. What do you think?'

Alice huffed a sigh of relief. 'So, we're not in trouble then?'

'No. Although your agents could be, if Mr Marks wasn't so determined in his quest to prevent 'indecipherables' getting through.' Miss Rivers replaced her teacup on the tray. She picked up a pen and began making notes on a sheet of paper. 'So, let's see. Yesterday was a terrible day. Of that, we are all in agreement. How are you both feeling today?' She pierced them with enquiring eyes. 'And don't pretend you're fine if you're not. Your work will show us the truth, I'm certain of that.'

Rita answered for both of them. 'We were saying, when we woke up, how glad we are to feel back to normal this morning. No headache or cramps. Well, not for me anyway...'

'No, nor me.' Alice was quick to reassure their superiors that all was well with her. 'Can we stay on the same shift until, well, next time, then? It makes it so much easier with sharing a room, to be on the same timetable.'

Rita sat nodding next to her. Miss Needham and Miss Rivers held a whispered conversation, the latter scribbling a few additional notes as they deliberated.

'Very well then.' It was Miss Needham's turn to speak. 'We'll keep you together for the next, shall we say, three weeks? Then one week on different shifts. Then, if all is well, you can return to your normal duty times for the next three weeks. And so on.'

Alice tried to thank the two women, but Miss Needham held up her hand to stop either of the girls before they spoke. 'On another matter. You will have noticed, I'm sure, an influx of 'guests' today? There'll be several more over the next couple of days. I can't say anything more, only that there is a great and urgent need to recruit and release new agents into the field with the utmost speed over the coming weeks. Besides the increase in personnel, you'll find a similar increase in skeds being received. You will have your work cut out for you, my dears, and we need you as sharp as you can be.'

'Tension in the field will be at its peak,' Miss Rivers continued. 'And, as you know, tension leads to mistakes. Some of our men — and women — will be at breaking point. We need to do all we can to ease as much of that tension as possible by getting their messages and communications through to those who need them as quickly and correctly as it is in our power to do so. We now have the charts provided by Mr Marks at our full disposal. Alice, I think you know how helpful they are proving to be?

'Over the next couple of days, they'll use a second new intervention by Mr Marks in the field. Rather than the agents relying on memory and a few lines of poetry, they will receive a set of Worked Out Keys from which to compose their messages. This will increase security and, hopefully, decrease error and hence indecipherable messages. We'll brief all you girls on those in a day or so.

'Rita, Alice, we need you to be at the top of your game. Really, it is vital. The other girls look up to you both, even those who are older than you. They take their cue from you — when you are calm, they believe anything is possible. When you appear concerned, or out of your depth, they too seem to sink.'

'Your daily temperament seems to make or break a shift.' Miss Needham's tone was midway between apology and pride. 'We have every faith in you, though. Now is the time for you to rise and do your bit. For King and country'

It was a rousing speech. Alice could not think of anything to say in response. Rita was also quiet.

'Yes well, sitting here won't get anything done, will it?' Miss Needham was brusque once more, the officer in charge of her subordinates. She looked at her watch. 'There will be a batch of skeds waiting for you already. Hurry along.'

The girls left the room in silence, speaking once the door was closed behind them and they were further along the hallway.

'Well, I never. I wasn't expecting that. How embarrassing.' Rita hurried along ahead of Alice, talking back over her shoulder. 'Fancy that, Mr Marks has been watching what we're doing so much, he even noticed that. Did you see Miss Rivers while Miss Needham was telling us? I think she was even redder than you. If that's possible.'

'Give over, Rita. To think our "friends" may have caused someone's cover to be blown. Worse, that it could have caused their deaths.' Alice tried in vain to dispel images of Tom, caught and tortured in a POW camp. Or Bill. *What if he's been caught too? He hasn't written in ages.* She sped up her pace, to both catch up with Rita and to shake the awful scenarios from her mind. 'What do you think they meant about the other thing, though? You know, all the extra activity? And those Worked Out Keys or whatever they are?'

Rita slowed, waiting for Alice. She was serious again. 'Something's up, that's for sure. Did you see the new ones arriving? They all looked so, I don't know, inexperienced. Didn't you think? There must be something big planned, to call up boys like that.'

'You sound like an old maid. Boys indeed. I noticed there were at least three who are way older than you and me.'

'Ah, older in years, but not in experience.' Rita laughed. Alice curled her lips in distaste.

'But what do you think about what they said about us? You know, being the life and soul of the decryption party, so to speak? What if it all gets too much and we get it wrong or something? I wouldn't want that on my conscience.'

'Well, what does your Mr Lewis say? Isn't that the entire basis of courage and bravery? Getting on with our duty, no matter what. Facing our fears.' Alice stopped walking, gaping at Rita in astonishment. 'What are you looking at me like that for? You've gone on about that book so much, how you see things differently since reading it. I thought I should read it as well.'

'Well, of course, I don't mind. I'm just surprised, I suppose. I didn't think you'd read that sort of thing. About religion and stuff.'

'I wouldn't have, before. But all this changes things, don't you think?' She swept her arm in a wide arc, encompassing in the gesture so much more than the hallway in which they stood.

'Yes. Yes, it changes everything.' Alice was quiet. 'I'm glad you borrowed Screwtape. I hope it helps you as much as it has me.'

They reached the coding room. Alice reached for Rita's hand. She gave it a squeeze. 'God be with you, Rita.'

'And you, Al. Come on, let's get on with it.' She took a deep breath and pushed open the door. 'Don't worry, girls, we're here to save the day.'

Alice rolled her eyes and ducked into the room.

Alice

Tension

●━　●━●●　●●　━●━●　●

A thick blanket of tension smothered Station 53a over the next few weeks. Stifling sound, suffocating conversations. Shortened tempers. The atmosphere snapped and fizzled with irritation. There were too many people in the dining hall and not enough tables and chairs for everyone. Not enough food, either.

The evening parties of music and dancing, the short comic revues and dramatic theatre stopped without anyone ever saying it was necessary. People held intense debates in private smoke-hazed huddles. Sentences went unfinished when a newcomer arrived or if someone walked too close for comfort. The girls in the radio room developed headaches from endless hours of pressing radio sets to their ears. The skeds were arriving more frequently, with more errors and mistakes. It was impossible to keep up.

Alice did her best. She and Rita worked extra long hours, overlapping shifts to finish whatever message they worked on rather than hand it over to a different girl. At mealtimes, Alice pushed her food around the plate before giving up and handing it over to one of the new young agents, who were still arriving daily. She grew thin and gaunt. Dark circles ringed her eyes. Her fingernails were bitten and ugly. *What would Vera say if she saw me now? Send me off for an urgent manicure, probably.*

At the end of each day — or night, depending on which shift they were assigned — the girls collapsed into their beds, exhausted. But neither slept well. Rita talked in her sleep, tossing and muttering in the stillness of the night. Alice lay hour after hour staring at the ceiling, re-running anagrams and messages through her mind, hoping her earlier choices were the right ones.

They both hated the weeks when they were assigned different hours of work. Sleep was even more impossible then. No matter how quietly each tried to get ready, they disturbed the other one. Rita huffed in frustration, pulling her pillow down over her head whenever Alice got ready for duty; Alice lay still, watching Rita through half-closed eyes, willing her to hurry and leave.

They spent little time with their other friends — Lucy, Marj, and a new girl, Carol. There were no picnics together, no walks down the lane to visit the village hall for a night of bingo. Every spare moment was spent trying to catch up on writing letters home or darning socks and sewing on buttons. There was no time to do anything enjoyable. And no interest in being joyful when there was any spare time.

Summer yielded to autumn one misty evening at a time. Brown and orange leaves drifted to the ground and gathered in discarded piles, dumped where the wind had grown bored with the dance. Rain spattered against the thin windowpanes, leaking damp patches onto carpets and curtains. Everywhere smelt musty and unaired, despite the draughts which made the girls shiver in their beds.

Not knowing what was going on or what was being planned made everything worse. Much worse. Rumours swirled around Grendon like the falling autumn leaves. The FANY girls in the code room heard of networks discovered and agents captured. Then they were reassured that messages highlighting any such reports were the deliberate spreading of false information. New code names appeared in the skeds, then, without warning, disappeared.

Alice found respite in the garden, wrapping up against the advancing cold in as many layers as she could find. The surrounding landscape was dreary. Bare trees, their exposed branches bending and twisting in the wind, the *clack clack* like skeleton bones knocking against one another a frequent soundtrack to Alice's thoughts. Although night shifts were long and tiring, they at least allowed her to catch a few hours of daylight between sleep and work. She sat now, a notepad on her lap, a pencil held between gloved fingers. She thought a while, then wrote a couple of sentences. Behind her, the shuffle of feet indicated someone's arrival.

'Oof, I am so tired. I didn't sleep at all this morning, did you?' Rita plonked down next to Alice, nudging her elbow as she sat. 'Oh sorry, I didn't mean to make your hand slip. What are you writing, anyway?'

'I got a bit of sleep, I think. Too many dreams, though. Not proper sleep, is it?' A series of pop-pops sounded from the field below. 'More shooting practice for the boys. I'm not sure how realistic shooting on a driving range is, though. Those targets stay still.'

Rita lit a cigarette. Alice hated them, but didn't want to add to Rita's stress by complaining. Everything was hard enough without her being petty. At least she didn't smoke in their room, only outside. Even when it rained. For that, Alice was grateful. She watched as Rita sucked in a deep breath of smoke, preparing to blow it all out again in slow, ringlike puffs. Despite herself, it always impressed Alice .

Wafting the smoke away with her free hand, Rita repeated her question. 'What are you writing?'

'A poem.' Alice laughed. 'I haven't been able to break the habit from when Mr Marks asked us to contribute to the poetry stock for the agents to use. Now, with those Worked Out Keys, I know poems aren't needed as much, but I keep writing them.'

'I don't miss the mistakes they caused. Some of those agents couldn't remember a line of poetry if their life depended on it. Which it did...'

They sat in silence, Alice lost in memories of agents and their terrible codes. 'Oh, I almost forgot. I've got something to show you.' Rita delved into her coat pocket with one hand while still holding her cigarette in the other.

'Mm? What have you got this time?'

Rita pulled out a square of fabric, waved it in front of Alice. 'Silk!'

'A new hankie? What are you showing me that for?'

'Not a hankie, silly. A silk. An agent's silk.' Rita's eyes shone with excitement. 'Look, it's got all the letters printed on it, just like Miss Rivers told us.'

Alice pulled off one of her gloves, taking the scrap from Rita. She rubbed the fabric between her thumb and finger, marvelling at how delicate it was. Tiny letters, stamped in neat columns, covered its surface. 'It's beautiful. Where on earth did you get it?'

'A friend of a friend. I never reveal my sources, you know that.' She circled her cigarette in the air. 'But isn't it wonderful? Mr Marks is a genius to think of it. It can be hidden in the agent's clothing, sewn into the lining of his coat or whatever. No crinkly sounds if he gets searched, like there would be with paper.'

They had all been briefed on the new system a few days after the embarrassing episode over their Monthlies. Some agents still used the poems, as that was what they were used to. But they gave new recruits sheets of silk with pre-designed code groups printed on them. Once the agent had used a column, they could tear it from the square and dispose of it without leaving a trace.

She stared at Rita in amazement and admiration. 'Well, I'm sure I don't need to know your source, but goodness, I never expected to see one of these. So simple and yet really so clever, don't you think?' She handed it back to Rita, who smiled her acknowledgement before stuffing the fabric back in her pocket. Alice closed the cover on her notebook. 'Seeing that has cured me of poetry writing, that's for sure. Why use a poem when you can have a silk?'

The following week, Alice received a pair of mittens in the post, knitted for her by Mother. With them a short, ecstatic note.

Tom found. All well. Being sent on home leave in next week or so. Will you be able to visit?

The stab of guilt this simple question provoked made Alice wince. A telegram from her parents had arrived a few weeks earlier.

No definite news but suspected alive stop In hiding question Pray ends

Its brevity annoyed Alice — *Can't you tell me more than that? And I'm already praying* — but knew that for her mother to say more would cost too much. No doubt a letter in the post would follow with a more detailed explanation.

Back then, Alice had longed to go home, even if only for a weekend. She wanted to check on her parents, reassure herself that they were coping as well as they said they were. She missed the parsonage, a castle of draughty rooms and passageways compared to her current billet. She wanted to chase the dogs along the path by the river, watch them as they sniffed for rabbits and hares. She even wanted to visit old Mrs Milton, sit in her cramped and stuffy sitting room, drinking milky tea and listening to the latest village gossip.

Time-off was not mentioned at the station for weeks; there was too much to do and too few people to do it. Of course, being a volunteer, she could just leave. But since the chat with Eve, Alice knew she wouldn't. And The Screwtape Letters added to her resolve. Something about being involved in a larger, unseen battle inspired Alice and lit her imagination.

In this invisible war, she wasn't just a backroom girl with a helpful brain, lending a hand when allowed; in this conflict, every decision she took made an impact, rippled beyond herself. Would she get up at dawn, eager to play her part on that day's shift, or would she roll over for an extra five minutes of sleep, leaving an exhausted night shifter to cover for her? Would she be kind and gracious to Rita, even though her choice of music drove her crazy and her perfume made her sneeze? Would she keep her promise to tell no one what she was doing, not even her family, or Bill, when she wrote?

'You alright? Is your mother's knitting that bad?' Rita's voice snapped Alice back to the present. She sat on her bed opposite Alice, twisting her hair into papers in a vain attempt to create a few curls. 'There might not be much fun going on right now, but that doesn't mean I shouldn't be ready for it. I heard about a dance planned for next weekend. With some of the new recruits. Give them something to write home about before there's nothing left to say.'

'Oh, don't Rita. It's bad enough knowing they're leaving soon, without joking about what might happen to them next. Poor Toby was a mess last night. His papers came through and he was told to be ready to leave first thing in the morning. I don't know where he's going, but he looked scared stiff. He was pretending it was all a jolly outing, like Boy Scouts on a jaunt. But I caught him being sick behind the hedge on my way back here. And he hadn't been drinking before you say anything.'

Toby had arrived at the weekend, full of happy bravado and cheerful grins. Alice and Rita had adopted him as their own. *Rather like a lost puppy.*

'Goodness, don't bite my head off. What's wrong with you?' Rita left her hair, swinging her legs off the bed to face Alice.

'Sorry. I didn't mean to sound so cross. It's just, oh here, read this.' Alice handed the brief note to Rita.

Rita skimmed the few lines. She looked back at Alice, her clear delight fading into confusion as Alice's eyes filled with tears. 'But that's amazing news, Al. Tom's on his way home. Why aren't you dancing a jig and packing your bags? Oh, don't cry, you silly goose.'

Alice sniffed into a crumpled hankie. 'I am pleased. Of course I am. It's what I've been praying for, hoping for, for so long. And it's finally happening.'

'So?' Rita moved to sit beside her.

'Don't you see? He's coming home, and there'll be parties and prayers, and he'll be the returning hero. And I'll be the transport driver. Or the typist. Or whatever I'm supposed to be. Why are you laughing? It's not funny.'

'Alice! You're jealous! I don't believe it.' Rita sat back, observing her friend as though seeing her for the first time.

Alice twisted the handkerchief into a tight ball. 'No, it's not that. Well, not really. I am a bit jealous, I suppose. You know, all the attention he's going to get. Always gets, actually.' She paused, marshalling her thoughts into some form that Rita would understand. 'It's more that I'll never be able to tell them what we've done. What I've done. Having to live a lie with the people I love the most. They deserve more than that. Tom deserves more. He's given his life for his country and he's going to hear that his little sister has done nothing more than drive lorries or something.'

She surged to her feet and paced their small bedroom. Two, three steps, turn, back. Frustration urging her forward. Rita allowed her to continue, uninterrupted.

'He's going to be so disappointed. They all are. And why shouldn't they be? First, they sacrifice to get me in to Cambridge, expecting me to get on and do better than they ever dreamt. The next they hear, I'm gadding about the countryside, staying in obscure country houses learning to...to... type, for goodness' sake.' Alice stopped pacing, coming to rest inches from Rita. She wrapped her arms around her chest, blew a lock of hair from her forehead. 'Well, doesn't it annoy you? Aren't you just bursting to tell someone — anyone — what you've been doing? Not for the praise or glory. Just so they *know*.'

'You'll never hear everything that Tom has been through, you know. He won't tell the half of it. He won't feel like a hero. He'll think he's a failure for getting caught, for being sent home.' Rita's voice was quiet, so low Alice stopped fidgeting to listen. 'He won't need you to tell him what you've been doing. He'll just know. He'll see it in your eyes. In how skinny you are.' She tried to smile, but Alice noticed the diamond-glisten of tears in her lashes.

'How are you so sure?' Rita shook her head, unable to speak. Alice returned to her place on the bed. She reached for Rita's hand, surprised to find it shaking. 'What's happened, Rita?'

'The last time I was home. You remember? It wasn't for long. But it was all I needed.' Rita bit her lip as the tears, now released, slid down her cheek. 'It was Henry. A family friend. A dear friend. He showed me. We didn't have to say a word, but we knew. I knew why he was home, why he jumped every time a door banged or someone laughed too loudly. And he worked out what I am. Oh, I told the stories and the cover-ups, and everyone else dismissed me without a further thought. My mother thinks I'm a nurse, I think. But Henry kept watching me. Observing me, really. I wasn't sure until I left. He came to say goodbye. Gave me a kiss. Then he held my hand and said, 'Thank you for it all.' We've never mentioned it again. In letters, or whatever.'

Alice bowed her head, ashamed of her self-pity. And yes, jealousy. *How quickly and easily I fall into the traps laid out to catch me.*

Rosie

Between Silk and Cyanide

$\bullet^{-}\bullet \quad ^{---} \quad \bullet\bullet\bullet \quad \bullet\bullet \quad \bullet$

'*This morning, we will be discussing one of the latest books in a recent explosion of World War 2 cyber and spy stories. But this time, it is all the more remarkable, because it is true.*

'*Mr Leo Marks was recruited as head of agents' traffic and communications in 1942. Passed over by Bletchley Park, he instead worked with the Special Operations Executive — SOE as it was known — in Baker Street, London. Like the fictional detective who lived in the same street decades before him, Marks sought clues which would enable him to unlock the mysteries of messages sent by desperate field agents operating behind enemy lines across Europe. He made it his personal mission to eliminate 'indecipherables', as he termed these seemingly unreadable communications...*'

The radio chatted away from its position on the windowsill in the kitchen. Rosie listened with half an ear, wishing her grandparents would tune in to one of the music stations rather than dreary Radio 4.

It was her first morning up and about at a reasonable hour since the bout of flu after her distraught walk to the river the other day. What started as the shivers and a bit of a sniff was soon a full-blown fever, aching joints and a persistent cough. Gran, insisting she stay in bed, nursed her with determined care. They said nothing about the reason for Rosie's mad dash down the lane. But there was lots of fussing, and trips up and down stairs laden with glasses of orange juice and bowls of thick chicken soup. *A guilty conscience, maybe?* Although the guilt lurking in her own conscience gave Rosie enough distress of her own. After all, she shouldn't have flown out of the house the way she did; she could have grabbed a jacket. She could have not gone out at all, trusting the conversation would calm down. Every time Rosie heard Gran's tread on the stairs, she struggled to sit up, to appear grateful for the attention and the supply of nourishment.

'Thanks, Gran. You really don't need to keep bringing me everything, you know.'

Gran placed a tray with a mug of tea, a bowl of chopped fruit, and a plate of toast on Rosie's bedside table. She gathered the clutter of discarded tissues, throwing them in the bin with a slight tut. 'You know I don't mind, Rosie-Posie. Here, have some tea.' She passed the mug over. Steam rose, tickling Rosie's nostrils. She sneezed, holding the cup as steady as possible to avoid spills. 'Bless you! How are you feeling? You look a lot better this morning. And I didn't hear you cough so much last night.'

'Oh, Gran, I've not been keeping you awake, have I?'

Gran waved away the objection. 'Ah, you know how old ladies are. We don't sleep that much anyway, so listening to a bit of a cough doesn't bother us. But are you feeling better?' She placed a hand on Rosie's forehead.

'Yes, thanks, I feel tons better. I thought I'd get up once I've had my tea.'

'Good idea. And it's a beautiful day outside, too. It would be a pity to waste the last few days of your holiday with us by being stuck in bed.' Gran was over by the window, pulling the curtains aside for Rosie to see. 'There you are, blue skies and not a cloud in sight. There is a bit of a breeze, mind you, so I'm not sure you should sit in the garden all day just yet. I thought we might head into town later, go for coffee or something. Bit of a treat.

'But first, let's get you up and get those sheets in the machine. I always need to wash everything when I've been sick. Helps me feel that little episode is behind me and I can get on with enjoying life again.'

'Good idea. Let me hop in the shower, then I'll strip the bed and bring everything down.' Rosie spoke through the half-eaten piece of toast she held to her mouth. 'I'll eat the fruit in the kitchen. With you and Gramps.'

'Oh no, you don't. You can have that shower while I sort out the sheets.' Gran was already grabbing the spare pillows next to Rosie, divesting them of their crumpled pillow cases.

Rosie tried to protest.

'Go on with you, before I change my mind.' Gran shooed Rosie towards the bathroom, flicking the pillow case at her to keep her moving.

Rosie now sat at the kitchen table, the untouched bowl of fruit in front of her. The effort of showering and getting dressed left her without an appetite. Or at least not an appetite for fruit. She kept glancing at the cake tin on the counter, hoping Gran would get the hint. She didn't seem to notice.

The bedsheets billowed on the washing line outside. Mitzy barked in a frenzy each time the fabric blew towards her. Gramps was busy filling the kettle for more tea. 'Silly animal. Why doesn't she just move herself out of the way? More tea, Al? Rosie-P?'

'Yes please, love. Won't you turn the radio up while you're standing there?'

'What for? It's just some book review, isn't it?'

'Mm? Yes, I suppose so.' But Gran wasn't listening to her husband. With her head on one side, she listened intently to the radio announcer.

'*And so, Mr Marks recruited and trained girls from across the country to aid him in his quest.*'

'Well, it wasn't quite like that.' Gran murmured to herself.

Rosie looked at her in surprise. 'Are you talking to yourself, Gran?' She asked nothing further. Curiosity had come close to killing the cat already.

But Gran didn't hear. She focused her attention on the radio. She leaned forward in her chair, straining to catch every word.

'*Of course, until now, this remarkable story has remained strictly secret. They gave official government permission to publish only towards the end of last year. Isn't that right, Mr Marks?*'

Another man began speaking. Gran gasped. Her hand flew to her mouth.

'Gran? Are you alright? You look as though you've seen a ghost.' Rosie was right. All the colour drained from Gran's face. Her eyes were wide, registering shock and something else? Fear?

Gramps was by her side. 'Alice, what is it, love?'

'Please turn that off...' Gran spoke in a whisper. A rustle of autumn leaves caught in the wind. She turned in slow motion to face her husband. Rosie leapt up and over to the window, twisting the volume button on the radio with such force it swayed forwards, in danger of falling into the sink below. The man's voice was silenced. Mitzy barked, making Rosie jump at the noise in the sudden quiet of the kitchen. Gramps was sitting next to Gran, a chair pulled close beside her. Like the man on the radio, they were silenced.

Rosie dared not move, certain the scene would shatter and break into a thousand tiny pieces. It reminded her of a toy kaleidoscope she once owned, a cardboard tube filled with tiny shards of coloured plastic at one end. Each time she turned the tube, the colours danced and shifted, forming a new pattern. She could never replicate one single pattern; once gone, it disappeared forever. The man on the radio had moved the tube and all the pieces of her life, her grandparents' lives were shifting and twisting. And she didn't know why.

Gran was speaking again. Rosie held her breath, straining to hear. 'It's all over, isn't it?' She looked at Gramps, seeking a reassurance that Rosie wasn't sure was his to give.

He reached for her hand, held it to his lips. With his other hand, he stroked hair away from her face. 'Ssh, it doesn't matter now, Al. It never did, not to me, you know.'

What on earth are they both talking about? How come Gramps seems to know, and yet Gran's hardly spoken a word?

'But it does matter, Bill. It always mattered. What was I doing? Where was I? All those unspoken questions. And all the ungiven answers. Four, five years that I've carried everywhere with me, years that shaped and made me, but that I've kept hidden. Even from you, dearest Bill. If he can tell the secrets, then so can I.' She spoke with a fierceness that Rosie didn't recognise as belonging to her grandmother. Not angry, or out of control, but determined. There would be no arguing, no contradicting. She pushed Gramps away, rose to her feet with a rush. 'Rosie, let's take that trip to town. Now. Go and get ready, dear.'

Rosie hurried from the room. Gramps was talking in a slow, careful tone as though calming a child after a tantrum. 'Al, you know you couldn't say some things. You know I couldn't...' Rosie was upstairs, out of range for the rest of the conversation. She took her time putting on make-up and gathering her bag and new summer sandals. She smiled at her reflection in the mirror, excited to be going out after the few days of sickness and bed rest.

By the time she was ready and skipping back down to the hallway, Gran and Gramps were waiting. Gramps wore his tweed flat cap — his favourite headgear of choice, much to Rosie's chagrin. And also to Gran's, if the eye-roll she gave Rosie was anything to go by.

'Ready? Good.' Gran's cheeks were flushed pink. She looked as excited to be going out as Rosie did. 'Are you sure you'll be warm enough with just that thin cardigan, Rosie love? You have been quite sick, you know.'

Before she replied, Gramps defended her. 'Oh, leave her alone, Al. You know these young things, they never feel the cold. Besides, it's a pretty cardigan and I'm sure Rosie doesn't want to cover it up with a boring old coat. Am I right?' He peered at Rosie. She grinned her thanks.

It took them half an hour to drive into town. They took the scenic route and got stuck behind a slow-moving tractor.

'I thought they had to move over, make way when there's a whole queue of cars behind them?' It was a question Gran often asked. Not that any tractor drivers Rosie knew paid much attention to the rule, if there was one. Even Dad kept trundling along until he reached a farm gate he was happy to swing into, rather than pull over before he was ready to stop.

Gramps grunted, concentrating on the road.

After navigating a series of roadworks and a set of defective traffic lights, they reached the main multi-storey car park on the edge of town with a collective sigh of relief. 'Let's hope it's not busy by the time we head for home. Never mind, we're here now. Let's get coffee first.'

They strolled towards the small coffee shop in the centre of town. It was Gran's favourite. Hanging baskets of pansies and trailing geraniums dangled at the windows. The smell of freshly ground coffee and baking greeted them as they pushed the door open. A bell tinkled above them as they entered. Inside, flowers arranged in delicate vases decorated the tables. Tea was served in dainty cups and saucers, gold-rimmed and decorated with intricate designs of flowers or birds. Square lumps of white sugar glistened in the sugar bowl. Rosie stretched across and popped one in her mouth. It was one of her favourite coffee shops, too.

They settled themselves at a table in the window. Gramps removed his cap, tucking it into his jacket pocket. Gran hung her handbag over the back of her chair. A young waitress hurried over.

'Good morning, Mrs Smythers, Mr Smythers. Oh, and you've got your granddaughter with you today as well. How lovely.'

'Hello, Yvonne dear. Yes, this is our granddaughter, Rosie. And how are you?' Gran knew all the staff by name. She waited while Yvonne gave a quick summary of her latest boyfriend — he's kind, Mrs S. Even buys the drinks when we're out — before asking about the cake special of the day.

'A spicy ginger cake. Coffee and walnut. And chocolate, of course.' She gestured behind her to a collection of cakes under glass domes arranged along the counter.

'So, a pot of tea for three and I'll have...coffee and walnut cake, thank you. Bill, for you? Do you want to try the ginger?' Gramps looked up from the newspaper he was already reading. He gave a slight shake of the head. 'No? Alright, chocolate then. And you, Rosie dear?'

'Also chocolate, please Gran.'

Yvonne bustled off to fulfil their order.

'Now, you both wait here for the tea. I want to pop over to WHSmith. Shan't be a minute.' Before either of them protested, Gran slung her bag over her shoulder and headed back out into the street, calling to Yvonne, who was already busy with their order. 'Back in a tick, Yvonne. Don't wait for me before serving. I won't be long.'

Rosie watched as Gran crossed the square and disappeared into the WHSmith shop opposite. Gramps didn't seem to notice his wife's absence. Bored, Rosie leant her elbow on the table, rested her head in her hand and gazed out of the window. A mother pushed a pram past the coffee shop, a young child trailed along behind her. A traffic warden wandered along the row of cars parked nearby. Rosie watched as she peered at one of the meters, then the car next to it. She pulled a book out of her brown shoulder bag. *Uh oh! Ticket coming.*

A man in a blue suit rushed out of a doorway next to the car. He waved his arms at the traffic warden, moving her away. She flicked the book open. The man delved into his pockets, held his palm out to show a pile of coins which he started feeding into the meter under the traffic warden's watchful gaze. She shrugged and closed the ticket book. The man beamed, gave a half bow as he shoved the new ticket under the windscreen wiper, and strode back into the office or shop from where he came.

Rosie chuckled at the pantomime. The traffic warden continued her slow progress down the street.

She was startled by Yvonne returning to the table with a clatter of crockery, and a cheery, 'Here you are Mr. Smythers. Mrs Smythers not back yet then? Hope she isn't much longer, or else her tea will go cold.'

Indeed, Gran was still nowhere in sight. Gramps patted Yvonne's hand. 'Don't you worry, my dear. She always knows when the tea's on the table. It's her sixth sense.' The rattle of the bell over the door behind Rosie announced a new visitor to the café. 'There, what did I tell you? Here she is.'

Gran slid into her seat, careful not to knock Yvonne's elbow as the waitress laid out the tea things. She held an orange WHSmith's bag in her left hand. The pink flush was again visible on her cheeks. It made her appear young and carefree, blown in on a gentle wind. 'What have I missed? My ears were burning — what were you saying about me, Bill?'

'Nothing, dear. Just explaining to Yvonne that you never miss tea.'

Gran turned to Yvonne. 'He is right, you know. Here, let me take that for you. Rosie, your cake.'

Rosie took her plate. 'Wow, that looks huge. Thank you, Gran.'

'It's my pleasure, my dear. I'm just glad you're feeling better, and able to enjoy it.'

Rosie nodded her reply, her mouth bulging with cake.

The lunchtime crowd were arriving by the time the three of them finished with tea. Gramps left a ten pound note under his saucer for Yvonne. She waved an acknowledgement, calling out, 'Cheerio! See you soon. Nice to meet you, Rosie.'

'You too. And thanks for the delicious cake. I never want to eat again, I'm so full.'

The three of them pottered around town for a while, collecting a few bits and pieces for tea, browsing the sale rail in Marks and Spencer. Rosie was fading, dragging her feet as she walked.

'I think it's time we headed back, Bill. Our Rosie here is nearly dead on her feet.'

'Oh, don't hurry home on my account. I'm just a bit tired, that's all.'

'I'll be glad to get home myself, Rosie-P. Enough shopping for me for one day.' Gramps put an arm around Rosie's shoulders and steered her in the direction of the car park.

The car was cool from the shade of the parking garage. Rosie settled on the back seat, resting her head on the side window. Before they'd left the outskirts of town, she was dozing. She woke up to the sound of the car tyres scrunching on the gravel driveway and Mitzy barking a riotous welcome.

'Poor Mitzy. She'll be all upset that she missed an outing with us. I should take her for a walk later this afternoon.' Gran released her seat belt and pushed open the car door. The dog bounded over, snuffling at Gran's legs as she climbed out from her seat. 'Down, Mitzy. Really, we weren't gone that long. Bill, Rosie, I've got some soup for lunch if you fancy it?'

'That would be great, if you don't mind. I'm still so full from that cake, but I need something to tone down the sweetness.' She followed Gran into the house and hung up her coat in the hallway. 'I'm just going up to leave my things, then I'll come and help.'

'Alright, dear. Bill, soup?'

Rosie eased the sandals off her blistered feet. *Why did I wear new shoes for a trip to town? These blisters will take ages to get better.* Dumping her bag on the floor beside her, Rosie leant back on the pillow. *Just a second. Then I'll help with lunch.*

The next thing she knew, Gran was shaking her by the shoulder. 'Did us old things wear you out this morning?' She was laughing, her eyes crinkled and kind. 'That flu really knocked it out of you, didn't it? Do you still want the soup I made? Or do you want to put your feet up for a little longer? You poor old soul...'

Rosie stuck out her tongue. 'Oh, ha-ha, very funny, Gran.' She swung her legs off the bed. 'Race you downstairs.'

By the time they reached the kitchen, the two of them were crying with laughter. 'Oo, you cheeky thing. You had a head start on me. Sneaking past me like that.' Gran grabbed the back of a chair, pretended to catch her breath. 'Taking advantage of an old lady.'

Gramps paused in the act of setting the table, a spoon held in mid-air. He snorted. 'You, an old lady. That'll be the day. Don't give her an inch, Rosie. You know she'll take a yard if you do.'

Gran served the soup — homemade leek and potato — with a roll warmed in the oven.

'That was delicious, Gran, thank you. I'll clear up. Why don't you sit in the conservatory while I finish off here? I'll make tea if you like?' Rosie gathered the bowls and plates.

'I'll do that. Don't worry about tea just yet, though. There's enough liquid sloshing around inside me to float the Titanic. Leave them in the sink for now. I've got something I want to give you.'

Deciding she might as well wash the dishes once she'd carried them as far as the sink, Rosie took a few minutes before joining Gran and Gramps in the conservatory. The last notes of the lunchtime concert poured from the radio. The dappled sunshine played around the open doorway. The air had the warm, sleepy scent of summer. Mitzy was curled up at Gramps' feet, all thoughts of a walk forgotten for the time being.

Gran sat upright and rigid, her hands resting on a parcel in her lap. 'Right then...' her voice cracked. She coughed and tried again. 'Now then, Rosie. Where to start? The beginning I suppose...

'I was meant to go to Cambridge. The University. I'd already started there when my friends — you know, Mavis and Vera — dared me to enter a competition sort of thing. A crossword competition.' Her voice trailed away. The concert crashed towards its finale. Gramps turned the volume down.

'Go on, love.' His voice was gentle, encouraging.

'Well, yes, you know this bit, Bill. It's the rest, isn't it though? Rosie, you see, I won the competition, in a funny kind of way. The prize was an invitation to work with the British government to help during the war.' Another pause, then a sigh. Rosie sat motionless. *What are you saying, Gran?* 'Oh, it seems so silly now, to keep it secret for all this time. Pointless now that *he's* written about it.' She tapped the parcel on her lap, shaking her head. 'It was such a shock to hear him on the radio this morning. That voice. Still the same as the first day I met him, you know. Like being back in that first lecture. Hearing what was really going on. Worrying about your Uncle Tom. And you, Bill, of course.'

Gran held her husband's gaze for a few seconds. Gramps leant forward in his chair, his elbows resting on his knees. He didn't speak.

'I'm getting ahead of myself. Where was I?'

'The crossword puzzle. And the prize...'

'Yes, that's right, dear. The prize. To work with the government during the war. To read messages.'

Rosie slumped in her chair, disappointed. *After all this, you were a secretary? Yes, it is silly to keep that secret. Silly and unkind.* A spark of anger flashed across Rosie's face. 'Well, that doesn't sound so terrible.' She didn't mean to sound so harsh. *Now who's being unkind?* 'Sorry, Gran, carry on.'

'Secret messages, Rosie. From agents. You know, spies.'

'Spies? Like James Bond, you mean?' Rosie was disbelieving. From Miss Moneypenny to 007 in two short sentences.

'Well, funnily enough, Ian Fleming did do a short stint at Bletchley Park.' Gran smiled, relieving some of the tension building in the room. 'But no, not really like James Bond. More, well, Leo Marks.'

'He was the man on the radio this morning, wasn't he?' Gramps spoke for the first time. 'I knew it. Always have, you know. Deep down. I knew, after Bedford, they'd want you for something big.'

Rosie was on the edge of her seat, her head swivelling between her grandparents. 'What? Gramps, what are *you* talking about? What was Bedford? I'm so confused...'

'That's why I bought this earlier. I want you to know, you see, but it really is too hard...too...hidden perhaps?...for me to do it properly. I thought if I gave you this, it would explain most things.' Gran handed the parcel over to Rosie. It was the orange WHSmith's bag. Rosie took it and peered inside. A book.

'I hope this is a bit easier to read than Screwtape, Gran.' She pulled the book from the bag. *Between Silk and Cyanide* by Leo Marks. 'Well, it certainly sounds like a spy book.'

'Of course, I haven't read it myself. I only found out about it this morning. But I do know Mr Marks — slightly — and I'm sure he tells a good story.'

Rosie stopped her flipping through the book. 'Did you say you know him? Oh, my goodness, Gran. How?'

'I worked for him, Rosie.'

Alice

Farewell

●▬ ●▬●● ●● ▬●▬● ●

A lice folded her winter coat and placed it on top of the other clothes. She didn't want it to get crushed in her suitcase, but it was too hot to wear. Especially on the bus to London.

London! Was it almost four years since she was last there? Four years since she met up with the girls. Four years since that day with Bill. She picked up the photograph from where it stood on her bedside table. It was the last thing to be packed. Well, almost. The copy of Screwtape, now well-thumbed, was still there. As was the gift from Rita.

Her roommate was already on her way back home, having left the day before. Alice found her first night alone since arriving at Station 53 unnerving. Of course, there were times when Rita was away on leave, or they were on those wretched alternate shifts. But then the room was inhabited by the essence of Rita, even if not by her presence. Clothes strewn across the end of the bed or hanging over the wardrobe door. The waft of Rita's perfume lingered long after the last generous spray her friend gave before leaving the room. Books threatened to topple off the bedside table, joined by a dirty cup and saucer, and some unfinished letters. All now gone, either packed into a trunk suitable for a world cruise, or given to friends and co-workers with notes of love and undying friendship.

The Bible was different. It was new. Rita said she bought it especially for Alice the last time she was home on leave. Its red cover embossed with gold lettering polished to a shine that would do an army officer proud. Alice picked it up, breathed in the smell of leather. And the scent of Rita.

'Rita, you shouldn't have. This must have cost a fortune.' Alice was mortified when she unwrapped the gift. She could never afford something like this for Rita.

They were lounging in the shade of the beech tree at the edge of the garden. It was a rare moment of quiet at the station; everyone sent out on their missions, and no new recruits arriving. The skeds were less frequent, and translated with less urgency. There were rumours about a final push across Europe. Alice wasn't sure if she believed it or not. Maybe it was the calm before yet another storm.

'That's for me to know and you not to find out. I wanted to get it for you. It was in pride of place in one of the shop windows back home. As soon as I saw it, I thought of you.' She took the Bible from Alice, tracing her fingers over the surface of the cover. 'I even wrote in it. Look.'

Alice leant over to see. The whorls and curls of Rita's handwriting were unmistakable.

But when you give alms, do not let your left hand know what your right hand is doing, so that your alms may be in secret; and your Father who sees in secret will reward you. (Matt 6:3-4)

Alice frowned. 'Why that verse? Do I need to give some money away or something?'

'Don't be silly, of course not. Alright, I know that bit talks about money. I'm not that uneducated in these things. Of course, alms are money. But don't you think they can also be a different sort of gift? The gift of ourselves?'

Alice was at a loss for words. This wasn't how the conversation usually went with Rita. Eve maybe, but not Rita.

'Don't look so surprised. We've given four years of our lives to this war, right? To helping others fight and win, without ever leaving the comfort of home.' Alice started to protest. Rita laughed. 'Well, you know what I mean. It's not like they parachuted us into France or anything exciting like that, did they? But we've given, Alice, we really have.'

Alice couldn't disagree. It wasn't as glamourous as the war fought by some. Nor as talked about as, say, Mavis and her land girls or Vera in the factory. But it was war, nonetheless. And there was a cost. Alice watched a swift arc through the air, its distinctive wing shape silhouetted against the blue of a perfect spring day. So many seasons come and gone — the stifling heat of summer, the bitter cold of winter, in an endless cycle of years all blurred into one. So few visits home. So many broken friendships, unable to carry the burden of stilted conversations and censored letters. Dreams of studying, or travel, even of courtship and marriage, lay dusty and unrealised in a distant corner of the heart. Was it worth it? Was it really a gift she gave? Or was it a treasure, stolen?

She thought of Tom. Her one trip home to see him had been too traumatic to repeat. Did he think it was worth it? Was his happiness, his peace, the gift he gave? Would any of them really know the price he paid?

'Yes, you might be right, Rita. Gifts — alms — given without anyone knowing. That's courage, isn't it?'

It was the only time they spoke in such a way. Even the farewells of yesterday were light and meaningless.

'You'll visit, won't you, Alice darling?'

'Only after you visit me.' They both knew it wouldn't happen. It was the easiest way. They could never meet under normal circumstances; the pretence would crush them. Family would want to know how they met and where; friends would intrude on their private memories. No, better a quick hug and cheery goodbye.

Well, that was what Alice believed yesterday. Today she wasn't so sure. She looked around their shared space, still clutching the Bible in both hands. 'Oh, Rita. I'm going to miss you. I hope you do write...'

'Talking to yourself, Miss Stallard?' Alice jumped and whirled around to face the door. It was Miss Rivers.

'Goodness, did I say that out aloud?'

'You did, yes.' Miss Rivers was in her full uniform, her hair pinned back under her cap. 'I'm just doing the last rounds, making sure all you girls are on your way. Is that everything?' She indicated the open suitcase.

'Yes. I'm all packed, thank you.' Alice bent to place the Bible next to Screwtape and pulled the lid of the case down over her belongings.

'You've done well, Alice, really you have. We're so proud of you. I'm so proud of you.' Miss Rivers turned as though to leave. She paused at the door. 'I understand it's hard to make sense of all this. You know, to hear what you have. To know what you do. And to share it with no one. You will carry this with you for the rest of your life, wherever you go. That is your burden. But this victory? That is your joy. Treasure it, my dear.'

My joy. The words raced and danced through her mind as Alice lugged her suitcase down the driveway towards the gate, to leave for the last time. The guard saluted her approach.

'Goodbye, Miss. And thank you.' He pushed the gate open. Standing aside to let her pass, he removed his cap and gave her a bow.

Alice smiled even as tears slid down her face. 'Thank you.' She watched while he closed the gate, watched as he retreated into his guard hut.

Turning away from him, Alice heard the distant rumble of an approaching aircraft. Lifting her hand to shield her eyes, she scanned the sky for any sign of the plane. Far away on the horizon, a speck appeared, growing larger and more distinct as it approached. Within seconds it was in full view, the air pulsing with the deep roar of its engines; a spitfire. Of all the planes flying above Grendon over the last four years, the spitfire was Alice's favourite. And Rita's. It was the favourite of all the FANY girls. The spitfire was romance and courage and bravery and everything they all wanted the war to be. Even on the days when it wasn't. Especially on those days.

Alice lifted her hand in a wave of greeting. *Silly, he won't be able to see me down here. I'm a dot on the road, a blur as he passes.*

Was it her imagination, or did the wings dip a fraction? *Had he seen me, after all?*

She lowered her hand, twisting her head to gaze one last time up the empty driveway behind her, imagining the grand old house hidden in the trees basking in the late afternoon sunshine.

'Goodbye, Station 53.' The roar of engines drowned out her words, as the spitfire soared out of sight.

Rosie

Truth

●ー● ーーー ●●● ●● ●

Rosie burst into the kitchen. Gran and Gramps were deep in conversation at the table, untouched mugs of tea in front of them. 'Gran, is this you?' Rosie poked the book under Gran's nose. 'This bit, about the FANY girls and working at Grendon? "No more indecipherables". That's what the note is about, isn't it?'

Rosie waved the book again. She sniffed. 'Is something burning? Oh, the toast...' A curl of smoke rose from the toaster. The automatic pop-up button was broken. She hurried over to switch it off at the plug. The charred remains of a slice of toast shot into the air. 'Well, I don't think you'll be eating that one. Can I make you some more?'

'No, thank you, dear. I don't feel much like breakfast this morning. I've even let my tea go cold, look.'

'Well, at least let me make another pot. I'm dying for a cup.'

'Alright, then. Here you are.' Gran pushed the teapot in Rosie's direction. 'What were you saying?'

Rosie busied herself filling the kettle and finding fresh tea bags. She picked the book up from the counter where it had dropped when she tried to rescue the toast. 'The book, Gran. I started reading it last night, but I was too tired and the style is a bit, well, funny. So, I didn't get far. But then I started it again this morning.'

Forgetting about the tea, she riffled through the pages until she found the part she was talking about. 'It says here he decided to pay an unauthorised visit to the "girls at Grendon". Explain to them why their job was so important. And then he put up a message on the board.

"There shall be no more indecipherables." Gran! That was you. You were there. Weren't you?'

Gran sat still and silent for so long, Rosie was about to return to tea-making, certain she was being shut out again. *I just want to know you, Gran. Like, properly. No more hiding, no more secrets. Tell me.*

'It was foolish of me to keep that note. Or at least to keep it where I did. I should have known it would be found someday. Maybe I wanted it to be found? I don't know.' She lifted weary eyes to her granddaughter's face, a face lit with the excitement of discovery and the romance of a war she would never really understand. Could never understand. 'Yes, Rosie, I was there. That was my home for close on five years.'

Rosie abandoned her place by the kettle, moving over to the table and pulling out a chair opposite Gran and Gramps. She rested her elbows in front of her, eager for more to be revealed and the story to be continued.

Gran was twisted in her seat, facing Gramps. 'It's how I know Rita, Bill dear. I know you've always wondered...'

'But never asked.'

'No, you didn't.' Gran's voice was soft, grateful. 'Thank you.'

Rosie knew the conversation was over before it even started. Again.

Rosie pressed on with the book, reading bits of it aloud in the hope that it would stir some memory, spark some kind of reaction. But Gran avoided answering any of her questions, or changed the subject each time Rosie broached the subject.

At night, in the stillness of the silent house, Rosie overheard her grandparents from their bedroom across the hallway. Gramps spoke in a low rumble, short exchanges followed by long pauses, giving Gran time to answer. Rosie couldn't understand it. She wanted to tell everyone how amazing and clever and important Gran was, to make them read the book and find out for themselves what took place behind the closed doors of some of the grandest homes in the country. And yet here Gran was, seeming able to talk about it only in whispered tones in the dead of night. During the day, she continued as though there was nothing of any interest to discuss; it was all runner beans and church events.

Rosie lay staring at the ceiling, trying to catch fragments of what was being said.

'...you were the best in class...I did think...but letters don't say, no, can't...' Gramps, gentle and understanding.

'...sorry...know how it was...wanted to...'

She fell asleep to the sound of lives tilting and shifting and rearranging.

By the time Rosie finished reading Silk and Cyanide, she was even more desperate to hear Gran's side of the story. To know first-hand, not just to read it on a page written by a stranger.

Before she could embark on another round of questions, Gramps intervened. 'That's enough for today, Rosie. Let's take Mitzy for a walk, shall we? The fresh air will do us good.'

'Are you coming, Gran?'

'No, dear, I'll stay here, I think. I'm a bit tired. Maybe I'm coming down with something. Your 'flu perhaps.'

Rosie grabbed Mitzy's lead. 'Oh, I hope not. Yes, you stay here and rest. You can read some of the book.'

A slight shudder passed over Gran. 'Maybe another time...'

'She doesn't want to read it, does she, Gramps?' They were halfway down the lane. Mitzy, released from the constraints of her lead, was sniffing along the hedgerows.

'She lived it, Rosie. She doesn't need to read it. She's spent the last, what, fifty years pretending none of it happened? That's half a century of silence.' He paused, waiting for Mitzy to catch up with them. 'The war was hard for all of us. But it's especially hard for those who couldn't talk about it. I don't think anyone knows the half of what I was doing. It didn't seem important by the end. We just wanted it over. So, to drag it all up again? No. I don't blame her for not wanting to read your book.'

They continued in silence until they reached the bridge over the stream. Slow ripples meandered and eddied around the rocks with a gentle murmur.

'Are you cross with me, Gramps? For wanting to know?' Rosie's voice was small.

'Cross? No, child, how can I be cross when I want to know just as much as you do?' He spread his hands out on the stonework in front of them. 'I always knew she did something different during the war. It was the fact she never spoke of it that gave it away. All the rest of the girls — Mavis, Vera, some others we were friendly with at the time — they were all full of silly stories and escapades. Whereas Alice — Gran — never said anything. Oh, she mentioned a couple of parties and spoke about Eve and Rita a fair bit. But never where the parties took place, or where she'd met her other friends.'

'When did you meet her again? She said you worked together for a bit. Bedford?'

Gramps chuckled. 'Ha, Bedford. The "typing course" she was on. I think even the family she was billeted with knew that wasn't true. Though I'm sure she never let the cat out of the bag.' They watched a duck glide beneath them. 'Mitzy, don't even think about it. We went our separate ways after that. They sent me to Scotland to work with a group trying to get into — or out of — Norway...'

'Norway? But that gets mentioned in the book. Apparently, there was an engineer working at the factory who was willing to help the resistance. He sent tons of communications back with detailed information, but he was a rubbish coder. It took Leo Marks hours and hours to figure out his messages.'

'Really? That is interesting. I met a few of the team sent to help with that operation. They all struck me as very clever. I don't think they would have trouble with their Morse.'

'I wonder if Gran knew about him? Do you think I could ask? You know, as it links with what you were doing?'

Gramps stared down at the stream. He was silent for so long, Rosie wasn't sure if he'd heard.

'Gramps...?'

'Do you know, I think you could? If your gran knew how she helped — *who* she helped — it might help her make sense of it all. Shall we give it a try?'

'Yes, please. If you don't think it will upset her?'

'If it does, it will be my fault. We'll figure something out, don't you worry.'

They ambled back up the hill, Mitzy panting alongside them.

'Alice, we're back.' Gramps called from the hallway while he hung up Mitzy's lead. 'Where are you?'

'In the conservatory. It's lovely in here. Not so hot. How was your walk?'

Gramps bent down, kissing his wife on the top of her head. 'Al love, we want to ask you something? No, wait, don't run away. I think it will help.'

Gran sighed and settled back into her chair. 'I won't get any peace until I let you interrogate me, will I? Go on, then.' She folded her arms, fixing her attention on Rosie.

'Well, Gran, did you know the names of the agents whose messages you decoded?'

'Decrypted. And no, of course not. That was definitely Top Secret.' She paused, remembering something. 'We did know a few code names, though. They were silly, types of vegetable, things like that. Why?'

'So, if you didn't know the actual agents, did you know where they were working? Like, where the messages were being sent from.'

Gran uncrossed her arms and tapped a pattern with her fingers. 'I'm not entirely sure if we did or not. I think on some occasions, we did. Really, I haven't thought about all of this for years, you know. It's hard to recollect those kinds of details.'

Rosie wasn't convinced. Neither, it seemed, was Gramps. 'Mm, so you say. I've never known you to forget a thing in your life. Or mine, for that matter.' He reached for her hand. 'Would you know if you ever dealt with anyone connected to Norway?'

'Norway. Now, why does that ring a bell?' Gran relapsed into silence. She closed her eyes. If it wasn't for the constant tap, tapping of Gran's fingers, Rosie could have assumed she was sleeping.

'Gran, that's Morse code, isn't it? Dot dot dot, dash dash dash, dot dot dot. SOS!'

'Oh yes, I suppose it is. I hadn't noticed.' Her eyes widened. She stared at Gramps. 'Norway, you said, didn't you? I know why I remember that. Oh goodness, one of the worst nights of my life. There was one agent who made terrible mistakes all the time. In his coding, in his Morse. It was awful. I got stuck with one of his messages. Mr Marks usually did them. I wonder why he didn't that night?'

She retreated into her memories again.

'Gran? You were saying?'

'What? Oh, yes. Anyway, nothing more to tell, really. We managed to work out the message at about dawn. I remember the birds singing as I wrote it out. That was a close-run thing, I can tell you. Ow, Bill, you're squeezing my hand rather tightly. Are you alright?'

'It was you. You saved us, Alice.'

Gran shook her head. 'What are you talking about?'

'It's in the book, Gran. There was some big event supposed to happen at a power plant or something in Norway — '

'Heavy water. Used for making nuclear bombs. We simply couldn't let the Germans have it, you see — '

'And anyway, there was an engineer at the factory, and he said he'd help the Allied agents with information. He even came to England. They showed him how to transmit messages, use poems, all that sort of thing. But he was here for only three weeks, so didn't really grasp it very well.'

'That message you got, Alice, the close-to-impossible one. From someone in Norway. It must have been from him.'

'What, the indecipherable of all indecipherables? Yes, it may have been, I suppose.' Gran paused, her head on one side as she considered this new possibility. 'But what are you so excited about that for, Bill? It was bad, but it was only one of so many.'

'It was such a critical time. The Germans were so close to succeeding in their plan. It would have ended the war if they had. Ended it the wrong way...'

Rosie watched as realisation spread across Gran's features. She gasped, her free hand plucking at the fabric of her armchair, eyes wide and unblinking. 'Oh...Bill...you went to Scotland, didn't you?'

'And the Norway missions were launched from Scotland.' Rosie wanted to finish the story. 'Weren't they, Gramps?'

'Yes, Rosie-Posie, they were.' But he wasn't looking at his granddaughter. He had eyes only for Gran.

With just a few days left of her stay with Gran and Gramps, Rosie was determined to spend as much time as possible following Gran down the pathway of memories. It wasn't an easy journey. At times, Gran was full of stories, regaling Rosie and Gramps with tales of a party or dance the girls of Grendon had attended.

'I remember one time. We hitched a lift back from Oxford. A young farmer bringing supplies to us, or something like that. Anyway, he was so distracted by Rita and her silly chit-chat, he missed our turning completely. Before we realised it, we were miles from where we should be. And of course, back then, all the village signposts were taken down — to confuse any German airmen who happened to crash land in Britain, or so we were told. Confused us locals, more to the point. We were lost for hours. We nearly missed our shift. Goodness, that would have been trouble. Rita laughed about it for days.'

Other times, she struggled to share more than a sentence or two. Dark shadows flitted across her face, clouds hiding the sunshine of fun and laughter.

'I felt for the children, the evacuees. They looked so lost. There was a party. Everyone went...everyone who wasn't working. We wanted to cheer up the poor mites a bit, ease the strain of being away from home. There was a brother and sister. They didn't join in the games. Didn't eat, I don't think. I sat next to the lady they were staying with. Didn't know that's who she was at first. Their home was bombed, she said. Parents didn't get out in time. She thought there was a granny too.' Silence. 'I think I'll go upstairs for a rest.'

Gran pushed out of her chair and shuffled across the room, stooped with the burden of another's loss.

'I'll never forget their eyes, you know. They were blue. Like yours, Rosie. So like yours.'

Rosie toiled on an arduous journey of discovery herself. Each night, as evening shadows melted into moonlit darkness, she rode a dipping, rushing rollercoaster ride of emotion. Overhearing Gran and Gramps talking on into the small hours, chasing the missing years, she tossed and turned in restless agitation.

Her young ears, alert to her grandparents' whispered conversations, caught snippets that puzzled and intrigued, challenged and confused her. It was nothing like the history books or films she'd sat through in the last two years of A-level study. Those had been two-dimensional, the people and passions as black-and-white as the photographs and newsreels in which they featured. This was different. This was heartache and loss, and decisions made and held, regardless of the sorrow trailing in their wake.

Why, Gran? Why didn't you just break the rules and tell someone? Tell Gramps, at least. And Gramps, what about you? You didn't ask, you didn't question. I would want someone who loved me to know me inside out, to know everything about me. I would tell. And I would ask. No secrets. No lies. Surely that counts for more than winning a fight I didn't start? And as for the government, why did they ask that of you both? Surely that's against your rights? Or something.

Sympathy swooped in, overtaking anger.

Oh Gran, why did you carry this for so long, with no one knowing? All that you've seen and heard, held inside for all these years. And then to have it spilled out over everyone's breakfast tables, with the morning news. Letting us believe you were just a typist, when really, you saved lives. How you must have bitten your lip.

Pride followed, mingled with resolve.

I want courage like that. Courage to be silent, to endure, to see beyond myself and my selfish dreams.

Rosie

The Secret

•⁻• ⁻⁻⁻ ••• •• •

'Are you ready, Rosie? Mum will be here any minute, I'm sure.'

'Yes, Gran, trying to do up my suitcase.' Rosie grunted with effort, squashing the contents of the overstuffed bag in an attempt to pull the zip closed. 'What on earth have I got in here? We didn't go shopping that much, did we?'

Gran appeared in the doorway, chuckling. 'That does look like a lot. Hang on, let me help. Here, you lean on that corner and I'll pull it closed. There. Teamwork!'

'Thanks Gran.' Rosie planted a kiss on a wrinkled cheek. 'And thanks for a really great holiday. It was the best holiday ever, honestly.'

'Ah, it's had its moments, that's for sure. But all's well that ends well, I think, don't you?' Before Rosie could reply, a car horn sounded in the lane below the window. 'That'll be them, then. I'll get your dad to come up and fetch that case. Don't you try to lift it.'

As she stepped out of the bedroom, the doorbell rang.

'Coming, coming.'

Rosie hung back for a couple of seconds. She stroked the duvet cover smooth, patted the pillows. She was eager to get home, to meet up with her friends and wait for their exam results together. She wanted to help on the farm, enjoy the rest of summer in the fields. She wanted to plan for going to university. But she was sad to be leaving — leaving Gran and Gramps and Mitzy, leaving the slow, laid-back days of tea and cake and lazing in the garden. And leaving the story of a life she hadn't known existed and now couldn't bear to lose.

'Rosie? Are you coming down?'

'Yes, sorry, just finishing up.' She took a final glance around the room, smiling at the two books left on her bedside table. 'Thank you for opening the door, Screwtape. And thank you for leading us through, Mr Marks...On my way!'

She hurtled down the stairs and into Mum's waiting arms.

'Well, hi, Rosie. It's good to see you too.' Mum was laughing, pushing Rosie away to get a better look at her. 'You look as though you've had a great holiday.'

'I have, Mum. There's so much to tell you.' Rosie gulped, noticed Gran and Gramps standing motionless in the doorway to the kitchen, arms linked together as they waited. Mum raised an eyebrow in question. 'Yes, you see, we've been growing beans and marrows for the harvest festival competition. You must come and see. I'm sure Gran is going to win.'

Without waiting for Dad to come in from the car, Rosie dragged Mum off towards the garden. She heard the exhalation of held breath as she stepped around Gran and Gramps, felt the release of anxiety like a cool breeze on a summer's day. She was pleased.

It's not my secret to tell, is it Gran?

THE END

Afterword

December 2018

We arrived in the car park in the near dark of a winter's afternoon. Glancing at our watches, we hoped there would be enough of the day left to properly explore the site. At least the tickets allowed for a repeat visit, should we be able to find the time.

We opened the doors and were greeted by an icy blast of air and a flurry of snowflakes. As we got out of the car, we shuffled our way into hats and gloves and scarves. Our South African skins shivered.

'We'll see you inside.' I called to Craig as I ran towards the entrance, kids following behind.

'Yes, thank you...' Craig laughed as he struggled to grab the bag out of the car and lock up before dashing in our direction.

Pushing open the glass doors, we found the inside of the building only slightly warmer than the car park. As we made our way to the ticket office, I looked around at the yellow painted walls and green doors and window frames. I was less than inspired.

'Welcome to Bletchley Park!' The attendant on the other side of the ticket counter greeted us with a smile, outstretched hand awaiting our money.

My sister lives a short distance from the town of Bedford where Bletchley Park is situated. On one visit to see my sister, my parents went with friends to explore the World War II secret communications centre. And they were enthralled. So much so that they returned several times,

and encouraged my family and I to go the next time we were visiting the
UK from our home in South Africa.

So here we were, paying for a full-price ticket at the end of a cold, wet
day to walk around an essentially outdoor museum. I hoped we weren't
wasting our money.

A few steps beyond the ticket office, and I was sure we weren't.

Arranged around the large, echoing main hall were photographs of
women hunched over desks, display cases of notebooks and machines,
quizzes for the kids to try. We browsed and played. And glanced at our
watches.

'If we want to see anything else today, we'd better get a move on.' Craig
led the way through the main doors out into the grounds of Bletchley
Park.

We stood in the gloom of a winter's afternoon and looked around us.
To our right were a series of low, brick-built huts, green roofs glistening
with the still-falling rain. Ahead loomed Bletchley Mansion, all Victorian
gables and red brick walls. In the middle, surrounded by muddy grass
lawns, a fountain splashed into a pond.

Having collected a map from the Visitors' Centre which we now
consulted, we realised we were going to have a hard time deciding what to
see and what to miss, hopefully for another visit. With the cold chilling
us to the bone, we hurried over to the museum displays housed in Block
B to better understand codes and how they are broken.

Now, I have to confess, I am no mathematician. Nor am I any good at
crossword puzzles or anagrams. The displays in Block B left me feeling
a little dispirited and, frankly, not very clever! Having wandered around
gazing blankly at all the tricks of a coder's trade, I decided it was time to
move on.

And it was in Hut 3 that the world of Bletchley Park finally touched
my heart, left those familiar footprints in the dust of my soul. For here,
amidst the clever reconstructions and the sound effects, the draughty
passageways and the dim lighting was a story of secrets. Not the secrets
of nations fighting nations, but the secrets of men and women huddled
around heaters in the cold mid-winter, or swatting flies in a sultry
summer; of trying to stay alert when presented with yet another page
of letters and numbers, the understanding of which could mean the

difference between winning and losing, life or death; and of not being able to tell anyone, even for years afterwards, the service they performed for their country.

After the tour of the site, we spent a happy half-hour browsing the shop, in particular the bookshelves. We couldn't resist buying a volume — or three.

Once back home in South Africa, my fascination with the secret side of World War II grew. I heard a radio interview with Giles Milton, author of 'The Ministry of Ungentlemanly Warfare: Churchill's Mavericks: Plotting Hitler's Defeat' and promptly added that book to my collection. I found a copy of 'The Heroes of Telemark: The True Story of the Secret Mission to Stop Hitler's Atomic Bomb' by writer and TV presenter Ray Mears and devoured that; the story of sabotage and secrecy in the frozen highlands of Norway became more personal when I discovered Craig's sister-in-law, Cecilie, had spent some of her teenage years living in the region.

And then a friend leant us 'Between Silk and Cyanide: A Codemaker's War 1941-1945' by Leo Marks. I was captivated. Young women recruited to decrypt some of the most vital messages of the War, housed in country estates dotted about the English countryside, keeping the secret of their wartime lives for generations to come. Bletchley Park, the enigma machine, Alan Turing — all so well known. These girls? Far less so.

It is these 'secret lives' who inspired this novel. I hope you enjoyed meeting Alice and her granddaughter Rosie as much as I enjoyed creating them. Alice, her family and her friends exist only in my imagination, but by making use of information available in the public domain, I trust they have lived a believable life on these pages.

Finally, I pray that, like Alice, you would discover your own secret life is seen and rewarded by your Father in heaven.

But when you give alms, do not let your left hand know what your right hand is doing, so that your alms may be in secret; and your Father who sees in secret will reward you. (Matt 6:3-4)

Anna
JENSEN

Acknowledgments

As with any novel, there are many people I need to thank for their time and effort in crafting Secret Lives.

So here goes. Thank you to...

Craig, Caragh and Leal for listening to all the early ideas and flights of fancy before the story becomes real.

Alison Theron for an excellent first draft reading. Your corrections and comments were invaluable.

Gwethlyn Meyer for your friendship and gentle correction when I'm not writing at my best.

Allyson Koekhoven of Allyna Author Services for your editing of the final manuscript.

My mum, Maureen McNally, for driving me to Grendon Underwood for a visit to what is now a prison. I'm grateful neither of us were arrested for our surreptitious attempts at taking a few photos!

My sister, Jane McKinnon, for taking me along the lanes and backroads around Banbury until we found Overthorpe Hall, now the Carrdus School.

The staff of the Carrdus school and to Susie Carrdus, former school principal. It was lovely to be in touch with someone who walked the same corridors, popped in and out of the same rooms as my Alice and her FANY friends.

James, of the Grendon Underwood Village and Archive, for the time spent poring over grainy photographs and slides in search of anything which could add flavour to my story. I'm happy to report we found a few bits and pieces which I have incorporated into the time Alice and Rita spent at Grendon Hall, Station 53a. If you'd like to visit the archive, you'll find them on Facebook.

Ian and Erika Biscoe, leaders of Emmanuel Church in Bicester, for allowing me to share my writing journey with you and for introducing me to more of the people and places associated with this special piece of history.

Also thanks to Peter and Carol Hill, also of Emmanuel Church, for an afternoon chatting over coffee and gaining further insight into the history of Grendon Hall.

Thank you to the fantastic group of friends who read Secret Lives, shared their reviews and helped me spot the errors I'd missed. It really does take a village to raise a child — and it takes a team to launch a book.

About Anna

I'm a British expat who has lived in South Africa for a little over twenty years. My husband and I live with our two teenage children on the east coast, a few miles north of the city of Durban. We overlook the Indian Ocean where we have the privilege of watching dolphins and whales at play.

My first book *The Outskirts of His Glory* was published in May 2019. The book is a Christian devotional and poetry collection, exploring the many surprising ways that God can speak to us through His creation. I have drawn on my travels in and around South Africa, as well as further afield, to hopefully inspire each of us to slow down and perhaps listen more carefully to the whispers of His ways (Job 26:14) that are all around us.

Since publishing *Outskirts*, I have had the privilege of speaking at a number of local churches and even have a weekly slot on a Christian radio station. I have also continued writing by contributing to a variety of blogs and online writing communities as well as developing my own website and blog.

Want to know more? Check out my website at www.annajensen.co.uk

Make it easier to hear about all things Anna and sign up for my free more-or-less monthly newsletter. You'll receive a gift of the ebook, 'A little book of words' when you do — which you get to keep even if you decide to unsubscribe later. You'll also be sent an invitation to join my Subscriber Family Birthday Club. Sign up today at www.annajensen.co.uk/news

Follow me across my various social media platforms. Or email me directly at hello@annajensen.co.za I'd love to connect with you.

Scan the QR code to access clickable links.

The Ripples Through Time series

Ripples Through Time is a series of novels telling stories of the past and showing how they inspire our present. Stories of how God takes the ordinary and transforms it into something extraordinary. The smallest of stones, tossed into smooth water, will create waves; concentric circles spreading outward to reach beyond the immediate or seen. So too, the seemingly insignificant actions of today can leave ripples that are felt into eternity.

There is the village of Eyam and her inhabitants' love and sacrifice which saved a generation, the Bletchley Park codebreakers' dedication to fight a war far from public praise, the adventure and ingenuity of diamond hunters settling in the impermanence of the Namibian desert, and the discovery of a 2000-year-old fishing vessel believed to date to the time of Jesus and his disciples. Campaigns and conflicts, castles and cottages – tales to uncover and histories to unfold.

These are the pebbles and the ripples they leave.

The *Ripples Through Time* series is dedicated to my personal mentor, author Marion Ueckermann, who sadly passed away on 25 June 2021. She included a devotion entitled *Reflections in Pebbles* in the multi-author boxed set, *In All Things* (a set which I also contributed to). I would like to leave you with this quote from Marion:

'God has chosen you to be His pebble in the sea of humanity. What ripples of hope could emit from the splashes of your life? What giants could tumble from the impact of one small stone, one random act of kindness?'

May you, like Marion, become a pebble in the hand of God, leaving ripples in the world as you pass.

More From Anna

I f you enjoyed this novel, you might like to check out my other books. You'll find all the books on Amazon, or you can buy directly from my website www.annajensen.co.uk

 A Candle for Christmas
Four candles. Four stories.
One Christmas Day.
The vicar of St Saviour's is preparing for Christmas. Four Sundays, four services, four advent candles to light.

Richard loves Christmas. And he loves the ritual of the advent candles. Only this year is different. Memories and regrets threaten to spoil his favourite season.

Joelle is tired. Tired of the streets; tired of the weather. Tired of being unseen. Could the preparations for Christmas at St Saviour's herald a new beginning?

Tamara knows this Christmas is going to be different. She's been planning for weeks. But will it be in the way she expects or is there a surprise in store?

Ellen realises her new-found freedom isn't as wonderful as she expected it to be. Can she retrace her steps and find restoration? Or is it too late?

Christmas Day. Richard ignites the final candle...

The '14 Days of Devotions' Series

A Seat in a Garden
14 days of reflections and poems from seven gardens of Africa
What better place to enjoy the presence of God than from a seat in a secluded garden? Take a moment to wander with Anna Jensen through seven of her favourite African gardens in this book of 14 daily devotions.

Discover with her the delights of quiet contemplation, finding glimpses of the Creator in every leaf and flower. Pause and rest for reflection on a 'bench' – a space created through poetry and prayer.

Rugged Roads
14 stories and poems from seven journeys in Africa
Take a journey off the beaten track and enjoy the drama on seven journeys of adventure and discovery through South Africa and beyond. Take the warned-against route from Harare to Victoria Falls, Zimbabwe, or discover the twists and turns of a mountain pass into Lesotho. Stumble through the sand of a Namibian desert or feel the adrenalin rush of being charged by a rhino or threatened by an elephant. In this collection of 14 daily devotions, reflect on the whispers of God heard when driving off-road.

Through stories and Scripture readings, poetry and prayer, find the joy of choosing 'rugged roads'.

Poems and Prayers
14 reflections from a year of change
The year 2020 started like any other – full of promise and hope. Within a few months, it was clear this was to be no ordinary year. By March, the World Health Organisation had declared a global pandemic of the hitherto-unknown coronavirus Covid-19. For Anna Jensen, it was a time of bewilderment, but also an opportunity; an opportunity to press in afresh and hear all that God wants to whisper.

In this collection of 14 daily devotions, Anna reflects on those early months of the pandemic, articulating her thoughts through poems and prayerful reflections.

A Gratitude Challenge
14 days of choosing thanks
In November 2020, Anna Jensen embarked on her first 'gratitude challenge', a series of social media posts giving thanks on a daily basis.

Anna found herself being grateful for the serious and the silly, and everything in between (on one of the days, she was thankful for shoe shops, after her son climbed into the car from school with a 'flapping sole', which needed an urgent remedy).

This book of 14 days of devotions is the pick of Anna's month of gratitude, shared with you in the hope that you will see the delight in the daily and the mundane. There really is so much to be thankful for.

Other books by Anna

The Outskirts of His Glory
Join Anna Jensen and her family as they travel to seek out and experience the odd and unexpected of God's creation.

Captivated by the Creator (paperback only)

Be inspired afresh by the voice of the Creator through the beauty of His creation. Be guided by Anna Jensen as she describes her own journey of discovery through articles and poems. This beautiful journal contains pictures for you to colour and space for your own thoughts and prayers.

Twenty Years an Expat

Read about Anna's experiences when she left her native land and learned to embrace the different and the new as she settled in South Africa. At times funny, at others poignant, the one constant is God's love and purpose for Anna in all she experiences.

Find all my books on Amazon

GIVEN LIVES

A village. A plague.
An extraordinary love

Anna
JENSEN

Given Lives.

A village. A plague. An extraordinary love.

Foreword

E yam (pronounced Eem) is a small hamlet in Derbyshire in the north of England. I grew up in the city of Sheffield, a mere half hour's drive away from this ancient village which we visited often on school trips and family outings.

Stone cottages cluster around a central green, dominated by the tower of St Lawrence's Church. Lush fields populated by sheep and wildflowers, quiet woodlands and gently rippling streams create a haven of peace and tranquillity.

Although it's a beautiful destination and a great place for a day out in the country, that isn't the reason I climbed on a school bus as a ten- or eleven-year-old and lurched out of the city clutching my lunchbox and pencil case, headed for Eyam. Nor was it the reason why I have returned again and again over the years. I go because I am drawn to a story – a story of seventeenth-century England, of tragedy and of triumph.

The mid-seventeenth century was a time of turmoil across England, Scotland and Ireland. In January 1649, the reigning king, Charles I, was executed and a new Commonwealth of England declared, led by Oliver Cromwell. A bitter civil war was the result, with Parliamentarians (Roundheads) pitted against Royalists (Cavaliers). Thousands died on both sides; communities were destroyed and families torn apart.

On Cromwell's death in 1658, his son, Richard, took over the Protectorate, a move which proved unpopular and was doomed to fail. By 1660, the son of Charles I had been returned to England and crowned King Charles II. The Restoration had begun.

Not only was the monarchy restored and parliament put in its place by King Charles II's coronation, but the church was also reformed. During the Commonwealth period a new breed of preachers and church leaders had flourished. Their strict teaching and behaviour led to them being known as the non-conformists or Puritans. Orthodox church services and formats were removed, and the concept of the divine right of kings abolished – an idea that was understandably unpopular with the newly crowned king.

By 1662, all such ministers had been outlawed by the Uniformity Act. Everyone was required to follow the prescribed pattern of service as laid down in the Book of Common Prayer. Anyone refusing to do so was banned from the church and forced to move away from their congregations.

Amidst all this change and upheaval, an outbreak of a disease in the poor St Giles district of London seemed of little consequence at first. In May 1665 the number of deaths from the bubonic plague, or Black Death, was recorded as just 43. In June 6,137 died; at its peak in August some 31,159 people died, or fifteen per cent of the city's population.

Such events were far removed from the concerns of the inhabitants of a small village in the north of England. Although they had experienced the trials of the civil war, and although their own church minister had been banned and a new, unpopular incumbent brought in to take his place, happenings in far-off London were relatively unimportant. Life was a daily struggle of farming or mining, finding ways to work together or feed a family.

That is until September 1665 when the plague arrived in Eyam and left a community battling for survival.

This is the story of Eyam – the story that keeps me coming back to visit, the story that stirs my soul.

Each person mentioned in the following chapters really lived in Eyam, and each date recorded is accurate. Only Kitty Allenby and her Sheffield family and friends were birthed in my imagination. The Scriptures read on particular Sundays in my book were those required at the time, and a letter from Reverend Mompesson to his children, included in my manuscript, was written by an ancient hand.

Some details may confuse the observant reader. For example, New Year's Eve celebrations taking place in March. During the 1660s, different calendars were used in different locations – Europe used the Gregorian calendar exclusively, while London used a combination of both the Gregorian and the Julian. Away to the north, in the wilds of the Peak District, the Julian calendar was all that was known. Amongst other things, this stated that the new year began in March each year.

Truth is the outline and imagination the colour to this story. I hope you will be as captivated in the reading as I have been in the telling. I pray these given lives would touch your heart as you hear them speak down through the centuries.

Prologue

We lined up on the playground clutching lunch bags and pencil cases, all ready to board the awaiting bus. Clattering down the stone steps to the pavement, I pushed my partner along to hurry her up. I wanted a good seat beside the window. Having climbed the few carpeted stairs into the dark interior of the coach, I joined the crush of boys and girls eager to start our school excursion. Mrs Bawcutt appealed unsuccessfully for calm as the cool kids commandeered the back row. At last we were all seated and ready to go. The doors closed with a gentle whoosh, the low rumble of the diesel engine roared eagerly into life, and we were off.

The driver drove to the end of the street where my school, Hunter's Bar Middle School, dominated the corner with its Victorian grey stonework and black railings, then we turned right and nosed onto the roundabout, taking the first exit leading out of the city. The bus lumbered past the park where we held our yearly sports day, past the fish and chip cafe my Nan, Aunty Betty and Uncle Ron frequented every Friday, past the rows of conjoined houses and past the strips of local shops.

The landscape quickly changed from city sprawl to rugged countryside, where the granite tors and soaring ridges of the Derbyshire Peak District came into view. Our route took us past lush green hillsides dotted with sheep prevented from escape by higgledy-piggledy dry-stone walls. Overhead the sun shone, and cottonwool clouds lazed across the blue sky.

After a while Mrs Bawcutt stood up, wedging herself between the two front rows of seats. Turning towards us, she began issuing instructions and information for our day out. Swaying to the rhythm of the bus, she occasionally lurched to one side or the other as the driver changed gear or navigated a particularly sharp corner.

'We will soon be arriving in Eyam,' she declared, glaring at any who were still absorbed in their own conversations. 'When we stop, remain seated while I hand out the worksheets and put you into your groups. You will then be able to get off the bus, making sure to stay together with your group and teacher. Please take a moment now to pick up all your litter and to collect your belongings. Don't forget your coats!' She sat back down, rustling through the backpack at her feet while we shrugged our way into coats and jackets.

'The crisp packet isn't mine so I won't pick it up!' someone yelled.

'Gimme back my pencil case!' wailed another.

Around a few more corners and we were there; the driver brought the bus to a hissing stop. We cheered and jumped up, full of pent-up energy after eating too many sweets. Mrs Bawcutt blocked our escape as she waved a fistful of printed papers aloft. 'Sit quietly and wait for the worksheets to be passed around.' She looked at me. 'Anna, please take one and pass the rest back.'

I grabbed the proffered papers, delighted that my favourite teacher had chosen me as her first recipient. I licked my finger and took one for me and another for my friend Alison sitting next to me. Stretching my arm up and over the back of the seat, I passed the sheets to the next pair. When I glanced at the page I saw there was a map, some pictures of a few cottages and space for lots of writing. It was going to be a busy day. Mrs Bawcutt eventually motioned for the driver to open the door and we were released. A shoving mass of noisy school children unleashed onto the unsuspecting streets of the village of Eyam. A story of tragedy and loss, of sacrifice and love, unleashed into my unsuspecting heart.

Like footprints in a dusty room, the villagers of Eyam have left their imprint.

It all unfolded in the summer of 1665

August 1665

Kitty stood and waited as the rest of the family clambered onto the donkey cart. Ma, her skirts hitched high to avoid tripping, was the first to be seated. Pa passed her the baby, Oliver, already nearly asleep with his thumb plunged deep into his mouth. Joan was next, insisting that she climb in unaided, much to their father's irritation. Hampered by the straw doll she was clutching in one hand, she struggled to get hold of the cart's sides and would have landed in a heap in the mud if both parents hadn't grabbed her at the last minute. Finally settled next to Ma, she turned to regard Kitty with her solemn brown eyes, dark blonde curls sticking to the heat of her forehead. 'Isn't tha coming, Kitty?' she implored. 'I'll cry if tha doesn't.'

Kitty swallowed hard. She would not cry. She had vehemently asserted that a year away from family was *exactly* what she not only needed but also desperately longed for, and she would not now show herself to be wavering in that assertion. 'No, luv,' she finally managed to say, suppressed emotion causing her to sound a little less gentle than she had intended. 'Tha knows I'm not coming with thee now. I'm going to stay with Aunt Anne and Uncle Robert, and help them with t' cousins and farm. I'll see thee soon though, I promise. Now, mind tha takes good care of t' baby there while I'm gone.' She indicated the doll cradled in Joan's arms – a parting gift won at the fair by Kitty's surprisingly accurate throw of a ball, dislodging as it had the one remaining skittle on the shelf.

'Alright,' snuffled Joan, clearly somewhat torn between bidding her big sister farewell and caressing her cherished 'baby'.

'Right, time we were going,' declared Pa from beside Kitty. 'Now, be good, be helpful, and don't forget to read,' he enjoined.

Pa had been a school teacher until five years before, imparting to young minds his love of words and contemporary theology. That was until Charles II returned from Europe and turned the country upside down. Again. Those deemed sympathetic to the old regime were immediately removed from positions of influence; Kitty's father was one of those who lost his job. Since then, he had been engaged by a string of wealthy Sheffield industrialists willing to turn a blind eye to his political and religious beliefs in their desperation that he teach their lazy children something of value. In his spare time, he had determined to teach Kitty to read and write. An unusual move, perhaps, in a city dominated by men, but one he hadn't regretted for a moment. Kitty had loved learning, finding joy as strange patterns on the page became words and phrases she could read and understand. Her own writing had become neat and easily legible – in her eyes a work of art to be perfected. They had both revelled in the camaraderie of learning, she in the focused attention she had received from him, and he finding her a pleasant antidote to the stream of disobedient and disinterested boy-children he frequently found himself saddled with.

'I've left thee something in t' bag which I dropped with Uncle Robert earlier.' He winked. Kitty gasped, guessing it would be the giant family Bible. She hugged him around the neck, breathing in the scent of home as she did so, drinking deep from his steadfast strength, his vibrancy and stability.'Thank you, Pa.' She smiled, aware of the sacrifice it would be for him, not having his Bible close at hand. However, she also knew that he had committed many passages to memory and seldom needed to leaf through its pages when in search of comfort or direction.

He raised his hand to her chin, holding her steady just as he had back when she was a young girl. Kitty felt the warmth, love and confidence contained within that one simple gesture and again found herself gulping for fresh, calming air. Pa said nothing more, just smiled and let his hand fall to his side as he turned, a sudden burst of energy released as he realised the lateness of the hour and the distance of the journey that lay ahead. He climbed on to the front of the cart, gathered the reigns and urged the donkey forward with a 'mst, mst' through his teeth.

'Goodbye, darling Catherine,' Ma called, waving her removed glove high in the air, a flag of farewell wafted for all to see.

'It's Kitty,' Kitty muttered, knowing it would make no difference, even if Ma could have heard. She would always be Catherine to her mother.

The cart lurched and bumped into motion, throwing Joan against the hard wooden side with a cry. Her wailing woke the sleeping Oliver, who in turn started up a great howl of indignation at the injustice of being woken so abruptly by his overly dramatic sibling. Ma ceased her exuberant waving, turning her attention instead to those offspring in far closer proximity than Kitty. Pa shook his head and seemed to settle lower in his seat, preparing himself for the road ahead and its upcoming joys. Even the donkey's ears had flattened against its head, and its braying laugh seemed to indicate it was enjoying the moment.

Kitty giggled, her eyes dancing in mirth as she watched them turn the corner, relieved that the tension of farewell had been broken by predictable Allenby chaos. Another group of friends tucked in behind the Allenby cart, following them on the road through the hills and back towards Sheffield. The Wakes Festival, the annual workers' holiday and fair, was over for another year; Kitty would only see her family again at the next one.

'Catherine – a pretty name.' Someone was standing at Kitty's elbow, having arrived quietly and unnoticed in all the confusion of farewells.

'Kitty, actually,' she muttered, not bothering to turn and address the newcomer directly, preferring to keep her eyes fixed on the road down which her family had now disappeared.

'Oh well, Kitty is nice too,' came the reply. 'Personally, I prefer to use my full name – Catherine.'

Kitty turned in embarrassed confusion, realising the lady at her side, another Catherine, had probably thought her disdain for their shared name was unfriendly at best and downright rude at worst.

'Ah, I'm that sorry...' she began, only to find any other words had flown from her thinking at the look of delighted amusement on the face of her namesake. The other Catherine's face was alive with the mischief of the moment, her already pretty features accentuated by the suppressed laughter Kitty could see bubbling under the surface. Dark, humour-filled eyes invited Kitty to join the merriment, erasing any of the awkwardness originally felt. Kitty let out a breath of relief and broke into a broad smile herself, grateful that this stranger had chosen kindness over offence.

'Pleased to make your acquaintance, Kitty. I'm Catherine Mompesson, wife to the newly appointed vicar of St Lawrence's Church. Is this your first visit to Eyam?'

The lightness of the exchange was suddenly engulfed in a cloud of shame and discomfort for Kitty. How could she not have noticed the careful accent, the fine clothes, the unmistakable symbols of a sort above her own? The woman before her represented all that Kitty distrusted and, yes, feared. She was one of the privileged, the well-connected, the ones who now ruled the world and, worse, the church. And yet, even as memories of overheard conversations held deep into the night between her father and his non-conformist friends threatened to deprive her of even the most basic of manners, Kitty was aware of something different. The look of concern that had replaced the mirth earlier so evident on Mrs Mompesson's face hinted that perhaps here before her stood one with a more sympathetic heart. She could only hope so.

Kitty ducked her head, gathered her skirts and bobbed the slightest of curtsies in outward response to this disconcerting revelation. She hoped Mrs Mompesson would accept that as sufficient recompense for her earlier presumption.

'Oh, no, please don't do that!' Catherine exclaimed in a rush, reaching out her perfectly gloved hands in entreaty. Kitty straightened, hiding her own bare and filthy hands behind her back. 'There's no need, really. I'm sorry if I embarrassed you, Kitty, that wasn't my intention in the least. It was so lovely to see a new face here in the village and then find we share a name, that I quite forgot myself in my desire to greet you. I do hope you'll forgive me and we can perhaps start again?'

'Yes ma'am,' agreed Kitty, still avoiding looking directly at Mrs Mompesson. At that moment her aunt, Anne, arrived, carrying a red-faced, angry looking cousin Sarah. Cousin Mary trotted behind, trying to keep up with her mother's focused strides.

'Kitty dearest, we need to get going. T' children are hot and tired and have had more than enough excitement for one day. Could tha hold Mary's hand...' her voice trailed off into silence as she noticed Mrs Mompesson standing next to Kitty. 'Oh, good day to thee Mrs Mompesson. I trust you and t' reverend have enjoyed t' day?' she asked, somewhat coldly, Kitty felt.

'Yes, thank you, Mrs Fox, it has been wonderful. Kitty, I didn't realise you knew Mrs Fox here?'

'She's my aunt, my ma's sister. I've come to stay till Wakes Fair next year. Help with t' kids and t' farm, that sort of thing.'

'Marvellous,' beamed Mrs Mompesson. 'Then I shall have the opportunity to get to know you after all. George, stop pulling your sister's hair. Elizabeth, don't scream so. Oh dear, I think it's time we left for home too. Good day, Kitty, good day, Mrs Fox.' And with that, she hurried after her warring offspring.

'Ma'am,' came Aunt Anne's muted response. 'Come now, our Kitty, we must be off.' For some reason Aunt Anne seemed cross and flustered, as though the encounter with Mrs Mompesson had unsettled her more than Kitty would expect. After all, the vicar's wife had been surprisingly friendly to her, a stranger in the village. Mind you, maybe that was just the good manners of a better position in life and not a real expression of warmth or companionship. Perhaps Aunt Anne knew something that Kitty didn't yet. She held her tongue and went to reach for Mary's outstretched hand. As she did so, she saw out of the corner of her eye a slight movement, as though the light had changed and caught someone standing in the shadows.

John.

Her breath caught and her hand dropped to her side, as Kitty forgot all about her little cousin who stamped her foot for the attention she had been so eagerly anticipating. Aunt Anne, ever attuned to the vagaries of her daughter's moods, stopped fussing with Sarah and looked up to see what could possibly have happened now. Her gaze took in her furious daughter, her frozen niece and the rapidly approaching young man.

'Oh, John,' she greeted the young man with a smile of welcome. 'Are thee getting ready for t' journey back t' town? Nice tha's had a break from labour these couple of days. But I suppose tha must get back to it, right? Well, we'll leave thee to bid Kitty here farewell, without the musical accompaniment of our Mary's lungs and foot stomps!' She grabbed the loudly protesting Mary by the wrist, hitched baby Sarah a little higher up her hip, and took her young brood a discreet distance away. 'See thee in a bit, our Kitty. But not too long, mind.'

Kitty hardly heard the commotion of her departing aunt and cousins, so loud was the thump of her heart in her ears. She clenched her palms, bitten fingernails digging painfully into the flesh as she sought some degree of self-control. This was the moment she had been dreading; had almost hoped wouldn't happen. She'd hoped Aunt Anne would have needed her back at the house earlier and she would have already left the fair. Or that, in the hustle and bustle of departure, caught up with his friends and fellow labourers, John would simply forget to find her. But he hadn't, and now he stood in front of Kitty, looking down at her even though she herself was tall for the girl she still was. His face was all red and freckly from the unaccustomed sunshine burning his miner's skin. The smell of ale, slight but distinct, caused a nose-wrinkling protest from Kitty as he drew closer. He grinned.

'Well, lass, we're off. Work's on again tomorrow so we can't be late.' He tried for a jovial, *just popping down the road, back in a minute* sort of approach, but Kitty could tell his heart wasn't in it. He was going to miss her, and they both knew it. Oh, miserable were the rules for apprentices! Even should he get placed with one of the cutlery masters he desperately wanted to work for, he wouldn't be allowed to marry until he was 21. Three whole years to wait! It seemed a lifetime for the two of them, grown up and into friendship almost as soon as they could walk and talk, now betrothed sweethearts.

Kitty knew that was the real reason behind Ma suggesting she spend some time with Uncle Robert and Aunt Anne. Yes, of course, they'd be grateful for the extra help, especially after Sarah was born just last Christmas, but she also knew they could cope perfectly well without her. This way, Kitty had something to keep her occupied while John worked his apprenticeship – not that he even had one yet. She sighed; it all seemed so unfair. A cloud covered the sun and a chill breeze lifted the dust at her feet.

'Don't be sad, Kitty, 'tis hard enough having to leave thee here. All this space and green grass and big skies – not right when tha's a town lad. And as for t' animals...' This as a chicken pecked at his boot and the sound of a desperately squealing pig caught their attention. 'Sounds like someone's just won t' greasy pig contest.' Suddenly he was laughing, the sound scattering the terrified chicken at his feet. That only made him laugh even harder, doubling over as he held his aching sides.

'Stop, stop!' Kitty cried, tears pouring down her cheeks as she too shook with laughter. 'Oh, my tummy hurts. Stop, oh stop!' Slowly John straightened, breathing deeply in an attempt to control himself. Kitty wiped her eyes and pressed her hands over her mouth to make sure she didn't get started again.

'Ah, Kitty, I'm going to miss thee, lass. We always have such fun together, don't we?' The mood changed, their hysterical outburst silenced by the reality that this was goodbye until the same time the following year. With his rough miner's fingers coarse against her damp cheek, he caught the newly flowing tears of a bereft heart as they traced their way down Kitty's face. 'It'll go quick,' he promised, trying to convince himself as much as her. 'And if tha needs anything, anything at all, tha only needs to get a message to me and tha knows, I'll get here – somehow. I need to go now, though. Don't hold me so – the lads are calling and will leave without me, tha knows they will!'

Sure enough, the other miners and apprentices were all shouting and jeering, whooping at John as he leaned closer to Kitty, whispering parting words of love and brushing her forehead with a kiss. She grasped his hand, willing him not to go, squeezing so tight her knuckles were white with the effort. Gently he prised her fingers open, blew her one last kiss and ran to leap onto the wagon that would take him away from Eyam – away from the treasure he held most dear.

Kitty watched the boys follow the same road her family had clattered down earlier. She stood perfectly still, alone for the first time in her seventeen years of life, trying to make sense of the torrent of feelings now rushing through her. Kitty suddenly remembered a day when she had been young; it had been pouring with rain for days, so much so that little rivulets and streams had formed in the street in front of their home. The water burbled and bubbled, forging a channel through the hard summer-baked earth. Swirling in a waltz of water, individual threads came together then parted, moving on to their next dance partner.

Once the rain had finally stopped falling from the leaden sky, Pa had grabbed a few sheets of paper, expertly folding and refolding them until there appeared in his hand, to Kitty's delight, three or four little boats. Perfectly triangular sails jutted proudly upwards, ready to harness the power of the air and toss, wild and free, to unknown worlds and destinations.

The two of them had gone outside, mindless of the cold and damp, and had released their vessels into the strongest flow of the deepest of the streams coursing past their door. With a squeal of excitement, Kitty had watched hers take to the high seas, tumbling and tossing its way to freedom and the end of the street. All of a sudden a gust of wind had caught its uppermost edge, and the boat flipped and flopped, dangerously close to capsizing. At the last second before disaster struck, the plucky little ship righted itself. Cheered and clapped on by Kitty, it continued down the street and around the corner.

'Where has it gone? What will happen to it now?' Kitty anxiously questioned her all-knowing father.

'To seek its fortune and find adventure,' Pa had responded.

'But it may get stuck, or break, or worse, sink.'

'Aye, but it may float and float and reach t' River Sheaf and then float some more and reach t' sea,' her father declared.

Kitty exhaled, releasing the tension in her neck and shoulders she hadn't even realised was there. Yes, that was it. She felt just like that paper boat, cast onto rough waters to be tossed whichever way they took her. Would she flounder and flail, be dashed upon the rocks of loneliness and difference and heartbreak? Or, as Pa had said, would she float and float and find the sea – her place and her purpose? She uttered a silent prayer for help and guidance from the Lord she had been told would always be there. *I hope He is,* she thought.

'Kitty, Kitty, look at me, Kitty.' The spell of introspection was broken. Racing towards her, on the unsteady legs of a chubby four-year-old, was Mary. Her dimpled cheeks were pink with exertion, her arms flailing wildly as she tried to keep her balance on the slippery slope of grass down which she was hurtling. Skidding to a breathless halt inches in front of a somewhat alarmed Kitty, Mary reached up and stretched her arms as far round Kitty's legs as she could. She burrowed her head deep into the coarse fabric of Kitty's skirts, her shoulders heaving from the effort of having run so far and so fast, and sighed a deep and contented sigh. 'I's loves thee, Kitty.'

'And I love thee too, darling Mary. Now, how about tha lets go of my legs and holds my hand instead, for I think it's time tha took me home. What say tha?'

Mary dutifully extricated herself from Kitty's skirt and began instead to skip in dizzying circles around her favourite cousin.

'Mary, stop doing that. Tha makes me feel all sick and wobbly just watching thee!' Aunt Anne had finally caught up with her daughter, slowed as she was by the burden of baby Sarah in her arms. 'Alright, Kitty, my luv? I know saying farewell is never fun nor easy, and I can see thee is mighty fond of that young John. And a find lad he looks too. Tha'll do well to wait for him.'

Kitty murmured a blushing word of acknowledgement. To prevent any further conversations of such an intimate nature, she tapped Mary's head and with shouts of 'Race thee!' she set off for the village. Going at barely more than walking pace, she was soon caught by a triumphant Mary.

'See, I's faster than thee!'

'That's the truth,' chuckled Kitty, grabbing Mary's hand to prevent her from running off again. Together they waited for Mary's mother to catch up, then they all clumped their way towards the little stream which marked the outskirts of Eyam itself. They stopped when they reached the brook, eager to take a moment to rest in the cool shade of the overhanging beech trees. Mary kicked off her small wooden clogs and wriggled her way to the edge. She dipped her feet in the gently flowing waters. Summer had been hot and rainless that year and rocks were clearly visible just below the surface.

'Any fish for tea?' asked Aunt Anne, with a wink at Kitty.

'I don't see any.' Mary, now leaning further forward trying to reach the waving fronds of waterweed with her fingertips, wanted to be certain. With a sudden 'splosh', Mary lost her balance and fell forward into the stream, frantically thrashing her arms around until she stood up in the shallow water. One second of stunned silence passed, then Mary filled her lungs with air and screamed. Kitty jumped up – Aunt Anne still being hampered by the baby – and waded in, boots and all. Her skirts dragged and caught in the mud at the edge, but she soon reached the terrified Mary, who she whisked into her arms and back to the safety of the bank.

'There, there. Tha's alright, my precious. Just a little wet,' she softly comforted. 'And it has been a mighty hot day, so now tha'll be all cooled down ready for bed.'

Mary hiccupped, holding tight lest she fall and get wet again. Shaking her head at her daughter's antics, Aunt Anne pushed herself up off the grass, baby Sarah still nestling her head in her shoulder. Kitty reached down for Mary's shoes, now the only dry part of her, and together they waded across the stream.

'I'm so glad tha's here, Kitty.' Aunt Anne smiled gratefully. Kitty smiled back, feeling this had been a sign that she was here for a reason; she was here to help, and already she could see she was going to be needed.

They emerged from the cool of the trees into the early evening sun. To their right lay the cluster of stone and slate-roofed homes that formed the central street of the hamlet. Kitty noticed a group of men making their way to the Miner's Arms, intent on extracting every last moment of pleasure from the short holiday. Wives stood in small groups, chatting and remarking on the people they had met or the gossip they had overheard. Unsupervised children chased each other, the boys pulling the girls' hair, the girls, in turn, knocking the caps from the boys' heads. A glowing beam of sunlight graced the tower of St Lawrence's Church – a divine smile of approval brightening the countenance of this watchful sentinel.

The sight of the tower reminded Kitty of their encounter with Mrs Mompesson. She wondered again at the diffidence shown by her aunt.

'Aunt Anne, tha didn't seem to like Mrs Mompesson overly?'

'Ah, she's alright enough in herself I reckon. It's just, well, her husband is t' Reverend Mompesson isn't he?' As though that settled the matter.

Confused, Kitty pressed harder. 'And?' she prompted, shifting the weight of a sopping wet Mary to her other side; the child seemed to have dozed off after her fright.

'Alright, let me explain,' her aunt sighed. 'But tha mustn't say anything to t' others in t' village. I'm not wanting to make trouble or stir up an argument; there's been enough of that over t' last few years, as you well know.' She shook her head sadly. 'Did tha notice t' short, plump man at t' fair? He was on his own most of t' time, bit on t' outskirts of things? Well, he was t' previous reverend. Mr Stanley – Thomas Stanley. He was none too happy when t' king returned and changed all t' rules. He wouldn't use that new book of prayer they insisted on, nor would he agree with t' goings-on in church on a Sunday – kneeling and all that. He's such a lovely man, knows us and cares about us in t' village more than anyone else we've had.

'Anyways, Reverend Mompesson came and took his place. He's not from round here; he's not one of us, nor does he want to be. He just likes telling us what to do, preaching and praying from that book of his. Mr Stanley lost his job and his home, now he has nothing. They wanted to make him leave t' area completely, but a few in t' village insisted he stay. They found him a house and provide a small living for him. Some of us,' her voice dropped to a whisper that Kitty could barely hear, 'still have him come home and give a sermon or pray. But tha doesn't know anything about that if asked!'

Now Kitty understood. The civil war between Oliver Cromwell and the monarchy-supporting Cavaliers had been long and bitter. Her own family had been affected too; her father's brother had gone to support Cromwell's New Model Army and not returned. Dissenting preachers, as with school teachers, were removed from office and taken away from their precious flock. Many now found the open fields their pulpits, the painting of an early morning sunrise their stained-glass windows. It seemed even a place as remote as Eyam hadn't escaped the turmoil.

They walked on in thoughtful silence, speaking only to greet their neighbours or exhort a wayward child to 'get on home'. Kitty became aware of the song of a bird hovering high in the sky, its beautiful notes piercing the soft blue of an August evening. She stopped walking, arrested by such a glorious sound so unfamiliar to her town ears. Aunt Anne carried on a few paces before she realised her companion had left her side.

'What's up, luv?'

'That bird song – 'tis beautiful. What is it?'

Aunt Anne chuckled at her educated, uneducated niece. 'That's a lark. There are plenty round here. Tha'll hear lots of them while thee's here!'

They paused to enjoy the bird's song a little longer before continuing on their way. A bee buzzed lazily alongside them, attracted by the scent of pink foxgloves and white sweet cicely growing in profusion along the edge of the street.

Eventually, they reached Water Lane on the other side of the village and climbed the short incline to their destination. Kitty saw the small cottage, nestled in between two others just like it, its leaded windows winking in the evening light, welcoming them. Aunt Anne hurried on, eager to feed Sarah who was once again awake, hungry and grumpy. Mary too had woken and wriggled her way out of Kitty's arms, refreshed and full of energy once more. Kitty let them go ahead, turning away for a moment to reflect on her new surroundings.

Seeing Eyam spread beneath her, now quiet and itself resting from the day's activities, she wondered what the upcoming year had in store. Would she come to love these people, to call them her friends? Would she learn to embrace the way of the country – the wide sky with its opera of birdsong, the hum of insects, the scent of flowers? Or would she pine for the familiarity of town, for paved streets and narrow alleys, shrouded so often in the coal smoke of a hundred fires?

'Kitty, hurry.' Again it was Mary who disturbed her. Kitty inwardly rolled her eyes, realising here was a little imp determined to intrude as often as she could. And she'd thought Joan was a nuisance!

Giving herself a shake of admonition, Kitty turned and skipped the few steps needed to reach Mary. She wiggled her fingers, preparing to tickle and chase her young cousin. Mary retreated through the open door and tried to seek refuge at her mother's feet.

As Kitty followed Mary through the door, she immediately felt the embrace of home. She had visited the house a few times over the years, usually like now at the time of the Wakes Festival, when her mother would take the opportunity to meet up with her sister, but she had never stayed longer than a few hours.

The ceiling was low and hung with sweet-smelling herbs and dried flowers, ready for use by her talented aunt. In the grate, a small peat fire glowed amber and crimson, a pot of water already steaming at its edge. In the centre of the room stood a thick-legged wooden table, around which were tucked an assortment of small chairs and stools. In the far corner, a spinning wheel caught her eye. *I hope I get to try that out,* she thought, little knowing how frustrated she would become when she did get the opportunity. She could hear the contented snuffle of Sarah finishing her feed on her mother's lap, watched by a striped tabby cat that jumped off the windowsill and prowled towards the newcomer.

'Girls, really! Quieten down! I've just got Sarah fed and back to sleep. Time for thee to go to bed too, Mary. And Kitty, tha must be worn out from t' day. Let me show thee where I've put thee.' Hitching Sarah onto her hip. Anne nudged Mary up off the floor and shepherded her – complaining bitterly at the injustice of one of the greatest days of her life being forced to a close – up the narrow stairway to the bedrooms under the roof. There were only two small rooms, one for Uncle Robert, Aunt Anne and the baby, the other for Mary and, obviously, Kitty. Each had a window overlooking Eyam and the hills beyond. Kitty could just about make out the shapes of the last few sheep nibbling away at the grass on the hillside opposite. The sun was dipping behind the distant ridge, although she knew it would still be some time before full darkness drew a curtain over the magnificent view.

As she ducked under the low doorway, Kitty saw her bag neatly stowed in the corner of the room, and a small bed made up under the slope of the eaves. On the opposite side of the room was Mary's pallet. She was already dressed in dry clothes and being snuggled under a thin blanket by her mother. Aunt Anne covered Mary's tiny hands with her own work-worn palms and, kneeling down at her bedside, whispered quiet words of thanksgiving and prayer over her daughter. She watched as eyes heavy with a day of fresh air and excitement drooped closed, fluttered open again briefly, then closed again for the night. Long lashes rested peacefully on the little girl's cheek, and Mary was soon breathing the deep contentment of the young.

Suddenly exhausted, Kitty turned to Aunt Anne. Before she could say a word, she had been kissed and hugged and left blissfully alone. She plopped onto the bed, reaching up with arms almost too tired to lift, to take off her cap. Releasing her flow of wavy brown hair to cascade down her back, the girl leaned forwards to unlace her boots. Stubborn fingers refused to comply, and it took what felt like an age to undo the knots. Finally, her feet were free, allowing her toes to stretch for the first time all day. She had needed new boots for a couple of months already, but they were not considered an essential household item, so Kitty had been left hobbling. Next, she untied the apron strings from around her waist and pulled her simple dress over her head. She stretched, lying back on the bed in her lightweight smock to stare at the beams of the roof above her.

As she lay in the twilight, watching the shadows lengthen, Kitty allowed her mind to recap the events of the day. Pa, Ma, Joan, Oliver and herself had risen at dawn and clambered up onto the donkey cart, waving at friends and neighbours who weren't lucky enough to get a day out in the country. Kitty had enjoyed the journey despite the early start and the bumpy road surface jolting her at almost every turn of the wheels. They had crossed the town boundary and begun the ascent into the depth of the moors. The fields and meadows were a patchwork of purples, greens and yellows spread before them. Others travelled alongside them, and there was much chatter and banter between all the families. Some she knew, others she didn't. Eventually they had arrived at the fair where they found Uncle Robert and Aunt Anne watching out for them.

After being helped from the cart, Kitty had gone on alone to explore all that was on offer. There was the skittle competition where she'd won the straw doll for Joan, and further along was a strong man contest – big, muscular miners and farmers battling it out to be declared the winner. The smell of roasting mutton enveloped the whole hillside, making her mouth water, and the stall selling ale was several men deep as they sought to quench their thirst. Children ducked and ran, chasing any sheep or chickens unfortunate enough to stray into the main arena. Women enjoyed the time to simply rest and chat with their friends and relations, while in the background choristers sang and troubadours played their instruments and told their stories.

The sun had shone all day with barely a cloud in the sky, but a gentle wind blowing down the valley prevented everyone from overheating. It had been a truly magical day. Kitty had lost sight of John soon after they arrived, until he had sneaked up behind her. He'd placed his hands over her eyes, blocking the light, and hissed a hello in her ear. She jumped with fright, then collapsed back against his chest as he removed his hands from her eyes and placed them briefly, instead, around her small waist. Then he was gone, only to be seen again at the end of the day when he came to bid her farewell.

At the rawness of the memory, Kitty slipped onto her knees and laid her forehead on her clasped hands where they rested on the bed in front of her. Asking for a strength beyond herself for all that the future held, tears collected in the cup made by her palms. *Thou tellest my wanderings: Put thou my tears into thy bottle: Are they not in thy book?* A verse she had recently read floated across her thoughts. A sense of peace and tranquillity which had eluded Kitty until then washed over her, and she knew she would be able to sleep. Moving quietly lest she disturb Mary, the young woman climbed back into bed, curled onto her side with her hand tucked under her ear and fell into a deep sleep.

Early September 1665

Over the next few weeks, Kitty learned to adapt to country living. Uncle Robert got up early each morning, Aunt Anne rising at the same time in order to make him breakfast before he left for the lead mine a few miles outside the village. Once he had gone, Kitty would hear her aunt pottering around downstairs, clearing away the breakfast things, stoking the fire, shooing the cat outside. Then there would be a creaking of a particular chair and a few minutes of silence. Kitty knew this was Anne's time for prayers and quiet contemplation before the day – and the children – were fully awake.

Kitty had been surprised at how devout her relatives were. She knew from her own mother that they had been raised in a God-fearing home, but she hadn't realised how deeply personal their faith was. Her aunt and uncle seemed to hold regular intimate conversations with God, and emerge from the experience looking somehow lighter and more at peace.

Kitty's parents had become involved with some of the Puritan preachers who visited their local church back in Sheffield, and her pa was always bringing out the family Bible – the one she now had beside where she slept – when he sought guidance or direction. But neither he nor Ma had seemed to be special friends with God in the way that her uncle and aunt were. And although she herself knelt at her bedside and said prayers each evening – calling on God to look after her family back home, her uncle and the other miners underground, and the crops as harvest approached – she wasn't sure if anyone was actually listening. Except for that first night; that had been unusual.

Now, listening to the blackbird singing at the bottom of the lane, Kitty yawned and threw off the covers. The mornings were definitely feeling cooler. The trip to the nearby brook to fetch water was less appealing than when she had first arrived, but it was her job that needed to be done, and do it she would. The young woman glanced across at the still sleeping Mary, her arm flung above her head in trouble-free abandon, little bubbles of moisture forming then bursting as she breathed in and out. Carrying her boots and outdoor clothes, she tiptoed down the stairs. Aunt Anne looked up as her niece descended, smiling wide as she saw Kitty.

'Morning, luv.' She got up from her chair as she spoke. 'Tha's off out to fetch t' water then?'

Kitty nodded and greeted her aunt with a kiss on the cheek before sitting on the recently vacated chair to put on her boots. Aunt Anne gave the girl's shoulder a gentle squeeze and started upstairs to wake Mary, then baby Sarah.

Kitty unlatched the door and went out into the misty September morning, grabbing the water pail from outside the door. The air was damp and full of the sound of birds not yet ready to leave for the winter. As the sun peered over the rooftops of the row of cottages, it burnished the slate with its glow. Collecting water was just one of the jobs Kitty had been assigned after the fun of the Wakes Festival was over. She also had to feed the chickens each morning, releasing them from their overnight coop before mixing together some grain and any leftover breadcrumbs from the day before, and scattering it in the yard. Once they were busy pecking and scratching for their breakfast, she foraged through the straw of their hen house in search of eggs; these all needed cleaning and preparing for sale later that day. After the eggs were packed carefully for their journey down into the village, Kitty would have a breakfast of ale and oatcakes while sitting at the large table with Aunt Anne and Mary. It was one of her favourite times of the day. Breakfast finished, it was time to attend to all the other chores that seemed to occupy her new country existence. To begin with, the sheep in the pen behind the cottage were led into the fields, expertly guided and cajoled by Patch, the farm dog. Once the sheep were happily nibbling away, Aunt Anne and the girls walked the mile or so to the strip of land on the other side of the village where their crops of oats and barley grew. Kitty could never quite understand why everyone's fields seemed to be randomly located rather than all grouped together in one place. She had tried asking her aunt and uncle, but they just looked at her blankly, not seeing a problem with the arrangement. As they walked, neighbours were greeted and eggs were sold. Mary taught Kitty the names of the flowers that still adorned the dry-stone walls they passed, and Kitty tried to teach Mary the alphabet – 'B' for 'buttercups' or 'H' for 'heather' helped both in their lessons.

By lunchtime they needed to be at the entrance to the lead mine where all the husbands would emerge, faces and hands blackened, sweat staining their shirts. The men lugged up the baskets of ore collected during their morning's work, exchanging them for parcels of food – bread, a couple of eggs, an oatcake or two, perhaps even some cold pie from the night before. After washing down the food with a mug or two of cold ale, they returned to their work like moles returning to their holes.

For the women, the hardest part of their day had just begun – the ore needed to be dressed and prepared for collection. The sound of hammers against rock echoed across the meadow as the large chunks were broken up and swirled through sieves of water. The heavy lead deposits settled at the bottom of the sieve, then they were retrieved and safely stored for the men to collect on their re-emergence from the mine later in the day. The older children helped where they could, the younger ones being left to play or doze in the grass. Kitty worked until her fingers were red and sore from the effort of prising apart pieces of rock and ore, or from fishing tiny pieces of lead out of the cold washing water.

As the women worked, they broke the monotony of the chore with gossip or singing, breaking off mid-sentence to admonish a wayward child or nurse a crying baby. Whether their own or not, it didn't matter – all were mothered by all.

The afternoon wore on, and when the tasks were completed the women gathered their belongings and began the slow walk home, children trailing behind them. Once home, Kitty would bring the sheep back in from the fields and fetch more water and firewood as Aunt Anne prepared the evening meal. It was usually a vegetable stew topped with fluffy dumplings, or pigeon pie with rich gravy, depending on what was available on the day.

By the time Uncle Robert arrived home, Kitty was ready to go to bed, but she loved the evenings spent with her uncle and aunt, enjoyed the gentle way they spoke to one another about their respective days, or exchanged news from the village. They often sat outside in the evening cool listening to the larks singing, just as Aunt Anne had promised they would. While the family relaxed, the cat prowled on her incessant search for mice, and Patch flopped at their feet, his tongue hanging out. Finally, Uncle Robert would declare the day over and, in his deep, dusty voice, pray for each of them in turn.

Once she was settled in her small bed under the roof, Kitty used the time to write letters home – if her stiffened fingers would allow. She regaled her parents and John with stories of her new life, marvelling as she did so at how much she had learned in a short space of time. She would have preferred the ease of face-to-face conversations, especially with John, rather than the stilted exchange of words on a page, but this was better than nothing. Eventually, the paper would slip from her lap and flutter to the floor, country air and hard work catching up with her at last. The young woman's sleep was sound, undisturbed by nightmares of the trouble that would stalk the households of Eyam in only a few days' time.

This measured pattern of their lives changed forever one early morning in September.

Kitty had left the cottage as usual to fetch the water. Swinging the pail backwards and forwards as she strolled along, she hummed a tune she had heard the women singing the previous day. Suddenly there was a great commotion on the road below her and a line of stamping horses pulling a large, covered wagon clattered into view. It came to a halt beside the stocks, empty at this hour of the day. The young woman watched as the driver helped a young man climb down; he then turned to drag a large, heavy-looking chest onto the grass beside him. Kitty was fascinated, not having seen this much activity since she left Sheffield. She wondered who the young man was, where he had come from and why he was here, in Eyam. Hoping to find out more, she continued to linger, waiting as the driver bullied the horses back into motion and took his place walking alongside them out of the village and into the open countryside beyond.

Returning her attention to the disembarked traveller, Kitty watched as he hefted the box onto his shoulder and wearily made his way back to the row of cottages behind him. The man pushed open the gate of one of the cottages and knocked on the door, which was soon opened to him. Kitty couldn't make out who had welcomed the stranger, but she did know the house belonged to the tailor, Alexander Hadfield.

Kitty suddenly realised she had taken far too long with her errand and, pulling her skirts high in one hand and clutching the bucket firmly in the other, she ran the remaining distance to the stream.

On her return, she shoved the cottage door open with her shoulder, being careful not to spill any of the water it had taken her so long to collect.

'Where on earth's tha been, our Kitty? Tha's taken an age and a half. I was thinking tha must have slipped and fallen or something!' Aunt Anne had never raised her voice the whole time Kitty had been staying there, but anxiety and irritation made her speech loud and edgy. Sarah wailed at the sound, and Mary joined her in protest; the calm of the morning was shattered. Kitty lowered the bucket apologetically, cross with herself for having upset her dear aunt. She pulled off her muddy boots and went straight to Mary's side, shushing her as she went. Aunt Anne, meanwhile, had successfully convinced Sarah that she was still the kind and gentle mother she had always known.

'Come and collect t' eggs with me, our Mary,' persuaded Kitty, knowing this was a task Mary loved because Kitty told her stories of pirates and buried treasure while they searched through the straw.

By the time that was done, breakfast eaten and they were all ready for their walk down to the village, Kitty had forgotten about the stranger's arrival. She only remembered the episode as they walked past the lychgate leading to St Lawrence's Church, the tailor's cottage being a few doors further on.

'Oh,' she exclaimed, 'I completely forgot. There was a reason I was so late with t' water this morning.' Aunt Anne raised her eyebrows, wondering what story she would hear from her niece's fertile imagination now.

'No, really, this isn't made up!' Kitty was stung, but persevered, so unusual had the actual event been. 'A caravan cart came in on t' Sheffield road, all huffing horses and bumping wheels. It stopped by t' stocks and a man got out, carrying a big box on his shoulder. He went in t' Mr Hadfield's place. It was ever so exciting.'

'Oh, that's George. He's come up from London to bring Mr Hadfield some cloth and do a bit of work for him. I was talking to the new Mrs Hadfield – Mrs Cooper as was, till her first husband died, God rest his soul – and she was telling me they were expecting George, with a parcel as well. I'm glad he's arrived then. Alexander – Mr Hadfield – was getting quite desperate, it was taking so long.'

Mystery solved, they carried on their way with Kitty somewhat crestfallen that the box only contained some boring old bits of fabric, and the stranger himself was nothing more than a tailor's helper.

After lunch at the mine site, they settled themselves in, ready for the long afternoon of hard, tedious work. Sarah snuggled into a bed made up of cast aside shawls, while Mary found her playmates and was soon happily rolling down the hill with them, getting dizzier and dirtier by the second.

Kitty wasn't the only one who had seen George arrive, and the village women were soon discussing the news he'd brought to Eyam along with the box of fabric.

'Did tha hear t' news from London? That fellow who arrived this morning to Tailor Hadfield's place was saying as everyone in t' city has been infected with a pestilence of some sort. All t' wealthy folks are leaving town and moving to their country places, and all t' poor folk are dying like flies. So he told them.'

'No, surely not! 'Tis London – streets there are paved with gold, so they say.'

'Tsk, get away with thee. My Samuel went there once and he said as how London is filthy; that river they have stinks, and there isn't a sight nor sound of gold anywhere.'

Kitty listened closely to the conversation, wanting to hear if the object of her morning's distraction had had anything else to say.

'Even t' king's left town, so Mr Viccars says. That's t' name of t' lad who's come all t' way from London with that parcel.' Bridget Ashe shared that final snippet; she was the mother of one of Mary's best friends, four-year-old Joan. 'He says so many have died, they can't even bury them properly. At first, they were taking t' bodies out at night, trying to hide how bad it was, but now tha's so many they're being carted around in broad daylight!'

Pausing for breath, enjoying the sensation of having everyone hanging on her every word, Mrs Ashe continued: 'Tis a terrible sickness, Mr Viccars says – starts with a hot fever tha' won't break, then big boils full of foul poison all over t' body. Nothing to be done to help t' poor patient, he says. Just a matter of time, and then they die. And t' worst is, if one in t' house catches it, everyone else also gets sick and passes.'

The women listening all shook their heads, inwardly grateful that they lived miles away from London and such problems. They turned their attention back to the more pressing and immediate needs their work presented, happy to dismiss such gloomy news from their conversation.

Kitty, however, was alarmed by what she heard. Growing up in the city as she had, she knew only too well the dangers of disease when living on a crowded street. She had seen a mere cough spread to the end of her own street, leaving each family touched by the finger of illness as it spread. She was grateful to now be living in the pleasant and open environs of Eyam but concerns about her family, and John, wouldn't be silenced. Would this disease reach Sheffield? Would it travel through the air, carried on the autumn winds like so much smoke from a fire? Or would one of the nobility flee the capital city, unknowingly carrying infection with him?

Suddenly the women around her broke out in raucous laughter, jolting Kitty away from the dark spectre of a city fighting for survival and back to the pleasant meadow where they all sat.

'Aye, so when they opened t' box brought up from London,' another woman – the tailor's next-door neighbour, Kitty thought – was saying, 't' cloth was all wet and damaged! Mary hung it out in t' kitchen, above t' fireplace, so's it could dry out, and as it warmed up, what should happen but a whole nest of fleas awoke and started hopping about all over t' house! I heard her screaming from my place.' Some of the women again laughed, others shook their heads in sympathy as they imagined themselves having to deal with an unexpected infestation of fleas.

Aunt Anne said little, merely whispering to Kitty, 'I's glad that we live at t' other end of t' village, away from t' tailor's and his visitors.' Kitty couldn't help but agree, grateful that they wouldn't now have to go home and clean in every corner to ensure no fleas had hopped over into their cottage. Imagining poor Sarah getting bitten, big red bites marking her delicate skin, and Mary itching and scratching all night in their shared room, she shuddered.

Soon enough it was time to finish for the day and return home. The women walked back together, waving farewell to Mrs Hawksworth as she went in at the house next to the tailor's where all the windows were flung wide and the sound of slapping and sweeping could be heard. The laughter was more muted this time, partly so Mrs Hadfield wouldn't hear them and think them uncaring, partly as they observed the enormity of the nuisance that had arrived with a simple bundle of cloth from London.

That evening Kitty took herself to her room early, for once not joining her aunt and uncle as they discussed their day. She didn't want to hear any more about the incident with Mr Viccars, the cloth and the fleas. Even more, she couldn't bear to listen as Aunt Anne related the details about the London sickness to her uncle. As she lay in bed, unable to fall asleep, Kitty could hear their quiet conversation – the soft whispers of her aunt and the low, deep answers of her uncle. It seemed he had already heard about what was happening in London but had chosen to say nothing for fear of alarming his wife. He tried to offer words of reassurance, saying that London was far away, and that it was unlikely such a distemper would ever reach their beautiful, wild corner of England. However, the tremble in his voice as he prayed his customary evening prayer seemed to Kitty to belie that confidence. She wondered what he knew that they didn't.

Want to read more of Given Lives, the story of the plague village of Eyam? Get your copy today.